Ja
Elaine
Joan Johnston
Kasey Michaels

"FROM THIS DAY FORWARD . . ."

Two lives become one—two hearts are forever
joined by love, glorious and true. From four
stunningly accomplished storytellers comes a
magnificent quartet of unforgettable romantic
tales that celebrate the sacred vows of eternal
devotion—stories of passionate dreams and
destinies realized that will raise your spirit . . .
and live in your heart for a thousand tomor-
rows.

Avon Books Presents

Avon Books Presents

TO HAVE AND TO HOLD

JANE BONANDER
ELAINE COFFMAN
JOAN JOHNSTON
KASEY MICHAELS

AVON BOOKS  NEW YORK

AVON BOOKS PRESENTS: TO HAVE AND TO HOLD is an original publication of Avon Books. This work, as well as each individual story, has never before appeared in print. This work is a collection of fiction. Any similarity to actual persons or events is purely coincidental.

AVON BOOKS
A division of
The Hearst Corporation
1350 Avenue of the Americas
New York, New York 10019

The Spinster Bride copyright © 1994 by Jane Bonander
The Bride of the Black Scot copyright © 1994 by Elaine Coffman
The Man from Wolf Creek copyright © 1994 by Joan Mertens Johnston
The Ninth Miss Noddenly copyright © 1994 by Kathie Seidick

Published by arrangement with the authors
Library of Congress Catalog Card Number: 93-91007
ISBN: 0-380-77691-X

First Avon Books Printing: June 1993

AVON TRADEMARK REG. U.S. PAT. OFF. AND IN OTHER COUNTRIES, MARCA REGISTRADA, HECHO EN U.S.A.

Printed in the U.S.A.

RA 10 9 8 7 6 5 4 3 2 1

CONTENTS

The
Spinster Bride

Jane Bonander

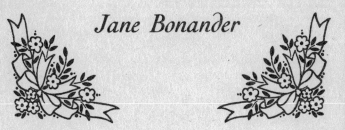

Prologue

Rural Ohio—May, 1887

The first letter had come a few months before, sending Kate McCurdy's world crashing down around her.

It had been bad enough that Brynna, the niece she'd raised after the deaths of both their parents, had come under the spell of a handsome drifter and gone off with him. That had nearly broken Kate's heart. The first letter had been from *him,* the devil who'd stolen Brynna away, telling Kate that her niece and the child she bore were dead.

Now, Kate stared down at the second letter, the anonymous one which she'd just received, her insides quivering and her hands shaking as she tried to tell her friend, Millie, about it. Speech had never come hard to Kate, but right now, she couldn't talk because one minute she wanted to bawl, and the next, she wanted to commit murder.

"Here." She thrust the letter at Millie and went to bring bread and tea to the table. As she returned with the tray, she watched surprise register on Millie's face as she read the missive.

"There was another child? Did you know Brynna'd had twins?"

"Well, of course I didn't," Kate answered, unable to curb the scolding tone of her voice.

"What did the original letter say, again?"

Kate closed her eyes, able to recall every word, every letter ... every crease and line in the paper, even though she'd received it eight months before. "It said, 'Brynna and the baby have died in an accident. They had a Christian burial. I'm sorry.' "

Opening her eyes, she gave Millie a baleful look. "He was *sorry?*" She sat down at her battered kitchen table and stared at the tea. "As if that canceled out everything he'd done and made it right. I won't ever forget the nightmare that man put me through as long as I live," she added, feeling tears crowd her throat. "If he hadn't coaxed Brynna into leaving with him, she'd be here with me now. Safe."

"Oh, no she wouldn't," Millie argued soundly.

Kate bristled, finding her friend's bluntness annoying. Honestly, though, what Millie said had a horrible ring of truth to it. Brynna had been in such a hurry to leave the farm, she'd have left with just about anyone. And, in Kate's mind, she had. *He* was a revolting man. The hostile knot that had formed in her stomach years before had returned, and tightened with a vengeance.

Millie reached for a piece of bread and slathered it with blueberry jam. "He was a handsome devil, though."

Kate fumed. "He was the devil, all right. But his looks were just bait for his trap."

Millie rolled her eyes. "So," she said between mouthfuls, her expression sympathetic, "what are you going to do?"

As she watched her friend eat, Kate's stomach continued to twist, and she was certain she'd never be able to eat again. "What I should have done long before all of this happened. I have to . . . to go to Texas, take the child from that . . . that *man,* and bring her home with me." She was ready for battle.

"I see. Well," Millie added, daintily licking jam off her fingers, "at least you have a little money now that you've sold the farm."

Kate glanced away. She had some money, but no one knew just how deeply in debt she'd been when she'd finally found a buyer for the property.

Although Millie continued to eat, Kate felt her gaze. "You've always been hard on him, you know that, Katie."

Kate kept her face turned away, hiding her pain. Maybe she did have a blind spot where he was concerned, but she couldn't help it. He'd been merely a hired hand, recruited among many other drifters to bring in the crops. Yet, by the end of the summer, he'd had Brynna falling all over him, slobbering like a lovesick calf.

"He didn't seduce her, Katie. I think it was the other way around."

Kate swung around and glared at Millie, anger replacing the threat of tears. "Don't say that. She was only seventeen. What did she know about seduction? And he was . . . Lord in heaven, he was twenty-eight. *My* age. He should have known better."

Millie merely shook her head, sighed, then glanced down at the letter again. She picked it up and reread it. " 'Brynna had twin daughters. One still lives.' Who wrote this? It isn't even signed."

"I don't know," Kate said on a sigh. "It wasn't *him,* I know that. I'm the last person he'd ever contact."

"Maybe it isn't even true, Katie."

"Oh, it's true all right. Brynna's mother was a twin. It makes sense. And why would someone write such a thing if it weren't true?"

Millie studied her. "No one can talk you out of this awful trip?"

Kate glanced around the tiny kitchen of her small apartment over the general store. Eight years. It had been eight years since her parents and Brynna's had been killed in that fire over in Dayton. Brynna had been barely ten. Oh, how the little darling had cried and cried. . . .

Kate hadn't had time for tears. She'd known that her survival and Brynna's meant working the farm. Backbreaking work that went beyond simple housework like baking, cooking, and cleaning. There had been cows to milk and crops to plant and harvest. But in the end, everything she made went to paying her hired help.

No, she thought, giving the kitchen another grim glance, she could hardly wait to leave. To have purpose again. To return with a part of Brynna that she could raise and call her own.

"No one," she answered, almost absently.

When Millie rose to leave, Kate hugged her, promised to see her before she left, and to try to think more highly of the man she was going to face. But when she was once again alone, Kate's anger festered like a sore.

Sage Reno. A godless name for a godless man. When she first met him as he swaggered onto the farm looking for work, she'd thought he'd made the name up.

No one was truly named after a prickly desert bush and a devil-filled, uncivilized border town in Nevada.

1

Sage Reno poked his head around the corner of the small nursery. He fought the catch in his throat as he watched Annie respond to her nurse's gentle chatter. A mop of russet curls crowned his daughter's head and she smiled and giggled, dimples denting her plump, pink cheeks. She was his world; he would protect her with his life.

Sarita, the pretty young wife of his wrangler, Luis, spoke to her in Spanish. Sage smiled and felt a sense of contentment. He'd been grateful she'd offered to continue to help with Annie even after the child had been weaned from Sarita's breast, for she had a baby of her own to care for. Most days, she brought her little girl with her, but today, she'd left her with Luis's mother, because the baby had a slight fever.

Sage and Luis were able to take care of the small spread Sage had purchased from a friend on the edge of the plains. But it was his job as deputy sheriff of the nearby town of Cedarville that put food on their table.

Sarita was singing to Annie in Spanish now, holding Annie's tiny hands in hers and clapping them together. Although Sarita and Luis had a place of their own where they lived with Luis's mother, they were Sage's family, too. All he had, now.

Stepping into the room, he said, "What's this I hear?

7

Spanish, again? You keep this up, Sarita, and she'll never learn English."

Sarita, still holding Annie on her lap, looked up and smiled at him. She was a beauty and Luis was crazy about her. Sage often felt a sense of regret and even some envy that he'd never found the kind of love they had.

"I teach her pat-a-cake, *Señor* Reno. All children must learn pat-a-cake." She studied him, none too favorably. "That's why you should get another wife. Annie needs a mother."

Sage heaved a dramatic sigh and rolled his eyes, hoping to make light of Sarita's announcement. "Haven't you got better things to do than try to marry me off?"

Annie wriggled off Sarita's lap and toddled to her father. He bent down, picked her up and planted a noisy kiss on her cheek. He breathed in her sweet baby smell, reveling in the easy, innocent way she'd enchanted him.

She said his name over and over again, then kissed him back.

"See? My little Sweet Pea and I get along just fine."

Sarita murmured something in Spanish. "But a handsome man like you shouldn't be alone."

Sage didn't want to think about it. Wounds were still fresh. Guilt still ate at him daily. He didn't want another wife. He'd had enough trouble with the first one. "I'm not alone, Sarita. I have Annie. And she has me." He gave her a teasing grin. "And we both have you."

Sarita waved away the comment and began straightening the blankets on Annie's tiny bed. "You have no other family? No one else?"

Sage remembered a cold, green-eyed spinster with hair of fire. He remembered the hate and distrust in those eyes when Brynna had followed him around the farm. A man could freeze in a pit of fire trying to soften a woman like that. It hadn't surprised him that she'd never married. It would take a lifetime and a man of infinite patience to thaw her glacial freeze. Hell, no. He had no one. He'd made damned sure he severed those ties when Brynna and her other twin daughter had died.

"No one else, Sarita."

"Hmm." She gave him a skeptical glance, then turned and began folding Annie's flannel squares. "I thought your wife had a *tia* back east."

Even mentioning out loud that the woman existed made Sage uncomfortable. And angry as hell. She'd prejudged him, finding him guilty of a sin he hadn't committed. "It'll be a cold day in hell before I'd ever let her know about Annie."

Sarita glanced up briefly, then bent to her duty again. "Ah, *sí*. You don't like her?"

"Sarita," Sage began, "if that cold, heartless witch ever finds out I have Annie, she'll be out here so fast, she'll make your head spin. And," he added with a sarcastic smile, "she'll probably arrive on a broomstick."

Sarita dropped what she was doing, crossed herself and scurried past him. As he watched her leave the room, he wondered a little sheepishly which of his words had offended her the most.

Kate thanked the buggy driver and fanned away the dry dust that swirled in the air as the wheels spit gravel. Bringing her handkerchief to her mouth, she coughed, trying to dislodge the disgusting clump of dirt in her throat. She ran her tongue over the grit on her teeth and shuddered.

The multicolored mountains in the distance seemed only a painting, a bedeviling enticement that skirted the dull, flat prairie on which she now stood. Lord, she thought, her heart sinking, even the land was godless.

Turning slowly, she surveyed the house ... if one could call it that. Her heart sank further and she choked up, thinking about how her sweet Brynna had put up with such a shack. Hopefully, the inside was decorated with her niece's gentle, feminine touch.

Breathing a determined sigh, Kate picked up her valise and marched to the door, stepping gingerly over the warped and rotted boards on the slanted porch. She took another deep breath, squared her shoulders, and knocked.

She couldn't hide her surprise when the door was opened by a young woman. She was a very pretty thing, of Mexican or Spanish heritage. Her hair was black and shiny, and she had a thick braid, as big around as Kate's fist, resting across one breast. A fleeting fear stormed her brain. Had the godless bastard remarried? If he had, it would make it more difficult to take the child away. She tried not to let the thought deflate her.

The young woman gave her a curious look. "Yes?"

Kate swallowed. "Is . . . is this Mr. Reno's house?"

"*Sí, Señor* Reno lives here."

Kate tried to smile. She had a feeling she wasn't succeeding. "I'm . . . I'm here to see him."

The young woman looked her up and down. "He is not home yet. He will be late, maybe after dark."

Kate stepped inside, gently squeezing past the other woman. "Then, I'll wait."

"Oh, but I—"

"Are you his wife?" Kate held her breath, expelling it heartily when the girl shook her head. "Then, it's important that I talk with him. I've come all the way from Ohio to see him, and I won't leave until I do." She dropped her valise on the floor and folded her arms across her chest.

Briefly, having discovered that the bastard was away, she'd thought how easy it would be to grab the child and run. It was tempting. The sooner she had the poor baby out of Sage Reno's clutches, the better. Hopefully, the baby was too young to be permanently damaged by such a man.

The young woman gasped. *"Dios mio!* You are too young to be the dead wife's *tia.* Um . . . auntie."

Startled and just a little pleased, Kate stared at her. "Oh . . . oh, but I am. How did you know? Did Brynna speak of me?"

The young woman shook her head and quickly turned away. "I didn't know her. I came to work for *Señor* Reno after the . . . the accident."

Kate was dying to know exactly what had happened, but feeding her curiosity would have to wait. And anyway, each time she thought about the death of those two sweet, innocent human beings, she lost all reason. Now was not the time to fly into an uncontrollable rage.

"I'd love to see the . . . the baby, if I could." She kept her feelings in check, for she was being studied. The young woman seemed to size her up, but there was no hostility in the look she gave her. No anger. Only interest.

"Sí," she finally said, then left the room.

Kate examined her surroundings for the first time. She was shocked and surprised at the paucity of furnishings and the lack of any visible feminine touches. The room was clean, and the furniture was of good quality, but there was no real sense of 'home'. What had happened to Brynna's handiwork? Had *he* been anxious to toss everything that reminded him of Brynna out into the dust? Perhaps. To stave off his guilt.

She fumed inwardly, but knew she had to hide it. A plan had begun to form as she rode west, and in order to implement it, she had to force a calm she didn't feel.

Hearing a movement behind her, she turned and watched the Mexican woman come toward her, carrying the child. Kate's heart melted, and she felt tears sting her eyes. The child was beautiful, but that didn't surprise her. Kate was just grateful, and heartsick, too, that the child looked so very much like Brynna. She would always be a reminder of what Kate had lost.

She swallowed, trying to clear the tears from her throat. "What . . . what's her name?"

The woman brushed the child's russet curls from her forehead. "She is Annie."

Kate bit her lip, overwhelmed by her feelings. "Oh, Annie. What a beautiful child you are," she whispered.

Annie put her thumb in her mouth and nestled her head against the woman's shoulder, her leaf-green eyes studying Kate solemnly.

"How old is she?" Kate guessed she was older than a year.

"She is one year plus almost one-half."

Kate continued to feel a maternal pull. "Yes, I would have guessed her to be about that." When she glanced up, she found the Mexican woman watching her carefully.

"You got my letter?"

Kate stepped back, surprised. "The letter?"

The woman nodded. "The letter about Annie."

"*You* wrote me that letter?"

"*Sí.* I am Sarita, *Señor* Reno's housekeeper and friend."

Kate was nearly speechless. "It . . . wasn't signed."

Sarita shook her head. "I did not want to sign it. I did not think it was necessary."

"Does . . . Mr. Reno know you wrote me?"

"No, he knows nothing." She gave Kate a conspiratorial look that turned into a frown. "I am not sure I should have done this. He is not liking you very much."

Kate almost snorted. *The feeling is mutual.* She pretended surprise. "He said that?"

Sarita shrugged, then turned back toward the bedroom. "Come," she said. "Annie needs changing, and we must talk."

She followed Sarita into the bedroom, resisting the urge to pull Annie into her arms and cuddle her. She watched as Sarita changed Annie's flannel diaper, then slipped her into a long, pink flannel dress.

"*Señor* Reno, he is a kind man."

Kate begged to differ, but kept her mouth shut. "Why did you write me?"

"Because he is lonely. And because Annie needs a mother."

The words stunned Kate, and she almost fell to the floor in a heap. "But ... but surely," she sputtered, "you ... you didn't expect me to come out here and ... and ..." She couldn't even say the words, much less finish the sentence.

"And marry *Señor* Reno?"

Kate nodded dumbly. Her chest ached and she had trouble catching her breath.

"Well," Sarita answered on a sigh, "now I don't know." She studied Kate again, then shook her head. "He call you a heartless witch. And," she added, looking embarrassed, "he say that if you find out about Annie, you would surely come try to take her away."

Grateful there was a rocking chair in the room, Kate stumbled to it and sat down. She continued to study the child, trying to keep her self-control. "He knows me only too well. But I suspect his remarks were a bit more sarcastic than that."

Sarita glanced away. "*Sí*, they were. He say you would arrive on a broomstick."

Kate kept quiet but lifted a cynical eyebrow. Her hatred for Sage Reno hadn't abated, nor had his for her, it appeared. "As you can see, the two of us have locked horns from the very beginning. No doubt you wrote me the letter before you found out his feelings for me."

"*Sí*, this is true." Sarita put Annie down and the child toddled to Kate and touched her shiny green skirt.

Sitting quietly, not wanting to frighten the child away, Kate held her breath as Annie poked and probed her skirt. She already loved the girl; she'd known she would. She put out her hand. Annie grabbed her finger and played

with her ring—the one with the tiny emeralds that her father had given her mother on their wedding day.

"And now what do you think?" she finally asked.

"I think," Sarita said, "that when you first arrive on
Señor Reno's doorstep, I make a big mistake. Now," she
added, smiling at Kate, "I think I must hurry home to my
own daughter and leave you to care for Annie until *Señor*
Reno gets home."

Sarita's plan sent shivers of fear over Kate's skin. "Do
you really think that's such a good idea?" Suddenly, to be
left to face Sage Reno alone was at the bottom of Kate's
preferred list of things to do. Oh, she was still angry with
the man, but. . . .

"*Sí*, I think it's a fine idea."

Kate gazed down at Annie, who played with the black
fringe that edged Kate's bolero. The child was good-
natured, healthy and well cared for. Was this Sarita's
doing, or was the man actually a competent father?

Stop it. She refused to soften toward him just because
the baby looked healthy. All at once, she wanted to face
him. She was ready for a confrontation; she'd been itching
for a fight for too long to let the desire for it dwindle and
die. "How do you know I won't take her and leave?"

"Because if you do, *Señor* Reno will be angry with *me*.
I think you want Annie very much, but I do not think you
are a coward who would steal her away."

Kate sighed. So much for her earlier thoughts. They had
been ill planned at best, anyway. But she refused to dis-
miss her idea entirely. Who knows, maybe the godless
Sage Reno would be only too anxious to rid himself of a
burdensome child.

Sage walked his horse toward the barn, surprised to find
it dark. Sarita usually lit a lamp when he was late. He
laughed softly. Obviously Annie had been a handful at

bedtime, and Sarita hadn't even had a chance to leave the house.

As he prepared oats for his mount, he realized that keeping Sarita so late had been unforgivable. She had her own family to care for. Something had to be done, but he didn't know what. He needed more permanent help with Annie, especially on long days like today when he had to be in Cedarville.

Yeah, he thought, wincing as the bandage across his chest pulled on his chest hair. It was days like this when Tessa's whores decided to kill each other that he wondered why he'd accepted the deputy's position. He'd heard the shrieking from the jail, and by the time he'd gotten to Tessa's place, two of her whores were going at it. And all the thanks he'd gotten for breaking up the fight was a knife wound across the chest. Those women were tougher than most men he knew. And meaner, too.

Thankfully, he had a week off before he had to go back and tame whores, sober up drunks, and break up card fights. Time to rest and relax with Annie. Just Annie and him . . . God, it was about time.

He trudged to the house, anxious to collapse in front of the fire with a tall shot of whiskey. If Sarita caught a glimpse of his wound, she'd insist on cleaning it and changing the bandage. Hell, maybe he'd let her do it before she left.

As he climbed to the porch, he glanced around, surprised to find her mount gone. And usually, if he was late, Luis's horse was hitched to the post as well.

A pinch of alarm spread through him, and he bolted to the door, quickly shoving it open. The room was empty. At a swift glance, he saw the fire churning in the fireplace and a kerosene lamp flickering on the table beside the couch. Nothing appeared wrong, yet. . . .

He pulled his Colt revolver from his holster and moved stealthily toward Annie's bedroom.

* * *

Kate sat in the rocker beside Annie's tiny bed, unable to pull her gaze from the sleeping child. How trusting she'd been when Sarita had left. Deep in Kate's heart, she felt it was because Annie knew she was here for her. To rescue her from a father who cared so little for her that he worked himself to death just to avoid having to be with her.

Kate's promise to Sarita that she wouldn't whisk Annie away had begun to gnaw at her. She saw now, more clearly than ever, that Annie should be with her. Sarita appeared to be a fine young woman, but she had a family of her own to care for. And Annie needed someone. No, Kate amended, not just someone. Annie needed *her*.

Annie whimpered in her sleep, and Kate went to her knees beside the bed and touched the child's hair.

"Sarita, what's the—"

Kate's heart leaped! She jumped away from the bed and turned to face the door. Her gaze locked with *his*.

His expression went from confusion to fury in the wink of an eye. "What in the hell are you doing here?"

Her own fury was fueled when she saw his abhorrent gun. "Do you always sneak around your own house with a drawn weapon?"

He strode into the room, shoving the revolver back into his holster. "What in the hell are *you* doing here?" he repeated, not bothering to speak softly.

She stood and faced him, hands on hips, his mere presence heightening her own fury. "Don't you dare wake her with your loud, blasphemous voice."

Before she could think, he'd taken a step toward her, grabbed her wrist and dragged her from the room.

"Now," he growled, once they stood by the fire, "what in the hell are you doing in my home?"

Kate wrenched her wrist from his grip and rubbed it. As she stared up at him, she realized that she hadn't remembered him being quite so large. Or so strong. He could have snapped her wrist like a twig.

"You didn't tell me there was another child," she spat.

"And there was good reason for that." He stepped to the small sideboard and poured himself a drink, tossing it down quickly before pouring himself another.

She studied him then, allowing her gaze to roam his tall frame, up over his wide shoulders to the dark stubble over his cheeks and chin. His tobacco-colored hair was shot with sun-bleached gold threads that shimmered in the lamplight. His brown eyes were rimmed with dark, curly lashes.

He was handsome, no doubt about it, but he was also the devil. An enemy of the most forbidding kind, for she knew very well that he was capable of charming the eyelashes off a mule. Fortunately, she thought, albeit a bit peevishly, he'd never tried working his wiles on her.

That he drank so freely made her even more certain that taking Annie away from him would be the right thing to do. "That sweet, innocent child will rot and die here, just as her mother and sister did."

A brief flicker of pain flashed in his eyes before he gave her a scorching look. "I don't know how you found out about Annie, but it doesn't matter. She's mine, and no one, especially a dried-up prune of a spinster, is going to take her away from me."

Kate gasped and brought her hand to her throat. "You haven't changed. You're still a vile, godless bastard."

"You're absolutely right. And your corset is still so damned tight it makes your eyes bug out."

Kate stiffened and narrowed her gaze at him. "You can say whatever you want to, Mr. Reno. It's what I expect from the likes of you."

He glared back at her, his gaze moving over her slowly, almost provocatively. "You don't even know what happened, and you've already condemned me."

His words, and the look he gave her, sent alarm clanging through her. "Are you going to try to tell me that whatever happened wasn't your fault? That you're innocent? My Lord in heaven, you—"

"I didn't say I was innocent," he interrupted. He studied her between gulps of whiskey. "Nor did I say I was guilty. I am, however, the only one who knows exactly what happened that day."

Kate quelled the urge to snap at him. "Will you share this secret with me? As Brynna's only living relative, I think I have a right to know." She spun away and paced the room, beginning to feel as if she'd been locked in a cage with this man.

"You don't want to know."

At his cryptic statement, a shiver stole up her spine and sank into the roots of her hair. It required an effort, but she turned and faced him. "Of course I want to know. Brynna was my *kin*. She was all I had in the world until . . . until—" She couldn't finish. The pain of Brynna's death was suddenly as fresh as a new wound.

"Until I came and took her away from you?"

She whirled away again. "Yes. And until my dying day, I'll hold you responsible for what happened to her."

There was a long, yawning pause, during which Kate heard the sputtering of the fire on the grate, the howling of the wind around the cabin, and the hammering of her own heart.

"In a way, I *am* responsible."

Kate's pulse leaped, sending a fresh surge of blood pounding into her head. Suddenly the snug collar at her throat became a stricture, and she fought the urge to send the buttons flying.

Turning slowly, she stared at him. "You admit it?"

He tossed the remainder of his drink into the fire, causing it to smoke and hiss. "Would you believe otherwise?"

She gave her head a curt shake. "No."

"Then there's no point arguing about it, is there?"

"I guess not," she answered with a weary sigh.

"Which brings me to ask again, what in the hell are you doing here?"

Kate squared her shoulders and faced him. "I've come to take Annie home with me." For some reason, she held her breath, waiting for his answer.

He barked a laugh, picked up the kerosene lamp and walked toward the kitchen. "Like hell."

Kate trailed after him. "I'm doing what Brynna would have wanted. You can't honestly believe you'd be a better parent than I." It was the wrong thing to say.

He stopped short, causing Kate to slam into his back. In order to keep herself from falling, she had to grab him at the waist. He swore on a hiss of breath, flung her arms from him, and turned on her.

"I'm her *father*, damn it, and no one—I repeat *no one*—is going to take her away from me." He winced, staggered toward a chair and flopped into it, resting his arms on the table.

Kate frowned. He didn't look at all well. In the lamplight, he appeared ashen. "What's wrong with you? Are you ill?"

He snorted a laugh. "You'd like that, wouldn't you? My being too sick to care for Annie would give you just the reason you need to spirit her away from me in the middle of the night." He unbuttoned his shirt and shrugged out of it, exposing the bandage across his chest.

Kate's curiosity turned to concern. Without thinking, she rushed to him. "My Lord in heaven, you're hurt. What happened?"

He began peeling the bandage away, then allowed Kate to finish the job. "It's just a superficial knife wound."

The blood left Kate's face and she felt dizzy. "Knife? You've been knifed?" She sat quickly, afraid her knees wouldn't hold her as she pulled the bandage away from his chest. Sucking in a deep breath, she regained control and studied the wound. Infection had already set in.

"Not that I don't think you might have deserved a good stabbing," she said wryly, "but . . . how did this happen?"

Ignoring her remark, he said, "I'm a deputy sheriff in Cedarville. I . . . I was breaking up a fight."

Suddenly Kate felt a little stab of guilt. "You . . . you're a lawman as well as a rancher?"

He winced as she gently probed his wound. "It pays the rent."

Kate cleared her throat, willing away any sense of admiration or respect for the man. "The wound must be washed. Where will I find what I need?"

He nodded toward the single-door dry sink.

After gathering some supplies, Kate carefully dabbed at the wound, aware that he studied her. She'd tended many farm hands and their wounds and had never been moved by the sight of their naked chests. Most had thin, hairless bodies, whiter than her own. To her dismay, she did remember this man stripped to the waist, sweating and squinting against the hot summer sun as he so easily lifted hay bales onto the wagon. Though she would never have admitted it aloud, it had been a sight to behold.

Dark brown hair curled across the wide expanse, covering his nipples. His skin was warm, stretched tightly over bulging, well-defined muscles. His arms flexed tensely as she worked, and she tossed furtive glances at his sculpted, hair-dusted forearms, puzzled at the achy feeling that tunneled into the pit of her stomach.

He did not have an unpleasant smell, she discovered. It was earthy, a mixture of soil and fresh air, and a hint of sweat. As with the manly form of his naked chest and arms, his scent burrowed deep within her. She took a ragged breath and stepped away.

"You'll need a poultice to draw out the infection," she

said, hoping her voice was strong, without the simper of a woman affected by a man.

He grimaced. "What do you suggest?"

Standing well away from him, she was able to find her strident tongue. "Well, there's always cow dung."

He raised one lush brown eyebrow. "Any other suggestions?"

She kept her distance, finding it easier to spar with him. "Do you have any salt pork?"

He nodded. "You should find some packed in the cellar."

Kate hurried to finish her job, for she discovered that being near him tossed her insides into confusion. And that would never do. She was here for one purpose only, and couldn't allow anything about Sage Reno to interfere with her plans.

2

Sage studied the spinster as she busied herself cleaning up the remnants of her nursing. It was a damned shame she pulled her hair back so tightly, for when the light from the lamp fanned out over her, that flame-red hair crackled with life, almost glowed. He'd surprised himself by wondering if she ever wore it loose, hanging in deep waves over her shoulders and down her back. Fat chance. She probably slept with the old maid bun tight to her head.

And she had that fresh, flowery smell about her. Like she'd bathed in pools of jasmine. Vaguely, he remembered that from before. He'd wanted to believe it was a spinsterish, old-lady smell, but he knew it wasn't. It didn't make him want to help her across a busy street.... He wasn't quite sure what it made him want to do.

Yeah, now that she was around him again, he remembered the scent from before—and a lot of other things. Her sweet smell had seemed so contrary to her sour disposition. It still did. He decided it was too bad she didn't act like she smelled.

"How did you get out here, anyway?"

She arched a russet brow at him, her face so close to his that he could see the gold flecks in her green eyes. "By broomstick, Mr. Reno. I thought you knew."

He grunted and looked away. *Sarita.* Women always seemed to stick together.

Continuing to study the spinster again, he realized she hadn't changed a bit from what he remembered. She was still trussed up like a Thanksgiving prairie chicken, all the way to her lily-white earlobes, just as she had been every hot, humid day he'd worked on her farm.

Somehow he had to convince her that Annie was better off with him, but the spinster was a strong-willed woman, not likely to swoon and titter if he tried to flatter her. That would undoubtedly only offend her. And hell, he wasn't a sweet talker anyway, no matter what she believed. He'd never be able to carry it off.

Possession and love tugged at his heart. If she thought she could take Annie away from him, she had another think coming, damn it.

Now she stood, nervously stepping from one foot to the other. "Well," she said with a sigh, "I guess you'd best take me into town so I can get a room."

He swore again, tempted to tell her to ride her broom in. "At this time of night? Hell, it'll take over an hour to get there in the dark, and I'm not sure they'll have a room for you anyway." He studied her carefully. "Unless you got a room before you came charging out here."

She flushed, but refused to look away. "No. I . . . I guess I was too anxious to get here. I didn't think of it."

He released an exaggerated sigh and stood. "Well, now, isn't this a dandy situation you've gotten yourself into?"

She tossed a nervous glance toward the door. "Well, surely you must have an extra room—"

"No, I don't. There's my room and Annie's. Of course, there's that short couch in the other room. You're welcome to sleep there—for one night." *Before you get the hell out of my life.*

The spinster's flush deepened. "Actually, now that I really consider it, I don't think it would be proper at all for us to sleep under the same roof. No, not proper at all." She sighed. "Well, I suppose I could sleep in the barn . . ."

Sage was almost too tired to argue with her. If that's where she wanted to sleep, she could be his guest. The hay was fresh, and he'd give her a blanket. It would serve her right for charging out here like a renegade rider, threatening to take his Annie away from him.

But after he'd tossed her a blanket and watched her trudge toward the door, he knew he couldn't let her do it.

"Ah, hell," he muttered. "You'd better sleep in my bed."

She turned, relief apparent in every movement. "Oh, but . . . but your wound . . ." The words faded away, as though she really wasn't all that concerned.

On an exasperated sigh, he answered, "I've done it before. It won't hurt me to do it again." He grabbed the blanket from her and headed for the door. To make sure they understood one another, he turned and glared at her. "Both of you'd better be here when I wake up."

She brought her hand to her chest, drawing his gaze. Surprisingly, even though she'd hovered over him while tending his wound, he hadn't noticed before how well endowed she was.

"I have no intention of whisking poor Annie out into

the night, Mr. Reno. I have better sense than that, thank you."

Nodding briskly, he left the cabin and strode to the barn.

Kate let out a whoosh of air as she went back into Annie's room. She took one last look at the child's sweet face before turning out the lamp and leaving the room in darkness.

Her valise still sat by the front door. She picked it up and marched to the other bedroom—*his* bedroom. She turned up the lamp that kept the room lit in low, muted tones, and surveyed his domain. Oddly, it was very masculine, as though no woman had ever moved into it. But she knew that was wrong.

Her heart fluttered lightly. Brynna had slept here. With *him*. For some strange reason, she shivered.

After slipping into her long, white nightgown, she loosened her hair, sighing contentedly as she combed her fingers through the long, tangled mass.

She pulled the quilt back and slid into bed, gingerly stretching her legs toward the cold bottom. For all that she wanted to hate being in Sage Reno's bed, it felt wonderful. She'd had a reasonably comfortable train ride, but the stage she'd had to take from Amarillo to Cedarville had been ghastly, then there'd been that dirty, dusty buggy ride.

Sighing, she turned on her side and slipped quietly into a deep sleep.

A sound, coming from far away, threatened to wake her. She moaned softly and frowned, trying to burrow deeper into the bedding. Soon, however, she could no longer ignore it. Fighting through her sleepy fog, she blinked and squinted as she hiked herself up on an elbow.

Suddenly the sound registered. *Annie!* She tossed off the quilt and hurried toward the sound, stubbing her toe on a chair. Cursing mildly, she continued at a limping run to the door, crashing into a chest that stood against the wall.

Ignoring her lumps, she felt her way to the other room. The room was light; she remembered distinctly turning out the lamp. She rushed in, weaving from side to side, using the wall for support.

Annie was quiet now, cuddled in her father's embrace. He glanced up from the rocking chair as Kate stumbled into the room. "Good Christ, woman. Doesn't anything wake you?"

Ignoring his sarcasm and his blasphemy, Kate shoved her hair away from her face and dropped to her knees in front of them. "Is everything all right?"

They were an incongruous twosome, this father and daughter. She, so tiny, soft and sweet; he, so big, hard, and fierce looking. Yet they seemed to fit. Annie was nestled against her father's wide, bare chest, her thumb in her mouth, and her eyes drooping sleepily.

Kate's gaze went to his face; she found him studying her, dissecting her openly. She felt vulnerable and indecent, although her gown was buttoned clear to her chin. Her breasts suddenly felt heavy and her nipples grazed the soft cotton of her gown, pebbling tightly. It was a feeling she'd never experienced before, and it frightened her.

He looked away abruptly. "She had a nightmare. It happens sometimes."

Kate stood carefully, her body still betraying her. "And you heard her crying, even from the barn," she said, almost to herself.

He made a gruff coughing sound, but Annie back in bed and lifted the quilt over her. She grabbed her rag doll, put her thumb back in her mouth, and was asleep immediately.

As he lifted the lamp off the bedside table, he asked, "Can you find your way back to the bedroom without breaking my furniture or killing yourself?"

She blushed; he'd heard her slamming into things in her

groggy stupor. "I'm sure I'll manage, thank you." She lifted her chin, squared her shoulders, and left the room as gracefully as possible, given the circumstances.

The following morning, just as the sun was coming up, Sage awoke, sleepy and not just a little disgruntled. Once he'd gotten back to his blanket, he'd stayed awake thinking about his situation. He wanted to believe that he alone could care for Annie in the future, but he knew he was wrong. Every little girl needed a mother, especially out here where life was so bleak and hard. He died a little inside when he thought about his precious daughter growing up, working like a man in a land that was so hard on women.

And he needed help around the house. As much as he appreciated Sarita, he couldn't selfishly take up so much of her time. She had a home and family of her own to care for. Not that she wouldn't do it if he asked. He knew she would; he just couldn't let her. He needed a woman of his own. . . .

The spinster had some claim on Annie, of course. But he'd stayed awake most of the night trying to figure a way around it. Trying to figure a way to avoid having to confront the issue. Trying to find a way to be rid of the woman forever. In the end, though, in the quiet of the black night, he knew what he had to do.

As he approached the house, breakfast smells assaulted his nostrils, and his mouth watered. Hell, at least she was good for something, he thought caustically. Last night he'd heard Annie's cries immediately; they'd awakened him out of a not-so-sound sleep. He swore it had been a full five minutes before he'd even heard the spinster staggering into the bedroom furniture.

He cursed, the memory of her breasts loose and full beneath her nightgown boring into his brain. They were more than a handful, much more. And that hair. . . . All that rich, rusty red hair falling over her shoulders and down her back. She actually looked . . . human.

His mouth suddenly went dry and his groin tightened. Ah, hell. She was still a spinster, through and through. He'd just been surprised that spinsters had breasts that weren't either flat as fried eggs or as long and flaccid as hounds ears.

He stepped onto the porch, cringing at its state of disrepair. He had to fix it one of these days, now that he had some time off. When Brynna had been alive, he'd made excuses not to be around. After she died, he'd felt so much guilt, he couldn't stand to stay.

As he pushed open the cabin door, the breakfast smells grew stronger, and more delicious. He frowned, wanting to find fault where he knew there was none to be found.

He stopped at the kitchen door. Annie sat at the table in the special high chair he'd made for her, picking up bite-sized pieces of a biscuit and shoving them into her mouth. When she saw him, she clapped her hands and grinned, the chunk of biscuit she'd just stuffed into her mouth dropping into her lap.

"Papa!"

He went to her and kissed her cheek. When he looked up, the spinster stood before him, offering him a cup of coffee. She was all trussed up again, and he felt a twinge of disappointment.

He accepted the coffee then hovered near the table, suddenly uncomfortable in his own kitchen.

She was back at the stove. "How's your wound this morning?"

He sat down across from his daughter and tasted the coffee. It was delicious. He forced himself not to sigh audibly. "Feels all right. Maybe we can get rid of the salt pork, though." He watched her come toward him, a plate of biscuits and gravy in her hands.

His mouth watered again; she'd made sausage and milk

gravy. He remembered from his brief stint on her farm that it was the best he'd ever tasted. He forced himself to act civilized and eat like a gentleman.

"Where's Sarita this morning?"

The spinster sat down on the other side of him and nursed her coffee. "Just as I was getting Annie up, a young boy came by to tell me Sarita's child is still sick." She cleared her throat, a nervous sound to Sage's ears. "I guess she won't be here today."

"No, 'guess not." He ate heartily, enjoying the kind of cooking he'd grown up on. Sarita's cooking was fine, but he'd never quite acquired a taste for Mexican food. And Brynna ... well, Brynna had never acquired a taste for cooking.

When he was full and extremely contented, he sat back and studied the spinster again. With incredible ease, she'd cleaned Annie up and changed her, as if she'd been accomplishing such tasks since the beginning. The thought frightened him some, but it also solidified his earlier deliberations—those that had kept him awake most of the night.

"I think we've got some talking to do," he finally said.

She was holding Annie on her lap, allowing her to play with the tiny buttons of her dress that climbed all the way up to her pointy chin. "Yes, I do believe you're right."

He plowed right in, knowing that if he didn't, he'd turn chicken and run. "You know I won't let you take Annie away from me."

She toyed with Annie's hair, then moved her hand to his daughter's back, where she rubbed gentle circles. It stunned him for a moment. How could she know that was the best way to get Annie to sleep?

"It may have been rash to come out here, Mr. Reno, but I firmly believe I'd be the better parent, even if you are her father."

"Hell, you don't even wake up when she cries," he muttered darkly.

A blush crept into her cheeks. "You must remember that I'm unaccustomed to being awakened by a child's cries. Believe me," she added with determination, "it won't happen again."

"No, it won't. Because you'll be gone."

She gave him a frigid smile. "And how is that going to happen if I refuse to leave?"

He stifled a curse. With her feeling like that, how could he trust her not to take Annie and run? All right, time for the most drastic of measures.

"I have a suggestion." He held his breath, hating what he was about to suggest but knowing there was no other way, save tying her up and tossing her into the creek. But no, not even he could do that.

"I can't imagine what could benefit both of us, Mr. Reno."

"Marry me." He held his breath again.

Her jaw dropped and her eyes widened. Her face lost all color, then color flooded back in deep pink tones. Somehow he'd finally rendered her speechless. If he hadn't been so desperate, it might have been pleasant to watch.

Suddenly she put Annie on the floor and stood, steadying herself by gripping the table. "If you'll excuse me, Mr. Reno . . ." She walked from the room, obviously dazed.

Kate stumbled to the bedroom and sat down on the bed. Her heart pounded and her mouth was as dry as the dust that swirled outside on the godless plain. He'd actually proposed *marriage!* Although she was as shocked as she'd been when Sarita had mentioned it, she felt entirely different about it. Oh, it was still a repulsive notion, and he surely didn't expect her to accept. It was inconceivable. She still abhorred him. She'd hated him with every fiber of her being since the day she'd first seen him, tall, handsome as the devil and cocky as a rooster. He'd been a man to avoid then, and he was a man to avoid now.

Pulling in deep, measured breaths, she realized she felt better, back in control. She stood, went to the mirror and studied her reflection. No blushing bride type, she. She knew full well what his intentions were. *Fool.* He was a fool if he thought she couldn't see through to his shallow soul.

She marched from the room, back into the kitchen, stopping short as she watched him play *pat-a-cake* with Annie. Something akin to pleasure fluttered through her, but she shoved it aside.

He gave her a guarded look. "Feel better now?"

"Infinitely," she answered stiffly.

"My offer took you by surprise."

She poured herself a cup of coffee, aware that both of her hands shook badly. "Your offer is unthinkable."

He muttered a curse. "It wouldn't be a normal marriage." He let his gaze rake over her. "God knows you wouldn't have to worry about your damn, precious virtue."

For some foolish reason, his statement hurt. She'd known she wasn't a desirable woman, but coming from him, the remark bothered her. "The state of my ... my chastity is not a subject you are free to discuss, Mr. Reno."

He put Annie on the floor, where she immediately toddled over to Kate, who automatically picked her up and cuddled her.

Muttering again, he went to the window and stared outside. "It would be a marriage in name only. What have you got to go back to, anyway? The fact that you're here suggests to me that you no longer have the farm." He turned briefly. "Am I right?"

She lowered her gaze and nodded briskly, suddenly remembering her feelings of failure when she'd finally had to let it go.

"Annie.... Well, Annie seems to like you, and I....

Ah, hell. I need someone around here. Sarita has a family of her own. I can't keep expecting her to neglect their needs for me and Annie. And," he finally added, "I wouldn't touch you. I'd even put it in writing if you want. I'll never demand my ... my husbandly rights."

Kate knew she was losing her mind, because the idea began to sound reasonable. Marriage without all the troublesome emotional trappings appealed to her. "It would be more like a business arrangement, then?"

He turned, giving her his profile. "Exactly."

A thousand emotions rattled through her. What *did* she have to go back to? Empty rooms above a general store. Hardly an ideal place to raise a child, but she'd have done it. She still wondered if it wasn't the sanest, most sensible thing to do. And she'd always been a sane, sensible person.

Glancing down at Annie, Kate discovered she was asleep. How easily she'd fallen into caring for this child who was, in essence, a part of her. "You're crazy, you know."

He huffed a laugh. "Crazy as a damned loon. Pardon the language, ma'am."

She smiled as well. She was beginning to think she was no saner than he.

He turned fully now, studying her carefully. "What about my offer?"

"I would basically be Annie's nurse and your housekeeper."

He gave her a noncommittal nod. "Except that by marrying me we would legally share custody of Annie."

Kate's heart expanded, and for the first time she felt a twinge of excitement. "It sounds too good to be true. I must be going mad, too."

"Then, you accept?"

It was the anticipation of legally becoming Annie's

mother that caused Kate's heart to flip-flop in her chest . . .
wasn't it? "I believe I will accept, Mr. Reno."

"Fine, ma'am. I'll make the arrangements."

As Kate watched him leave the kitchen, she realized
that not once since she'd arrived had he called her by
name. It shouldn't have mattered, but somewhere, deep in
the recesses of her feminine soul, she wished he had.

3

The three of them rode in silence from the church.
Kate, uncomfortable in her new role as wife and
mother, wondered what insanity had taken possession of
her. Mr. Reno, too, appeared uneasy, for he sat stiffly beside her. Annie was the only one who didn't sense the tension; she slept in Kate's arms.

"It's all pretty normal, you know."

Kate turned and surveyed this man who was now her
husband. His size was still unsettling. And the way his
muscles bunched up under his shirt sleeves. . . . She had
the oddest notion to squeeze his arm just to see if it was
as hard as it looked.

"I beg your pardon?"

"People getting married without hardly knowing each
other. It's done out of a sense of practicality, ma'am. Most
women, and some men, too, wouldn't survive on the plains
and prairies of this country without a mate."

Kate shivered. 'Mate' was such an earthy, lustful word
to describe what he was to her. "I realize what you're saying is true in many cases, Mr. Reno, but it hardly describes
us."

He flicked the reins over the team, and the horses turned onto the dusty, rutted two mile road that led to the cabin. "Seems to me it describes us perfectly, ma'am."

She swallowed a snort, clearing her throat instead. "I doubt that every couple who marries out of convenience has a history of rancor, such as we have."

"You mean me, thinking you're a dried-up, mean-spirited, grudge-carrying spinster, and you, feeling certain I led your sweet little Brynna into the arms of the devil?"

Her reaction to his words was swifter and harsher than she would have expected. *Dried-up . . . mean-spirited . . . grudge-carrying . . . spinster. . . .* She hadn't thought of herself quite that way. For some foolish reason it hurt that *he* had. She sat up straight, holding her head high.

"I still feel that way, Mr. Reno. I sincerely feel that if it hadn't been for you, Brynna would never have left home." And she'd be alive now, she wanted to add, but didn't.

He released a lusty sigh. "We're often blinded by those we love the most."

She eyed him, daring him to mock the dead. "I gather you're trying to say that Brynna wasn't exactly what I wanted her to be."

He was quiet for a moment, then said, "Brynna was a lot of things you wouldn't have wanted her to be."

Her spine stiffened more. "I think you should explain yourself, Mr. Reno."

He took off his hat, combed his fingers through the thick, brown hair, then settled it back on his head. "Maybe. In time."

Kate would have insisted he explain, but just then Annie woke up and all mystifying conversation ceased.

"Are you sure you'll be all right out here?" Kate gave the corner of the barn a dubious look. Even though there were quilts over the hay, a table and a kerosene lamp, it was a pathetic bedroom for any man—especially one who had a perfectly good bedroom in his own cabin . . . one she'd taken from him.

He surveyed the corner. "It'll do."

Kate thought about the impending winter. This might be Texas, but she'd heard that the plains could be brutally cold.

"You know, Mr. Reno—"

"Sage," he interrupted. "You can't keep calling me 'Mr. Reno'. You'd better call me 'Sage'."

She swallowed hard. It was true, of course. But their marriage hadn't been made in heaven, and calling any man, especially him, by his given name seemed so . . . intimate.

Suddenly she turned on him, her Irish up. "And what will you be calling me?"

Frowning, he asked, "What do you mean?"

"I mean," she said, her hands clenched on her hips, "ever since I arrived, you haven't called me anything but 'ma'am'. Why, that's even more ridiculous than me calling you 'Mr. Reno'."

He raked his fingers through his hair again, a gesture she'd come to equate with his discomfort. "Yeah, I guess you're right. Trouble is—" He glanced away, appearing embarrassed.

"Yes?" He knew her name; she'd had to give it to the preacher just the day before. "Surely you haven't forgotten my name, already?"

"No, ma'am. I just don't know what you prefer. Kathleen, Kate, or Katie."

All of those names sounded surprisingly pleasant to her, especially rolling out so smoothly in his rich, baritone voice. For some bizarre reason, she had a quick flash of him kissing her and calling her 'Katie'. It left her skin clammy and her heart drumming painfully in her chest.

"Kate," she answered tersely, shoving away the pleasure. "Just . . . just call me Kate."

He studied her, a smile tugging one corner of his mouth. "Of course. Kate, it is."

Again, her name on his tongue sent an oddly pleasant prickly pins sensation through her scalp. She shook her head and cleared her throat. "Yes. Well. What I was going to say was, before winter sets in, perhaps we should purchase a cot and put it in Annie's room. I'll be happy to sleep in there and give you back your bedroom."

"Winter." He kicked at the hay with the toe of his battered boot. "And it'll be coming on soon. We could get a blizzard up here any day."

Kate was incredulous. "A blizzard? But . . . but we're so far south."

"Yes, but we're on the plain. Winter weather is unpredictable up here."

"Then . . . then we should order the cot quickly, shouldn't we?"

Nodding, he answered, "Yeah. I'll take care of it the first chance I get."

She heard Annie's cries from the cabin. As she scurried to the barn door, she said, "Lunch will be ready in an hour."

He watched her leave, the gentle swell of her hips moving her skirt from side to side. They'd been married only yesterday, and already he was cursing himself for promising he'd never touch her. Hell, not that he really wanted to. Her with her spinster hairdo and trussed-up wardrobe. But, damn it, he had normal male urges. What in the hell was he supposed to do about those?

You should have thought about that before, you stupid bastard. Yeah, well he hadn't. He still didn't know why he offered marriage so quickly, especially to a woman he *knew* hated every inch of him—hated him for something he hadn't even done.

God, there were times when he wondered if he'd lost his mind completely. Yet, even though this flame-haired harridan was a prickly, no-nonsense kind of woman, she'd probably survive the harsh existence of a Texas wife. Hell, a woman like that would probably survive alone, beating off cougars with her bare hands.

He cursed again, his gaze going back to study his bed of hay. Had he just imagined the sensuality beneath her grim exterior, or was it really there? He continued to assess his new 'bed,' his thoughts suddenly filling with pictures of the two of them having a good, sweaty roll in the hay. Her hair, loose as he'd seen it that night Annie had awakened, would fan out over the tops of her breasts, and her skirt would be up, her lily-white thighs splayed wide to accept him. He could almost see the thick thatch of rust-colored hair that no doubt covered her womanhood. . . .

Turning away, he cursed his instant arousal. Her soft sensuality was just wishful thinking on his part. Hell, she probably wore one of those old-fashioned chastity belts just to be on the safe side. He shook his head and grimaced. As if any sane man would seriously think about ravishing *her.*

He'd made a hasty decision, and because he'd married her so quickly, he was probably just frantic to find something redeeming in a cold, frigid relationship that would go on and on into old age. He shuddered at the thought, yet wondered how it could be any worse than the relationship he'd already had. . . .

Her new husband had taken some time off from his job. She'd learned that there were three other deputies, and they took turns helping the elderly sheriff keep the law in Cedarville.

He'd fixed the porch, replacing all the old boards with

new ones. Kate heard him outside and, against her better judgment, was anxious for a glimpse of him. She crossed to the window and watched him. He'd shucked off his shirt and was bare chested, save for the bandage over his wound, which was healing nicely.

It was sinful, really, and inexcusable how she sneaked peeks at him. Just as she'd remembered, he was a magnificent male specimen. Tall, broad of shoulder, thickly muscled, with dark curly hair covering his chest. . . .

As he labored, sweat ran in tiny rivers over his torso, tunneling into the chest hair, matting it to his skin. Oh, it did odd things to her insides, things that didn't seem decent, or proper. Things she'd never have believed she would feel. Things she hadn't even known existed until now.

He glanced up, catching her staring at him. Her heart did a strange flip-flop. She suddenly realized she'd been holding her breath, and she gasped for air. She'd be wise to remember just who he was, and what he'd done. She was dismayed that her bitterness was no longer automatic, that it was something she had to dredge up from deep inside her.

Opening the door briskly, she announced, "Lunch is ready."

He stood and arched his back, exposing his firm, naked chest to her hungry—no, deprived—gaze. It wasn't that she needed to watch him; it was just that she couldn't seem to get enough of it. It was purely educational. *Oh, right, Kate.* She frowned at her disloyal inner voice.

"Fine. I have to be gone for a while this afternoon. I'll put in an order for that cot while I'm at it. Might not get home until after dark. Will you be all right here, or should I ride over and tell Sarita to keep you company?"

She watched him go to the washstand and wash himself off. The sleekness of sweat was now replaced by the slickness of water. His skin, brown and warm, glistened. Kate swallowed hard and mildly cursed these new, mysterious feelings. "I won't have you disrupting that poor girl's life any longer. Annie and I will be just fine."

After he'd gone, she felt restless. Annie was napping, and the afternoon seemed to yawn in front of Kate like an endless canyon. She found herself tearing the kitchen apart, learning what supplies there were, and organizing them the way she wanted.

When Annie woke, Kate dragged the tin tub into the kitchen and filled it alternately with hot and cold water. After playing with Annie and feeding her supper, she undressed her and sat her in her bath. Annie squealed with delight, splashing gaily.

"Mama," she said, pointing to Kate, then slapping her plump little hands on top of the water.

A lump of emotion clogged Kate's throat. *Mama?* Fighting tears, she reached out and touched Annie's hair. Yes, she'd known she would be Annie's mama, but ... hearing the words caused Kate pain and not a little anxiety. The permanence of being Annie's mother didn't bother her. It was the unalterable state of being Mrs. Sage Reno that frightened her beyond words.

Kate eyed the bathwater. She was hot and sticky from toiling in the kitchen. She'd already unbuttoned her dress, nearly to her bosom. Sweat trickled over her scalp, soaking the hair at her temples. A bath would feel wonderful.

But what about *him?* He'd said he wouldn't be back until evening. Did she dare take the chance?

She eyed the water again, and could almost feel the pleasure it would give her to bathe and shampoo her hair. After retrieving her nightgown from the bedroom, she added more water, flung off her clothes, and joined Annie in the tub.

The first thing Sage had heard when he rode into town was that a cougar had killed a couple of horses at a neighbor's ranch. That meant every other ranch in the area was in danger of the cougar's visit until it was killed. He'd made it back to his ranch in half the time it usually took him to get there, because he had to warn Kate.

He swung from the saddle, tossed the reins over the hitching post, and bounded up the porch steps. As he strode into the cabin, he heard Annie's giggle from the kitchen, and he let out a pent-up breath. They were all right. Still, he had to warn Kate, alert her to the possibility of danger.

He stepped through the kitchen door and his jaw went slack. Annie and Kate were in the tub, Annie sitting between Kate's legs, splashing and playing with the suds that fell from Kate's long red hair.

He held his breath, knowing he should shuffle his feet or clear his throat—something to announce himself. Instead, he stared. At the soft, milky-white shoulders and the hands that now scrubbed her head. At the tiny patches of red hair under her shapely arms. At the pale pink nipples that crowned her high, firm breasts . . . breasts that before this were hidden beneath corsets and covers and high-necked dresses. It was a crime to hide such beauty.

Her breasts were magnificent, jiggling slightly as she moved her arms, and shiny from the bath water. Had she washed them with care, soaping them thoroughly, massaging them lovingly, or had she carelessly ignored them, unaware of their beauty or ashamed of their existence? Every inch of his manhood tightened, pulled, swelled, itched with desire.

"Papa!"

He heard Kate's grasp, and quickly turned away. "I'm sorry," he nearly stuttered. "I—"

"Oh . . . oh . . . oh, my . . ." For the second time since she'd arrived on his doorstep, the woman appeared to have trouble with speech.

He apologized again. "Here," he said, his eyes turned

away, "let me take Annie out. I'll, er . . ." He cleared his throat gruffly. "I'll get her ready for bed." He took a towel from the chair by the tub and lifted Annie out, carefully keeping his gaze averted.

"Mama," the child chirped, unaware of the provocative tension in the room as she pointed to the naked woman in the tub.

Sage quickly left the kitchen, Annie's words still singing in his head. Mama? She called her 'Mama'? For a brief moment, his desire fled and his anger at this woman resurfaced. She sure as hell hadn't wasted any time, had she? He couldn't help but wonder if, despite the vows of marriage, the woman wouldn't still spirit Annie away from him.

Kate quickly rinsed her hair, wrapped a towel around it and stepped from the tub. Her knees were so weak, she could barely stand. Oh, *God,* what had possessed her to do this? She could have done it at a time when he was aware of her plans, thus preventing such embarrassment. After drying off, she pulled on her long, white nightgown. Repeatedly, she tried to fasten the buttons at her neck, but her fingers shook so badly, she wasn't able to do it.

She wondered how long he'd stood there, ogling her. Long enough, no doubt. Her embarrassment faded slowly into anger.

She was sitting on the couch by the fire, drying her hair, when Annie came running up to her, all ready for bed. She pulled the child onto her lap and automatically kissed her on the cheek.

"Mama," she said sweetly, touching Kate's hair.

Kate looked up and saw Sage lounging in the doorway. His cavalier stance was an act, for although one shoulder rested against the doorjamb and one ankle was casually crossed over the other, there was anger in his eyes. What did *he* have to be angry about? He'd no doubt gotten an eye full. The idea that he'd seen her in such a state filled her with shame—and a multitude of other emotions that she didn't want to examine.

"Come on, Annie. It's time for bed." His voice was gruff, huskier than usual.

She kissed Kate's cheek and gave her a hug, then slid to the floor and toddled to her father.

Kate waited for him to return. Obviously there was something on his mind. The tension in the air was thick enough to cut. She continued to brush her hair even when she knew he'd returned and was standing behind her.

"It didn't take you long, did it?"

Surprised at the resentment in his voice, she turned and looked up at him. "What do you mean?"

"How long have you been coaching her?"

Kate frowned. "Coaching her?"

He strode past her to the fire, where he added another log. "To call you 'mama'?"

So that was it. Well, let him think the worst. He would, anyway. "I can't help but wonder why you're so upset about it. After all, by marrying you, I *did* become her mother now, didn't I?"

He went to the sideboard and poured himself a drink, then suddenly remembered his manners. "Care for some?"

Normally, Kate rarely drank. But tonight . . . "I'll have some sherry, if you have it."

He snorted a laugh. "Sorry. All I've got is whiskey."

She'd never tasted whiskey. At this moment, she didn't care if it was vile, she needed *something*. "F—fine. I'll take a little, thank you."

He nodded, poured her a small glass, and handed it to her. She took a grateful sip, swallowing it quickly to hide the taste. She shuddered at the bitterness, unable to keep her eyes from watering. It was truly wretched stuff, but after the first sip, she began to feel a warmth in her belly.

They sat in silence, staring at the fire. Suddenly Kate remembered that he wasn't supposed to be home this early. "Why did you come back so soon?"

His gaze moved slowly over her hair, her breasts, and the opening at her throat and neck. She felt a blush heat her cheeks, and the feeling in the pit of her stomach wasn't shame.

"Surely not to ogle me in my bath," she added tartly.

He glanced away. "I rode back to warn you that there's a cougar roaming the area. He's killed cattle mostly, but I just want you to be aware of the danger. When you're outside with Annie and I'm not around."

Kate felt a stab of fear. "And what am I to do if I see him?"

"Can you shoot?"

She gave him a hesitant nod. "I'm a fair shot."

"Just remember, the rifle is there, above the mantel."

She glanced at the weapon, experiencing another jolt of fear. It was her first shock of reality. Suddenly she realized just how dangerous it was to live here, how hazardous it was to try to raise a child here. Half the time he wasn't even home, but working a job in Cedarville. It stirred the coals of her anger, igniting them again.

"How dare you leave Annie out here in this Godforsaken place while you go off to work. It's a wonder you haven't lost her the way you lost Brynna. If it were up to me, I'd—"

"No!" He slammed his glass down on the table beside the couch. Turning, he grabbed her shoulders. "It's *not* up to you. None of it. Don't get any bright ideas about Annie. I admit this isn't the best place in the world to raise a child, but it happens to be where I am. I make every effort to keep her safe. I'd never risk her life. *Never.*"

His fingers pinched her, heightening her own fury, escalating her fear. "You're hurting me."

His gaze narrowed, his brown eyes darkened to black, and a nerve jumped in his jaw. His grip softened, but he didn't release her. "You've got to learn to trust me. I know you find it hard, considering what you . . . what you think you know. But I'd never let anything harm Annie. Or . . . or you. I don't take my responsibilities lightly."

It was too much, this concern. This caring. She tried to pull away, but he held her firmly. She pulled again, her hair flying over her face. She blew at it, moving it enough so that she could see him. His nearness made her weak, unsure of herself. "Please. Let go of me."

His gaze roamed her face now, and his pupils continued to darken. "You could turn into a handful, woman."

And he was dangerously close to cracking her waspish facade. They'd never been this close, and she'd never dreamed how it could feel. It was exciting. Terrifying. "I want you to let me go."

He nodded, giving her a crooked smile. "I know you do. And I will. But . . . but don't you think maybe one little kiss is in order?"

She swallowed, her breath then coming rapidly. "No," she said. "Oh, no. I don't think so."

"Even at the church, we didn't seal this arrangement with a kiss, Kate. Why, I'm not sure it's even legal unless we kiss."

She stared up at him. Was he teasing her? It . . . it was so unlike him. . . . "I don't think a kiss means anything."

"Then it shouldn't bother you if we do it."

She was torn. She knew that by not disagreeing she was, in essence, telling him she wanted him to kiss her. She stared into his face. He had a hard, firm jaw, and a heavy five o'clock shadow covering his cheeks and chin, although she knew he'd shaved before he left for town. He was big and rough, gentle and kind. His mouth drew her gaze and she knew she wouldn't turn away.

He lowered his head and touched her lips with his, moving gently, experimentally over hers. Frightened at the feelings that rushed through her, she gave him a quick peck and pulled away, her heart thundering in her chest.

He gave her a strange, lazy smile. "Ah, Kate. I think there's more to be had than that."

His mouth came down on hers again, harder this time, but still unthreatening. She wanted to push away, to turn her face away, but his hand suddenly came up and held her head firmly. She knew she couldn't fight his strength, but she refused to respond in any way.

Much to her dismay, her body thought differently. Deep in the recesses of that soft, warm place between her legs she felt an odd stirring, one that coiled up through her belly, touching magical secret places all along the way. Something long locked away, rusted from lack of use, began to soften, open, and she found herself kissing him back.

His tongue found hers, and she gasped into his mouth, surprised at the pleasure such an improper response summoned. The kiss went on and on, weakening Kate's defenses, softening her response even more.

Suddenly, all too suddenly, he pulled away and stared down at her. "So," he said, his voice dripping with drowsy sexuality, "there's a real live woman under that tight corset and old maid's hairdo, after all."

Confused at her conflicting feelings, she pulled away and smacked his jaw with the flat of her hand. As she stood, she glared down at him, wondering just who she despised more, herself or him. "Don't you ever try that again. *Not ever again.* If you do, so help me, I'll kill you as you sleep."

As she stumbled to the bedroom, drowning in a mixture of shame and desire, she knew that for better or worse, his kiss had changed her life permanently.

4

They squared off in silence, like predator and prey, for two days. Sage was reluctant to leave the cabin, fearing that Kate, in her anger, would ferry Annie away, out of his life. There had been many times when he'd wanted to tell her what really happened with Brynna. He would have to eventually, but he was also afraid, for he feared her response.

And the weather had turned cold. On the third morning of their standoff, he woke up in the barn and saw his breath as he cursed the rigid discomfort of his pallet. His other rigid discomfort made him swear, too. He'd dreamed of his new wife, finding her sweet and malleable, genial and generous with him. That *was* a dream, wasn't it? At times, he felt as though he were living another nightmare.

Despite the discomfort of his cold bed of hay, he lay back and closed his eyes, trying to recapture the fantasy. She was in the bath, as she'd been the day he'd returned from town. But she was alone; Annie was sleeping. Her hair, piled on top of her head, glowed in the firelight, and her flawless white skin was wet and slick.

She saw him and gave him a slow, sexy smile. *Hello, darling. Wash my back, please?* He rolled up his shirt sleeves and reached between her legs for the soap, barely grazing her secret place with his thumb. She closed her eyes and shuddered, squirming in the water. . . .

His horse nickered, dragging him back to reality. Yes, reality. They *had* kissed; that hadn't been a dream. There was fire there, deep inside where no one had touched her.

He'd meant to give her a chaste kiss, but once he'd tasted her, he knew he wanted more. The memory of her naked in the tub . . . her clean, shiny hair falling over her face as he held her . . . her virginal white nightgown . . . all these things made her desirable to him. He wanted to bed her. He chuckled, a dry, humorless sound. And she wanted to kill him.

Tossing his covers aside, he left his bed and strode toward the cabin and its warmth, hoping that on the way, the biting cold would zap his mounting desire.

Kate held Annie on her lap in the rocking chair by the fireplace and playfully tickled her tummy.

"Here comes the Sammy Spider," Kate said, walking her fingers slowly through Annie's curls. She felt Annie's smile of anticipation as she moved her fingers down her neck and on toward her stomach. When she got there, she gave the child a frantic tickle, sending Annie into shrieking giggles.

They lapsed into a comfortable quiet while Kate rocked gently beside the fire. Annie turned and played with the buttons at Kate's throat, sliding them out of the button-holes one by one until she discovered Kate's corset cover.

Kate settled Annie back against her, hoping she'd take a little nap. This room was nice and warm. She'd been surprised when she'd awakened, for the weather had changed dramatically. She glanced at the window, fearing she'd see snow. Thankfully, she didn't. A chill skittered through her. Not yet, anyway.

She was tempted to ask him about the cot, but something told her it was too soon to expect it. As many times as she told herself she didn't care if he froze to death in the barn, she knew it wasn't the truth. No matter what discomfort and mistrust lay between them, she knew it wasn't fair to keep him from his own bed. She'd even thought about sleeping with Annie, but Annie had a child's bed, meant for a child only. Her gaze slid to the short couch. Yes, there was always that, despite the fact that even she'd have to curl into a ball to lie on it.

The wind whistled about the cabin windows, seeming to scream for a place to get in. Kate cringed, wondering if her new husband had slept at all. Strangely, it worried her. She had a lot of unpleasant qualities, she knew that. She knew she had an acerbic tongue. She was well aware of the fact that it had probably kept men at a distance all of her life. And, she was stubborn, domineering, rigid and tough; she'd had to be, considering the life she'd led. How else could she have survived the hailstorm that killed her corn crop three years ago? Or the year the river overflowed its banks and drowned the wheat? Or the loneliness of the long, dark winters?

She'd had to be tough to single-handedly cook for a threshing crew while Brynna preened and pranced around in front of the men.

She clamped a hand over her mouth and took a shaky breath. Never before had she allowed herself to remember how little Brynna had helped her. Still, Brynna had been high-spirited and delicate. Or . . . had she just been spoiled?

Kate's thoughts went again to her husband. If she insisted that he sleep in the barn with the biting cold wind howling through the cracks in the boards, she would be acting inconsiderately. And it was terribly unchristian. As of late, she'd been more and more distressed about her unchristianlike behavior.

She looked up, her heart leaping against her ribs when she saw him standing there, tall, handsome, and to her great relief, not frozen to death. So often he caught her unawares. It was disquieting, yet strangely thrilling. And, she realized, that was a terribly foolish response, coming from such a levelheaded woman.

She took a shuddering breath and rose from the rocker. "I'll get you some breakfast."

He put up his hand to stop her. "Never mind. I'll get it myself."

Frowning at his retreating back, she shook her head. She was supposed to just sit here while he shuffled about in her nicely organized kitchen? Not likely.

She laid Annie down on the couch and covered her with a lovely quilt that was usually folded over the back. She'd noticed the quilt before and knew it had to be his, for Brynna had not had such a unique coverlet.

She stopped at the kitchen door for a moment and watched him as he stepped up from the cellar. He held three eggs, which she'd discovered earlier he kept fresh in limewater. Remarkably, he knew exactly what he was doing.

"You look strangely at home in the kitchen," she said, stepping into the room.

He gave her a half-grin. "Brynna wasn't much of a cook."

The almost shy half-grin kept Kate from spewing back a biting remark. She hadn't thought much about Brynna's cooking skills, and now, when she did, she realized that her niece had never done more than peel potatoes and snap the ends of the pole beans because she liked to hear the sound they made.

A picture was beginning to form in her head, and she didn't much like it. But for the first time, it was Brynna she was angry with, not the man who stood before her, deftly whipping up a bowl of eggs.

Kate glanced away. "I guess that was my fault. Things always got done faster if I did them myself. I was never very good at delegating responsibility, especially in the kitchen."

He poured the eggs into a hot skillet, and they bubbled and hissed, the sound remarkably loud in the quiet room.

After dumping in some cut up ham, he stirred and pulled the eggs away from the side of the pan as they cooked.

As he flipped the concoction over, he said, "She tried to be a good mother, though."

A fluttering of discomfort began in Kate's chest. "She *tried* to be?"

He slid the eggs onto a plate, took two of her freshly baked biscuits and sat down at the table. "Are you ready to listen to some things about Brynna?"

Was she? Kate pressed her fingers to her throat, suddenly realizing that Annie had unbuttoned her dress. With quick, nervous fingers, she buttoned them back up to her neck, aware that her husband watched her.

"I . . . I don't know," she answered honestly. More little memories had begun to come back to her. Memories of Brynna lolling about the kitchen while Kate worked. Memories of her lounging on the loveseat in the parlor while Kate polished the furniture. A painful memory of Brynna daring her to stop her from leaving with Sage, and of Brynna's spiteful, hateful words. She'd always known Brynna was spoiled; Kate was as much to blame for that as anyone. But Brynna had been her flesh and blood, her responsibility.

Oh, she thought, the hurt of her loss returning, it was so hard to criticize those one loved.

"She was a selfish girl," Sage said quietly.

Kate sat down across from him and lowered her head. "I know. And it was my fault—"

"Don't blame yourself. We are what we are. Nothing and no one can change us unless we want to."

She gave him an impatient glance, wondering how he'd suddenly become so wise. "Why did you take her with you? Did . . . did you love her?"

His laughter was quiet. Humorless. Almost sad. "Believe it or not, she threatened to tell everyone she was already pregnant if I didn't let her come with me."

A shock of concern spread through Kate. "She wasn't, was she?"

Sage looked at his plate. "No, and if she had been, it wouldn't have been mine, but there wouldn't have been any way to prove it. Just her word against mine."

"What are you saying?" Did she really want to hear?

He studied her. "The night before I left, she came to me and asked me to take her with me." He pushed his plate away and leaned back in the chair. "I told her she was only seventeen. Just a kid. Hell, I was almost ten years older than she was. That was my mistake, I guess. Suddenly she was all over me, trying to prove she was all grown up." He toyed with his fork. "I even told her it wasn't fair to leave you all alone on that farm. She said . . . ah, hell, she said you'd be glad to be rid of her."

His words had the same effect as a blow to the stomach. "But that's not true! You can't believe that's true—"

"No," he interrupted. "I'd seen how little she helped you, but I also saw how much you cared for her, overlooking the fact that she was no help to you at all."

Kate swallowed the news, sensing it was the truth. He looked too miserable to be lying about any of what he's said. "And . . . and then?"

He sighed and shook his head. "I thought I could sneak out early the next morning. Hell, I knew she was never up before the sun." He gave her a quick glance. "Not like you were."

A wash of pleasure warmed Kate, but she said nothing.

"I wasn't five miles from the farm that morning when I heard her riding hellbent for leather behind me. And I knew it was her. At that point, I thought it would be better just to let her ride with me until we got to a town where I could put her on the train and send her home."

"You . . . you tried?"

He gave her a dry chuckle. "Twice. After that, I thought, 'to hell with it.' She rode with me to Texas."

Kate thought back to her friend Millie's statement and knew that she'd formed a picture of Brynna that had been one of innocence and sweetness. She'd had to, for since she was responsible for raising the girl, what else could she think?

"Surely a mere girl couldn't force you into a marriage you didn't want," she finally said.

He studied her, as if measuring his words before he spoke them. "I didn't say I didn't want to marry her."

It was like a physical blow, albeit a small one. Why it bothered her to hear the words, she couldn't say. She should have *wanted* him to marry Brynna. She should have. . . .

"Then . . . then you loved her in spite of everything."

"I didn't say that, either." He rose from the table, went to the stove and poured them each a cup of coffee. After he'd put a cup in front of her and sat again, he added, "I felt she needed someone to look after her. She was stubborn and mule-headed." He gave her that shy half-grin again. "Must run in the family."

Kate felt the blush steal into her cheeks, then looked away. "I would have looked after her. You needn't have married her just to become her keeper." The thought made her a little angry, and she didn't know why.

"She got pregnant."

Kate looked at him, puzzled and more than a little angry. "*Then* you married her? After the damage was done?"

"I never slept with her."

Kate swallowed hard, hoping her heart didn't leap from her chest. "What . . . what are you saying?"

He rubbed his face with his hands. "I think it's pretty obvious. Do I have to spell it out for you?"

"Yes," she answered, "I think you'd better."

He dragged in a heavy sigh. "Brynna met a wrangler from a nearby ranch who was only too happy to keep her entertained."

Kate gripped the coffee mug with both hands, willing the warmth to seep into her suddenly frozen bones. She shook her head in disbelief. "You're telling me that Brynna followed you out here, slept with someone else who got her pregnant, then *you*, out of the goodness of your heart, married her?" She barked a laugh. "Well, pardon me, but I find that very hard to believe."

He studied her again. "Why would I lie about it?"

"Because it makes you sound more like the hero coming to the poor girl's rescue than the bastard who dragged her to this Godforsaken place."

"It also makes Annie some other man's child."

He couldn't have stunned her more if he'd hit her with a board. She could hear her heart pounding in the quiet room. "Oh, my God," she whispered, clutching her stomach. No man, especially this one, would admit to such a thing if it weren't true, because it would mean she had more right to Annie than he did. And she knew that he loved Annie more than his own life.

With her hands still clutching her stomach, she looked at him. "Do you know who . . . who . . ." She couldn't say the words; they were too painful.

"Yeah," he answered with a nod. "I know who he was."

"Was?"

"He was killed in a brawl over in Amarillo."

"Before he found out she was going to have his baby . . . babies?"

He shook his head. "Last month."

She let out a pent-up sigh. "Oh, my Lord. He never knew?"

Sage shrugged. "Might have. He just didn't care."

Kate let what she'd learned sink in. "Surely, if Brynna slept with him, she must have loved him."

The look her husband gave her bordered on pity. "Yeah, maybe she did. In her own way."

Kate had to believe it. The alternative was too painful to

comprehend. Had she failed so miserably in rearing Brynna? Had the girl needed love so badly, she'd gone out and slept with men thinking that was the only way to get it?

And Sage. She couldn't believe she'd misjudged him so. She'd been so blind to Brynna's faults that she'd placed all the blame on him. She'd put him through pure and absolute hell, and he hadn't been the villain in the piece, but the hero.

"Did . . . did she appreciate what you did for her?"

He gave her a soft laugh. "In her own way, I guess."

Something caught Kate's eye, and she glanced at the window. Her stomach fell. Snow flakes smacked against the pane.

He stood and crossed to the window, staring outside. "I should go to town and see about the cot."

A frown nicked her brow. "Should you go if it's snowing?"

He rubbed his neck. "I should, but I don't dare. I might not be able to get back, and I don't want to leave you and Annie here alone."

Knowing that he was concerned sent warmth curling around her heart. "We'll . . . make do."

"I can still bed down in the barn—"

"No," she interrupted, her voice sharper than she'd meant it to be. "I won't have you sleeping in the barn with a blizzard howling about your head."

He turned, giving her his lazy half-grin, no longer shy. "What do you suggest?"

Momentarily flustered, she turned away. "I'll think of something. Make no mistake about that."

The snow continued to come down, the flakes so thick and white, it looked as if the angels had snipped off the ends of a pillow and all the feathers were floating to earth. When Annie was in her heavy, warm, flannel, footed pajamas, she toddled to the window, climbed up on the yellow wooden stool with bluebirds painted on it, and stared outside, mesmerized. Kate learned that Sage had made the sturdy bench and the highchair in the kitchen. It was yet another thing that tilted the balance of her feelings for him in his favor.

She glanced at the window, surprised to see no moisture collecting on the sill. He'd built the cabin, too, and Kate could see that he'd done a remarkably fine job. Annie's room was warm, despite the fact that there was no fireplace in it.

"Is my little Sweet Pea ready for a bedtime story?"

Both Kate and Annie turned, and Annie held her arms out to the only father she would ever know. He scooped her up and put her in bed, tucking the quilts around her.

Kate bent and kissed her, then left the room. They had a bedtime ritual, and Kate didn't want to disturb it.

She went into the kitchen, but she knew there was nothing to do; she'd cleaned up everything earlier. She was restless and nervous and not just a little upset. She paced in front of the fire, tossing nervous glances at the short couch. Testing her earlier decision, she sat on it, laid down and tried to get comfortable. It wasn't easy. No, she thought, twisting against the hard wooden frame that poked up through the center of the cushion, it was impossible.

With a sense of purpose, she rose from the couch, went into the bedroom and hastily prepared herself for bed. No longer hearing him reading nursery rhymes to Annie, she picked up her brush and continued brushing her hair as she stepped out into the other room.

He stood before the fire, his hands clasped behind his back. He must have sensed her presence because he turned, his gaze moving slowly over her.

She cleared her throat. "You ... you can't sleep in the barn tonight."

He gave her a small grin, neither cocky nor shy. "You told me that earlier." He held her gaze. "I can, you know."

She shook her head. "It's ... it's not really necessary."

He walked toward her, his steps measured. "I promised not to exercise my rights as a husband. I don't suppose that will change, will it?"

Alarm, warm and foreign, spread through her. "Of course not," she answered crisply. "If you're a true gentleman, you'll keep your promise."

He rubbed his jaw. "But you're suggesting we sleep in the same bed?"

Her stiff composure melted away, leaving her fluttered. She turned away, wringing her hands. "Well, I don't know what else to do. I've tried the couch; it's short and lumpy and there's a board right smack in the middle. *I* can't sleep there, and I know *you* surely couldn't. And ... and Annie's bed is a child's bed. There's no room for me in there. And there's a snowstorm brewing that doesn't appear to want to let up, so you can't go back to the barn."

She turned, knowing her face held frustration and fear, but she didn't care. "Do you have any other suggestions?"

"I could sleep on the floor."

Sighing, she walked away, toward the window. "For how long? Forever? Until the snow stops, and we can get into town and pick up the cot? It's ... it's just not fair to make you do that."

In an odd, mad way, she trusted him. Yes, he'd kissed her, but she was certain he wasn't really attracted to her. After all, no man had ever been attracted to her before, and anyway, she'd heard that kissing women for no apparent reason was commonplace to most men. She found him very pleasant to watch, and yes, perhaps she was attracted to him in some small way, but nothing would happen unless she let it happen. *And she wouldn't.*

He came up behind her but didn't touch her. He might

just as well have; she felt his presence along her entire back.

"You're sure you want to do this?"

She swung around and faced him. He was only inches away, and she found herself studying the fine squint lines that fanned at the corners of his eyes and the parentheses that bracketed his mouth. The mouth that had kissed hers just a few days before. No, she was not at all sure she wanted to do this. But it was fair. They were, after all, legally wed.

"Surely you can sleep in a bed with a woman and not . . . not do . . . do what . . ." Her voice ebbed, leaving her feeling more foolish than ever. She took a deep breath, dredging up every bit of contempt she could find. "Surely you can control your animal instincts for a time, Mr. Reno."

He lifted an eyebrow and gave her his half-smile. "Oh, hell, yes, ma'am. I don't see a problem with that at all."

Kate blinked rapidly, aware of an odd feeling of disappointment. "Fine. We understand each other then, don't we?"

He started to undress, pulling his shirt from the waist band of his jeans. "Yes, ma'am," he answered, giving her a cocky grin as he walked past her toward the bedroom. "Only thing is, I'm sure gonna miss not sleeping with my horse."

Had she been in her right mind, she'd have told him, in her tartest tongue possible, to go right back out and sleep with the animal, then. But she said nothing.

5

Sage had made a production out of undressing, but only to throw her off balance. He almost enjoyed watching her confusion. Somehow it softened her.

He banked the fire, put the screen in front of it and crossed to the bedroom door. He'd purposely left her alone in there, hoping she would be asleep. It would make the damned night so much easier.

She'd left the lamp lit. It flickered on the table beside the bed, casting light over her bright hair. He quietly stepped closer, studying her as she slept. She looked soft in sleep. Actually, she seemed to have softened some otherwise, too. She no longer wore her hair so tight, and often she left the neck of her dress unbuttoned. And she automatically softened the minute she was with Annie.

He felt a sharp stab of apprehension as he remembered how he'd basically told her everything. Well, not everything. But what he'd told her, which was the truth, by God, hadn't sent her packing with Annie in tow. He'd gambled on her reaction to that. If she'd known the truth right away, she'd have taken Annie and fled. He had no doubt about that.

Somehow they'd settled into a restless, almost satisfying relationship. Everything just might turn out fine, as long as she didn't find out about the rest of Brynna's story. Although what he'd already told Kate was bad enough, he wasn't sure she'd believe the rest of it.

He pulled off his jeans and his wool socks, debating whether or not to sleep the way he usually did in his own bed. Glancing at her again, all soft and sleep-warm, he was sorely tempted. But he was a gentleman, at least he always attempted to be, although this woman tried his patience more than any woman he'd ever known. Except for Brynna, but strangely, for another set of reasons altogether. And this was no time to shock his new wife. Not when she'd actually met him halfway.

He crawled in beside her, careful not to wake her. God, it felt strange to be in bed beside a woman again. It felt damned good, but . . . strange. He could smell her, that light flowery scent that he'd wanted to equate with old maids and spinsters but couldn't.

Sucking in a deep, cleansing breath, he rolled onto his side and stared at the window. The wind still howled outside, but he thought the snow had stopped.

She moaned lightly and turned over. He stiffened when he felt her roll toward him and he tried to move away. He couldn't. He was already hugging the side of the damned bed.

He should get up. Hell, he should roll up in a blanket and sleep in front of the fire. Or, he thought, chagrined, trudge out to the barn and get his sleeping roll, the one he used when he and Luis slept out under the stars; he hadn't told her about that. He also hadn't told her that he hadn't been in town long enough to order a bed. He wasn't sure why he hadn't told her, but he cursed softly now, knowing she'd raise holy hell when she found out.

A voice in his head told him he was fooling himself, for he knew exactly why he hadn't dragged out his sleeping roll, and why he wasn't sorry about the extra bed. As much discomfort as her nearness caused him, he wanted it. He wanted her, but in a fit of madness, he'd promised never to take her.

In another fit of insanity, he'd thought that just sleeping beside her would be enough. He'd always enjoyed sleeping with women. They were so soft and compliant when they woke up in the morning, usually eager to be loved before he left their beds.

But that was the difference. He'd enjoyed sleeping with women because he enjoyed loving them. Oh, God, this was *so* different. He forced himself to relax. The bed was warm and familiar; his bed partner was warm, but not the least bit familiar. Did he want her to be? Hell, yes. But he had to watch it. *Don't screw this up, Reno.*

He just hoped he could make it through the night without embarrassing himself.

Kate awakened slowly, knowing she should get up and start a fire in the stove. But for some reason, the bed was warmer than usual, and she just wanted to stay there and enjoy it. Just another minute or two, she told herself as she snuggled deeper into the bedding.

Suddenly her eyes popped open and her heart was in her throat. Slowly she turned, knowing, sensing he was there beside her. She prayed briefly, hoping he was still asleep so she could scoot out of bed without him knowing it. Glancing at the foot of the bed, she saw the outline of his long legs beneath the quilts. Her gaze moved on up, over his hip to his shoulder. When her gaze met his face, she groaned quietly.

He was awake—and smiling at her. His eyes were half-open, his thick, curly chestnut eyelashes hanging lazily over them. He had stubble on his cheeks and chin, and his hair was messed in a sleepy, not unattractive way.

She knew she should scramble from the bed like the foolish virgin she was, but she felt like a museum statue filled with heat. She was unable to move, yet flames licked her insides and she began to wonder if the fire would ignite inside her, causing her exterior to explode into pieces.

"Good morning, Kate."

Shivering at the sound of him saying her name in his

husky, sleep-filled voice, she scooted backwards toward her side of the bed. "Good . . . good morning," she answered, a little breathlessly.

His hand snaked out from beneath the quilts and grabbed her arm.

She gasped at what his touch did to her, but didn't berate him, knowing the touch was pleasant and not disgusting. It puzzled her deeply. She glanced at his hand, brown and strong with sprigs of dark hair across the back. "What . . . what do you want?"

His hand moved up and down her arm, and she could feel the heat from his touch through the fabric of her nightdress.

"I behaved myself all night," he said softly.

Her insides were leaping around, bumping into each other. "Well, you said you would." Why didn't she pull away and leave the bed?

"I think I deserve a little reward, don't you?"

She could feel the throbbing pulse at the base of her throat, but she refused to just roll over and submit to her emotions. "Would . . . would you like biscuits and gravy for breakfast?"

He laughed softly, the sound intensely pleasant to her ears. "That's not exactly what I had in mind, but it sounds good, too."

"What . . . what did you have in mind?" Oh, God, she was actually playing his little game.

His hand moved up to her hair, and she felt his fingers move through the curls that hung over her shoulders. "Your hair is like the fire I know is inside you, Kate. It almost burns my fingers, just like your wit scalds me. I find both sensations very pleasant, although I'm pretty sure you don't mean to please me."

She swallowed hard. "You must be a man who enjoys pain," she answered as glibly as she could.

His fingers threaded through her hair, landing at the

back of her head. "Sometimes pain is more pleasant than feeling nothing at all."

Her head tingled from his touch, as did her breasts, although he hadn't come anywhere near them. "Is . . . is that supposed to be directed at me?"

"Do you think it is, Kate? Don't you ever feel anything?"

She still found herself eager to play, although she knew she was playing with fire. "I . . . I felt pain when Brynna went away with you."

"Ah, but that was the bad kind of pain, Kate. Have you ever felt the good kind?"

His fingers stroked the back of her neck, sending frissons of excitement down her spine. "Good pain? I don't understand . . ."

His hand left her neck and his fingers touched her cheek, moving over her nose to her mouth. She had no idea a man could be so gentle, yet so seductive, and she knew he was trying to seduce her. She might be virginal, but she wasn't stupid. Yet, she allowed it. Lord, she was truly going mad.

"Pleasure-pain, Kate. Have you never felt pleasure-pain?"

She glanced away from the magical arousal she found in his eyes. How could she know what he was talking about? She'd grown up building a fortress around herself, refusing to allow herself any pleasures at all.

"No, of course you haven't," he answered for her. "All I ask of you this morning is a kiss. Just a kiss, Kate." His hands were at her shoulders, where he pressed tightly.

"It seems you have me pinned down and at your mercy," she said, wishing she didn't sound so foolishly eager.

"You bet I do," he answered, just before his mouth touched hers.

He was exquisitely tender, gently nipping at her lips

with his. She hadn't known that anything so tender could summon up such deep, carnal feelings from deep inside her. Feelings that had only begun to exist since she came here . . . and was with him.

His tongue slid over her mouth, and she gasped, innocently allowing him entrance. He conquered her, touching her, teaching her to duel gently, then more zealously.

Her hand moved to his chest; she felt the beat of his heart, hard and strong, against her fingertips. His hand came over hers, and he moved it to the opening at the neck of his underwear. He coaxed her fingers inside, and she touched the crinkly hair that grew high on his chest, above his nipples. He had a sleep smell that drew her like a bee to nectar. It was all so intoxicating, so different . . . so new.

She could barely breathe. They continued to kiss as she touched him, shyly at first, then dipping down to touch his nipples, which stood up hard on the flat, hairy surface of his chest.

Suddenly she felt his fingers at her throat, and he began to unbutton her nightdress, slowly slipping each button from its hole. She stayed her hand on his chest, hoping her pounding heart wouldn't break her ribs, while he moved downward toward her breasts. His fingers occasionally grazed her skin beneath the gown, sending shivers of indecent delight over her body.

Oh, she thought she would die from the pleasure of it! When his hand moved inside her gown and touched her breast, she arched toward him, shuddering with a mixture of fear and excitement so strong, she thought she might lose her senses.

His lips claimed hers again, and she kissed him back, desire and inexperience making her frantic to have more. When his fingers found her taut nipples, she knew she would finally explode, shattering into a million ecstatic pieces. Then, suddenly—

"Papa! Mama!"

Kate pulled away from him, clasping her gown together and pushing against his chest.

A bright-eyed, smiley faced Annie had crawled up on the bed and was watching them.

Sage chuckled beside Kate, taking her hand and kissing her palm before she could scramble from the bed.

She looked at him, horrified that Annie had caught them, angry that it didn't seem to bother him.

"Thank you for the kiss, Kate." He rolled from the bed, grabbed Annie, and gave her a wet, noisy buss on the cheek. "Let's get you cleaned up, little Sweet Pea. When did you learn how to crawl out of your bed?"

Kate watched him cross to the door with Annie. There was a strange spasm in her stomach when she looked at the front crotch of his long underwear, for it stood out, high and full, like a pole holding up a circus tent.

She shuddered and closed her eyes, willing her own body to stop betraying her. There was a heavy feeling between her legs. It felt wet down there, too.

As she dressed, she wondered what she was going to do. There was an enormous temptation to follow her instincts and see what would happen. Hopefully, once she was busy with Annie or cooking, or cleaning, or *something,* this lustful feeling would go away and never, ever return.

As she left the bedroom, bound for the kitchen, she realized that she was beginning to understand the incongruity of the words, 'pleasure-pain'.

6

The snow continued, falling in such thick, white flakes that Kate often couldn't see the barn. Before breakfast Sage had made a fire in the stove and stoked up the one in the fireplace, then bundled up and went out to tend the animals.

Now, while Kate stirred the sausage and milk gravy, she kept remembering what had passed between them earlier in the bedroom. She was a little disappointed that she couldn't shake it from her mind, but told herself that as the day wore on, the whole incident would dissolve into nothing.

Putting her worries aside, she set the spoon down, went to the window again and looked for him. Before he left the house, he'd told her it was too early in the year for the snow to stay permanently. Now, as she watched its gentle, downward fall form deep, soft mounds, she wondered how he could be right. At this rate, they'd never be able to get in to pick up the cot.

The pulse at her throat thrummed when she saw him trudging through the heavy snow toward the house.

She quickly set the table, and by the time he entered the kitchen, everything was waiting for him, and she was sitting beside Annie.

His eyes lit up and he smiled. "Mm. Biscuits and gravy. My favorite." He sat down and tossed her a lingering glance. "Any reason for such a special breakfast?"

Straightening her spine, she answered, "I did promise, and I never go back on my word."

He ate lustily, appearing to savor every bite. "On everything, Kate?"

The question took her by surprise. "What . . . what do you mean?"

"I mean," he began, slathering a biscuit with honey, "do you keep your word about everything?"

She stiffened. "If you mean, will I promise not to take Annie away, just because you aren't her natural father, of course."

"No matter what else you might find out?"

His words sent a shiver of wariness over her. "What do you mean, what else I might find out?"

He gave her a nonchalant shrug. "It's nothing. I just want our agreement to cover everything, I guess."

Yes, she could understand that, given the circumstances. Her gaze moved over him. Over the wide shoulders and thick arms, over his hair, still wet and windblown from the weather, and his face, still a little red from the cold. A now-familiar feeling expanded inside her, not unlike a flower unfolding.

There were so many good things about him. Things she didn't see when he was working for her those long years ago. Of course, she hadn't seen anything but red back then, her anger so strong because of the way he allowed Brynna to—

No, she could no longer blame him for what had happened to Brynna. He seemed so honest and sincere, telling her things that must have hurt him to tell. He was a good man, a hard-working man, and a man who wasn't too proud to become father to another man's child. In many ways, she was very lucky to have married him.

"Looks like we're snowed in for a spell," he said, breaking into her reverie.

She glanced up and caught his gaze, which freely and slowly roamed her face, her neck . . . her bosom. . . . A blush climbed to her cheeks, rendering them hot.

Snowed in. Another night with him in her bed. The pleasure-pain settled deep in her pelvis. Her heart fluttered madly, and she covertly brought her hands up to cover it, lest it bound from her chest.

Kate sat across from him on Annie's bed while he recited Mother Goose; he'd insisted she join them. She was embarrassed to find that she couldn't keep her mind on the tale, for her thoughts leapfrogged ahead of her, to the time when she and her husband would go to bed.

When he finished reading, they both kissed Annie and left her room. He went to the fireplace, obviously allowing Kate time to prepare for bed. She did, but wondered how she ever got herself unbuttoned and untrussed with her fingers shaking the way they were.

Once in her nightgown, she buttoned it to her throat, quickly unbuttoned it down to her chest, then buttoned it up again. Oh, she just didn't know what to do!

Sensing him behind her, she whirled around, her hand still at her throat.

He leaned against the door jamb. "Nothing will happen that you don't want to happen, Kate."

Everything inside her shook, quivered like leaves on an aspen. Not trusting her voice, she didn't answer him, but merely turned away and stared at the bed.

He came up behind her and tenderly pulled her against his chest. He was so strong, so big . . . so much more than she'd ever dreamed he was. When his hands moved down her arms, his fingers gently grazing her breasts, she thought her knees would give way. He exposed her ear, pulling her hair to the side, and kissed it slowly, gently tugging on the lobe.

She nearly buckled, but he caught her, lifting her high in his arms. He gazed down at her then, his eyes filled with arousal and his jaw clamped tight. He carried her to the bed, allowing her to scramble under the covers.

"I'm going to undress, Kate. If you don't want to watch, then turn away."

She considered it. How could she just lay there and watch him drop his clothes? But she remembered that the night before he'd had his long underwear on. She could watch him shuck his jeans and shirt; that wouldn't be so hard. She just didn't want to act like a prude, not tonight.

He pulled his shirt out, unbuttoned it and tossed it on the chair by the bed. Next, he unfastened his jeans, letting them drop to the floor before stepping out of them. They were folded and laid on top of his shirt.

But when he began unbuttoning the top of his underwear, she swallowed a gasp and closed her eyes.

"What . . . what are you doing?" Her voice sounded so silly, so frantic.

"I'm undressing."

"But . . . but . . . are you taking off your . . . your underwear?" Only whores looked at naked men. How could *she,* even though it was so very, very tempting?

"It's the way I prefer to sleep, Kate."

Her eyes snapped open. "But . . . but . . . but . . ." She couldn't remember what she was going to say. It went clean out of her head, for the top of his underwear hung loosely around his hips, and his—Oh! It was so . . . so large, standing stiffly in that bush of dark hair.

Her gaze climbed up, over his chest and the small bandage that covered his healing wound to his face where she found him watching her carefully. "Can I come to bed, Kate?"

He spoke so softly, she could hardly hear him. Or maybe it was because her heart was beating so loudly, she could hear nothing else. Utterly flummoxed, she simply nodded.

She felt his weight as he slid under the quilts. In his effort to get comfortable, he accidentally touched her hip, and she thought she'd spiral right out of bed.

They lay quietly for a time. Kate's eyes were wide open, riveted at the ceiling. She knew he was on his side, watching her.

"I won't go back on my word, Kate. Not if you don't want me to, but I have to tell you that . . . that I want to touch you. Make love to you."

Kate shivered as though she were standing out in the snow. She was cold, yet parts of her felt hot. Oh, heavens, she didn't know just what she was at this moment, hot or cold, she just knew she would never be the same again once this night was over.

She took a deep breath, expelling it slowly. "I would like you to just hold me for a moment. I'm . . . I'm really quite cold."

He gathered her to him, and she went willingly, wondering how his body could be so warm without any clothing at all, when hers was bundled up in a flannel gown, yet cold anyway. She hugged her arms to her breast, allowing him to enfold her entirely. Her fingers again touched the springy hair on his chest, and she swallowed a delighted shudder, for to her great surprise, touching him brought her so much more pleasure than she'd ever thought possible.

They lay together for long, heart-pounding moments. At first his hands moved in chaste circles over her back. Slowly the circles began to get bigger, and when one hand dipped lower, over her buttocks, she stiffened. He must have felt her tense, for he stopped rubbing her.

She felt the pressure of his hand against her bottom, could feel the heat of his palm through her nightgown. With her heart in her throat, she realized she could also feel him in front, down there where the pleasure-pain had tormented her all day. The memory of him standing beside the bed, that part of him large and proud, sent tingling messages through her whole body.

He pressed her bottom with his hand, as if quietly urging her closer. She acquiesced, releasing her arms from their imprisonment between them and bringing them around his back. Oh, it was wide and hard as she shyly moved her palms over it.

She felt him down there in earnest now, for they were pressed together so tightly, she didn't think a hatchet could separate them. Her breathing changed; she took deep, shuddering breaths as his thickness pressed against her. She timidly moved her hand down, over his waist to the tops of his hard, firm buttocks and felt him shudder as well. The sound sent her heart soaring and her blood singing.

Somehow, her nightgown had ridden up in back, for she felt his hand on her bare skin. Every inch he touched—her waist, her bottom, her hip—sent tingles of desire into her pelvis, and she squirmed against him, suddenly needing so very much more, yet not really knowing what it was.

"I want you to touch me, Kate."

Her heart lifted again, for she knew what he meant. He pulled away slightly and took her hand, moving it down over his navel to the thick thatch of hair just below it. She had the most impossible ache between her legs, and felt that whatever he was doing, would eventually fulfill her.

Her fingers found him and her discovery dizzied her. She touched him, gasping at the size and the velvety softness of it. He put his hand over hers and moved it up and down on the enormous length. His breathing changed, too, his breath shuddering lustily on her cheek.

His hand stilled hers. "No more, Kate. I don't want to spend before you have pleasure," he whispered in her ear. He brought her hand to his mouth and kissed the back of it before he pressed her down on the bed.

She went apprehensively yet willingly, because somehow he just had to do something about the infernal ache that continued to throb and spread from somewhere deep inside her.

As he drew her nightgown high on her abdomen, his fingers grazed her skin. His big hand, so capable and strong, was gentle and tender as it moved over her tingling flesh.

She held her breath when his fingers found the place between her thighs, a place she'd been sure no one would ever know. As his fingers circled her, she instinctively flinched, for his touch was like lightning, sparking fires along her flesh.

"Ah, Katie, Katie," he whispered, his voice shaking with emotion. "You're ready for me, girl."

"That ... that may be," she answered, her own breath battering away in her chest. "I just ... just don't know what I'm ready for."

His fingers plundered her, creating pangs of ecstatic pleasure. She gripped his shoulders, pinching him hard as he stroked her. Spreading her legs in wanton abandon, she reveled in his touch, shivering and shaking, moaning and nearly weeping with the pleasure of it all.

Impulsively she reached for him, finding the soft tip wet with dewy moisture. He groaned aloud, raised himself on one knee, and moved between her thighs.

When the head of his manhood entered her, she was attacked with a spasm so strong, she raised herself off the bed. They lay there, breaths shuddering, bodies touching. Kate could feel him inside her, and though he barely moved, he pressed his hands against her bottom and held her, rocking gently against her.

She felt something begin somewhere deep inside her. Wanting it, needing whatever it was, she arched against him, wound her legs around his back and urged him to satisfy her.

His rocking motions intensified as he drove deep. A shock passed through her, sending her high against him. She closed her eyes, took deep, shuddering breaths, then felt every muscle in her body turn to liquid.

When she floated down from her ecstatic high, her husband was hugging and kissing her, and clasping her to him.

She reached up and touched his hair, amazed that her arms felt like lead. "What happened to me?"

He cuddled her close. "I think you've been successfully ravished, Mrs. Reno."

With a bemused smile, Kate cuddled closer. She was exhausted and had no desire to move away. Less shyly now she ran her hands over him, touching his hard flesh, delighting in the rough hair that covered him.

It wasn't long before she felt his root grow and thicken against her thigh again. Surprisingly, she felt a stirring within herself as well. She reached for him, gasping with delight when she discovered him growing harder with her touch.

They made love again, and this time, she felt the pleasure of their coupling more acutely and with more long-lasting satisfaction.

Afterward, he pulled her against him, spoon-style, and she slept. Deeper than she'd ever slept before.

7

Kate woke the next morning and found her husband up and gone. But beside her Annie was asleep, her sweet head on her papa's pillow. Kate envisioned her husband putting the child there, drawing the quilts up around her. With a shaky sigh, she realized he'd probably watched her sleep, too. She wondered if he thought about the night before as she did. She smiled, feeling a little dreamy.

Intent on watching Annie sleep, Kate drew her legs up and winced at the soreness between her thighs. *Small price to pay, isn't it?* Yes, she thought, it was. Despite the soreness, she felt chipper as a squirrel.

She glanced at the window, noting that it was barely dawn. Her husband would have stoked up the fire in the fireplace and made one in the stove. She could already feel the warmth in the room.

Annie scooted closer in her sleep, and Kate drew her near, hugging her little body against hers. Breathing in the child's exquisite baby smell, Kate realized she'd already become accustomed to it.

Knowing she was feeling too energetic to fall back to sleep, Kate merely closed her eyes and thought about the delicious night she'd just spent in her new husband's arms. It was her first, but she knew it wouldn't be her last. She felt some guilt at finding her happiness at Brynna's expense.

Suddenly she realized she still didn't know how Brynna and the other twin had died. For some reason, whenever they started talking about that, something interrupted them or the conversation changed. For her own peace of mind, she had to know.

Annie rolled over and touched Kate's cheek. "Mama."

Kate opened her eyes, smiled and touched Annie's nose. "We'll have to start teaching you some new words, Annie."

"Annie's nose," she lisped as she pressed her finger against her nose.

"Why, you already know that," Kate answered, her voice filled with pleasure.

"She already knows a lot of things."

At the sound of her husband's voice, Kate's heart fluttered and her gaze flew to the doorway.

"Papa!" Annie scrambled from under the quilts, tumbling into her father's waiting arms.

"Good morning, little Sweet Pea." He held Annie high in the air while she squealed and kicked merrily.

Watching the scene, Kate thought her heart would burst with happiness. When her gaze locked with his, she gave him a tremulous smile.

"Morning, Kate." He observed her openly.

Just the sound of her name on his tongue sent her heart soaring. "Good morning," she answered, almost shyly. "You should have wakened me," she added as she left the bed.

"I can't bear to wake a snoring woman."

Mildly indignant, she said, "I don't snore."

Sage gave his daughter a serious look. "Did you hear that, Annie? Your mama says she doesn't snore." He made a dreadfully exaggerated snoring sound at Annie's neck.

Annie shrieked with laughter. "Mama snork," she cried, then snorted at her father.

Trying desperately to be serious, Kate raised an eyebrow at them. "If the two of you are done making fun of me, will you please leave so I can get dressed?"

Her husband studied her, his gaze roaming over her long white nightgown. "I think I'd rather stay."

Still feeling chipper, Kate picked up a pillow and threw it at him.

He caught it and grinned, his eyes filled with devilish humor. "If you want to tussle a bit, Kate, I can put Annie back to bed."

Flustered at the feelings that scampered over her, Kate turned away and nervously fiddled with the buttons on her gown. "You'll do no such thing. Now, scoot. Get Annie dressed. I'll get breakfast going as soon as I can."

When she was sure he'd gone, she quickly dressed and hurried to the kitchen. As she prepared griddlecakes and sliced ham, she wondered, a giddy sensation making her tremble, how life could get any better than this.

* * *

The snow continued to fall. Annie was asleep, and Sage was out in the barn, modifying an old bathtub sleigh so it would haul hay.

Kate had just finished cleaning out her husband's paneled wardrobe where she'd found a small trunk of Brynna's things. A wealth of sadness pressed against her heart as she sat in the chair by the fire and stared at the items that had been her niece's.

She pulled out a familiar red wool cape with a quilted red silk lining. *Red.* Yes, that had been Brynna, never wanting to be subtle. Feeling suddenly chilled, Kate wrapped the cape over her shoulders and delved deeper into the trunk. She pulled out the book of poetry she'd given Brynna one year for Christmas. For all of Brynna's faults, she did love poetry.

Opening the inside cover, Kate stared at her inscription.

> *For Brynna,*
> *Poetry is music for the soul.*
> *Merry Christmas*

Kate's throat clogged with tears as she remembered the year she'd given Brynna the book. She'd tried her patience so often, it was a wonder Kate hadn't given up and tossed the girl out. Oh, the times she'd wanted to scream and rail at her. . . . There were times when she'd even *wanted* Brynna to go away and leave her in peace. Though she'd never voiced her feelings, Kate couldn't help but feel responsible for everything that had happened to the girl.

But once Brynna had left with Sage Reno, Kate's thoughts about her became selective. How long had she pushed Brynna's true personality to the attic of her mind? She wasn't sorry she had, for it was safer to think about Brynna the way she'd wanted her to be rather than the way she really was.

She dropped the book back in the trunk and lifted out

another. Thumbing through it, Kate realized it was a journal. With trembling fingers, she read an entry.

June 4—They told me not to tell anyone. Sometimes it's hard to keep them quiet so I can do other things. Sage gives me funny looks. They told me he can't be trusted.

Alarm spread through Kate like cold river water, sending fresh shocks of fear into her mind. She flipped to another page.

June 15—The babies cry all the time. They told me it wasn't my fault, but that doesn't help, 'cause they cry anyway. One said Sage was a danger to my babies. Another said he was a danger to me.
June 16—They haven't been around much, and the babies slept for a change. Sage gave me an evil look when he brought me my breakfast tray. I must watch him.

Briefly, because her hands shook so, Kate closed the book and put it in her lap. Who were these people Brynna wrote about? With mounting dread, she opened the journal and read on. Brynna's handwriting changed. It became a frantic scrawl.

July 20—This morning I saw Sage put a pillow over Alice's face. If I wouldn't have stopped him, he'd have killed my baby! Is Annie next? Am I? Sometimes I think he married me just to get even with me for sleeping with someone else. I think he really hates me and the babies.

Kate closed the journal again and fought for breath. She clutched the book to her chest and hurried to the window.

Her heart climbed her throat as she watched her husband trudge through the snow toward the house.

She had to find out what had happened; she had to ask him. But, she thought, her pulse hammering inside her skull, did she really want to know?

Shivering violently, she hugged herself and rubbed her arms with her hands. She had to remain calm. She couldn't let him see her doubts, her fears. She wanted him to have a reasonable explanation for this. Was Brynna right? Was her new husband dangerous? Some insidious voice in her head told her he must be, for she'd known Brynna all her life, and the man she'd married was a stranger. Dread knocked at the entrance to her heart. Had she been right about him all along?

He entered the room in his stocking feet, having left his boots by the door. "Well," he said, shrugging out of his heavy fleece-lined jacket, "I guess that old sleigh will have to do. I hammered a wide piece of wood on top of it—Kate?"

She glanced at his face and saw his puzzled look.

"Kate? What's wrong?"

Unable to shore up her courage, she answered, "Why . . . why nothing. I've been woolgathering, I guess."

He hung his coat on the peg by the door, then crossed to where she stood. When he attempted to touch her, she backed away. "Looks like more than that to me, Kate." Frowning, he touched the cape. "This is Brynna's."

Kate nodded, unsure she could speak. "I was making room for some of my things in the wardrobe and came across her small trunk."

Brow still furrowed, he continued to watch her. "Bad memories, Kate?"

"Bad enough," she answered truthfully.

She knew that if she didn't ask him now, she never would. Again, as before, she was tempted to take Annie and leave. "How did Brynna and Alice die?" She held her breath as she waited for his answer.

He shoved his hands into his back pockets. "We never got around to that, did we?"

She shook her head and studied the fire, clutching the cape around her. "No," she answered softly.

He crossed to the window and stared outside. "The babies cried a lot. Hell, one would have been more than Brynna could handle, but two. . . .

"I hired Sarita to come in and help her, but Brynna didn't trust her. Didn't want another woman in the house." He grunted a laugh. "After a week or so, she told Sarita to leave and never come back. I don't know why she didn't want her here. Sarita cooked and cleaned, tended the twins . . ."

Kate watched him warily, feeling the seeds of doubt grow deeper. What was going on here?

"Sarita told me she'd never met Brynna." Kate was amazed her voice was so strong, for her insides felt like pudding.

He turned and gave her a puzzled, hooded look. "She told you that?"

Heart pounding, she answered, "Why would she lie about something as simple as that?"

Sage chuckled dryly. "Probably because as Brynna's relative, you wouldn't believe what had happened to her so it was safer to pretend she didn't know anything about her."

The answer didn't mollify Kate. She clutched the journal closer to her heart. "What happened to her?"

Sage studied her briefly, then turned back to the window. "I'm not qualified to say, Kate. But something was wrong with her mind, that much I know."

Kate swallowed. "How did she and Alice die?"

He hung his head and his shoulders sagged. The only sound in the room was the crackling of the fire on the grate. "Even though Brynna didn't want Sarita around, I couldn't leave her out here alone. I figured that . . . that maybe Luis's mother would be less of a threat to Brynna. She stayed here as often as she could, but she's older, and Brynna tried her damnedest to make the old woman's life miserable.

"About a week after Brynna told Sarita to leave, I came home from work and no one was here. Not Luis's mother. Not Brynna and the twins. I wouldn't have thought too much about it, except that when I took my horse into the barn, there was Annie, asleep on the hay.

"I . . . I was damned scared, believe me. Why would Annie be here alone? God, I was so grateful she hadn't wandered off. . . .

"I don't know why I headed out toward the rocks, but I did. My heart damned near stopped when I saw buzzards circling. Then I saw her . . . and Alice."

Kate watched and listened, barely breathing as she tried to decide whether he was lying or telling the truth.

"And . . . and they were dead?"

He nodded, his head still bowed. "To this day I don't know how Brynna died. There wasn't a mark on her, but I'll never forget the expression on her face. It was filled with . . . terror."

Shuddering, Kate brought her hand to her mouth. "And Alice?"

Sage shook his head. "There was a pillow tied around her face. Brynna had smothered her."

Kate fought to stay calm. This couldn't end here. There were still too many unanswered questions. Clutching the journal in her hand, she shoved it at him. "Here. I want you to read this." Her voice was hard.

He turned and took the book. "Her journal?"

"Yes. I found it in her trunk."

Scowling, he thumbed through it. "I knew she kept one,

but I never bothered to read it. I figured it was her private business."

Kate stood her ground but wanted to bolt. "Turn to the July twentieth entry. You might find it illuminating."

He stopped and read the entry, still frowning. "Hell," he muttered, briefly tossing Kate a glance. "This is crazy. This isn't the way it happened at all."

Kate's heart was booming and her mouth was dry. "She says you tried to smother Alice with a pillow. She says you wanted to kill *both* of the children *and* her."

Sage shook his head, disbelief turning to anger. "And you believe these lies?"

Kate couldn't seem to breathe normally. "I knew Brynna a lot longer than I've known you, Mr. Reno. Why shouldn't I believe her?"

"What the hell are you saying? You're my wife, damn it."

Confusing emotions flooded her. "Just tell me why she would say such terrible things about you if they weren't true."

"How the hell should I know?" he growled. "But if you want a dose of the truth, let me tell you how it really was. I found *her* trying to suffocate Alice. That's when I hired Sarita, then Luis's mother. I knew damned well I couldn't trust Brynna not to harm one of her babies. She . . . she acted crazy sometimes." He thrust the journal at her accusingly. "This proves she was."

Kate didn't want to believe such a thing. Not of her own niece. She'd learned Brynna had been many things she hadn't wanted her to be, but surely she hadn't been crazy, too.

"How *dare* you accuse her of being crazy!"

He uttered another curse, went to the door and pulled on his jacket. Before he left the cabin, he turned to her and stared at her for a long, stifling moment.

"I should have known what we had together last night

was too good to last. I'm not that lucky. I can't prove a damned thing. But if you won't believe me, then maybe you *should* leave. But I want you to know that if you take Annie with you, I'll hunt you down. I'll sniff out your trail no matter where you try to hide."

He pulled on his boots and opened the door. Cold air whirled inside, sending the fire spinning in the fireplace. "I've gotta get out of here. You do what you damned well please. I don't know when I'll be back." He slammed the door behind him.

8

Kate stumbled to the fireplace, grateful Annie was still asleep. With the journal in her hands, she curled up at one end of the couch and read, hoping to learn more about Brynna—blood kin she obviously hadn't known at all.

She started at the beginning, the entry dated June fourth, 1886, just after Brynna had delivered the twins. As painful as it was to read, as the weeks and months passed, the entries became wilder, more troublesome, and harder to understand.

She read an entry that marked Sarita as an evil messenger sent by Sage to drive Brynna crazy and kill her children. Lord, Kate thought with a sigh, it was no wonder Sarita pretended she hadn't known her. Kate wondered who she would have believed just a few weeks ago—her beloved Brynna, or a total stranger?

Closing the book, Kate clutched it to her chest. Clearly something had happened to Brynna's mind. Maybe coming to this Godforsaken place and being expected to run a household and care for children had unhinged her.

But Brynna had never been strong. Was that Kate's fault? Could she have made Brynna a strong, independent woman? Oh, she didn't know ... she just didn't know.

What she did know was that Brynna's journal was filled with references to imaginary voices she heard and distorted pictures of reality. If she hadn't read anything beyond what she'd read before she faced Sage, she might have felt differently. But she'd read on, and by the end, there wasn't a shred left of the girl Kate had known.

She dropped the journal on the couch and sat back, studying the fire. Poor, dear Brynna. Tears clogged Kate's throat as she tried to imagine the terror that had imprisoned Brynna's mind. A mind that was gone long before she died.

With a sigh, Kate rose and went to the window. Fear clutched her, for it was snowing hard again. This time, however, the wind howled ruthlessly, and the wet flakes smacked against the windowpane.

Annie cried from the bedroom, and Kate hurried in to care for her, all the while wondering where her husband had gone, and if he was safe from the storm.

Her husband's supper grew cold. It was dark, but the storm had not abated.

Kate had valiantly entertained Annie the rest of the afternoon, thankful she had tired her out so she could put her down early. Most of her energy was centered on Sage. He'd left angry. Angry because she couldn't trust him.

Kate had thought of little else all afternoon. She thought about Sage trying to deal with Brynna, whose mind had snapped and who trusted no one. He had tried, perhaps more than any man could be expected to, to make an impossible marriage work. It was a worthy trait in anyone and made Sage just that much more admirable in Kate's eyes. All of her feelings about him grew.

She probably shouldn't have approached him until she'd read the entire journal, but what was done ... was done.

Clasping her hands to her chest, she paced the floor in front of the fireplace and prayed for her husband's safety. She crossed to the window, saw nothing, then paced again. Pressing her hands to her mouth, she prayed he was all right. It was her fault he was out there somewhere, maybe mired down in a snowdrift, unable to get home.

Her stomach twisted and hurt, and she couldn't keep from striding about the room. Pictures of Sage freezing in the snow, perhaps calling her name weakly, became paramount in her mind, and she felt every muscle in her body tense with fear. How could she ever forgive herself if he died because of what she'd said to him? Before she had a chance to tell him she loved him? It would haunt her forever. She would blame herself for his death as well as Brynna's.

She prayed again, promising never to send him away in anger just as long as he came home safely.

Although the room was warm, she shivered as she crossed to the window. Her heart vaulted upward when she saw him wading through the snow, leading his mount into the barn.

She waited, her heart in her mouth, until she heard him stamping off snow on the porch. She raced to the door and flung it open just as he reached for the knob. Stepping backward, she allowed him inside, then pushed the door shut against the intruding wind.

"Where have you been? I've been worried sick about you. You could have frozen to death out there!" Now that he was safe, relief turned to unrealistic anger.

He gave her an odd look as he brushed the snow from his jacket, took it off and hung it on the peg. As he removed his boots, he said, "You're still here."

She pressed the pounding pulse at her throat. "Of course I'm still here. Where would I go? God," she said, pulling in a tear-filled gasp of breath, "someone has to take care of you. Don't you *ever* scare me that way again, Sage Reno. I was so worried about you I almost made myself *sick.*"

He combed his wet hair with his hands. "I went into town to see about a cot, but I—"

"Oh, Sage, I don't give a *damn* about that cot. I don't give a damn about anything just as long as you're here and safe." She was close to tears.

He turned, his look more puzzled than ever. "You'd have missed me?"

"Oh, Sage, of *course* I'd miss you, you foolish man." Her gaze roamed over him hungrily.

"Kate?" There was uncertainty in his voice that held many questions.

She rushed to him, still wondering if she wanted to hit him for scaring her to death or throw herself at him because she was so relieved he was alive. The latter desire won, of course.

She studied him, knowing her expression was open, hiding nothing. "I'm sorry I didn't trust you, Sage. I'm sorry, I . . . I read the rest of the journal, and everything you said about Brynna was true. The poor dear, living in such imagined terror. Maybe there had always been something wrong with her, I don't know. I . . . I probably didn't *want* to know. After all, she was my responsibility, and if she turned out bad, I'd have to see it as my fault. I'm so sorry, darling—"

"Kate?" he interrupted.

She swallowed hard, stopping just short of touching him. "Yes?"

He touched her hair, drawing it loose from her bun. "You've just called me by name. Not just once, but four times."

A frown nicked her brow. "Wh——what?"

"Since the day we married, I've called you Kate. Never once, until now, have you spoken my name out loud. I've been waiting for it, Kate . . . needing to hear you say it."

She melted against him, hugging him hard, rubbing her hands over his wonderful back. "Oh, I've come to love you so much. Just the thought that I might have lost you filled me with terror. And I love you not just because of how you tend Annie, but because you are truly a warm, tender, wonderful man."

He chuckled, a tempting sound that rolled from deep within his chest. "And I'm also a man who can make you faint with pleasure in bed, don't forget."

She reached up and took his face in her hands, her gaze wandering over his handsome, beard-stubbled face. "Your supper is cold. Are . . . are you very hungry?"

He gave her an irresistible, lopsided grin. "My hunger for you is greater. The other can wait to be fed."

She stood on her tiptoes and kissed him the way he'd taught her to kiss. Without breaking contact, he lifted her into his arms and strode toward their bedroom.

Kate watched Sage light the lamp, his broad back naked to her gaze. He had loved her with a possession that shook her soul.

"Why do we need a light?"

He flopped back into bed and stripped the quilt back, away from her chin. She felt her nipples tighten.

"Because I want to look at you. I haven't really seen you since that day you and Annie were taking a bath."

Any self-consciousness fled when she saw the look of adoration in his eyes as he cupped her breasts. She raised her hand and ran it over his furry chest. "I might say I've admired you, too."

He nuzzled one breast, lazily licking the nipple, sending shivers over her skin. "I know."

She felt herself blush and swatted his shoulder. "Oh, was I that obvious?"

He made a contented sound and continued fondling her. "I sometimes wonder if you ever had daydreams about me like I had about you."

She ran her fingers through his hair while he adored her breasts. Things were heating up down below again. "Daydreams? Tell me about them."

"Well," he said after kissing her nipple, "first I wondered what it would be like to tumble you in the hay, strip you naked and make wild love to you."

Heat scorched her nether parts, rendering her damp. "R——really? Naked in the hay?"

"How does that sound?"

She cuddled against him. "I can't wait until spring." She kissed his shoulder. "What else?"

"Oh, well, after that day I saw you in the tub, I had this daydream about how you'd call me in to wash your back, and in order to get the soap, I'd have to reach deep into the water, sort of like this."

His hand moved between her legs, but his fingers barely grazed her. She throbbed for him. "Oh, that . . . that's very wicked, Sage Reno."

"What did you dream about me?" He stroked her stomach.

"Oh, my darling. I'm afraid I had no experience in wondering what we could do together. I just loved to watch you. Your body is so hard and strong . . . so beautiful."

"Then I guess it's up to me to teach you everything."

She ran her hands over him, gently claiming that part of him she'd so recently learned gave her pleasure. "I'm a quick study, darling."

He sucked in a breath as she touched him. "And I've got a lifetime to teach you, Kate. I can't begin to tell you how much I love you."

Tears of happiness pressed against Kate's throat. They

would have many wonderful years together, the three of them. They would make a success of the ranch; she would work beside him. And maybe one day they could give Annie a brother or a sister. Maybe both. Perhaps there was a child just beginning to grow inside her now. She touched her stomach lovingly. Protectively.

Whatever the future held, Kate knew it promised to be wonderful with Sage and Annie in her life.

Jane Bonander

I was so pleased to be asked to write a short story for *Avon Books Presents: To Have and to Hold.* The timing couldn't have been more perfect. My mother and father had just celebrated their sixtieth wedding anniversary, my husband and I our thirtieth, and our oldest son had just gotten married. It was a banner year.

All writers of historical romance who choose to set their stories on the rugged prairies of the frontier are aware of the hardships our pioneers endured to survive. That's not to say they didn't find some measure of satisfaction, as well. Through an old letter dating back to the late 1800's, I learned of one woman who found love and fulfillment in her new marriage. No doubt her day to day life was filled with adversity, but, as I discovered, her nights were filled with the passion.

I wrote "The Spinster Bride" for all the women who believe that love has passed them by, but I hope that everyone who reads it enjoys it.

Jane Bonander
P.O. Box 3134
San Ramon, CA 94583–6834

The Bride
of the Black Scot

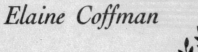

Elaine Coffman

For Jamie Mondragon
for all his help

1

Scotland, 1750's
In the Years Following the Battle of Culloden

He was the first naked man she had ever seen. Lady Juliette Pemberton fervently prayed he would not be the last.

Standing unclothed in the water herself, she knew no lady of breeding would dare ogle a naked man, but any lady who always did the expected had a very dull time of it.

There, across the pond, was the most splendid example of manhood that she had ever seen. Up until this moment, she had thought the Earl of Devonshire's wickedly tight breeches the height of male magnificence, but now she realized there was a higher level.

Not being one to pass by any of life's offerings, she felt not one shred of embarrassment as she gaped like a rustic. A situation such as this was simply too good to be missed.

After all, her very own father had sent her from her home in England to marry the most dreaded man in all of Scotland. And he'd done it by quoting Pittacus.

"Daughter, *know thine opportunity*," he had said.

Well, obedient daughter that she was, she was taking advantage of an opportunity right now.

Juliette stared into the mist that hung over the pool, considering her good fortune. In her mind, any woman who chose not to look would have to be worse than thick-witted. She would have to be dead.

Juliette's mind was fertile with imaginings. Only this morning she had prayed for a bit of adventure to bring some excitement into her life. A naked man ... yes, that was just what she needed. Some black-haired devil, proud as Lucifer, bare as the day he was born. With lip-smacking relish, she parted the reeds and craned her neck to get a better look.

Ah, Scotland. Here two days, and she loved it already. If there was anything the English nobility lacked, it was gloriously naked men without a speck of modesty. *If this is an example of Scottish manhood, then I most assuredly have something to look forward to....*

Hers might be a marriage forced upon her by the King of England, but in Lady Juliette's opinion, marriage to a man such as this black-haired Scot would be far, far better than any prospects she had at home, where many a maiden fished fair and caught a frog.

Naked as a needle herself, Lady Juliette hid among the rushes near the opposite shore, feeling her skin shrivel and knowing she had tarried overlong with her bath. She shivered. The water in Scotland was far colder than in England, but not even the likelihood of turning blue from the cold could lure her away.

From out of nowhere he had appeared like temptation, and for what seemed an eternity he stood on a rock that jutted out over the pool—as beautiful as sin, as perfect as the first man.

She felt as if she had partaken of the fruit of the tree of knowledge.

Desire spread its open wings before her, giving her a glimpse into a new world, velvet black and honey gold, sweet and forbidden. In spite of the chill water, something seemed to burn within her, some intense heat that came whenever she looked at him, an instinctive flow of need that made her want to do more than simply look. For the first time in her young life, she knew a thirst she could not quench.

Yea, the serpent had beguiled her.

At that moment, he glanced in her direction, and for a trembling instant she felt the heat of his gaze upon her. Everything within her seemed to melt. This is what she had been wishing for—a man such as this who would unlock all the deep secrets she yearned to have revealed. Faith! She didn't know her own body anymore. Everything above the water's surface was cold and confused, while everything below was as hot and steaming as a fresh baked pudding.

She told herself she should go, or at least duck down to hide, but she knew he couldn't see her, hidden as she was. Unable to look away, she stared back at him, and the rest of the world faded into oblivion.

And they were both naked, the man and his wife, and were not ashamed. . . .

Adam and Eve may have been ashamed, but she was fair to bursting with a desire to march over and take a closer look at him. She glanced down at her own bare breasts skimming the water's surface. Would he find as much pleasure looking at her as she did in looking at him?

"Psst . . ."

Lady Juliette knew all too well to whom that beckoning voice belonged, and she knew what her maid Edith would say if she looked in her direction. Ignoring Edith, she continued to drink in the sight of him, and felt the moment shatter with disappointment when he made a perfect dive into the pool. As the ripples spread outward and lapped against her breasts, she knew a new fear, for now he was in the same small pool. . . .

"Psst . . ."

This wouldn't do. Edith would persist until the two of them were caught. Juliette sighed. It was just as well, she supposed. As much as she was tempted to stay, it would not do for the betrothed of the Black Scot to find herself in a compromising position with another man.

A worried frown marred her small oval face. The King of England was exasperated with her as it was. If she angered him further, he might decide to lop off her head instead of send her to Scotland to marry the dreaded Black Scot.

With a sigh of regret, she watched the ripples of the pool spread in ever widening circles, then fade. Just as he surfaced, slinging water from his black head, she turned away, losing herself in the tall rushes that lined the bank.

A moment later, she reached for the blanket Edith handed her and wrapped it around herself as she made her way to the spot where her clothes hung on the branches of a tree.

"For shame, Lady Juliette," Edith said. "Looking at that naked savage when a lady of your breeding should have averted her head."

"I didn't see you averting yours."

Edith looked properly dignified. "I'm an old woman."

Juliette smiled. "But you still like to look."

Edith shrugged. "At my age, looking is about all I can do."

Juliette began to dress, her expression taking on an enraptured look. "He was the most beautiful man I've ever seen."

"And you saw plenty, or I miss my guess."

Juliette wanted to say she had not seen nearly enough. "Truly, Edith, he was like the angel of darkness, Lucifer before the fall, when he was the most beautiful of all the angels. Such dark skin and such long, black hair . . ." Her voice drifted off. She sighed. "Tell me, are all Scots so . . . so wild looking?"

Edith snorted. "The whole race is wild, child. They're no more than savages, but enough of that. You'd best be worrying about the particular beastly savage the king has promised you. I hear he uses human bones to pick his teeth."

Juliette laughed, clapping her hands over her mouth to muffle the sound. "Oh, Edith, you don't believe all those stories, do you? The king might be a bit put out with me for talking Papa into rejecting the offers of suitors he has sent our way, but he has always been fond of me."

"Your papa is far too lenient with you, m'lady, and I have told you so before. It is a fair shame, the way he has made your sisters wait on their own marriages until a suitable husband could be found for you. Your father coddles you overmuch."

Juliette smiled in fond recollection of her dear papa. "Perhaps he does, but I do know the king wouldn't promise me to a madman, no matter how exasperated he was with me for rejecting his previous suggestions."

"Every advantage has its tax," Edith said. "Besides, the king is more interested in soothing the feelings of these Highland savages than he is in making the likes of you happy. Your father's position as one of his favored earls only meant yours was the first name that popped into the king's head when he thought of an appropriate sacrifice."

Juliette barely listened. Her mind was on the man in the pool; she was convinced that marriage to a Scot would be no sacrifice. Nay, it would be pure pleasure.

"Come on," Juliette said, when she finished dressing, "we best be getting back to camp. You can finish scolding me there, while you braid my hair."

"Aren't you going to dry it first?"

Juliette looked around at the heavy mist that had lingered since their arrival the day before. "It will never dry in this weather."

"You could dry it over the fire, m'lady."

"And go to my betrothed smelling of woodsmoke?"

Edith snorted again. "It's probably better than what he's accustomed to."

Juliette smiled at Edith, knowing the woman who had served her since infancy was terrified of coming to Scotland. Poor Edith. She had no way of knowing how the image of the naked Scot was emblazoned in Juliette's mind. Not even marriage to the infamous Black Scot would dispel what she had seen today.

With all her heart Juliette wished that the man she had glimpsed in his magnificent nakedness was her betrothed. Even as she thought it, she knew it was foolish to think a man as important as the Black Scot, a Highlander whose realm lay far to the north, would be leisurely bathing in a simple Lowland pool.

Putting such thoughts aside, she headed back toward camp, Edith following behind. When they reached their tent, Juliette lifted the flap and went inside. A few minutes later, Juliette was sitting on one of her trunks, Edith standing behind her, brushing her hair. "Tell me more about what you've heard about my betrothed, Edith."

"I hear he drinks the blood of unbaptized babes for breakfast."

Juliette laughed. "Tell me the truth. Have you heard he is handsome?"

"Bah! As if handsomeness were important," Edith said, as she began to plait Juliette's hair. "Just who would be telling me such as that? The soldiers the king sent to escort us to the Scottish border?"

"So that's where you've been getting all those horrid stories. I'm ashamed of you, Edith. A woman of your years should know how soldiers love to pontificate."

Edith tied the ends of the long, blond braid that hung

down Juliette's back. "There now, it's finished, but mark my word, it won't dry in a plait like that."

"Perhaps the Black Scot will ride into camp this very day," Juliette said dreamily. "He will put me on his horse in front of him and we will ride like the wind back to his castle, drying my hair as we go."

"He is more apt to put your head on a pike," Edith said, wagging her finger. "You are English, Lady Juliette. Don't be forgetting that. And don't be forgetting that the Scots hate the English above all things. This bonny Black Scot that you fancy doesn't share your sentiments, I'll wager. He is probably angry enough to chew logs over the entire affair. The Scots don't like to be told what to do, especially by an English king." Edith shook her head. " 'Tis a pity, but I fear it is your wee body he'll be taking out his anger upon."

"Hmmm," Juliette said. She had a vision of a wickedly graceful man diving into the water and for just a moment wondered what it would be like to feel his touch. "Oh, trifle!" she said. "I don't think the Black Scot is half as black as his name makes him out to be." She looked thoughtful for a moment. "Edith, have you any idea what it must be like to have a name like Black Scot? Why, he was probably a darling baby who became a miserable man by trying to live up to such a horrible name."

"He *earned* the name, m'lady."

Juliette's expression remained wistful. "I don't believe it."

Edith shrugged, giving Juliette a self-righteous look. "That's your romantic side talking, not your sensible one, but suit yourself, m'lady." She turned away, mumbling, "Don't say I didn't warn you."

Juliette came to her feet and crossed to the tent flap, throwing it back and peering out. "It's getting late," she said, unable to hide the disappointment in her voice. "I had hoped the clansmen of the Black Scot would have been here by now."

"They were supposed to be here yesterday, waiting for us when we arrived. Of course, I didn't expect them to be. It will give them no small satisfaction to make us wait. They love to torment the English any way they can. Who knows? They may never come."

Juliette stared out into the sky, seeing the fringe of trees standing dark and sullen in the distance. Her destiny lay out there in that darkness. Out there, and with a man she had never seen, a man to whom she felt strangely connected.

"They will come," she said, taking up her cape and ducking through the opening. "I know it."

"You have been wrong before," Edith called after her.

Juliette smiled at Edith's babbling, dropping the tent flap behind her. She slipped the cape around her to ward off the chill.

"It will be night soon, will it not, captain?" Juliette inquired of Captain Morrison as he passed by.

The captain stiffened in rigid attention. "Yes, m'lady, black as pitch it will be. There's a darkness here like no place else I've ever seen. Can't see a star in the sky, or your hand in front of your face."

"I have found that to be true," Juliette said, pulling her cape more closely about her and suppressing an uneasiness that threatened to grip her. It was blessedly difficult to remain cheerfully optimistic when those about you were as pessimistic as spinsters. She glanced back at the tent, feeling suddenly consumed by loneliness. Faith! She was in Scotland now, just beyond the border, far from home and everything she knew—soon to be wed to a mysterious stranger with a foreboding name, and then surrounded by still more strangers. "I suppose I should prepare myself for bed, then. Perhaps they will come at dawn. I will need a good night's sleep."

"They will come when we least expect it, m'lady. It is the Scots' way."

"You know the Scots, then?"

"Yes, more than I would like."

Juliette started to inquire more, but the closed look on the captain's face decided her against it. "Do you know anything of my betrothed, Captain?"

"Only what I hear, m'lady."

"From a reliable source, I am sure."

"From a clansman of the Black Scot himself."

"You have talked with him?"

"I was there when he presented himself to the king and gave the Black Scot's reply to the king's suggestion of a betrothal between you."

Juliette's eyes rounded with fascination. "You were there? Tell me, what did you hear?"

"It was not something I would like to repeat, m'lady."

"I am of a strong constitution, captain. I will know what the Black Scot thought of this betrothal."

"The messenger said the Black Scot would sooner affiance himself to a sack of wet barley than to a whey-faced Englishwoman with a backbone of jelly and no more resourcefulness than a fresh-laid goose egg."

Juliette laughed. "Well, he will be pleasantly disappointed then," she said, "for I might be fair of skin, but I've backbone enough to face the likes of him without flinching, and as for resourcefulness . . ." She gave the captain a knowing look. "With six conniving younger sisters, I could be nothing but."

Captain Morrison coughed discreetly and Juliette knew he was trying hard not to laugh. "It grows late. The men are ready to eat," he said. "Shall I have food sent to you?"

Before she could answer, the pounding of horses' hooves shattered the stillness. She looked beyond Captain Morrison, still unable to see anything, but hearing the thunderous sound growing louder, interspersed with voices.

Suddenly, a band of men on horseback burst out of a wooded glen and descended upon them with great swiftness.

In a moment that was both wonderful and terrifying, Juliette looked up to see the horde thundering toward them as the most magnificent black horse and rider crashed through one of their tents, the canvas flying out behind him like the wings of some giant, mythological bird. With similar grace, the other horsemen tore through camp, following close behind their leader, pulling their horses to a rearing stop just a few feet from the very spot where Juliette and Captain Morrison stood.

She stared up at them, too struck by their sheer magnificence to speak. They were beings from another world, another time—wild and dangerous, free and without restraint. Something deep within her soul stirred, and she felt as if she had lived all her life for this one moment.

The black-clad leader of the group looked with haughty disdain at the English soldiers who surrounded them, before pinning his cold, blue-eyed gaze on Juliette. For the briefest moment, time was suspended, the man's great black cape swirling magnificently about him, his ebony horse tossing his head and pawing the earth that seemed to quake beneath her own trembling legs. The second their gazes met, something within Juliette leaped and she knew, knew without a doubt, that this raven-haired man with clothes as black as the night was the same man she had seen—and seen a great deal of—at the pool.

The black devil impaled her with a look that suggested he had seen a great deal of her as well. The idea was preposterous, of course; she had been too well hidden. Yet his knowing look made her glance away. But not before she saw the sardonic amusement on his face.

That look made Juliette confront him squarely and without fear. It would not do for these men of the Black Scot to report to her betrothed that he was about to marry a weakling.

With a creaking of saddle leather and harness, the black-cloaked leader urged his horse closer and drew him to a stop just inches from her. He leaned forward, crossing his arms over the pommel of his saddle as his gaze swept over her. "I ken *this* is the betrothed of the Black Scot," he said in a powerful, threatening voice.

"This is Lady Juliette Pemberton," Captain Morrison said. "And who might you be, sir?"

With one graceful movement, the dark stranger threw a leg over the saddle and dropped to the ground. He was tall and slender. His black velvet doublet and breeches fitted him well—too well—and she wondered if he wore the black of mourning in defiance to the king's banishment of the tartan.

It wasn't his tight breeches that drew her attention, however, but the sensual mouth beneath the hawkish nose, the raven hair that hung to his shoulders, the proud angle of his head, the devil's own blue-black eyes that seemed in harmony with a face that might have belonged to the Roman deity of the underworld.

"Stephen Gordon at your service," he said.

"You are a kinsman of the Black Scot?" Captain Morrison asked.

His smile was mocking. "The Gordons are all clansmen, but I ken it could be said that I am closer to our laird than anyone," he said, drawing his gaze from Captain Morrison and giving Juliette the once-over before stepping closer and taking her by the chin, tilting her face toward the fire.

The moment his fingers made contact with her skin, she jumped as if touched by a red-hot brand. He took no notice, studying her as casually as he might a pedlar selling hot cross buns.

"You hide your fear well," he said.

Her heart hammered in her chest; her palms grew damp. Breathing became something of a labor. "I see nothing to fear," she replied, praying the sound of her knocking knees did not reach his arrogant ears.

He had the audacity to laugh and her first impulse was to take her revenge against his shin, but she surmised such an attempt in soft slippers would only crush her toes. There would be another chance, when she was wearing riding boots. She returned his stare. "Were you hoping I would be afraid of you? Is that why you came dressed in black and tore down half the tents in camp as you arrived?"

His smile was wicked. "You seem remarkably determined in your refusal to show fear, mistress."

"Fear is bondage."

"And pride consoles the weak."

"We shall see," she said, tilting her chin up and keeping her gaze steady on him.

"Aye," he said. "I ken I like nothing better than a challenge, lass."

Towering over her as he did, she thought him unbelievably tall. His face was half-hidden in shadow, but the firelight revealed his sensual mouth curving in a slow, satisfied smile. Was he toying with her?

"Then consider yourself challenged, m'lord."

"Proceed with caution, lass. Only a fool rides headlong into the unknown."

Perhaps she *was* a fool. She had been looking for adventure, a diversion from the boredom of the English court. But now, standing in the presence of this man, she realized her folly. She had once seen a cat stand idly over a mouse, purring deeply in its throat, just before it struck so swiftly she did not see it move. This was no game he was playing.

Still, strength would serve her better than weakness. It

remained to be seen if the strength would be real or feigned.

Stupidly, she looked straight into his eyes and wondered if she would ever be able to look away. His eyes were so dark a blue that they looked black, unfathomable, against his sun-darkened skin. She had been right to liken him to Lucifer. As she watched, his eyes seemed to change, illuminated by a light from within that blazed brilliantly silver. Her breath caught in her throat. The very trees around them seemed to grow still with expectancy, the mist that had plagued them for two days hanging motionless. Even the fire seemed to grow dim.

She needed the assurance of something living, knowing she could not command her own cowardly voice. She looked toward Captain Morrison. Blessedly, the dear man seemed to sense her distress.

"We have tarried longer than we expected," the captain said. "We were told you would meet us here two days ago."

"We were delayed," Stephen said, offering no further explanation.

"We are two days behind schedule and the king is anxious for our return," Captain Morrison replied. "He awaits word that our mission has been completed, that Lady Juliette has been delivered safely into the hands of the Black Scot."

The devil's expression was mocking now, and he nodded in understanding, as if taunting the captain with the knowledge that they were uneasy on Scottish soil.

Captain Morrison's face went suddenly red with embarrassment. "Of course it would be foolish to expect you to escort a lady at such a late hour. Please join us for a light repast. Afterward, there are some documents that will need your hand. Tomorrow will be soon enough for us to depart."

Stephen Gordon frowned. "Documents?"

Captain Morrison nodded. "To attest that Lady Juliette was delivered in good health and without harm into your hands."

Before Stephen Gordon could look back at her, Juliette spoke. "I grow weary. You do not require my presence. I will retire now." Giving the Scot a direct look, she could not resist adding, "Pray continue your discussion of me."

She had gathered her skirts and turned away when the Scot's voice rang out, stopping her.

"Ready yourself, mistress. We leave in a few minutes."

She spun around, remembering Edith's warning that the Scots would take their revenge out on her body. "Leave now!" she cried. "Do you mean to exact my punishment already?"

His eyes glittered with silver fire. "You expect punishment?" He smiled. "Have you done something wrong, lass?"

"I am English," she said. "I thought that reason enough."

His expression darkened and she wondered if she had gone too far.

"I am not in the habit of making war with women," he said.

"Yet you expect me to travel with you now . . . at this late hour, like some fat, obedient cow you have just purchased?"

"The comparison is yours," he said. Then without further discussion, he ordered, "Make yourself ready, mistress. Direct my men to your belongings. We leave in half an hour."

He turned back to Captain Morrison and Juliette realized she had been well and truly dismissed.

She began to sing under her breath.

"There were two cats at Kilkenny;
Each thought there was one too many

So they quarreled and they fit,
They scratched and they bit,
Till, excepting their nails
And the tips of their tails,
Instead of two cats, there wasn't any."

He turned toward her. "Did you say something?"

"I was singing."

"Sing something else."

"As you wish."

He looked as if he were waiting for something. When she remained silent, he said, "You surprise me, lass. I would have thought you had more mettle. You offer me no challenge?"

She recognized a master at verbal sparring. He had the advantage for now. She would wait for a better time to even things between them.

"You have nothing more to say?" he asked.

"The devil is seldom outshot with his own bow," she replied.

2

Stephen watched Juliette duck into her tent. Standing beside Angus, he saw a worried frown stretch across his friend's ancient forehead.

"You didna tell the lass the truth about who you are, lad," Angus said. "Do you think that wise?"

"Aye . . . for the time being."

"I dinna ken what harm it would be to tell the lass the truth. You canna keep it from her forever."

"No, but I can keep it from her until I am certain why she is here."

"You suspect treachery from the lass?"

Stephen turned to look at him. "We are dealing with the English, are we not?"

"Aye," Angus said, nodding. "And you suspect everyone . . . even the lass?"

"Especially the lass, until I have reason not to. She may be as innocent as we were led to believe—chosen on a whim of the king's, a name selected to barter, an innocent pawn in a game of politics between two long-standing enemies. But she might also be coming for a different reason entirely. She could be a spy for the King, sent to bring about my downfall. I'll no take to wife a woman who is capable of putting a knife between my shoulders while I sleep. I have lived with treachery enough to know I can trust no one. I will know where her loyalty lies before I tell her I am the Black Scot."

"She is a comely lass," Angus said, scratching his chin, "and abundantly dowered."

"Aye," Stephen said, "but I care far more for her loyalty than her wealth." As he spoke, Stephen let himself remember, his mind picking out details—a fall of golden hair in a thick braid down a back, full breasts, small waist, oval face, eyes so blue a man could swim in them. She was not beautiful enough to take his breath away, but she was comely. He had a flash of memory of her at the pool, standing in waist-deep water, her nakedness calling out to him. Aye, her body bore the classical perfection her face did not possess. A comely lass with a body a man could worship. If she proved to be loyal, he would be more than satisfied.

But Stephen had been seduced by such beauty before. Seduced and betrayed by a woman, as had his father before him. Treachery seemed to run in the veins of the women whom the chiefs of the Gordon clan took to wife.

A woman's betrayal had ended his father's life. Stephen himself had barely escaped death at the hands of the faithless woman he had wed. He would not risk his heart or his life again.

"Loyalty is worth more to me than a comely face," he said at last.

Angus shrugged. "Perhaps this time you will have both."

"Aye, perhaps I will," Stephen said. "Either that or I will have neither."

A sturdy mare was brought for Juliette to ride, a surefooted chestnut of gentle disposition, according to Angus. He gave her a boost into the sidesaddle and rode beside her for the first part of their journey into the darkness that lay beyond the bright fires of the English camp.

Shortly after they mounted, Juliette noticed they aimed their horses toward the distant mountains, where the white-globed moon hung low, as if it was too heavy to climb higher. From time to time she stole a glance at Stephen Gordon, who had taken place behind them. He seemed so stern and distant—untouchable even—garbed in his black clothes and cape. She remembered the way she had first seen him and felt a twinge of regret, for she had liked him ever so much better when he was naked.

Strange, how I could feel closer to a man when he is without clothes than I do when he is fully dressed . . .

She felt the impact of Stephen's gaze upon her. Again she thought of him naked at the pool, and felt she had the advantage. She gave him a sweet smile that said *I know something you don't know.*

He returned it with a smile that seemed to say, *I know something as well.*

Her composure was shattered. Her thoughts flew back to the pool. She recalled the moment when he had looked in her direction, and her whole body had suddenly felt warm. *He couldn't have seen me. I am certain I was too well hidden.*

Still, the thought brought added heat to her face and she turned away.

She could have sworn she heard him chuckle just before he dug his spurs into his horse's sides. She watched his back as he pulled ahead of them and disappeared into the darkness.

The moon was high in the sky when at last they drew rein. Six of the fifteen men led the pack animals to a road they had come upon. As she continued down the trail with the remaining eight, she glanced at Angus. "Where are the others going?"

Angus did not speak. Juliette repeated her question. "Pardon me. Could you tell me where those men are going with my belongings?"

"The pack animals will fare better on the main roads," Stephen said, seeming to appear out of nowhere, riding his horse between her and Angus. "We will make better time on the trails. If all goes well, we should reach Craigmoor Castle a good two days ahead of them. Dinna fret over your silks and satins, mistress. They will be well guarded, even at the risk of men's lives."

As a child Juliette had been taught that anger in a world controlled by men was only a waste of time, that a woman had more effective, diplomatic ways to get what she wanted. But looking at this towering man, she did not think diplomacy would gain her one whit. Besides, she had never much followed what she had been taught.

"I was not fretting over the safety of my garments," she said. "I was merely asking their destination. Clothes can easily be replaced."

A grim smile played on Stephen's mouth. "You think the Black Scot would be so charitable?"

"I cannot speak for the Black Scot since I have yet to meet him. I can only surmise that a man honored and respected as the chief of his clan would be kind and honorable to the woman he took to wife."

Whatever principles Stephen Gordon held to, admitting he was wrong was apparently not among them. In spite of that, she felt some satisfaction when his face turned dark and glowering. Not one to bask overlong in sweet victory, she looked past Stephen to where Angus rode silently, half-hidden in the darkness. "Does he ever speak?"

"Only when he has something to say, or he feels it is his place to do so," Stephen said, nodding at Angus, who took off at a gallop.

Stephen inclined his head in the direction Angus had taken. "Let us ride," he said.

She remained stubbornly where she was.

With a *swoosh*, Stephen drew his broadsword. Juliette saw the flash of moonlight dancing off metal before the blade swept toward her in a descending arc. She had no time to react, only to fear.

The broadsword swept past her, the flat side coming down against her horse's rump. The horse reared, then jumped, and broke into a gallop, heading down the trail Angus had just taken, the sound of Stephen Gordon's cursed laughter ringing in her ears.

After what seemed like hours of riding at a full gallop, her posterior growing numb, they slowed enough to cross a narrow stream, and then began to climb upward. The trail narrowed, forcing them to go in single file.

She was thankful it forced them to slow their pace, which did little to ease the ache in her joints. *Faith! Are these Scots always in a hurry?*

Once, Juliette paused long enough to look behind her, her gaze moving over the column of men to locate Edith. She was bouncing along on a small, but sure-footed pony, and judging from her expression, she was praying her heart out. Juliette could not help but smile.

The smile faded when Stephen said, "Keep moving, lass. We are in MacBean territory."

His tone was softer than it had been earlier. She had been right to stand up to him. "Is that bad?" she asked.

"Aye, it can be bad, if they see us. We are small in number."

"Why did you not bring more men?"

"That is an English habit . . . legions marching into battle, drums rolling, their red coats brilliant in the sun."

"Do you answer every question with platitudes?"

He shrugged. "More men is a sure way to draw their attention," he said. "Satisfied?"

She nodded "I am always gratified to receive an honest answer," she said. "Are you an enemy of the MacBeans?"

He laughed. "If your name isna MacBean, then you are their enemy. Have you no heard that the clans are always fighting each other? Today we are enemies of the MacBeans and the MacAlpins. Tomorrow it might be the MacDuffs and the Sinclairs."

"Why would they attack you? You carry no valuables. What could they possibly be after?"

"You, mistress."

His words sent a shiver through her. "Me?" To her shame, her voice was lost somewhere between a croak and a warble. She tried again. "Surely they would not wish to anger the king by abducting me."

"After you were forced to marry one of their clansmen, they would expect the king to be more lenient toward them."

"But Scots hate the English. Why would any Scot go out of his way to have an English wife?"

His eyebrows rose. "They would see the sacrifice of marriage to an English lass as a fair exchange."

"For what?"

"Security. For gaining the favor of King George. You are a pearl of great price, mistress. The clan so favored with your marriage would hold considerable power and influence."

A pearl of great price . . . She almost laughed out loud at the thought. What would her dear, beloved father say if he heard such poppycock. Why, in England, there had been times when her father would have gladly *given* her away. She chewed her lip and considered the prospect of being taken by yet another band of Scots, just when she was settling in with this one. Faith! She could not help wondering if she would spend the rest of her days being kidnapped and bartered about, for it did seem that was all these bloody Scots thought about. Suddenly marriage to the Black Scot sounded like a blessing. The Scots might be barbarians, but at least they were Christian barbarians. Once she was married, she would no longer be fair game.

The very idea of being fair game to anyone did not sit well with her.

"Are you worried about the MacBeans, mistress?"

"You are here to guard me, so there is no reason to be afraid. However, I am not enamored of the idea of being kidnapped. How about you? Are you afraid of them?"

She realized immediately she had said the wrong thing. His dark look told her that this man did not like being called anything that even vaguely resembled a coward. She opened her mouth to explain what she'd meant, but he cut her off with a curt answer.

"I am no coward, mistress, but I am no fool either. We are only eight men. I respect their large numbers," he said, putting spurs to his horse and riding off.

Her mouth still hanging open, she watched him go, thinking he had such a subtle way of ending a conversation.

3

Some time later, they reached the top of the mountain and began their descent, down a rocky trail that ended in a small glade. She had almost reached the bottom when her horse faltered. Before she had time to react, she felt the iron weight of an arm slide around her waist. An instant later, she was pulled from her horse and thrust across rock-hard thighs. Her head hanging upside down against the sweat-glistening side of a much larger and darker horse, she knew immediately that it was Stephen Gordon who had rescued her from taking a nasty tumble.

It was an encouraging thought, for the man had showed little regard for her so far. There were times when she wondered if he was not disposed to dropping her along the wayside and riding off without her, not really caring if she was taken by the MacBeans, or the wolves.

"You can put me back on my horse now," she said.

"You will ride with me for awhile."

"Why? Are you afraid my horse will stumble again?"

"Perhaps . . . or perhaps I like the feel of you here."

He might like the feel of her tossed over his horse like a sack of barley, but she was quite uncomfortable.

She righted herself in front of him—which took some doing—and shifted her weight to a more comfortable position, then stared up and back at him. "I have no inclination as to whose idea it was to travel at such a pace," she said, "but I will tell you this: I am not as soft as you assume. If you think I am going to beg you, or ask for leniency, you are mistaken. You can ride until this black beast drops out from under you and I will still be beside you."

He did not say anything, so she went on. "I will not be treated like some bit of cumbersome baggage. I will toss myself off the nearest cliff before I submit to such." She would not have dared, of course, but for someone who did not have much to barter with, it sounded reasonably heroic.

She waited for his response, but he simply reached inside his cloak and pulled out an oatcake and took a bite, offering it to her. "Hungry?"

Here she was talking of suicide and he was thinking of food. She shook her head. "No thank you," she said with haughty dignity. "There are some things more important than food."

Seeing his amused expression, she said, "I might be English and I might be a woman, but I can keep up with the likes of you."

He gave her an amused look. "You think you are as good as any Scot?"

That ruffled her. "I *know* I am as good as any man . . . English or Scottish."

He chuckled. "We shall get along. I like a strong woman."

"Then find your own. I'm already promised to an ogre."

His eyes narrowed. "You will find, lass, that when baiting a mousetrap with cheese, it is best to leave some room for the mouse."

She shrugged. "He that makes himself an ass, must not take it ill if others ride him."

"Scotland is a wild, unforgiving land. Provoke me overmuch and I may leave you behind. I am all that stands between you and certain death."

"Leave me behind and you will infuriate the King of England, m'lord. I am all that stands between Scotland and another war."

"There have been many wars, but none have broken us. Scotland will outlive both you and the king," he said.

Juliette ignored him.

"You have no comment?" he asked.

"It has never been my intention to inspire braggarts. An ass will bray, whether encouraged or not."

"You seem to ken a great deal about asses," he said.

"Yes, and I'll wager I'll know a great deal more before we reach Craigmoor Castle."

He ate two oatcakes without replying.

They rode on in silence and Juliette drifted off to sleep, cradled in his arms.

It was still dark when she awoke, although the first, pale-gray, hint of morning was beginning to creep over the tops of the mountains that lay in the distance. She had been awake for some time now, but felt no compunction to speak. In spite of being in a strange land, and finding herself cradled in the arms of a stranger, she felt safe and secure.

She did not venture to look at him, but had a sense that he knew she was awake. Not much went on that missed Stephen Gordon, she decided. She wondered if that was why he was entrusted by her betrothed to go on a mission such as this.

Her betrothed.

That reminder sent her thoughts drifting into another direction entirely. She wondered what kind of man the Black Scot was. How old was he? Was he fat? Did he have all his teeth? Was he a learned man? Would he be kind to her? Would he be gentle? She sighed. Answers to these questions would come, in time. In the meantime, she would simply have to be patient.

But one question still loomed in the back of her mind.

What did the Black Scot look like naked?

After riding in silence for some time, Juliette could

stand neither the silence or the suspense any longer. "Tell me about the Black Scot," she said.

"What do you wish to know? The typical things? Is he handsome? Does he beat his women?"

"His handsomeness matters not, but I would like to know something of his appearance. Is he tall and dark like you? Or is he short and squat like Angus?"

"He favors me a great deal."

His words warmed her. "Tell me something about him."

"He is the Black Scot, the leader of our clan. What else is there to tell?"

"What is his proper name?"

"His proper name is Alexander Gordon, Seventh Earl of Gordon. Does that satisfy your curiosity?"

"Partly. Tell me what kind of person he is. What he likes."

"He likes silent women," he said, pushing her head against his chest. "Why don't you go back to sleep?"

Her head popped up. "I would rather talk."

"That doesna surprise me. You do little else."

"Then we are well matched, for you hardly speak at all. Why is that?"

"Perhaps I have nothing to say."

"No, I think it is because you distrust me. Am I right?"

"Aye. I have no reason to trust you, or any Englishman."

"You have no reason to *dis*trust me, either. True, I am English, but I will soon be a Scot. Does that make no difference?"

He scoffed at that. "Marriage to the Black Scot doesna make you a Scot."

"Being born in England doesn't make me untrustworthy."

"Perhaps," he said, adding no more.

Juliette could not help thinking about this solemn-faced Scot, wondering at the strange relationship they seemed to be forming. She would have to admit that she was more than taken with him and she was convinced he was not indifferent to her, yet his dark glowers and sharp replies said otherwise.

She stole a glance at his grimly set features. In spite of his stoic presence, she felt completely at ease with him. Yet never in her life had she met anyone who went to such extremes to discourage her. With a sigh, she leaned back against him, deciding she needed to think about this man in depth. His breath was warm and moist, brushing across her like an ocean breeze—a touch of human contact as reassuring as the first signs of spring, as comforting as her favorite blanket. It stirred the fine hairs that curled around her face. She sighed and closed her eyes, absorbing the warmth of his great body curled around hers. It both satisfied her and left her with a strange longing. She kept thinking thoughts she had no business thinking.

She wanted him to kiss her. She wanted to be with him as they were at the pool—naked and unashamed. She wanted to feel his unclothed body curl around hers as it did now.

But that would never happen. They would never be permitted such liberties. They would go on as they had been doing, each hiding his thoughts and feelings. Despair filled her at the prospect. She decided then that she would not hide her feelings. In truth, she did not think she could.

They continued in silence, until her curiosity got the better of her and she could contain herself no longer. "Why are you so sad?"

His laugh was low and bitter. "Those are your words, mistress."

"But you *are* sad. I can feel it. I see it in your eyes. Oh, I know you try to hide it, and you probably fool a lot of people, but you do not fool me. You are not as happy as you would have people think. You carry a burden m'lord, and it grows heavy."

"I *am* burdened," he said. "You are a heavy lass."

"I am not *that* heavy," she replied, wanting to throw her arms around his neck because of the way he tried to make light of something that obviously pained him. "Who has caused you so much suffering? Was it a woman?"

Even in the dim light, she could see the muscle working in his jaw. He did not say anything for a long time. When she repeated her question, he said, "Aye, it was a woman."

Now we are getting somewhere, she thought, priming herself for a long discussion of this man's past. "Want to tell me about it?"

"No."

A minor setback, nothing more. Don't give up, Juliette . . . "Sometimes that helps . . . you know, talking about it."

"I dinna need any help," he said harshly. "Contrary to what you think, it doesna bother me."

"*Something* bothers you . . . unless you've always been this way. Were you always solemn, even as a little boy?"

"If I was, I ken it was because I had something to be solemn about. Everyone is no as fortunate as you, lass. We canna all be born into gilded perfection."

She would have said a word in her defense, but there was something in his tone, a woeful lilt, a hint of melancholy that made her want to understand this complex man more than she wanted to defend herself. Suddenly, it was very important to understand him, to know what made him so unhappy as a lad, so distrustful as a man. "Did you get on well with your brothers and sisters?"

"I had no brothers or sisters."

"Oh," she said. "I am sorry."

"I was a bastard," he said, "born out of wedlock. My father was married to another woman. Now, does that satisfy your curiosity?"

"Not completely," she said. "Why didn't your father claim you as his own?"

"Do you never sleep?"

"No, do you?" she asked, then heard his resigned sigh.

"He would have, but my mother took me away. She preferred living in secluded poverty to giving me up."

"She must have loved you a great deal."

"Aye," he said, in a way that made her think his thoughts were spinning backward, to another time, another place.

"Did your mother ever marry?"

"Aye. She married my father . . . eventually. His marriage to his first wife was a childless union. A few years after I was born, his wife died. I was five years old when my father found and married my mother."

A bastard, raised in secluded poverty . . . She had visions of him, a ragged little urchin, teased and taunted because of the circumstances of his birth, a child with no one to love and comfort him, save a mother who was as much an outcast as he. She thought of her own family, the rich, full life she had enjoyed. Her heart went out to him. The look she gave him was a tender one. "But by the time they married, it was too late to erase the burden of being illegitimate," she said, her voice low and full of feeling.

"Aye," he said. "By then it was too late."

She put her hand on his sleeve, feeling him flinch. "I am sorry, Stephen."

He drew back. "It doesna matter now," he said. "It was a verra long time ago."

"But it does matter," she said, knowing even before he spoke that he would tell her no more about himself.

"We have talked overmuch about me," he said. "It is time you spoke of yourself. Why were you the one chosen to marry the Black Scot?"

She sighed and leaned her head back against his chest, staring at the fast fading stars overhead. "It is a long story, and not very interesting," she said, wishing there was some way she could bring a smile to his tightly held mouth.

"It is a long way to Craigmoor lass, and I have nothing to do, save looking at the backside of Angus's horse."

She smiled. "I am the daughter of an English earl. I am the eldest of six sisters who are anxious to be wed, but my father said I must marry first."

"Ah, as Katherine did in *The Taming of the Shrew,*" he said.

Her heart lurched. *A learned man.* She prayed her betrothed was such as well. "You read Shakespeare?" she asked.

"I have been known to indulge. But we are not talking about me," he said. "Are you trying to tell me that your father allowed the king to use you as a pawn simply so your sisters could wed?"

She nodded. "Yes, I suppose I am, although it sounds far more cruel when you say it that way."

"It *is* cruel," he said. "Why did he not simply find you a suitor in England? You are no great beauty, but you are comely enough to find a husband."

She smiled inwardly. If he thought to provoke her by baiting her with a comment about her plain looks . . . well, she was not so vain as to fall for that old trick. "It is true that I am not the beauty some of my sisters are," she said with forced sweetness, "but I had enough good qualities to attract many offers."

"And a large dowry?"

"It is true that my dowry is large, but according to my father, it was my intelligence and wit that drew the offers. At most of the gatherings I would find myself surrounded by men, while many women more beautiful than I were left alone. I never understood why, but for some strange reason men seemed to find it challenging to carry on a discussion with me." She looked up at him with an impish grin. "Perhaps it was because I am a worthy opponent in chess. Do you play, m'lord?"

"Aye."

"Then we must have a game sometime."

"I have a feeling you would beat me."

"I would try," she said, looking up at him and smiling. For a moment she thought he might smile in return, but he curbed the inclination, keeping the discussion on the target he had set earlier: Herself.

"If you had many suitors, why would your father marry you to a Scot? Surely he knows we are no verra fond of the English?"

No verra fond. . . . I do love the way he speaks. Faith! I think I am beginning to love everything about him. . . . Danger. . . . Danger. . . . Danger. . . .

She ignored her own inner warnings. "I fear I was too particular. Each time the king suggested a suitor to my father and the poor man came to call, I found him not to my liking and my father sent him away."

"Your father is very indulgent of you, I take it."

"Yes, he is. Of course he would like my sisters and myself to think him gruff and stern, but in truth, he is the kindest of fathers. He would sooner lop off his own hand than cause one of us grief."

"And because of your ease in manipulating your father, the king became annoyed with you, so he banished you to Scotland."

"He made it sound as if he were doing me a great honor," she said, turning her head to look at her companion, but seeing only the square thrust of his chin.

"It is the way of kings." Stephen looked down at her, and for a moment he studied her face. He was so close she could feel the moist heat of his breath, a warm caress against her cheek. For a time she simply stared at him, her gaze fastened upon his full, sensuous lips. She could not help wondering what it would be like to kiss him. She could not help herself. She was attracted to him, and despite the way he acted, she knew he was attracted to her as well.

"You talk overmuch."

"I know, but there doesn't seem to be anything else to do, save look at the backside of Angus's horse."

She heard his soft chuckle. Looking up, she saw the expression in his eyes and recognized his intention, just as his head came toward her. Her breath quickened. There were a dozen things she could have, should have done to dissuade him, but all she did was make a small noise deep in her throat before her eyes drifted closed. His lips touched hers softly, then withdrew. It was not a kiss of passion, but merely one of inquiry. When she did not turn away, he lowered his head again. This time, he kissed her with slow, lingering thoroughness, tracing her lips with his tongue, then drawing her lower lip inside his mouth. The sensation made her gasp and she had to dig her fingers into the soft folds of his cape to keep from falling off the horse. As if humored by her action, he broke the kiss, dragging his lips back and forth across hers until she melted against him. She moaned softly when he drew back, studying her face intently.

She bore the scrutiny of his dark gaze. "Why did you do that?"

"Because you wanted me to."

She smiled, losing herself in his eyes and forgetting for a moment why she was here and who he was. "Yes, I did," she said, her voice barely audible. "What would you do if I wished it again?"

"I would tell you to remember you are promised to the Black Scot," he said in a chilling, unemotional tone.

His words slapped her in the face with cold, hard reality, and it took only that one reminder to draw her thoughts up short. She felt too many things for this man that she should not be feeling. Suddenly she was terrified of herself, yet even more terrified of him. This was no foppish boy like the ones she dallied with in the drawing rooms of England. This was a man in every sense of the word. Suddenly, she felt as if she had stepped off a cliff and was falling into a bottomless abyss. Her body trembled.

If she had been on her own horse, she would have ridden ahead, leaving the tempting reminder of him far behind her. As it was, she could only feign indifference, praying the heat she felt on her face was not as red as it felt.

Ignoring her obvious discomfiture, he said, "Now, tell me why you seem so accepting of your fate."

"Is there a reason why I should not be accepting? Should I have cause to fear this union?" she asked, fighting to regain her composure. "Is the Black Scot an animal? Will I grow to hate him?"

"He is a fair man. One who holds the responsibility for the welfare of the clan and must act accordingly. He cannot think of what he wants, but only of what is best for his kinsmen."

"He is a lot like the king, then."

"Aye, perhaps he is. Why are you so inquisitive about the Black Scot?"

"He is to be my husband. Is that not reason enough?"

"Perhaps you want to find out his weakness, the place where he is vulnerable." He looked deep into her eyes. "Are you Delilah, come to cut Samson's hair, or Salome, ready to dance for his head?"

She returned his gaze, praying he would see the truth in her eyes. "Perhaps I am Esther."

"The Jewish girl who became queen of Persia."

"The Jewish girl who told the Persian king of a plot against his life. I am not a seductress or a warrior, m'lord. My motives are simpler ones, and more gentle. It is only a woman's natural curiosity that prompts my questions. I have no doses of poison hidden in my jewels, no dagger tucked into my boot, no code memorized to send the King of England secret messages. Why are you so hesitant to tell me about him?"

He shrugged. "What is there to know beforehand? You will have time enough after you are married to learn of him and his ways. Why is it so important now?"

"Because it might help me to be a better wife to him."

He looked surprised. "You plan to serve him?"

She stiffened at the sound of that. "I come as his betrothed—soon to be his wife—not as his servant. I will be his equal, but that does not prevent me from wanting to know and understand him."

His voice was scoffing. "I ken he would value your allegiance more than your understanding."

"He has that already."

The look he gave her was one of open surprise. "Ah, but how do you know *you* can trust *him*, lass? Have you no heard? He is no called the Black Scot for naught."

"Oh, I have heard he picks his teeth with the bones of his victims . . . that he drinks the blood of unbaptized babes."

"And still you dinna fear him?"

"He has your trust, does he not?"

"Aye."

"And the trust of his clansmen?"

"Aye."

"Then I have no reason to fear him." She glanced at him, saw his worried frown, and smiled. "Trusting must come difficult for you," she said.

"I never trust a strange dog, an unknown horse, the deepest part of a river, or a talkative woman."

"I feel sorry for you then. Yours must be a lonely existence."

Anger flared in his eyes. She felt his body stiffen. "Perhaps I prefer it that way."

"And perhaps you don't."

"You are a troublesome lass," he said.

After riding for a while longer, Stephen drew rein and they came to a stop. He remained astride his horse until

Angus approached, then he handed Juliette down to Angus, and dismounted behind her.

"We will take a short rest here," he said.

"How long is a short rest?" she asked, rubbing her posterior and looking around for Edith.

"You would be wise to spend the time walking, to ease the discomfort of your legs, rather than exercising your tongue."

"I know I talk overmuch. It is a habit that has plagued me since my mother died and I found myself caring for six younger sisters. It is the one thing I found I excelled at. I talked enough for myself and my sisters, too." She smiled at him. "My father always said, 'talk won't cook porridge.' "

Her words seemed to soften the hardness in Stephen's eyes, but his expression made her more uncomfortable than his hardness had done.

"It is said a man is hid under his tongue," he said.

She broke into musical laughter. "I assure you that I am hiding nothing."

She made the mistake of looking at him. He was watching her with an intensity that frightened her. Her every instinct told her to run, to reveal nothing more of herself to him, yet she knew she should remain steady. "As much as I would like to continue our conversation, this is, as you said, a short rest. I find I am in need of some privacy . . ." She looked around for a hidden place. "That is, I would. . . . I need . . ."

Stephen chuckled and nodded toward a cluster of low shrubs. "That should provide you sufficient cover to ease your distress, lass."

She eyed the low cluster. "Cover? A suckling pig couldn't hide behind that," she said.

"I ken it will cover the important parts," he said. "You may go that far, and no further. You decide."

She stomped off toward the bushes, complaining under her breath. *Thickwit ... numskull ... overbearing brute ... dictatorial tyrant. ... The man must have a bladder the size of the king's coffers.*

She heard Edith puffing as she ran up behind her. "M'lady, where are you going?"

Juliette paused, waiting for Edith to gain her stide. "To relieve myself, Edith. Have you a need as well?"

Edith looked properly horrified. "I could not do it *here.*"

"You could if it were necessary," Juliette said. "Go back, then. I will only be a moment."

"I would sooner step into a den of hungry lions," Edith said. "Those men have lust in their eyes."

Judith smiled and glanced back at the clearing, where no one seemed to be taking any notice of them. "What makes you think that?"

"A woman can tell," Edith said. "Old as I am, I am beginning to fear for my virtue."

Juliette looked astonished. "You mean you still have it?"

Edith seemed to swell with righteous indignation. "Of course I do. And I'll not be loosing it on the likes of these rugged creatures. I don't mind telling you, m'lady, that being with these men does not sit right with me."

Juliette was thinking that at Edith's age, she should be happy to lose her virtue anywhere she could. She didn't say that, of course, simply tried to soothe Edith, but it was difficult to remain serious. "I think you worry overmuch, Edith. Why, Stephen told me himself that his men were most honorable."

"Honorable? A Scot? Begging your pardon, m'lady, but I'd sooner trust a starved wolf. I would die before I would give the likes of these a second glance."

Juliette could not help smiling. Edith needed a diversion. Out of the corner of her eye, she caught a glimpse of

Angus. "Perhaps you would reconsider if it was a man who recently said to me that an honorable man would seek only marriage."

Edith went on fuming. "Marriage is of no consequence," she mumbled, then paused. "Which one said that?"

Juliette pointed at Angus, laughing to herself when Edith took off like a trained falcon, in hot pursuit of Angus.

Laughing outright, Juliette continued to the bushes and glanced back. Seeing no one was watching her, she decided to go a little further, where the land sloped away, over a jumble of tumbled stones, down to where a small burn spilled down an embankment. She stepped across the burn and found the perfect spot, sheltered in a low stand of trees.

A few minutes later, her task completed, she left the screen of trees . . . and her heart leaped into her throat as she came upon three large, burly men mounted on shaggy horses blocking her way.

MacBeans!

One of the men snarled something and the three of them eased their horses forward, one of them reaching for her. Juliette screamed and turned away, running for the cover of trees that lay just ahead.

Suddenly, a shout rang out, and Juliette whirled around. The three men turned to stare at the sight of a lone rider galloping toward them—a rider garbed in black, his dark cape billowing out behind him, sparks flying from the rocks struck by the hooves of his black horse as he rode like a demon.

Juliette heard the *whoosh* of air as he drew his claymore.

Two of the men shouted and spurred their horses forward, riding toward him. Juliette's first reaction was to turn away, but she found she could not. What she saw then would live in her mind for the rest of her days.

It was a moment both magnificent and terrifying, the most ungodly, uncivilized act, and yet the most graceful deed she had ever witnessed.

Stephen rode between the two men, wielding his claymore to the right and catching one of the men at the neck, between the head and shoulder. Before the man toppled from his horse, he slashed to the left, catching the other man across the chest before riding toward the third man, who rode toward him with his claymore held in both hands, high above his head.

Stephen rode his horse toward the man, his own horse never veering from the course, but staying true and striking the other horse, causing it to stumble, unseating its rider. Before the man could come to his feet, Stephen pinned him to the earth, driving his claymore through the man's sleeve. Blood seeped from a cut on his side.

"Tell your chief that I keep what is mine," Stephen said.

The back of her hand against her mouth, Juliette watched in horror as the man staggered to his horse, then mounted and rode away. Stephen whirled his horse around and rode toward her. For a terrifying moment she thought he might cut her down as well, but it was only his arm that came out to grab her and throw her across the saddle in front of him.

His horse never slowed as they rode back to the clearing where the others waited. She could see from her upside-down position the rest of the men watching them. She squirmed and was about to say something about her discomfort when she felt the flat side of his broadsword come down against her backside.

It wasn't very hard, and what force there had been was absorbed by her petticoats, but she gave a yelp anyway, just as he jerked her upright and gave her a shake. "The next time you disobey me, I won't be so kind." He dropped her to her feet.

Backing away, she stared at him, unable to speak. There was something about what she had just seen—something that was both terrifying and exciting. She had thought this man dangerous, but she realized now, with absolute clarity, that he was far, far more dangerous than she realized.

"You are appalled?" he asked.

"Yes."

"Why?"

"That was the most barbaric thing I have ever witnessed."

"Perhaps, but they would have done the same to me, mistress, if given the chance. It is the way of the clans."

"It was still uncivilized."

His look was direct. "I spared the third man, did I not?"

Her throat was too dry to respond.

When she did not speak, his brows narrowed. "You should not judge that which you know nothing about," he said.

Speechless still, she stared at him. In the moonlight he had been a thing of beauty: the strong angles of his face; the play of firelight on his dark hair. She did not realize the man she teased with reckless ease was such a mighty warrior.

Her first thought looking at him in the bright light of day was that she had jumped into water way over her head.

Dumbstruck, she allowed Angus to give her a leg up. The moment she was in the saddle, she collapsed in a weak heap.

Stephen rode up beside her. "Perhaps your speechless state is a sign of wisdom," he said.

"Every man has his weak side," she said in her defense, then urged her horse forward.

"Aye," he said softly, "and you may prove to be mine."

At that moment, Edith came charging forth on her small pony, looking a bit worse for wear, her hair flying about her face, bonnet askew. "M'lady, are you all right?"

"I am fine, Edith," Juliette said. Then seeing the concern on Edith's face, she smiled and said, "Truly."

"Oh, m'lady, when I saw him riding back with you . . . his sword all bloody . . . oh, my heart fair dropped to my feet. How many of them were there? Did they touch you? I have never seen such a bloody display of vengeance. I do hope you turned your head away, m'lady. It wouldn't do for a lady of your breeding to witness such barbaric acts as blood drawing I must—"

"Silence!"

Stephen Gordon's voice ripped through the air and echoed through the trees beyond. Juliette started to say something, then thought better of it.

Stephen looked at Edith's slack jaw then at Angus. "If she so much as opens her mouth, gag her."

"Aye," Angus said, showing no emotion when Edith snapped her mouth shut.

4

Soon they were on their way again, Juliette taking the place Stephen assigned her, to ride beside him on her own horse this time. In spite of what he said about gagging Edith, Juliette found she could not be quiet. Perhaps it was simply a way to ease the stiffness from her body, or to keep from thinking about the bloody scene she had witnessed earlier.

"How much further?" she asked Stephen.

"To where?"

"To Craigmoor Castle, of course!"

"Four days ride . . . more or less."

She sighed in exasperation. "And where exactly is Craigmoor Castle located?"

"Near the village of Craigmoor."

Juliette gritted her teeth and prayed for patience. It would not do, she supposed, for her to knock him from his horse. In truth, she was ready to throttle the man. "And where, pray tell, is the village of Craigmoor located? Is it near the coast?"

"In Scotland, you are never more than forty miles from water, lass."

She nodded. "Thank you for that interesting bit of information. I shall try to remember it, for I am certain there will be many times when I will want to pass such enlightenment on to others."

He didn't say anything, but that didn't bother Juliette. She had spent half of her life being ignored by her father and her younger sisters. "Are you going to tell the Black Scot about the MacBeans?"

He gave her a suspicious look. "How do you know they were MacBeans?"

"Just before we stopped, you said we were in MacBean territory, so naturally I thought . . . they *were* MacBeans, were they not?"

"Aye, they were MacBeans."

"Were they after me?"

"They tried to take you, did they not?"

"Yes, but did they come looking . . . particularly for me?"

"Aye, I told you about that before. They would have seen the taking of you as a good way to humiliate me, nettle the King of England, and fill their coffers with ransom money."

"Oh . . . ransom. You mean they wouldn't have forced

me to marry the leader of the MacBeans?" she asked, remembering what he had said earlier.

"You sound disappointed, lass. Want me to call the man back?"

"Don't be foolish. I was merely curious, that is all. It is easy for you to be jocular. *You* would not be the one forced to marry a MacBean."

"Dinna fash yourself, lass. I ken if you had given them as much trouble as you have given me, they would have returned you before nightfall. You are a troublesome lass."

"You have told me that before, m'lord."

"And you talk overmuch."

"Well, at least *I* answer questions," she said, giving him a direct stare and not caring if he noticed.

He noticed, but he didn't say anything. He simply sat there, with his back to the sun, staring back at her as if he were trying to figure her out—as if a man could figure out a woman by looking at her. Now, looking at *him* was a different matter entirely.

She found herself momentarily absorbed in the way the sun seemed to highlight the black tones of his hair and turn them to silver. The hard elegance of his face, however, needed no sunlight to hold her attention. It was difficult to ignore a mouth that offered such sensual promise, eyes that touched her with such heat. Her gaze drifted to his mouth and seemed content to stay there. Enraptured, she recalled the feel of those lips against hers.

"Alexander MacBean is already married," he said, interrupting her reverie.

The blissful memory was shattered and she could not hide her disenchantment. She sent him an irritated look.

He had the gall to look taken aback. "You are no disappointed, are you?"

"No, of course I'm not. I am not such a dolt, m'lord. If I must marry, I much prefer marriage to the Black Scot."

"You have never met him. How do you know you prefer marriage to him?"

"I like his name."

Stephen choked. "His name? You would marry a man because of his name? A man with a reputation like the Black Scot?"

She scowled. "Not even the devil is as black as they paint him. Besides, I am marrying a man simply because the king ordered me to. Now, I don't see that liking his name is any more ridiculous than that. At least I know there will be *one* thing I like about him. Besides, you told me that he looks a great deal like you, did you not?"

"Aye, I did."

She nodded. "Well, suffice it to say that that pleases me."

He grunted. She recognized a skeptical sound when she heard one, but she stubbornly remained quiet.

That didn't seem to deter him, however. "An intriguing name and a fair face . . . you dinna ask for much in a husband, I ken."

"Oh, I hope for more, but until we have met, I know only what you tell me. Please, will you tell me more about him?"

"Lady Juliette, you are a great deal of trouble."

Juliette sighed and looked off, speaking softly. "Yes, I fear that is primarily the reason I am here."

Stephen threw back his dark head and laughed.

Juliette watched him spur his horse and ride ahead of her. When he gained Angus's side, he slowed down beside him, leaning low over his saddle as he spoke. If Stephen's words had any effect upon him, Angus did not show it. As far as Juliette could tell, his face was as blank as the white cliffs of Dover.

A moment later Edith's pony came trotting along, slowing down as it drew even with Juliette's.

"That black devil seems to enjoy your company, m'lady," Edith said.

"Sometimes," Juliette said, looking wistfully at Stephen's broad back. "I don't know why, but I keep having the feeling that he is playing games with me."

"It is a man's way. They act that way till the day they die."

Juliette took a deep breath. "Stephen Gordon is a perplexing man. He is like a gem with many facets."

"I don't know about facets," Edith said, giving him the once over, "but he is a handsome devil, even when naked as the truth."

A slow smile stretched across Juliette's face. "Especially then," she said, and they both laughed.

Just when Juliette thought she would never get off the back of her horse, Stephen announced that they would stop for the night and make camp.

With a weary sigh, she slid from the saddle and collapsed into a weak heap the moment her booted feet touched the ground. Angus, who happened to be passing by, gave her a yank, hauling her to her feet.

"Thank you," she said.

Angus walked on, saying nothing.

"Faith! The man is as dumb as death," Juliette said.

"A man's silence will never betray him," Stephen said.

Not having known Stephen was nearby, Juliette jumped, her hand coming to her chest. It riled her to have him sneak up on her like that, and she put a little venom in her words. "Neither will it gain him a friend," she said.

"Dinna be so quick to judge, lass. He will be there when you need him. What better definition of a friend is there?"

Juliette shrugged and walked off, not liking the way she always seemed to come out looking like a fool. She hated it . . . really hated it when a man got the upper hand. His words came back to haunt her. *Silence will never betray him. . . .*

Stephen, she thought, might have a point.

A short while later, she watched one of the men called Dougal spread tartans upon the ground for her and Edith to sleep upon. Scots made camp in a strange way, Juliette noted, and could not help commenting upon it. "Where are the tents?"

Dougal looked at Stephen.

"I suppose he doesn't speak either," she said.

"Only when he has something to say," Juliette and Stephen said in unison. Then Stephen grinned and said, "We dinna use tents."

"What if it rains?"

"Roll up in your tartan."

"Now, why didn't I think of that?"

"Because you are English."

"Well, don't go blaming the rain on the English," she said, suddenly remembering something. She frowned, staring at the tartans spread upon the ground. "I thought the king outlawed these."

"He did," Stephen replied.

"But you are using them."

"Only when the English are no around," he replied.

As Juliette thought about that, she watched Angus disappear into the darkness, just behind a stand of pine trees. She noticed Stephen start off in the same direction. "Where are you going?"

"To catch some fish."

"You are going fishing? Now? In the dark?"

"The fish dinna mind. Do you?"

"No, of course not, but fishing in the dark . . ."

"You are hungry, are you not?"

"Yes, but—"

"Do you ever stop talking, lass?"

She smiled. "Only when I sleep."

He almost smiled. Almost. "Ah, blessed relief. I pray that is true," he said, turning away and disappearing into the darkness, the sound of his voice drifting back to her. "Relax, lass. I willna be gone long."

"Ah, blessed relief," she echoed, and heard his soft chuckle.

After he left, Juliette sat beside the small campfire, watching the men tether the horses, build a fire, and spread their tartans on the ground. Edith came to sit beside her, inquiring if the one called Angus ever said anything. "Only when he has something to say," Juliette replied. "Did he speak to you?"

"After a fashion," Edith replied.

Juliette was surprised by that. "Well, what did he say?"

"He said I should be cropped, for I had no need of ears."

"Well, at least he said something. That's a start, I think."

"You really think so, m'lady?"

Juliette smiled. "Of course I do. He certainly won't talk to me."

Edith seemed pleased by that, looking in the direction Stephen and Angus had taken earlier. "Where did they go?"

"Fishing for our dinner."

"Good. I am starving to death. I was wondering if they were going to feed us, or torture us. I have never ridden such an uncomfortable animal. God's teeth! That horse is nothing but backbone."

"Backbone seems to be something all Scots have in common," Juliette said.

"Whether they be two-legged or four," Edith added.

Juliette smiled, looking off into the darkness.

"I cannot help admiring such strength," Edith said in an enraptured way that told Juliette she was thinking of Angus. Then catching herself, she stammered and said, "Of course Stephen is a strong man as well ... strong and seemingly wise for his years."

"I reserve judgment," Juliette replied. "It remains to be seen whether he is more Samson or Solomon." She rose to her feet.

Edith watched her, but made no move to get up. "Where are you going?"

"I think I shall see how the Scots catch fish."

"Mayhap m'lady hopes for another glimpse of the naked truth."

"One takes one's blessings where one finds them," Juliette said with a shrug, following the same route Stephen and Angus had chosen before.

The burn lay quite close to camp. Juliette heard the low murmur of voices before she left the residual light of the campfire.

A moment later, Stephen's voice reached out of the darkness. "Hearing you approach makes me wonder how the English ever perfected the sneak attack."

"It is wiser to be heard and recognized than to be shot for sneaking," Juliette replied.

She saw the dark outline of two shapes sitting on a boulder that the burn seemed to curve around, its surface spangled with moonlight. Just as she reached them, Angus came to his feet. Stephen handed him two fish, strung through the mouth and gills with a length of string. "You'd better see to these," he said. "I ken I am about to be talked to death."

"Aye, talk gushes like water from the Sassenach lass. I ken all the English are smitten by Aaron's rod," Angus said.

"We are a friendly lot," Juliette replied with a shrug, looking at Stephen.

"Have you no heard, lass, that silence catches a mouse?"

"I thought to inject a few currants of conversation into this tasteless gruel of existence."

He laughed. "Well then, lass, sit yourself down. Angus has left the spot warm for you."

She glanced in the direction Angus had taken. "Had he known that, I am certain he would have stood the entire time."

"Win his trust and you will have a strong ally."

"Faith! I think it easier to catch leviathan with a hook, than to win that man's favor."

Stephen laughed and Juliette sat upon the spot Angus had warmed, watching Stephen roll up a piece of string with a hook on the end of it.

"Do you ever use a rod?" she asked.

"No. I learned at a young age that a rod is nothing more than a stick with a hook on one end and a fool at the other."

"When I was young, I tried to learn how to tickle fish, but I never mastered the art. My father said the water was too clear."

"Aye, fish are tickled best when the water is muddy." He finished rolling up the string and put it in his pocket. "You are close to your father, I think."

"Yes. My aunt says it is because I have no mother, but I think it is because my father is such a wonderful man."

"When did you lose your mother?"

"When my youngest sister, Ellen, was born." Her look turned wistful. "You were fortunate to have known yours for such a long time."

"How do you ken I knew my mother for a long time?"

"Because, in spite of the sadness in you, there is also a gentleness . . . a patient understanding of women that could have only come from a mother's love."

"Maybe it is because I have always been a lad who was fond of the lassies," he said.

"No, it is much deeper than that," she said, seeing that her words made him uncomfortable. It was proof that she had spoken the truth.

He looked at her strangely.

"Is something bothering you?" she asked.

"Aye. I can no help wondering why your father would agree to your betrothal to the Black Scot," he said. "From the way you talk, I gather he is extremely fond of you."

"I told you before. It was simply because the king commanded it. Perhaps I made it easier for him to accept."

"How?"

"Because I wished for excitement."

"Then you are a fool."

"Perhaps I am, but it hasn't been too bad so far."

He turned his head to look at her. "Has it not?"

She smiled at him. "No. I find I have a taste for adventure."

"Our journey is young, lass. You are speaking prematurely."

"I don't think so. In fact, I have a feeling that I will come to enjoy the next few days more than I have enjoyed the past ones."

"Ours is a dangerous journey. There are many clans like the MacBeans. Do not take it too lightly, or you will be caught off guard," he said, watching her with his disturbing blue eyes.

She looked at his face. "I fear that has already happened," she said softly.

He gave her a questioning look. "What are you thinking, lass?"

"If you knew that, you would think me past foolish," she said, wishing she could call back her words. She had always been too free with her tongue, speaking her mind when she should have remained silent. Perhaps being around these closedmouthed Scots would be good for her.

"Perhaps I think you past foolish already. You did say you were agreeable to this betrothal to the Black Scot, did you not?"

She looked off. "Yes, although I must confess I have come to regret that already . . . at least in part."

"Changed your mind, have you?"

She turned to look him full in the face. "I find myself wishing . . ." She caught herself.

His eyes seemed to gleam in the moonlight. She felt a shiver of apprehension. The warm touch of his hand against her cool cheek made her jump. His gaze seemed to penetrate hers, and she could feel the sudden pounding of her heart.

"I find myself curious about what you were going to say," he said in a musing, almost careless voice as his hand dropped lower, his fingers spreading between her breasts where her heart lay, beating in triple time. "You are strangely quiet now," he whispered in her ear, his lips brushing the sensitive skin there. "I wonder why?"

She swallowed, trying to force away the lump in her throat. "I . . . I find I have nothing to say at the moment."

He nuzzled the skin below her ear. "Are you afraid of me, lass?"

"No," she croaked.

"You should be," he whispered, his words coming from the velvety darkness to brush softly against her skin.

"I am only afraid of the unknown," she said, wishing for the first time in her life that she knew more about what passed between a man and a woman.

"Your heart beats fast," he said, lowering his head, his mouth touching the sensitive skin of her neck, as if he were tasting the very pulse that hammered so wildly. She shivered again, feeling both hot and cold. She dared not move.

"Tell me," he whispered, his mouth dangerously close to hers. "Tell me what you were about to say. You found yourself wishing ... what?"

She closed her eyes, swallowing hard as he nuzzled her neck. "Wishing you were the Black Scot." She expected him to kiss her, or at least for her words to shock him.

She felt disappointed and strangely bereft when he drew back. "I ken you feel that way because I am the one you met first."

"No, I say it because I like you."

"Liking isna the same as loving, lass."

"No, but it is a beginning," she replied, feeling suddenly shy. Her voice dropped so low, her words were barely audible. "I know I could come to love a man such as you."

"Aye, you probably could," he whispered, turning her toward him, his mouth brushing hers. He rose to his feet, reaching out and taking her hand and hauling her upward. "Save that kind of talk for your betrothed," he said harshly, "or dinna you have any scruples? Is one man as good as another to you?"

In her benumbed state, she could only answer what was in her heart. "If that were true, I would not be so troubled. I fear it is my scruples that cause me such distress. I have never felt this way around a man before. You do strange things to me ... things I do not understand." She shook her head.

He stood holding her hand and looking down at her. He drew her toward him and his gaze searched her eyes as if he were looking for some hint of truth. "You had best be careful, lass. That kind of talk sets a man to thinking things he has no business thinking."

"Then that makes us well matched, for I have been doing so all day."

"Come on," he said, pulling her along.

"Where are we going?"

"Back to camp before we both do something we will regret."

"You should speak for yourself."

"That is what I am trying to do," he said, and she wanted nothing more than to go to him, to kiss that hard mouth into such passion he would take her for his own—take her and never let her go. She realized suddenly that it was truly what she wanted, that she had thought of little else since the moment she had first seen him. It took every ounce of pride she had to keep from asking him to take her in his arms, to kiss her as he had kissed her before.

"Are you really afraid you might do something you will be sorry for?" she asked.

"Aye, I ken I already have."

"You should never say something like that to an impressionable woman," she said. "If it is your wish that I wed the Black Scot, you should be doing all you can to dissuade me, instead of telling me you find me appealing."

He jerked to a stop. "You misunderstand me, lass. I dinna find you appealing in the least," he said harshly. "My desire to return to camp was only my desire to spare you the humiliation of my rejection."

"You don't lie very well," she said, thinking his dark, cynical beauty made him only more attractive to her. She came up on her tiptoes and kissed him softly on the mouth. "You like me more than you are willing to admit . . ."

He opened his mouth to speak, but she cut him off.

"I know you better than you think, m'lord, and I find you transparent as glass," she said. She didn't find him transparent at all, but it sounded good and made her feel as if she had some power in this situation, which had gotten terribly out of hand.

He jerked her against him, his hand coming behind her head and holding her there, so her mouth was against his.

He kissed her fiercely, possessively, using the pressure of his mouth to force her lips apart.

She kissed him back with all the untutored passion she had within her, knowing it was an inexperienced kiss at best. He seemed to take over, his tongue coming roughly into her mouth again and again, as if he were trying to frighten her. She moaned, not frightened at all. The kiss turned suddenly gentle. She arched against him, melting when he groaned deep in his throat, his hand coming up to close warmly over her breast. A desperate craving consumed her and he whispered something in a language she could not understand.

He released her suddenly. "There will come a time," he said bitterly, "when you will find you dinna know me at all."

Stephen sat before the fire, staring over the smoldering coals to where Juliette lay sleeping in his tartan.

"I ken it is hard looking one way and rowing another," Angus said.

Stephen looked at him. "What is that supposed to mean?"

Angus sat down near him. "You seem to find yourself sinking deeper and deeper into the quicksand of deceit. You should have told the lass who you are while you had the chance. Before it was too late."

"It isna too late."

"Aye, it is."

"What makes you say that?"

"You waited overlong, lad. The lass's heart is involved now."

"It doesna matter. I will simply tell her."

"Aye, but not without suffering her hurt and anger."

"What do you think I should do then?"

Angus shrugged and picking up a stick, stirred the fire. "The lass cares for you."

"Aye, that complicates things for now, but it makes the future look a bit brighter."

"Aye, if you can tell her the truth without losing her trust. I wouldna want to be in your shoes, laddie. A precipice in the front; wolves in the rear."

"I will find a way," Stephen said, "for I will not lose her."

5

They rode hard for two days, taking few breaks to rest, and only a few hours to sleep. The pace was difficult, and they were plagued with a misting rain that seemed in no hurry to end.

For hours they had been riding without stopping. Cold, wet, and fighting a headache, Juliette sat wearily upon her horse, listening to Edith complain, thinking Stephen had been right to covet silence.

Stephen.

Her heart warmed at the mere thought of him—even knowing that he had been avoiding her all day. For the hundredth time, she allowed her gaze to search him out, her mind doing what it enjoyed of late: wistfully thinking how different things would be if it were Stephen she was to marry instead of the Black Scot.

For a moment, she allowed her thoughts to stray off in that direction, something she found both pleasurable and agonizing. There was no point in denying the truth. She could not lie to herself. She was falling in love with him. The question that bothered her was whether or not Stephen could come to feel about her as she felt about him—in the little time they had together before they reached Craig-moor.

And if he *did* come to care for her, would he turn against the leader of his clan for the woman he loved?

One look at the broad back and proud carriage of the man in question and she knew the answer. Dishonor was as foreign as French to him. Since infancy, Stephen had been fed liberal doses of pride and honor right along with his porridge. He might come to care for her. He might kiss her a time or two. But he would never, ever betray his laird.

Oddly enough, she found she would not want him to.

At that moment, she realized he was riding toward her and her heart hammered. *Come to me, Stephen. Take me. Hold me. Tell me you care....*

She smiled shyly, her heart pounding furiously in anticipation. She looked longingly at his dark, impassive face as he rode past her, without so much as a brief glance in her direction.

Her heart shattered, trampled like her dreams in the mud beneath the hooves of his horse. If there had been any lingering doubt as to where things stood between them, he had clarified it now.

A deep, stabbing pain twisted her heart. She wanted to cry, but in private ... not bouncing along on the back of an obnoxious beast and in the presence of eight stubborn, uncaring Scots.

She glared at Stephen's back. She wanted to ride to where he was and shove his arrogant face into the mud. If she were a man she could do just that.

"Take heart, lass. The lad fares no better than you."

Juliette jerked her head around to see that Angus had ridden quietly next to her. If she had not been so disheartened, she would have been in awe that he had spoken to her at all.

Instead, the words of consolation coming from such a

stalwart man made her ache with emotion. She felt sorry for herself. Wounded. Abandoned. Tears burned her eyes and she prayed she would not cry. Not now. Not in front of this silent old man who seemed to know her heart.

"Taking heart is easier said than done, I fear."

"It is no as difficult as you make it, lass."

She sniffed. "You don't understand. I made a fool of myself. I kissed him and now I think he hates me."

The corners of his mouth twitched and Angus cleared his throat. "I wouldna be too upset, lass. If Stephen hated every lass who kissed him, there wouldna be any lassies left for him to like."

She shot him a dark look. "If *that* was supposed to make me feel better, it didn't."

"Weel, would it make you feel better if he did hate you?"

She lifted her chin, feeling a sudden surge of pride, determined that he would not know how much it really did matter. But her resolve seemed to crumple immediately. She felt a tear slip down her cheek and she wiped it quickly with the back of her hand. "I have never felt so young and naive," she said. "I have always been taught to be honest, but I have learned that honesty can also be a ruinous mistake. I spoke what was in my heart. I see now that I blundered in thinking he would respect that. Now I feel as if I made a fool of myself. I know I should not have kissed him, that I should never have spoken to him so honestly. What I did was wrong, but there is no way to undo what has been done."

She wiped her eyes again, not looking at him for fear she would burst into tears.

Angus's unexpected friendliness exasperated her and raised her ire until her tears were all but forgotten. She wanted to tell him to take his meddling old self out into the forest and pet a mad wolf, but she managed to hold herself in check, though she still couldn't understand why this dour Scot's decision to suddenly take her into his confidence should make her want to cry.

"Dinna fret, lass. No one whose heart is in the right place will be denied paradise forever," he said. With that, he spurred his horse ahead, leaving her alone, the tears she had fought to hold back streaming down her face, mingling with the now pounding rain.

The rain slowed again to a penetrating, thick mist, and the rest of the day passed without event—another long day with too few stops, another day during which Stephen ignored her.

When the sun should have been settling comfortably on the horizon, they rode into the yard of a ruined abby.

"We will make camp here," Stephen said gruffly, and dismounted.

Juliette looked around. Only the abby walls remained standing, offering little protection from the elements or the Gordon's enemies.

Angus came to help Juliette down. The moment her feet touched ground, she turned abruptly and almost ran into Stephen.

His hands came out to grab her. He did not release her.

She glanced up at him, uncertain. Having been taught that one gained more with honey than vinegar, she smiled.

He returned the smile with a lazy one of his own. It caught her unawares, leaving her confused. Smiling was a mistake. She had a feeling he had learned while in nappies to use that smile with such knee-weakening effect.

Too bewildered and weary to sort through her emotions, she turned away, wrenching herself from his grasp before he had a chance to say anything, or give her another mocking smile.

As she hurried away from him, she realized this was the first time she had even been in love. Why anyone would covet this miserable feeling was beyond her. Seeing that

Edith, as well as Stephen's men, had disappeared behind the walls of the abby, she went looking for them.

She had gone no more than a few feet when she heard Stephen coming up behind her. "You look tired," he said.

She stopped, clenching her fists at her sides. She spoke without turning around. "I *am* tired," she said.

He came around her, blocking her way. "These walls will give you some comfort tonight. Dinna expect a roof over your head."

She nodded, ready to leave. "If I have learned anything about the Scots," she said, "it is not to expect anything that resembles understanding or comfort."

That seemed to amuse him. "There is a burn nearby that feeds a small pool. I thought you might be wanting to take a bath."

Her heart lurched at the thought, for she could not help remembering what had happened the last time she had taken a bath. "Yes, a bath would be welcome," she said, putting the thought out of her mind. "Thank you. I shall report to my betrothed that you treated me with the utmost courtesy."

"I ken no man could ill treat a lass as kindhearted as you. Do you think I would be capable of such?"

She looked at his dark face and hard mouth. "Will my betrothed be so understanding when I tell him how I made a fool of myself by kissing you?"

He hid his surprise well. "Those are your words, lass, not mine. But since you ask, I dinna see why you have to tell him at all."

"I would not have him thinking me something other than I am," she said, trying to maintain her dignity and finding it difficult with her hair hanging limp and wet, and knowing her damp clothes gave off the odor of a wet sheep. "I admire honesty in others. I can expect no less from myself."

He lifted his hand to her face, stroking her cheek with

the back of his fingers. "Take heart, lass. As you once said, the Black Scot is not as heartless as his name implies. I doubt your revelation would start a war with the English," he added with good humor.

She said nothing.

Stephen continued in a light tone. "He might have *me* drawn and quartered, but he would no harm a hair on your golden head."

"He might if he knew what was in my heart."

His hand dropped to his side, but the look in his eyes told her he desired her. No amount of harsh or jovial words could dissuade her from believing that. She had no doubt that if she were not the betrothed of the Black Scot, Stephen Gordon would do more than stroke her cheek.

And that is what hurts the most. I want him to do more. As God is my witness, I do. I do. . . .

The sound of his voice pulled her back from her thoughts. "And what is in your heart that is sure to provoke his anger?" he asked.

She looked at him with hurt in her eyes. "Don't mock me," she whispered, intending to turn away.

He caught her before she could move. "Come here, lass," he said.

"No."

Unexpectedly, his arms came around her and he drew her against him, kissing her slowly, thoughtfully, and quite thoroughly. She felt herself drawn to him, as if she were sinking into a warm, long-awaited bath.

Then suddenly his grip tightened. He loomed over her, dark and dangerous, crushing her mouth until her senses reeled. His tongue forced her lips apart, expertly probing with ravishing implication. His gentle softness had become punishing roughness.

She knew that he deliberately meant to frighten her, and thus snuff out the desire that still burned inside her.

He did not want her to want him. She understood that.

She was forbidden to him, dangerous and destructive, yet there was something within him that was unable to resist. His struggle touched her.

Is that what love was?

Her thoughts vanished as he continued to kiss her, allowing his mouth to do to her the things the rest of his body could not. She arched against him in complete surrender. Her hand came up to rest against his bristled cheek. His jaw was hard and masculine. Her hand slid around his neck. His hair was silky and cool to the touch.

She knew they should not be doing this, but something strong within her pushed her further into his embrace, until it was difficult to know where she ended and he began. Everything he did touched her more deeply than anything she had ever experienced. She made a small sound of need. He responded by drawing her even closer, close enough to feel the hardness between his legs. She moaned again, floating ... drifting ... wanting. ...

Suddenly, he broke the kiss, and she understood that he had not mocked her, that he had revealed his feelings in the only way he knew how.

His voice came to her from out of the mist that seemed to surround her. "Now you know," he whispered, releasing her completely.

A moment later, she was left standing cold, wet, and lonely in the rain.

6

Juliette entered the roofless abby and found Edith, who was leaning over a fire that boasted a cooking pot.

She paused in the archway, watching Edith stir the pot and talk to Angus.

Angus wasn't saying anything back, of course, but that didn't dissuade Edith.

With a tired groan, Juliette found her tartan spread in a corner and sank down upon it, gazing at the starless sky overhead. Stephen had warned her not to expect a roof. Well, at least it had stopped raining.

With a weary sigh, Juliette watched as Edith handed Angus the spoon and instructed him to stir the pot. Then, she turned away, coming toward Juliette with a springy bounce in her walk. "Angus said you could have a bath, m'lady."

"I am too tired to bathe, Edith. Faith! I am too tired to eat."

"Rest then," Edith said, and hurried back to the cooking pot. Taking the spoon from Angus, she returned to stirring the pot herself.

Juliette lay down and closed her eyes.

Some time later, the savory smell of food wakened her. Juliette opened her eyes to see Edith hovering over her with a steaming cup in her hand.

"I brought you some soup."

Juliette sat up, taking the cup with thanks, drinking the soup down, in spite of its scalding temperature. After she finished, she decided the bath she had been offered earlier sounded better now.

Gathering fresh clothes, she slipped through the open doorway of the abbey, making her way in the last rays of the day's light.

Rising out of the mist like a well-hidden secret, the pool was everything she had hoped it would be.

Located low on the side of a cliff, it was fed by a thundering waterfall that hurled its icy burden over the cliff, then formed a rushing, gurgling beck that ran down the fellside. There the water's mad rush mellowed as it slowly wound its way through the gently rolling heath, glistening like a string of amber, until it widened into a placid pool.

Juliette followed a trail that ran alongside the pond to where the water lay still and smooth.

There, she also found Stephen swimming.

She froze. She couldn't bring herself to look away. He was waiting for her in the cool, misty darkness. She could feel his gaze upon her as she came closer.

"Go back to the abby," he said when he saw her.

She wasn't about to move ... not with him swimming in the water, as deliciously naked as he had been that day when she first saw him. Stubbornly she held her ground. "You said I could have a bath."

"I'll come get you when I am finished," he offered.

"I will wait here ... on this log, thank you," she said, and seated herself at the pool's edge.

He swam toward her and waded out of the water until he stood waist deep. She felt a twinge of disappointment when she saw he was coming no further. She thought it a pity that she would not have the chance to see what she had seen the other day, only closer.

"You had best be getting back before I come out and embarrass you," he said with a wry twist to his lips.

She felt it again. The same warming heat as when she had seen him naked at the pool that day. She tossed him the tartan she had brought to dry herself with. "Put that around you, if you are modest," she said, "but don't cover yourself on my account. I have seen you before ... when you were swimming at the pool that day ... before you took me from my English escort."

He wrapped the tartan around himself and waded out of the water, coming to stand before her. "I am sorry, lass, if the sight of me frightened you."

"I was never frightened," she said. "I thought you were the most beautiful man I had ever seen."

He cleared his throat. "Weel, I ken it must have been a shock . . ."

Weel . . . I love that word, too, she thought. "No, it was no shock, believe me."

He raised a brow. "You have seen naked men before?"

"No, never. Oh, I know this sounds preposterous. Faith! I don't understand it myself. Only there was something about you . . . something that seemed to reach out to me across the distance. I felt warm all over . . . which was foolish, I know—especially since my teeth were chattering from the cold."

"I ken you had your first taste of desire, lass, nothing more."

"I *ken* I had more than a taste . . . enough to make me want to taste it again."

He closed his eyes, as if to cut off the flow of her words. She knew it was wrong to speak to him of such things, especially after she had so foolishly declared her feelings for him last night. No lady would ever dare speak of such to a man she was not married to.

If her father ever caught wind of this, he would tear out his hair. This man was not her betrothed. She knew very well what could happen to both of them if they went beyond the roles that had already been dictated to them. But something compelled her to tell this dark and taciturn man how he had touched her, in a way no man ever had, or ever would. She knew now, with every breath she drew, that she could not become the bride of the Black Scot, not even if rejecting him meant losing her father and displeasing the King of England. Her destiny lay with Stephen Gordon. She knew it. And, God help her, but she sensed he knew it, too.

"Would you kiss me?"

"You are playing with fire, lass."

"Please," she whispered, and found herself in his arms. She closed her eyes, absorbing the heat from a body that was cool to the touch, feeling the pleasing hardness of him against her softer parts. His face was mere inches from hers and she trembled like a newborn fawn in anticipation. A long restrained cry pulsed from her throat when his mouth closed over hers.

He had been the first man ever to kiss her.

She knew with all her untutored heart that there would never be another.

His body was close ... so close his warmth became her warmth. His scent washed over her, the fresh, wild smell of the Highlands, where every bit of heather, every blade of grass whispered the secret aroma of life. Bathed in warmth and excitement, she felt a deep sensation of desire begin to swell within her. She wanted ... what, she did not know, but some intuition said he knew. ...

"I knew it would be like this," she whispered. "Make love to me, Stephen."

He groaned. "I canna," he said. "Not now, not this way."

Through a sensuous haze, she looked into his face, seeing something akin to pain in his eyes. Her heart hammering wildly in her chest, she could not speak. A sigh of despair and need escaped her. She gave him a look that said she did not understand.

He kissed her softly on the lips, his voice coming to her in a whisper that seemed to caress her flesh. "It isna because I dinna want to, love. I want you with a fierceness that makes me ache. But I wouldna have anything come between us. You have been honest with me. I can only be the same with you. Aye," he said, his voice laced with pain, "I will make love to you, and well, but not until I speak what is in my heart. Not until I right a wrong."

Suddenly she was afraid. She knew that look, knew what it meant. She did not know what horrible thing he had done, what unimaginable deed he burned to confess. In truth, she did not want to know—for she sensed it would bring an irrevocable change, driving them apart. She saw the agony in his face even before she heard it in his voice.

"This thing between us . . ."

"No," she whispered, pressing her fingers to his lips. Just this once, her heart cried. Just this one time, and no more. She did not want to know what he had to tell her . . . not now, not when she was so close to fulfilling her dream.

Reality was her betrothal to someone else. Stephen could never be hers—not really. She knew that, and accepted it. But now, at this moment, he would be hers.

"Don't tell me," she whispered. "If you don't say it, it won't be true."

"Lass, I canna . . ."

Tears welling in her eyes, she shook her head. "Not now, not when everything between us is so beautiful. I will not have you change that, Stephen. Make love to me," she whispered. "Make love to me now . . . and break my heart afterward."

He held her close, whispering her name, covering her face with kisses. "Tell me to stop," he whispered.

"I cannot."

"Aye, you canna, but you will come to regret this."

"I will never regret it," she said. "Never. And neither will you."

"Then God help us both," he said, his mouth closing over hers in a soft and gentle mating. He backed her up against a tree, kissing her deeply, his knee coming between her legs. He kissed her with agonizing tenderness, his hips flat against hers, the burning length of him searing and hard.

She began to remove her clothes, watching him as he dropped his tartan. Her hungry gaze wandering over his body, drinking in the sight of him. He was as beautiful as he had been the first time she saw him, and she made no effort to hide her desire.

"Jesus," he whispered, reaching for her and wrapping her tightly in his arms. "Dinna look at me like that, lass, unless you mean it."

"I mean it."

Her response fired his hunger and he groaned, his mouth claiming hers with renewed possessiveness. They dropped to the ground and he rolled over her, his body crushing her against the mossy earth, his hand skimming the tender, sensitive skin of her breasts which ached for his touch. She gasped, feeling agonizing pleasure when his mouth began to tug at her nipple. Shuddering, she arched her back. His hands went lower, stroking her belly until she wanted to scream. He seemed to be ceaseless in his assault upon her body and she felt her own excitement build until she wanted to sob. His hand moved between her legs and she gasped from the shock of it, realizing she had not known before what exquisite agony was.

She was panting now, wet with wanting, consumed by urgency. His movements seemed to go slower as he stroked her with infinite patience, driving her to a frenzy. His mouth claimed hers, and he blocked every image from her mind except the delicious weight of his body pressing into hers, the feel of his skin hot against her own.

She moved against him in an unconscious gesture of passion, strange feelings washing across her, unknown yearnings driving her forward. His hands touched, caressed, inflamed the bare flesh, making her writhe.

"Flesh of my flesh," he whispered. "I want you."

She longed to tell him that she wanted him, too, but her body seemed to take possession of her.

"Dinna hate me," he whispered.

She could reply only by raising her hips, meeting him as he came into her. She held her breath.

The pain was no more than a sharp stinging sensation,

soon replaced by a feeling that was infinitely better. Her legs tightened around his as he filled her completely, and then he was guiding her, sweetly teaching her, his hands gentle, his kisses demanding, until she felt she had given him everything, even her soul.

Her small, choked cry was absorbed by his mouth as he deepened his kiss. Juliette was filled with tension, an aching need she did not know how to release. But Stephen did.

As he began to stroke her intimately, she began to breathe more rapidly. Without looking at his face, she knew he was watching her, knew that he, too, was waiting for something to happen.

It happened. And when it did, Juliette stiffened with surprise, then went limp with disbelief. "I never knew," she whispered afterward. "It was beautiful. Absolutely, perfectly beautiful."

It was the act she had heard described a dozen times, but actually experiencing it was so different than she had been told. Faith! It was all she could do to keep from passing out from the pure pleasure of it, and when it was over, and he rolled to his side, taking her with him, she felt she had never known such peace. How any woman could find this joining distasteful was far beyond her imagining. She looked at Stephen. Of course, not every woman was so fortunate as to have such a man make love to her.

With a satisfied sigh, she lay her head against his shoulder, but immediately his body stiffened. He lay unyielding and unresponsive. He was withdrawing from her and she felt an aching loss. Perhaps it was her fault. He had wanted to bare his soul in confession, but she had persuaded him not to.

"You won't give me any more than I asked for, will you?" she asked, thinking she had asked him to make love to her and he had done just that. He had made love to her, and beautifully, but abruptly the closeness they had shared was gone.

He was troubled—troubled by something that she instinctively knew would destroy the beauty of what they had shared. As she gazed at him, sadness swept over her. He was separate from her now. Distant. Withdrawn. Alone.

Had she been wrong to deny him his confession before he made love to her?

Taking her hand, he drew her to her feet and wrapped the tartan around her before slipping into his own clothes.

She felt suddenly chilled. "If you must tell me, then tell me now. You will not rest until you do."

Even in the dim light, she could see the muscle in his jaw work as he threw his head back and stared up at the sky. "I have misled you. I am not the person you think I am. I had good reasons for deceiving you, but they dinna seem verra important now."

Her heart seemed to stop. She stared at him with a look of disbelief upon her face. She did not want to hear what he had to confess. She did not want to believe what she suddenly knew was the truth.

"Forgive me, lass. I am not who I claim to be."

"You are my betrothed," she said. "You are the Black Scot."

"Aye," he said, "but never have I been less proud of it."

"All along, it was you. I should have known from the beginning . . . the way your men revere you . . . your fondness for wearing black . . . the hundreds of hints you gave me along the way."

He took a step toward her. She backed away. "Stay away from me," she said. "You are both my heart's desire and my terror. You watched me fall in love with you, little by little, knowing the pain I suffered, when all the time it was in your power to give me that which I most desired. You could have eased my agony."

"I am sorry, love."

She knew that expression on his face, knew he wanted to come to her, to comfort her, but something held him back. Perhaps it was the look she gave him . . . the look that said he was not welcome.

Not now.

Perhaps not ever.

She had done the unpardonable. She had thought herself betrothed to one man while she had shamelessly thrown herself at another, begging him to make love to her, in spite of all he did to dissuade her. Shame and desire warred within her, and she turned away, her low voice filled with anguish. "Too much," she whispered. "There has been too much deception between us. I cannot go on pretending it does not matter, for that would go against everything I believe in. For above all else I respect honesty and abhor deceit."

His look was soft, gentle. "It wasna your fault. I was the one who wronged you, but if you will give me the chance, I will make it up to you."

Her look was incredulous. "You cannot mean you expect me to go through with this mockery of a marriage."

He gave her a dark look. "We just made love, Juliette. In the eyes of God you are my wife already."

"I cannot marry you, Stephen. I want to return to England."

Stephen stood staring at her slender back, her bent head, unable to believe her words. *Return to England? Was she daft?* He reached for her, taking her by the arms, turning her around. She kept her gaze fastened on the ground.

"What did you say?" he asked.

A horse nickered in the distance. The wind stirred the trees. She looked at him, her face twisted with anguish, and a wrenching pain tore at him. "I said I want to return to England."

"You are here by order of the king. Do you no understand what would happen to you and your family if you defied that order?"

"Then I will go to France . . . *anywhere* . . . but I cannot marry you. Not now."

"Did our lovemaking change so much?" he asked, but in his heart he knew it had. He had acted dishonorably. He had deceived his betrothed. He had made love to her without revealing who he was. The thought of it sickened him. How could he have stooped so low, when he knew how much she had come to care for him—when he knew it was love that had compelled her to ask him to make love to her in the first place? Frustration ate at him. How could he make her understand why he had had to test her, why he had had to be sure?

"Leave me," she said, turning away.

He reached out his hand, touching her shoulder gently.

"Oh God . . . Leave me! Please! Grant me this small dignity, at least."

His other hand came up to touch her shoulder and he drew her back against him. His heart twisted. He did not know what to do. Never had he felt so inadequate. Her feelings for him ran deep, he knew, but they were also new and terribly fragile. Anguish tore at him. He wanted to take her in his arms and make love to her again, to make love and keep on making love, until he made right everything that was wrong between them.

"Stephen . . . please leave me."

He sighed wearily and threw back his head, staring at the dark canopy of trees overhead. "Ah, lass, have I ever told you that you are a great deal of trouble?"

"Yes," she said, "but I promise I won't trouble you any more."

Before he could say anything else, she dropped the tartan and waded into the water. A second later, she dove under, disappearing from his sight.

He sighed, his hands dropping to his sides as he stared into the darkness, his thoughts troubled.

7

The roofless walls of the abby seemed to close in upon Juliette as she sat staring morosely into the fire, ignoring the sounds of sleep coming from Stephen's men, who lay scattered around her. She felt so alone, yet only Angus and Stephen were absent. She did not know where they had gone.

She drew her legs up, wrapping her arms around them, resting her chin upon her knees, staring blankly into the fire, her mind combing her memories for a dozen or so clues that should have told her that Stephen and the Black Scot were one and the same.

He favors me a great deal . . .

There will come a time when you find you dinna know me at all . . .

That much was certainly true. She was betrothed to a man she did not know.

The more she thought about it, the more she realized that she was having a great deal of difficulty accepting the fact that Stephen and the Black Scot were the same. Stephen was a living, breathing man, someone she knew. Someone she had once trusted.

The Black Scot was just a name, a man cloaked in mystery.

Her shoulders slumped. Tears threatened, but she swallowed back the hurt, keeping the bitter aftertaste. No longer would she worry about loving one man while being married to another.

How could she marry Stephen now? A man she could not trust? She could never be happy in a marriage based on lies. She had always been an honest person. She could accept no less in the man she would marry.

She sighed deeply, uncertain what to do. She would have to return to England, of course, thereby disgracing herself and her family. But that would be better than becoming embittered in a failed marriage, or allowing her hurt to be transformed into an angry need for revenge.

No, that wasn't her way. Nary an ounce of vengeance flowed in her veins. She was hurt, but not so hurt that she felt any desire to destroy Stephen. Love could not turn to hate so easily . . . at least, not for her.

How easy to think of what she did not want to do; how difficult to know what she did want. She was like a child with a piece of ice, neither able to hold it, nor willing to let it go.

"Indecision brings nothing but delay, lass."

"Hello, Angus," she said, without looking at him. "I fear I am not very good company at present." She heard the rustle of clothing as he lowered himself to sit beside her. She tilted her head to see firelight skip over the creases in his face. "You have talked to him?" she asked.

"Aye, as much as I could. 'Tis easier milking a wildcat than getting conversation out of the lad when he doesna want to talk."

"I think he has said enough for one night."

"So that is the end of it, then? You are calling the wedding off?"

She picked up a stick and poked at the fire, drawing circles in the dirt. They reminded her of wedding rings. She smoothed the dirt, destroying the image, only to find herself drawing it again. That is what her mind had been doing: Making decisions and cancelling them, only to make the same decisions again.

"What are you thinking, lass?"

She sighed heavily. "I am thinking that I don't have many choices, and none of them are to my liking."

"Weel, you canna remain like the ass 'twixt two bottles of hay, without ever moving an inch either way."

She sighed again. "I know."

"Would it help lass, if you ken the reasons why the lad kept his identity from you?"

"I don't suppose it would make it any worse."

"I ken he never intended to deceive you, lass. It was only his intent to be sure of your loyalty before he revealed himself as your betrothed. If he hadn't lost his heart to you, he would have told the truth sooner."

Her head came up off her knees and she stared at him. "Be sure of my loyalty? Had I given him any reason to doubt it? Did he think I sent the MacBeans?"

"Nay, he didna think that, but the lad hasna had many reasons to trust the lassies. His aunt betrayed his father, you ken, and it cost the old laird his life. He died in Stephen's arms."

She dropped her chin down to her knees again. "And so I suffered the consequences of her betrayal."

"Aye . . . hers and Stephen's first wife."

Her head jerked up. Her mouth went dry. "His first wife? I did not know he had been married before."

"It wasna for long, and it was a long time ago."

"And she betrayed him?"

"Aye. Even before her betrayal she tried to tell him his son was another man's bastard."

"Why?"

"It was an arranged marriage between two clans. Neither of them was happy about it, but Stephen was willing to try. She wanted no part of him or the marriage, you ken, because she loved someone else. When she discovered she was with child, she taunted Stephen by telling him it was another man's child she carried."

"But it was really Stephen's child?"

"Aye, though he didna ken the child was his at first. Even so, he loved the lad as his own."

"How did he learn the boy was his son?"

"By the time Robbie was two years old he looked so much like Stephen . . . weel, a blind man could have told the lad was his son. He wanted nothing more to do with her, you ken, but the child . . . it was his intention to hold the marriage together because of Robbie."

"Was?"

"She betrayed him to his enemies—to the man she fancied she loved—thinking Stephen would be killed. Stephen and his men were ambushed. It was a fierce battle and Stephen was badly wounded, but he returned home, ready to kill her with his own bare hands. She was standing on the south wall of the castle, watching his return through the parapets. Just as he reached the castle, she threw herself over the side."

"Oh, how terrible."

"Aye, she took Robbie with her."

"Oh, God."

"There hasna been much tenderness in the lad's life. His mother was the only woman close to him who never betrayed him, but she died soon after his father. It isna that he distrusts all women, you ken. It is simply that he would be certain of a woman's allegiance before he puts his trust in her."

Juliette remembered what Stephen had told her of the Black Scot. *I ken he would value your allegiance more than your understanding . . .*

"Weel, I ken I have confused you enough," Angus said. "I will leave you with your thoughts, lass." He started to rise to his feet.

Juliette touched his arm and he turned back to her. "Thank you," she said.

Angus nodded, then left as silently as he had come.

Juliette sat staring into the fire, feeling peace within her at last. She ached for Stephen, yearned for him to come to her, to tell her there would be no more lies, no more deceptions between them, that he loved her and wanted her to become his wife. She breathed deeply, hope flowing back into her heart. At last, she knew what she must do. Stephen would never come to her, but she could go to him.

A few moments later, she was walking down the trail with nothing but the light of the moon to guide her. The mist was beginning to gather, the wind that came after the rain having died down.

She saw Stephen standing where she had left him, his back to her. She stopped, uncertain what to say or do.

"I willna let you go," he said, "if that is what you came to ask me."

"I came to talk to you."

Still, he did not turn around. "Why?"

"Because there are many misunderstandings between us that I would have resolved before . . ."

"Before you return to England?"

He turned around now, and looked at her, his expression neither accusatory nor understanding. For the longest time they stood there, as if searching for the answers to many unasked questions. "I would have come to you," he said at last.

"When?"

He smiled. "Soon enough to prevent your leaving." His expression darkened. "I meant what I said, lass. I willna let you go."

"I am glad to hear that, m'lord, for I can think of no other place I would rather be than with you."

Suddenly, he was crossing the distance between them.

He was standing close enough for her to reach out and touch him. But she did not.

She had taken the first step by coming to him. If this man was to be her lifelong mate, he must tell her that he cared. She would walk back to England if she had to—and face King George's wrath—but she would not commit herself to marriage with an inflexible man.

As if sensing her thoughts, he caressed the side of her face. "You are a remarkable woman, Lady Juliette. Not many would be so forgiving."

"I am not being charitable, m'lord, nor am I too witless to know when I have been wronged. I came back because I want you to know I understand why you did it. Angus told me about your father." When he looked off, she put her hand on his sleeve. "Why would his sister betray him?"

Stephen's gaze returned to her face. "Because she favored my father's younger brother and wished him to be the laird of the Gordons."

"But you would have become the laird after your father's death."

"Not if I was dead."

Juliette's heart lurched. "She meant for you to die as well?"

"Aye. But when the battle was over, it was her favorite brother who died in my stead."

His arms came around her tightly, drawing her hard against him, as if he feared she might bolt and run.

"Did Angus tell you anything else?"

"He told me about your wife and son."

She heard his sigh of relief, then felt his body relax. "I should have told you, but I couldn't. I have been standing here since you left, trying to think of a way to tell you— groping for the right words to say, the words that would make you understand."

"I understand now," she said softly.

"And I thank you for that. All I can say in my defense is I was so afraid of being betrayed, I didna think how I would feel if it turned out that you had come to Scotland to marry me for honest reasons."

He dropped his head, his warm breath sending tremors of delight over the sensitive skin of her neck. He whispered his next words against her ear. "Forgive me. There has never been much softness or gentleness in my life, and precious little understanding. I was reared with a broadsword in one hand and a shield in the other. Your openness, your honesty, your straightforward manner disarm me." He dropped down to one knee before her. "I lay my arms at your feet, mistress mine. I desire to atone for what I did. What would you have me do?"

"I would have you stand up first, m'lord," she said, tugging at the sleeve of his coat. He came to his feet and drew her against his great body. "I never thought I would see a man such as you surrendering to a mere lass," she said. "Does this mean you are my prisoner?"

"I ken I was that from the first moment I saw you . . . as naked as a newborn, you were, and as shy as a fawn." He rested his chin on top of her head. "It was never my intent, you ken, to care for a wife who'd been forced upon me by an English king."

"And have you come to care for me?"

"Aye," he said, "I have. I am glad you came back to talk to me, lass. It gives me a small glimmer of hope."

"Have you need of hope, m'lord?"

"Aye," he said, "much to my surprise, I find I do. It would seem a certain English lass has captured my heart and my good sense along with it." He drew back, looking down at her. "I never intended to keep my identity from you for so long, but by the time I felt I could trust you, I realized how much I had come to care for you. And then I was afraid to tell you for fear of losing you. When you asked me to make love to you . . ." He threw his head back and closed his eyes. "I have never felt so dishonorable than I did at that moment." He opened his eyes and looked down at her. "Can you find it in your heart to forgive me, Juliette?"

"I told you I have already forgiven you, m'lord."

"But have you forgiven me enough for us to marry?"

"I have forgiven you enough to persuade King George to go to war with the Scots if we don't."

"Did I ever tell you that you were a troublesome lass?"

"Aye," she said with her best Scottish brogue, "you have."

Before Juliette could say more, Stephen kissed her with a driving hunger that left her weak with wanting. She kissed him back with all the feeling she could show him, experiencing a warming satisfaction when he groaned and pressed himself more intimately against her, so that even through her clothing she could feel the fierceness of his need, the shape of his desire.

His hand came up to cover her breast and she shuddered. Suddenly, his body stiffened and he pulled away.

"What is it?" she asked.

He remained motionless, his head turned slightly, as if he were listening for something. A second later, he shouted, "Run, Juliette!"

Before she could obey his command, he whirled around. Stunned, she watched him run toward his broadsword.

There was no sound at all, and when she first saw them, she thought they were figments of her imagination, mere specters of her fantasy created from the shadows of the night.

A great shout arose, and the reverberating echo of horses' hooves rang in her ears as a band of thirty or so men came thundering out of the trees. She jerked her terrified gaze from the approaching hoard of men to where Stephen was running toward her, his great claymore in his hand. And then at least a dozen riders cut him off.

The leader of the group rode forward and looked down at her. She had never seen a man with such red hair. She had never seen a man who looked so primitive, or so large. Juliette swallowed painfully and stared up at him.

"I thank ye, Lady Juliette, for making the taking of ye simple for us. I dinna ken that kidnapping an English lass would be so easy."

"Who are you and what do you want with me?"

The man swept his bonnet off his head and dipped toward her in a low, mocking bow. "Robert MacAlpin at your service. Now, if ye will be so kind as to settle yourself behind my son, Calum, we will be off."

She felt as if frigid air had seeped into her very bones. Her blood ran cold. Tears gathered in her eyes with a sudden rush. She looked from MacAlpin toward Stephen, just as a younger man with the same red hair and beard rode toward her.

Stephen's voice rang out. "Touch her and I'll kill you!"

What happened next passed with such rapidity that it was no more than a blur. A clammy coldness gripped Juliette as she watched Stephen charge, saw the flashing arc of a broadsword as a rider seemed to come out of nowhere and cut a gash in Stephen's arm before the flat side smashed against his head.

Juliette screamed. At that same moment an arm lashed out to encircle her like a band of steel, and she felt herself being hoisted into midair and thrust across a saddle.

Her abductor shouted, his horse lurching forward and breaking into a hard gallop. The thundering repeat of horses' hooves came behind them, shaking the earth and sending a throbbing pain through her head. The last thing she saw was Stephen going down.

8

Consciousness returned, and with it came the aware-ness of a sticky wetness seeping onto his face. He felt the stabbing pain and put his hand up, feeling the blood oozing from a wound on his head.

Stephen opened his eyes, feeling the burning throb of the cut on his arm as Angus kneeled over him, tying his arm with a bandage. The fuzziness in his mind cleared, and with it came the blinding reminder that Juliette had been taken.

He tried to rise, but Angus and Dougal held him down. "Easy lad. Let me finish binding this," Angus said.

"Juliette?"

"They took the lass. Did you get a look at them?"

"MacAlpins."

"Aye. I thought as much," Angus replied, tying a knot in the bandage he put around Stephen's head. "There you go, lad. 'Tis the best I can do until we get you home."

"Help me up," Stephen said, closing his eyes and grit-ting back the pain.

"You dinna plan to go after your lass now, do you?" Angus asked.

"Aye, as soon as I can stand." With Angus's help, he rose, wobbling, to his feet. "Was anyone else hurt?" he asked, looking around at his men.

"No," Dougal said. "They were gone by the time we got there. We came as soon as we heard your lass scream."

"We canna go after her now. We will need more men," Angus warned.

"I ken they have taken the lass for ransom," Dougal said. "They willna harm her."

"Aye," Angus said. "She will be well cared for."

"I am no worried about that as much as I am worried they will try to marry her off to one of their own," Stephen said.

"Considering the way she feels about you, she wouldna allow that to happen. Dinna fret, lad. Your lassie is smarter than you credit. She will find a way to hold them off. Mayhap we could trade Edith for her."

Stephen saw Angus's smile and knew he was trying to lighten the situation. He grimaced, fighting back dizziness, refusing to acknowledge the truth of Angus's words.

"I suppose the best thing would be to return to Craigmoor ... at least for now," Dougal said. "It's only a half day's journey from here."

"Aye, I ken that would be wise, considering Stephen is bleeding like a lanced boar and can barely stand. I ken it will be awhile before he will think with a clear head. A week of rest will serve him better than rash actions." To Stephen he said, "Dougal is right, lad. The MacAlpins willna harm the lass. She is worth more than a year's reiving."

"I willna wait," he said. "I will go after her now. I only need time to gather the men. I am fine," Stephen said, and fainted dead away.

Stephen spent the next week at Craigmoor Castle, recovering from his wounds.

Hearing of their laird's condition, the men were worried, their faces grave. The MacAlpins had taken their chief's lass. They would not rest until they had the lass back. Knowing the Black Scot would have need of them when he was better, his men readied themselves, honing their skills with the same steadfast devotion they gave to caring for their weapons.

As the week passed, Stephen tried more than once to go after Juliette. The first time, he was too weak and passed out. The second time, he pulled the stitches from his arm. The third time, he punched Dougal in the jaw. The fourth time he found himself tied to the bed. His bellowing rage assured the Gordon clansmen that their leader was on the mend. Their spirits lightened.

Their chief would soon be strong enough to go after his lass.

On a mist-shrouded morning Stephen and his men set out for MacAlpin land. They had spent the previous evening in the chapel, listening to the minister's prayers for the safety of their hides and the success of their mission. If all went well, they would retrieve their lass and be back at Craigmoor within a few days, ready to celebrate a wedding.

They had ridden less than half a league in a heavy mist that turned to rain, when a rider suddenly emerged from the thick mist before them, surprising Stephen, who reined in his horse with such sharpness, the black beast reared, pawing the air.

"Who goes there?" Stephen shouted.

"A MacAlpin," the man called back.

Stephen drew his claymore with a *woosh*, hearing a similar sound as his men did the same. "You are a little beyond the boundaries of MacAlpin land. Are you lost, or a fool?" Stephen answered.

"Neither," the man answered. "We are on our way to Craigmoor Castle. We have business with the Black Scot."

"And what business would that be?"

"We wish to return something that belongs to him," the man replied, coming closer.

A long column of riders emerged from the mist behind the rider. Stephen recognized Robert MacAlpin in the front. Juliette rode beside him.

The MacAlpin drew rein when he saw Stephen. "We have something to return to you, Stephen."

Stephen looked at Robert, then rested his gaze upon Juliette, satisfied that she looked well. "So I hear."

"May we come forward?"

"You may send the lass forward," Stephen said. "Return her and you may go in peace, with no bloodshed."

"I would have a word with you before I hand the lass over to you," Robert said.

"And you think I should trust you?"

"Do you have any choice? You want the lass, I ken."

"Aye," Stephen said, then he nodded and rode forward, meeting Robert MacAlpin at the midpoint of the clearing between them.

"Are the MacAlpins now taking women into battle to act as their shield?" Stephen asked.

Robert smiled. "I canna blame you for thinking that, lad," he said, "for if I told you the truth, you wouldna believe it."

Stephen remained silent.

"After we took the lass from you at the abby, we were attacked by the MacBeans. Seems they thought they had a claim upon the lass as well."

"Go on."

"My only son and heir, Calum, was wounded. The blow would have been a mortal one, if your lass hadna ridden her horse into the MacBean deflecting his blow. While we continued to fight, she staunched the bleeding and bound Calum's wound with her petticoat. If it hadna been for the lass, he no would have lived."

"And you rode all the way over here to tell me that?"

"Aye, and to bring the lass back to you."

"You are returning her, simply because she saved Calum's life?"

Robert looked a bit uncomfortable. "Weel, that and the

fact that. . . . God's bones, lad, I dinna ken the lass was so much trouble. She has a tongue on her, she does. In truth, I never knew anyone who could talk so."

Stephen was finding it hard not to laugh. So, the MacAlpins found her to be a troublesome lass. At least he spoke the truth. But a MacAlpin was a MacAlpin, and could not be trusted. Stephen forced a stern countenance. "So, you are bringing the lass back?"

"Aye, with my blessings."

"And how much do you ask for your kind gesture?"

"You wound me, lad. I ask nothing in return. In truth, I only wanted to show my gratitude, so I granted the lass anything she wished, thinking she would wish to be returned to her family in England. To my surprise, she asked to be taken to you at Craigmoor."

His words pleased Stephen, but still he did not trust him. "What is your real motive, Robert?"

"As God is my witness, I came only to give the lass safe conduct to your keep." With that, Robert turned in his saddle and waved Juliette forward. A moment later, she galloped up to them.

She smiled when she reached Stephen's side. "I did not think I would have the good fortune to see you so soon. How have you been, m'lord? Are you recovered?" she said, her gaze traveling over him, as if each part of him were dear to her.

He smiled back. "Well enough," he said, returning her inspection. "And you, lass? Did they harm you in any way?"

"I am fit, as you can see, m'lord. They extended every kindness to me."

"Except the kindness of leaving you in our care to begin with."

"Well, they regret that bit of doing and are anxious to make amends. Have they not shown it by this gesture?"

"I will answer that if we make it as far as Craigmoor without being attacked from the rear."

Robert laughed. "You are a distrustful lad, but I ken the way of it. Take your lass. She has already formed an attachment for you. God knows, I heard of it often enough."

MacAlpin laughed and whirled his horse around. A moment later, he joined his men at the edge of the clearing. The sun broke through the mist, striking his red hair and turning it the color of fire. As he rode past, the MacAlpin warriors turned and followed him into the trees.

Stephen looked at Juliette, thinking he had never seen anyone who more resembled a drowned rat, or anyone more dear to him.

She put a hand to her wet head. "I fear I am a mess, m'lord. It is not how I would have desired you to see me for the first time in many long days."

He kept his mouth tight, but knew the pleasure he felt at the sight of her showed in his eyes. "Are you trying to tell me that you missed me?"

"Yes, m'lord. That is exactly what I am saying. Did you not miss me as well?"

"Aye," he said. "I found I didna enjoy stripping for my bath half as much as when there is a certain lass about to spy on me."

"Then I shall endeavor to spy on you often."

"I shall give you the opportunity soon."

"It can not be too soon to suit me," she said, seeming to take delight in Stephen's laugh.

"Am I to believe Robert then? Is it true you fair talked the MacAlpins to death?"

"I fear that is the truth, m'lord, but it was not without a purpose. The MacAlpin is not much of a talker, you see. He rarely says a word until after the evening meal."

"Aye, Angus says he is like a bagpipe. He never talks till his belly is full."

She laughed and he found himself drinking in the beloved sight of her. "I have missed you, Juliette."

She smiled. "But you said I was a troublesome lass," she replied.

A smile played about his mouth. "Aye, that is the part I missed most."

"I think we shall get along, m'lord."

"I *know* we shall," he said. Then, holding out his hand toward her, he added, "Come, lass. Let us go home."

"Home," she said, placing her hand in his. "I like the sound of that." With a teasing smile, she asked, "Which way is home, m'lord?"

Stephen barely had time to nod in the direction of his men when Juliette said, "I'll race you." Kicking her horse into a gallop, she rode toward the group of astonished Gordons.

For a moment, he watched her ride, then he turned his horse around and dug in his spurs until the black beast leaped forward. "You are still a troublesome lass," he called out to her.

"Aye, and you like it," she shouted back.

"Aye," Stephen whispered. "I do at that."

Epilogue

They were married in the chapel at Craigmoor Castle a few weeks later, Lady Juliette Pemberton becoming the bride of Alexander Stephen Gordon, the Seventh Earl of Gordon, Laird of the Gordon clan.

As the minister said the words that joined her to him forever, Juliette was reminded that good things do come to those who seize the opportunity. With a satisfied sigh, she realized she had fulfilled her destiny.

She had become the bride of the Black Scot.

But in her heart, she knew she would always be simply Stephen's wife.

Elaine Coffman

I started to begin this letter by telling you about my own wedding, then I decided against it for one simple reason. You would all be reaching for the fast forward button. There is nothing more boring than reality.

Being a bride is a beautiful experience, but creating a love story is much more fun. Perhaps I feel this way because I spent so many hours playing "dress-up" when I was a little girl—and what better way to prepare for writing about brides than to spend time fantasizing about them? The only problem was, by the time I finished the lavish descriptions of my wedding dress and expounded upon the masculine attributes of my Prince Charming, my playmates had all fallen asleep. But, no matter. That is the beauty of pretend—we can enjoy it all by ourselves.

Always the true romantic, I faithfully created fantasies with happy endings. I've poured more passion into a kiss than Scarlett did in rebuilding Tara. I've married more men than Elizabeth Taylor. And like Mae West, I've been in more laps than a napkin. I took Spencer Tracy away from Katharine Hepburn and threw William Holden over for Gregory Peck. Cary Grant and Gary Cooper fought a duel over me, and I married both of them—thinking that was what made a "double wedding."

These were all a part of my youthful fantasy, but the love stories played out in my mind left indelible images in my memory. Love really does make the world go around, and nowhere is the magic of make-believe more profound than in romance. In "The Bride of the Black Scot," I've written about two of my favorites—Scotland and the power of love. So I hope you enjoyed your visit to an enchanted land of mist and make believe, discovering for yourself that love really is where you find it.

Keep believing,

Elaine Coffman
Box 8300-519
Dallas, Texas 75205-8300

The Man
From Wolf Creek

Joan Johnston

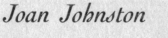

1

Cale shivered in his buckskins as he pulled the bear-skin coat tighter around his chin to fend off the sting of blowing snow. He hadn't precisely expected this spring blizzard, but he had lived in the Teton Mountains long enough to plan ahead for the unpredictable weather. There was no one to save him if he got into trouble. He was on his own in this lonesome wilderness. It was a choice he had made ten years ago, when he was twenty-four. He had never regretted his decision to leave the civilized world behind.

Cale had checked most of his traps before the storm hit and had already started back to his cabin while the snow was still falling in flakes that slowly, gently buried the June flora. Now the wind whistled down the back of his neck, and the snow was deep enough to slip into his knee-length moccasins and melt around his toes. Best he could figure, he had another half mile of uphill walking to do before he could settle down in front of a roaring fire and wait out the storm.

The sight of a saddled mule sitting on its haunches between two lodgepole pines stopped him in his tracks. Cale shook his head in disgust when he saw the figure of a man yanking on the mule's bridle, trying to get the animal on its feet. The man wasn't wearing a coat, and despite his slouch hat, his eyebrows and mustache were white with snow. Cale considered making a detour around man and mule, but another look at the flannel shirt and denim trousers the old man wore convinced him the idiot would freeze to death if left on his own.

"Need some help?" Cale asked as he stepped into the stranger's line of vision.

The man let the reins drop and turned to face Cale. His eyes crinkled with pleasure, and he shoved his hat back and brushed the snow from his mustache with two quick flips of his wrist. "Glory be! Figured I was gonna freeze to death for sure. Didn't look like snow when I left the valley this morning." He held out his hand. "Name's Orrin Schuyler. You got a cabin somewheres close? I'm about to freeze my arse off."

Cale grimaced and ignored the outstretched hand. "About a half mile up. Follow me."

"Why, I'd surely like to do that, son, but Betsy here, she ain't moving. Can't leave her here. The two of us have been together a long time."

Cale walked over to the animal, murmured a few words into the mule's ear, turned his back and began walking away. Betsy brayed once as she struggled to her feet and followed docilely after him.

Orrin gathered up the reins and hurried after Cale. "I'll be hornswoggled. What did you say to her?"

"That if she stayed where she was, some Blackfoot or Arikara would have her for supper."

Orrin guffawed and slapped his knee. "Guess you told her, all right. Didn't catch your name, son."

Cale gave Orrin a cold stare. "I'm not your son, old man."

"No offense meant," Orrin said with a hop-skip through

the deep snow to catch up with Cale's longer strides. "So what are you called, boy?"

Cale frowned ferociously at the old man. *Boy* wasn't much of an improvement over *son*. Being alone so much, Cale wasn't used to talking. He found the old man's questions irritating. But Orrin Schuyler looked stubborn enough to keep yammering until he got an answer, so Cale said, "Name's Cale Landry."

"Cale Landry," Orrin murmured. "Heard tell of you at the last rendezvous down in Willow Valley. You the one can shoot the eye from a turkey at two hundred paces?" Without waiting for an answer Orrin continued, "Heard you don't come down from the mountains much, but when you do, you got the finest beaver pelts a body's ever seen. Story is some Flathead Injun woman taught you how to cure them skins so nice and purty. That so, boy? You an Injun lover?"

Orrin chuckled deep in his throat. "Guess folks'd call me an Injun lover too, seein's how I got me a daughter by one of them squaws. The girl's ma was one of them Nez Perce Injuns. Always stood so tall and straight, like she was some kinda queen, when she wasn't no such thing. Made you feel like you oughtta bow down to her. Raven— that's my daughter—turned out the same way. That girl fairly oozes pride."

Orrin clucked his tongue. "Her ma was some woman, all right. Died 'fore I learned the secret from her of how to cure skins so nice. Didn't seem no need for it while she was alive, and once she was dead, well, it was too late then. You're a lucky man, Cale Landry."

Right then, Cale was regretting the impulse that had led him to save the talkative old man. He caught sight of his cabin through the blowing snow and heaved a sigh of relief. Which turned out to be premature. Once the old man was warmed up, his lips loosened even more.

" 'Preciate you putting Betsy in the lean-to with your

horse. Mighty fine bunch of furs you got stored in there, Cale. You must've had a right fine winter of trapping. Beaver and marten and muskrat, all three. Me, I ain't been doin' so well lately." The old man pulled a deck of worn cards from his vest pocket and shuffled them in his hands. "Wasn't for my girl selling buckskins with fancy Injun beadwork, we'd'a gone hungry once or twice this past winter. Figured I'd hunt us up some venison for supper tonight. Woulda had a fine buck too, hadn't been for this blizzard."

Cale went on with his regular routine, gutting and cleaning the rabbits he had caught and making a stew from them. He did his best to avoid Orrin, who wandered around the small room shuffling his cards. Cale hoped the snow would stop by morning. He didn't want to put the old man out in the storm, but he had learned that when it came to survival, a man had to do what a man had to do. He wouldn't last another day with Orrin Schuyler yakking away in his cabin.

"Nice place you got here." Orrin slapped his deck of cards on the trestle table that dominated the center of the room. "Mighty comfortable. That pine bed of yours looks big enough to share."

"You sleep in front of the fire." Cale pointed to the huge buffalo robe he had put down to keep the drafts from seeping in under the wooden floor of the cabin. He didn't intend to knock elbows with the other man in bed. But he had a feeling it wasn't going to be easy to ignore Orrin Schuyler's presence. With his luck, the old man probably snored.

Cale turned a deaf ear to Orrin's chatter and surveyed his domain. The log walls were well chinked with a mixture of mud and grass, and the single window was covered with an animal skin scraped thin enough to let in a shadowy light. The door hung on leather hinges, and he had used strips of buckskin to seal it around the edges. Several kerosene lanterns provided light to work by. It was an extravagance he allowed himself, like the books he bought. After all, there wasn't much else he could do with his earnings, living alone like he did.

Maybe the place was a little cluttered, but that was one advantage of living alone. He knew where everything was, because there was no one to move things around. And maybe he didn't clean as often as he should, but there was no one he had to impress. It stunk a little, but that was the natural result of his trade. He worked outside as much as he could because the cabin was too small to be truly comfortable for a man his size. Adding a second person had made it downright crowded.

"Do you suppose it's snowing down in the valley, too?" Orrin asked. "Or just up here? Hope that girl of mine has sense enough to find some shelter."

"You don't have a cabin?" Cale asked.

"Naw. Been camping out under the stars, waiting for everyone to show up for the rendezvous next month in Pierre's Hole. Figured to bunk in a tent with some friends of mine."

"How old is your girl?" Cale asked, suddenly alarmed at the thought of a child left all alone in the storm.

"Be nineteen this summer. Believe me, Raven can take care of herself. She's got gumption, all right. Just ain't been tapped yet. Little bit shy, is all. Don't cotton much to white folks. Which ain't surprising, considering she's half Injun."

Cale had seen how capable an Indian woman could be on her own, but he wondered how much this white man's daughter knew of the Indian ways. "How old was Raven when her mother died?"

" 'Bout six, I guess. She lived with her ma's people for a few years after that, till I could get back to pick her up."

"Get back?"

"I traveled 'round a mite in those days. Couldn't be

bothered with a kid. Came and got her soon's she grew up enough to help me out."

"When was that?" Cale asked.

"Couple years ago. Been a lotta men sniffing after her lately, I can tell you."

It had been so long since Cale had been with a woman, just the thought of touching female flesh made his groin ache. For a moment he considered following the old man down into the valley to get a look at the girl. But he knew from experience it was worse to look and know you couldn't touch.

In the middle of winter, when he was alone, he would think about getting himself a squaw in the spring. When he was no longer snowbound, he found himself reluctant to take such a step. Once upon a time he had loved a woman, and the experience had brought him nothing but pain. Not that he had to love a woman to bed her, but neither did he underestimate the power of sexual desire. That kind of need could bring a man to his knees before a woman. Queenly presence or not—and he didn't doubt Orrin's description of his daughter—Cale Landry had vowed he would bow to no woman, ever again.

The day passed slowly. Orrin never stopped talking. Cale was glad when the sun began to set. The wind still whistled, the storm still raged, but they were snug, if not warm, in the cabin. He joined Orrin at the table while they each ate some rabbit stew. Cale left his empty bowl on the table and stood. "I'm going to get some shut-eye. I've got work to do tomorrow."

"Can I talk you into a game of cards?" Orrin coaxed.

Cale was tempted. Once upon a time he had been a sharp himself. But he couldn't handle any more of Orrin's chatter, and he knew it was too much to hope the old man would hold his peace. "No," he said, then added a conciliatory, "Thanks anyway."

He left Orrin playing cards at the table while he stripped

down to his long johns. He blew out two of the three lamps and snuggled under the warm furs on the bed. "Put out the light when you settle for the night," he said to Orrin.

Orrin grunted a reply.

Cale was no longer paying attention. He was thinking of a woman with long blond hair and eyes the soft blue of a robin's egg. He could feel the fullness of her lips, the smoothness of the skin at her throat. His body responded immediately to the image in his mind. His pulse pounded; his shaft hardened.

He gritted his teeth against the memories that threatened to engulf him. And reminded himself of what had come later. The lying smiles. The betrayal. The sight of her flesh joined with another man's.

Cale swallowed the grating sound of pain that sought voice. Damn Orrin Schuyler for coming into his life. For reminding him that he needed a woman. For making him want again.

He heard Orrin leave the table, and turned on his side away from the man. He didn't want that old man seeing his misery. He hoped Orrin would blow out the lamp soon. He needed the darkness.

Cale heard footsteps and felt the old man breathing beside the bed.

"Cale? You awake?" Orrin whispered.

Cale figured if he said yes the old man would start up a conversation. He kept his breathing steady and pretended to be sound asleep.

"Good," the old man said. "This won't hurt so much."

Cale reacted an instant too late. The heavy frying pan hit the crown of his head with enough force to knock him cold.

2

Raven woke to the sound of a man's deep, threatening voice.

"Where are my furs?"

She heard her father's strangled reply.

"Gone. Gone."

"Where's the barter you got for them?" the harsh voice demanded.

"Gambled away," her father rasped.

In the gray, predawn light she could just make out the hulking shadow crouched over her father's body. The intruder was huge and hairy, a ferocious human beast. He held a Green River skinning knife slanted across her father's throat.

She reached slowly, silently for her father's Kentucky rifle.

"Don't move!" the voice commanded.

Raven froze.

The hulking figure rose abruptly, bringing her father upright with his throat caught in one giant hand. "Who's there?" he called.

"Raven," she whispered.

"It's my daughter," Orrin said with the little air the mountain man's fierce hold allowed down his throat. "She's yours, if you'll just let me go."

Raven gasped as she realized the enormity of her father's offer.

The beast also hissed in a breath of air.

"No, Father," Raven said, struggling out from beneath

188

the blankets she had been wrapped in and rising to her feet. There must be some other way to pay the menacing man for the furs her father had lost. She knew better than to plead with the beast. There was no mercy in the dark, haunted eyes that stared into hers.

Suddenly, her father was free. He coughed and spat, clearing his throat. "Figured you'd come hunting me," Orrin croaked, rubbing his throat. "Didn't think it would take this long, though."

The beast turned his shaggy head toward her father. "You damn near killed me!" he snarled. "Saw double for two weeks. And that was a low thing to do, hiding my clothes. I had buckskins half made when I found the set you hid under the bed."

Orrin grinned, exposing tobacco-stained teeth. "Worked though, didn't it?" He reached out to touch the sleeve of Cale's bearskin coat. "I surely hated to leave this behind, but I've got my scruples. Knew you'd need a coat."

The beast growled. "Lucky for you my horse was still there."

Orrin looked affronted. "I ain't no horse thief!"

Stealing a man's horse often condemned him to death, considering the long distances between water in the West. Thus, there was nothing lower than a horse thief, and he was killed when he was caught.

"Don't think much of a body who'd steal after accepting a man's hospitality," the beast said.

Orrin shrugged. "Couldn't help myself. Got a weakness for gambling, you know. Needed a poke and figured yours'd do."

Raven noted the look of disbelief on the beast's face.

"You lost them all?" he asked.

"Every one," Orrin confirmed. "Took near three weeks to do it, though. Too bad you didn't show up here sooner."

Raven took advantage of the opportunity to light a lantern. She stirred the fire with a stick, and when she found live coals, added kindling to build up the fire.

"How 'bout some coffee?" Orrin said. "Find yourself a seat, and we can discuss the matter of my debt to you."

Raven stiffened. So, her father had meant it when he offered her to the mountain man as though she were a pile of furs to be bartered. She kept her face turned away from the big man. She did not want to encourage his attention, and she still had hopes of escaping the trap her father had sprung on her.

The mountain man settled himself cross-legged on the ground beside her father with surprising grace. He kept his peace, listening as her father related how he had arrived early at the rendezvous site at Pierre's Hole and found a score of free trappers as well as nearly a hundred men who had hired themselves out to the Rocky Mountain and American Fur Companies. Besides the trappers, there were numerous lodges of Nez Perce and Flathead Indians.

"Found plenty who'd play cards with me, I can tell you," Orrin said. "Started out lucky. Almost doubled what I had." His slightly bucktoothed grin flashed. "Or rather, almost doubled what *you* had. Then my luck turned." He shrugged. "That's the way of it."

"That was a season's work you gambled away," the beast said. "I figured to make a couple thousand."

Orrin whistled. "That's a mighty lot, all right. But I've got something worth at least that much," he said, eyeing Raven.

"If I'd wanted a squaw, I could have bought one for a lot less than a season's worth of furs," the beast said.

Orrin's eyes narrowed. "One that speaks English? One that can cook white folk's food? One as pretty as my Raven?"

Raven felt her father's finger under her chin, forcing her face up to be observed by the mountain man. She lifted her eyes, refusing to be cowed, and met the stranger's gaze, then bit her lip to keep from gasping again.

His eyes had a hungry look. His nostrils were flared for the scent of her. His mouth, nearly hidden by a full beard, flattened to a thin line. Heavy lids hooded dark eyes in a way that did nothing to hide his naked desire. He wanted her.

Raven felt a terror she had experienced only once before, when a man had come upon her sleeping and nearly forced himself on her before she had managed to reach her knife and stab him. He had lived to embellish the tale of the Nez Perce bitch who had cut a man to pieces rather than give herself to him. Her fierce reputation had saved her from further unwanted advances at the past few rendezvous.

If her father gave her to the beast in payment of a debt, she would belong to him. She would be honor bound to obey him, to serve him in whatever he asked. And she had no doubt he would wish to couple with her. No doubt at all.

Only, she did not wish it. A surge of rebellious anger forced the words from her mouth before she could stop them. "I will work for you, as I work for my father, to repay his debt. But that is all I will do for you."

There. It was said. It was her father's problem if the beast would not accept what, and only what, she offered.

Cale couldn't take his eyes off the girl called Raven. She was beautiful beyond words, her body slim beneath the beaded buckskin dress, her face a delicate oval framed by shiny black braids from which tendrils had escaped during sleep. Her eyes were exotic, almond shaped, dark and wary. Her nose was small and straight, her mouth wide, the lips full and very, very kissable. The mixture of white and Indian blood had resulted in skin a rosy peach color that looked so soft it begged to be touched.

He wasn't the least bit pleased with the bargain Raven

had offered. She had left out the one thing he truly wanted from her! His groin tightened at the thought of bedding her. He knew deep down it was a mistake to let the old man pawn the girl off on him in payment for the furs he had stolen, especially if he agreed to the girl's terms. And yet, he couldn't bring himself to turn down the offer.

"I'll take her," he said abruptly.

"For three months," Orrin qualified. "Or thereabouts. Until the first snowfall."

Cale frowned. "Three months?"

"Or until the first snowfall," Orrin repeated. "I couldn't let her go for longer than that. I can't manage without her during the trapping season, you see."

Cale swallowed hard. Maybe Orrin was doing him a favor. If he had the girl around any longer than that, he was liable to start depending on her. Better she should go back to her father. "All right," he agreed. "Three months, or until the first snowfall."

"I will go with you," Raven said in a quiet voice, "because my father owes a debt to you. But only with the understanding that you will not take what is not offered. Otherwise, I will fight you. To the death."

Cale started to laugh at the ferocity of her challenge. The sound died in his throat. She was serious. Her eyes flashed with defiance, and her body was tense as she waited for his response.

Raven's ultimatum certainly put a hitch in his plans for her. But Cale was quick to note that she had not said he could *never* bed her. She had said she would fight if he took *what was not offered*. Which meant that if he could win her trust, he could have her.

In days long past, Cale wouldn't have questioned his ability to convince a woman she would find pleasure in his arms. But there was something about Raven that left him wondering. He smiled wolfishly. The challenge would give him something to do to help pass the time until winter.

He would have her, he decided. Somehow, some way, he would have her.

"I won't take what isn't offered," he said.

She nodded her acceptance, but the wariness didn't leave her eyes as she handed Cale a tin cup of coffee.

"You're welcome to camp here with us," Orrin offered, "and get an early start home when daylight comes."

"I need to buy supplies before I leave," Cale said.

"Sure. Take your time. Raven isn't going anywhere. We'll be here waiting for you—"

"Raven comes with me," Cale said. "You'll understand if I don't trust you to be here when I've finished my business."

Orrin grinned. "Once burned, twice chary, eh? Raven will be ready to go when you are. Right, girl?"

Cale turned his head toward the young woman. She met his gaze without flinching.

"I will be ready."

3

Cale glanced over his shoulder. Raven was still there. It was as though he had dreamed it all. The old man appearing on the snowy mountainside. His furs being stolen and gambled away at the rendezvous. Accepting Raven in exchange for Orrin Schuyler's debt. He hardly believed it had all happened.

Except the girl was real. He knew it from the eyes of the mountain men who followed her progress as she walked several paces behind his horse. He felt a sense of possession that was totally alien to him. He wanted to shield her from sight, so she couldn't be ogled by all those other men. Of course, he did nothing of the kind.

"Didn't figure you to take a squaw."

Cale slipped a leg over his piebald gelding and landed on both feet in front of a curly-haired man with pale blue eyes who was dressed in grease-slick buckskins. One word served as greeting and welcome. "Laidlaw."

Cale held out his hand, and the other man grasped it at the elbow.

"It's been a long winter, Cale," Laidlaw said. "You're a sight for sore eyes."

Cale had met Laidlaw, who was from the hills of Tennessee, his first winter in the mountains. Laidlaw had taught him everything he knew. How to survive the bitter cold, how to trap beaver, how to avoid the Blackfoot and Arikara, and how to trade with the Flathead and Nez Perce. It was Laidlaw who had encouraged him to remain a free trapper rather than hire himself out to work for one of the big fur companies. Laidlaw's advice had kept him alive and made him a rich man, though he chose to save his money, rather than spend it.

"Got time for a smoke?" Laidlaw asked.

"Sure." Cale headed with Laidlaw toward his camp.

Laidlaw's mouth curved in a crooked smile. "Aren't you forgetting something?"

Cale glanced over his shoulder and experienced a moment of chagrin. The girl. Raven had stopped in her tracks when he joined the other man. "You coming?" he called to her when she hung back.

She glanced around her at the men whose eyes ate her alive. He could almost feel the shudder that shook her small frame. "I am coming."

Cale felt that odd protectiveness again, the urge to comfort her. He shrugged it off. He knew better than to let himself feel anything for Raven Schuyler. She belonged to him, like his horse or his furs, for the period he had agreed upon with her father.

Only, there was another factor involved that made her more than that. He had been in a state of half-arousal ever since he realized she was his. He had resisted the urge to drag her into the trees and take what he wanted. Partly, it was because of the threat she had made. Partly, it was because he knew there really was no privacy to be had here. There would be time enough later, when they were alone in his cabin and certain not to be interrupted, for him to woo her into his bed.

Cale wondered whether she would really fight him. He hoped she didn't. She had to know what he wanted from her. His avid looks hadn't exactly been subtle. Still, he didn't want to hurt her. From what he had gathered, she hadn't lain with a man before. And she was tiny in comparison to his over six-foot height. She couldn't weigh more than a single pack of furs.

The mental picture of her bucking beneath him brought his shaft to hardness. He grunted with annoyance at his body's fierce reaction to the mere thought of his flesh pressed close to hers. But what did he expect? He was a man who had been without a woman for better than a year. And he wanted her.

Cale welcomed Laidlaw's interruption of his carnal daydreams, until he realized the subject Laidlaw had chosen to discuss.

"Where'd you find the girl?" Laidlaw asked.

"She's payment for a debt."

Laidlaw raised a dark brow and whistled. "Must've been some debt."

"It was."

Laidlaw was an intelligent man, and he must have realized from the curtness of Cale's replies that he didn't want to discuss the woman.

"How was the trapping?" Laidlaw asked instead.

"Beaver aplenty. A few muskrat and marten."

"So you have lots of furs to trade?"

Cale's upper lip curled wryly. It seemed all roads led back to his possession of the girl. "It's a long story," he said. "I'll tell you over a cup of coffee."

Laidlaw's camp wasn't much, a ground cover thrown over a bed of pine boughs and a ring of stones where a fire had been laid. The two men settled themselves comfortably on opposites sides of the warm stones.

The valley called Pierre's Hole was about thirty miles long and fifteen wide, bounded to the west and south by low, broken ridges. The land spread north in a meadow of grass as far as the eye could see. Cale found himself with a view of three snowcapped mountain peaks called the Grand Tetons to the east.

Laidlaw set a battered speckled blue coffeepot on the fire and offered Cale some tobacco for his pipe.

Cale realized Raven was still standing nearby, holding the lead rope of a newly purchased mule loaded with his supplies for the coming year—gunpowder, a new ax, a dozen five-pound steel beaver traps with double springs, and the scented castoreum to attract the beaver, with which he baited the traps. He had also purchased foodstuffs he craved—sugar, coffee, flour, beans, and bacon.

Raven was apparently waiting for permission, or a command, to sit. He started to say "Join us" and realized that wasn't what he wanted, after all. It wasn't that he thought she would be embarrassed by the discussion of her father's perfidy, but rather that it would be uncomfortable to have her listening with that martyred expression to every word that came from his mouth.

"Gather some wood for the fire," he said.

Raven tied the mule's lead to a nearby scrub tree and turned wordlessly to obey him.

Before she had taken three steps he said, "Don't go beyond my sight."

Raven shot him a quick look of . . . disdain?—before heading across the meadow toward a stream fed by rivulets and mountain springs. It was bordered with willow and cottonwood that had grown so thick it was nearly impassable.

Cale found himself watching the gentle sashay of her hips as she moved away, which set the buckskin fringe on her skirt to swaying. When he turned back he saw Laidlaw grinning at him.

"She's prime, all right," Laidlaw said.

Cale was grateful for the beard that hid his flush. "She's payment for a debt."

"You already said that," Laidlaw replied with a chuckle.

Cale shook his head like a baited bear. "It's not like I planned to get myself a woman," he began. "It just happened."

Laidlaw poured Cale a cup of coffee and handed it to him. "I'm envious," he admitted. "Have you had her yet?"

"We just settled the debt this morning."

"She's the one who stabbed Jack Pelter a few years back, isn't she?"

"I wouldn't know."

"She is," Laidlaw confirmed. "Man had so many cuts on him by the time she was through, they started calling him Ribbon Jack." He pursed his lips. "Naw. You haven't had her yet."

"What makes you say that?"

Laidlaw smirked. "Don't see any marks on you."

"What happens between me and the girl is none of your business," Cale snapped.

"Ain't that a sack o' hell. Man's got a pretty woman for his bed and won't share the details with his best friend."

"Get your own woman. There's plenty to be had here."

"Not like that one," Laidlaw said wistfully.

Cale didn't dispute him. He himself thought that Raven was an extraordinary woman. She carried herself with a sense of presence that was every bit as majestic as her father had suggested. Cale was surprised to hear she was the one who had cut up Ribbon Jack. He had seen the slashes on the man's face at the Wind River rendezvous two years ago. He would have to make sure Raven didn't have a knife on her when he was ready to bed her. But then, he planned to have her naked. There would be no place for her to hide a knife.

"You gonna tell me what happened to those furs of yours?" Laidlaw said.

Cale explained everything that had happened over the past month, from finding Orrin Schuyler in the mountains, to their confrontation that morning.

Laidlaw whistled in appreciation. "Sounds like you're lucky you came through with a whole skin—no pun intended."

Cale grinned. His smile faded as he caught sight of Raven returning with a load of firewood. Not far from the stream, she was surrounded by a rowdy group of drunken men.

Without bothering to excuse himself, he rose, grabbed his Hawken rifle, and headed toward her.

Raven had spent the better part of the morning trying to reconcile herself to her fate. The more she thought about the situation, the less she liked it. The man-beast was much larger than she was. Even if she remained constantly on guard, there was always the chance he might catch her unawares and take what he wanted by force.

Despite his shaggy-haired, beastlike appearance, Cale Landry did not appear to be a brutal man, but appearances could be deceiving. Her uncle had seemed a kindly man. She had been more than willing to stay with him when her father had brought her to live with the Nez Perce after her mother had died. But Two Bears had been a bully and a brute. She had suffered many a bruise before she learned to stay out of his way.

Raven had been ready and willing to leave the Nez Perce camp when her father returned for her several years later. Though Orrin Schuyler worked her like a beast of burden, at least he did not slap or cuff her. As they spent more time together, they had struck a wordless bargain in which she helped him with the work that must be done, and he kept her safe from the men who sought to use her for their pleasure.

Only, in the end, her father had sacrificed her to save himself. She had only agreed to the bargain because ... because she had seen something in Cale Landry's face beyond mere lust for a woman. His eyes had held a longing, a loneliness she had recognized and understood, because it dwelled within her as well.

Raven forced her thoughts away from contemplation of a physical joining between her and the huge, hairy beast. She could not help feeling afraid. She reassured herself with the knowledge that she had told Cale—it felt strange to give the beast a name—that she would not lie with him. If he tried to force her, he would find out she meant what she had said.

Raven became aware of a group of men coming toward her at about the same time she realized she didn't have her knife. It was a fatal error to be without a weapon, a mistake she had not made for a long time. But the events of the morning had been extraordinary, and she had been concerned about getting away from Cale and having time alone to think, so she had left her knife with her pack on the mule.

Slowly, carefully, Raven shifted the bundle of sticks off her shoulders and down to the tall grass at her feet. To her dismay, the drunken men didn't stay in a group. They shifted around her, like a pack of wolves stalking its quarry, making it impossible to keep her eyes on all of them at the same time.

One shouted to draw her attention, while another rushed her from behind. Raven eluded him and darted between two others, who both grabbed for her and ended up running into each other. She sprinted for the spot where she had left Cale, but she hadn't gotten far before she was dragged down from behind. She lashed out with her feet, catching one of her tormentors in the shin with a lucky blow. Another man took his place.

The thunder of a Hawken was followed by the painful yelp of one of the men who held her down. He fell sideways with an awful howl. The rest of the men froze in a tableau of stunned surprise that made Raven want to laugh. She was too busy yanking her dress down over her exposed thighs to find humor in the situation.

"The woman is mine," a harsh voice announced. "Anybody wants to dispute that can deal with me."

To Raven's astonishment, the men each took a cautious step backward. It seemed no one wanted to contest Cale's claim on her. One look at his face and she could see why. Death waited for the unlucky soul who challenged him.

Raven stumbled to her feet in time to see that there was one foolhardy man who seemed determined to fight. Undaunted, he stood with fists perched on hips and feet spread wide.

It was Ribbon Jack.

Raven felt a shiver of revulsion travel her spine. On his best day, Ribbon Jack had not been an attractive man. Now, with several bright pink scars across his right cheek, he looked even less agreeable. His brown eyes glittered with malice as he eyed her. She made an unconscious move backward toward Cale.

He put a hand on her shoulder and shoved her behind him, handing her his Hawken. "Stay out of the way," he ordered.

Cale took his eyes off Ribbon Jack just long enough to make sure that Raven was free of harm's way. It was a mistake that nearly cost him his life.

Ribbon Jack lunged with a knife he had pulled from the sheath tied between his shoulders. His blow would have caught Cale in the heart if he hadn't thrown up his arm at the last instant. Instead, the knife caught in the thick sleeve of his bearskin coat.

In seconds the two men were surrounded by the drunken crowd, which was ready to enjoy this entertainment as a welcome substitute for the fun they had been denied with the squaw.

Cale hadn't realized how much he needed this fight. It gave him the opportunity to release the anger he felt over being fooled by Orrin Schuyler. It helped that Ribbon Jack was a strong adversary. Cale was taller than the other man, but Ribbon Jack was thick with muscle. Apparently Jack hadn't drunk much of the rotgut that passed for alcohol among the mountain men. His reflexes were quick, and Cale was hard-set to keep from being stabbed, even though he now had a knife in his hand as well.

Now that he was locked in mortal combat, Cale realized he didn't want to kill the other man. Not that he hadn't killed before, and wouldn't again, but it seemed to him that Ribbon Jack had already suffered for his encounter with Raven. Living with the knowledge that he had been bested by a squaw was punishment enough for any man.

Cale feinted in one direction, but held his place. When Ribbon Jack lunged, Cale managed to catch the man's wrist and forced the knife from Jack's hand. Jack would have continued the fight with his fists, but Cale held the tip of his Green River knife to the other man's throat and said, "I'm satisfied. Enough for you?"

Ribbon Jack had no choice but to grunt his assent. Once he was free, he snatched his knife from the ground and returned it to the sheath between his shoulders. "That woman is trouble," he muttered to Cale. "She should be taken care of."

Cale was left with no doubt how Ribbon Jack would "take care of" Raven if he ever got his hands on her. But he said, "I'll take care of her. You just make sure you keep your distance."

Ribbon Jack didn't bother to answer him, just turned and headed away by himself, too humiliated to try and join the men who had watched the fight. They never missed him. They were already passing around the kettle of rotgut.

Cale headed back to the campfire, where he found Laidlaw waiting for him.

"Business finished?" Laidlaw asked.

"I can't help feeling sorry for the man," Cale said. He shoved a hand through his long black hair as he settled down beside Laidlaw. He found his Hawken lying beside the fire, but no sign of Raven. "Where's the girl?"

Laidlaw shrugged. "Took her pack off your mule and headed toward the trees. Figured you must have told her to go hide herself somewheres so she couldn't get into any more trouble."

Cale swore a blue streak. He came to his feet like an avenging fury, Hawken in hand. "Damn that squaw! I knew it was a mistake to get myself involved with a woman."

"What's wrong?" Laidlaw asked.

"I didn't send her anywhere," Cale said. "Damned female must've run off."

Laidlaw laughed. "Why not just let her go?"

"She belongs to me," Cale said in a hard voice. "Until the first snow falls, she's mine. And I don't give up what's mine."

He didn't bother explaining his fierce desire to possess

the woman. He didn't quite understand it himself. He only knew he wasn't going to let her go.

Cale mounted his horse, grabbed the lead rope on the mule, and headed in the direction Raven had gone. She wouldn't get far on foot. And when he caught up to her . . . she would pay.

4

Raven was woken by a hand clamped over her mouth. She struggled to rise, but a heavy weight bore her down. It was pitch black, and there was nothing to tell her who her captor was. Only she knew. From the musky smell of him. From the size of him. From the harsh sound of his voice when he spoke.

"Don't scream," Cale said.

The thought had never crossed her mind. She felt a breathless, paralyzing terror. She had run away, and he had come after her. And caught her. He was likely furious. Men, she had discovered, did not like to have their will thwarted by women. And this man was a stranger to her. She had no idea what form his revenge would take.

The hand that covered her mouth also half-covered her nose, so she had difficulty breathing. She grabbed for Cale's wrist and shoved with all her might to move it enough so she could catch her breath.

"Don't bother struggling. You can't get free," he said.

Her fear made it even more difficult to draw breath, so she fought him harder, clawing at his large, powerful hand with her nails. Her efforts were futile.

Then she thought of the knife she had tied to her thigh

before she began her flight, where it would be readily available in just such an emergency. She abruptly stopped fighting and reached surreptitiously toward the slit in her skirt that allowed her access to the weapon.

"That's better," Cale said.

She noticed his voice almost crooned, as though he were attempting to calm a wild animal caught in the steel jaws of a trap. He did not know it yet, but she was fully capable of being as vicious as a cornered wildcat. The moment she was armed with the claw-sharp knife now resting in its sheath, he would see he had underestimated her.

Raven drew the knife and plunged it toward Cale's heart all in one swift movement, because she knew she wouldn't get a second chance. Cale was bigger and stronger. Her only advantage was the element of surprise.

She heard his grunted "Oooff" and felt the knife catch on something. Suddenly his hand fell away from her mouth.

"Beast!" she hissed. "Animal! I hope I've killed you!"

She felt the warm wetness of blood on her hand and struggled frantically to free herself from beneath him. His legs straddled her waist, and as he fell forward with his full weight, she was trapped beneath him.

"No!" Raven shoved against Cale's shoulders in an attempt to move him, but without success. She bucked with her hips beneath what she believed to be his dying body, hoping to move him off of her.

To her dismay she felt him shift his hips farther into the cradle of her thighs. It became immediately, undeniably plain that he was not a dead man. For in that most intimate of places she could feel the length of him, hot and hard and ready for a stabbing wound that she was convinced would be the death of her.

"No. Please," she whispered. "I . . ." She had to swallow over the painful lump of fear in her throat before she could continue. "I will not run away again. I will serve you as I promised. If only you will not . . . will not touch me."

She held herself stiff beneath him, unyielding, ready to fight, drawing all her resources together for the battle she feared was about to begin.

To her relief and astonishment, he grunted once and rolled off her onto his back.

She clambered to her feet and stumbled backward several steps to put some distance between them. Raven wasn't sure why Cale hadn't taken her, since he obviously wasn't wounded badly enough to affect his ability to do the deed, but she wasn't going to give him a chance to change his mind. The night air was frigid without the striped wool blanket she had wrapped herself in. She felt, rather than saw, the clouds that formed as she panted, drawing explosive breaths into starving lungs.

"This wound needs some attention," Cale said. "Build up the fire so you can see what you're doing."

Raven hesitated only a moment before she dropped to her knees and felt for the stones she had laid in a circle to keep the fire from spreading. She stirred the ashes and found a glowing ember to which she added some dry grass and a few twigs until it burst into flame. In that tiny, orange light she saw Cale Landry's face for the first time since she had left him fighting Ribbon Jack.

His eyes gleamed in the dark, like some beast of prey. His teeth were bared in a grimace of pain. His fingers, shiny with blood, framed the hilt of her knife. It was clear that the bearskin coat had taken the brunt of her thrust. Only the mere tip of the knife was imbedded in his skin. She was disgusted to see that she had only caught his shoulder, missing his heart by several inches.

"Go ahead and pull it out," Cale said. "I'd do it myself, but it's at an awkward angle for me to reach."

Raven's lips flattened in distaste. The sight of blood made her sick. She had learned, out of necessity, to swallow her gorge and to work with her head averted from whatever animal she was slaughtering for supper. But she would need to pay attention to what she was doing in order to pull the knife from Cale's shoulder without doing him further injury. Not that she would have minded if he suffered further, but she feared that if she provoked him by hurting him, he would finish what he had started.

The big man made no sound as the knife came free in her hand. She stared at the tip darkened with blood, both fascinated and nauseated. She had started to sway dizzily when he plucked the knife from her fingers and put it down out of sight.

"There's water in my canteen to clean up this blood. Have you got anything you can use as a bandage?"

He was sitting up now, slipping the bearskin coat off his arms so it created a puddle of fur around his hips. Raven had never seen Cale without the coat, and she was surprised to discover that it wasn't the fur that had made him look so big. He *was* big, with shoulders as broad as an ancient tree. It was equally apparent there wasn't a shred of fat on him. His body narrowed to a slim waist and his legs were long and muscular.

She approached him with the canteen she had taken from where it hung on his saddle. "Perhaps, since your shirt is already covered with blood, we could use it to wash your wound."

Cale looked at the long john shirt that was soaked with blood at the shoulder. He made a disgruntled sound and started to draw the shirt up over his head. He hissed in a breath of air as he jarred the knife wound. He handed the shirt to Raven.

Raven forced her eyes away from the sight that now greeted her. The mountain man was an awesome being, half-naked as he was. The promise of strength she had seen when he dropped the coat was fulfilled in the man sitting before her. It surprised her to discover that, although he had a patch of dark hair in the center of his chest, he was not the hairy beast she had suspected. A thin line of black down ran into his buckskin trousers. She resisted an urge to see if it was as soft as it looked.

Raven lifted her gaze guiltily and found herself staring into lazy, hooded black eyes that seemed to laugh at her.

"See anything you like?" he asked.

Raven was grateful for the dark that hid her flush of embarrassment. "Lean back," she said curtly, "and I will clean your wound."

Cale obeyed, and Raven dabbed at the wound with the dampened long john shirt until most of the blood was cleared away. She kept swallowing her gorge, hoping she wouldn't humiliate herself by losing the contents of her stomach before she had finished.

"It needs to be stitched," she said when she could see the extent of the wound.

Cale pursed his lips. "There's a needle and thread in my pack."

Raven used the excuse he gave her to get away. Once her back was turned to Cale, she took several deep breaths to clear the stench of blood from her nostrils. It was the smell, the coppery, oily odor of blood that was the worst. Sometimes, she would tie a bandanna around her face to avoid it. But, she wasn't willing to display her weakness to this man, at least not so soon in their relationship. She would have to use the other remedy she had found that sometimes worked. She would put herself in another place, doing something else, and not think about the blood.

She remembered a time when her mother had taken her to the river to swim. The water was icy cold, and they had laughed as the trout nibbled at their toes. The sun had sparkled on the water, and the wind had soughed through the firs in a haunting cascade. It was a nearly perfect day, a happy day. Now, the only image of her mother that remained was a look of tenderness in a pair of dark eyes and a sweet, gentle smile.

Raven focused on that memory as she opened Cale's packs, searching for the needle and thread. With Cale directing her where to look, she found what she needed. Raven took her time threading the precious steel needle, then settled on her knees at Cale's side, where she would have access to the wound. She took a deep breath and thought of sparkling water and the heady scent of pines.

"This will hurt," she warned him.

"It won't be the first time I've been stitched," he said. "Do what you have to do."

It was only after he mentioned it that she realized there were more than a few scars on his upper body. She had been so overwhelmed by the whole of him, she hadn't looked at the parts. She noticed a round, smooth scar near his collarbone that appeared to be from a bullet. There were three stripes that she realized had been left by the claws of some wild animal. She reached out tentatively to touch them and felt Cale flinch.

Raven glanced up and was caught by the look in his eyes. His gaze seemed soft, almost tender. She quickly lowered her eyes to the unusual scar, but not before she felt a peculiar warmth flood her body.

"Cougar?" she asked as she softly traced the marks.

"Grizzly," he replied.

His voice was husky, and the sound lifted the hairs on her neck. "Big brute I've come to call Three Toes, seeing as how he lost the rest to a trap I laid for him." Cale touched the striped scar with his own fingertips. "He repaid me for the insult. We've had a war going ever since."

Raven couldn't help respecting a man who was willing to face down a grizzly. She shuddered at the thought of confronting one of the huge animals. Her only previous encounter with a grizzly had resulted in the loss of a childhood friend who was mauled to death. She had developed a deathly fear of bears.

"You going to stitch me up, or sit there thinking about it some more?"

Raven felt a flash of resentment. He was lucky she was willing to help him. But she had learned from past experience to hide the temper that sometimes flared and got her into trouble. Instead she said, "I don't want to hurt you." She added in a taunting voice, "Do you want to drink some whiskey before I begin?" She would soon see just how brave he was.

"No," he said. "Just get it done."

Raven took a deep breath and let it out. She swallowed hard, then stuck the needle into his flesh.

He didn't make a sound.

She looked into his eyes and saw the pain he hadn't expressed. She worked quickly, pulling the flesh together with tiny stitches, careful not to pucker the skin, keeping it flat so it would heal cleanly.

"This is the last stitch," she said.

"Damn good thing," he muttered.

As she tied the last knot, she realized there were beads of sweat on his forehead. His hands were clenched into fists. She had thought he must not feel pain quite as other men did, but now she saw he had only endured it well. She could not help admiring him for it. It was the Indian way, to act stoically in the face of suffering. She compared her father's howls to Cale's silence and found herself wondering in what other ways he might be different from other men.

Cale shivered, and she realized he must be cold. The air was frigid, and he was naked to the waist. Without saying a word, she threaded the needle through the shoulder of her buckskin dress so she wouldn't lose it, then stood and reached for the bearskin coat to draw around him.

"Thanks," he said.

"Are you hungry?" Raven had asked because she knew from experience that a man with an empty stomach was more troublesome than one who had eaten. If she were to tame the beast, she had best keep him fed.

"I need sleep more than food. Let's get some shut-eye. I want to get an early start in the morning."

Raven felt Cale's eyes on her as she cleaned the needle and returned it to his pack. She rinsed the blood from his long john shirt as best she could, then laid it on a bush to dry. Finally, there was nothing else to do. Unfortunately, he was sitting on her blanket. When she started to pull it out from under him, he stopped her.

"Uh-uh. You'll be sleeping here, where I can keep an eye on you."

"I will not run," she said in a breathless voice.

He snickered. "You've been too much in your father's company for me to trust you. Come here, Raven. I want you beside me."

"You promised—"

"I'm not going to touch a hair on your head," Cale said irritably. "Just get your tail over here so I can get some sleep." He lifted an edge of her blanket, making it plain that he expected her to roll up in it and sleep within his arms.

Raven debated the wisdom of running again. He would be weaker with the wound she had given him. The look in his eyes convinced her he would never let her go. And the next time he caught her, he might not be so willing to forego the pleasures of the flesh.

She lowered herself onto the blanket with her back to him and felt him circle her with both the wool and a bearskin-clad arm. He pulled her snug against him, so her bottom spooned into his groin. She tried shifting away from him, but to no avail.

"Lie still," he said. "It'll be warmer if we sleep this way."

She couldn't deny that. In fact, a fierce heat had suffused her body. Her heart thumped a brisk tattoo and her whole body was wired taut with a strange tension.

"Raven," he whispered against her ear. "You're about the most beautiful thing I've ever seen in the mountains. And that's saying a lot."

Frightened by the sensual tone of his voice, by the delicious tickle his mouth created, she shook her head as though a fly had buzzed her ear, catching him in the nose.

He grabbed one of her braids and wrapped it around his fist. "Be still," he murmured. "Be still."

His other hand flattened against her stomach, pressing her back into his groin. He was aroused. She could feel the length and hardness of him. Her breath came in shallow pants. Her heart thundered in her breast.

Raven was aware of each fingertip splayed across her belly. Of the warmth of his breath in her ear. She felt dizzy, almost as if she were going to faint. She resented Cale touching her but was forced to admit he wasn't hurting her. She was ready to fight him, tooth and claw, if he tried to do what it was clear he was primed and ready to do.

Only, to her dismay—disgust, displeasure, delight—the next thing she heard from Cale Landry was a long, stertorous snore.

5

"This is it." Cale watched Raven closely to see her reaction to his cabin. It wasn't much, but it was home. He tried to see it with a woman's eyes, but it was all too familiar to him. He admired the table hand hewn from Douglas fir and the two chairs on either side of it. It was odd, he realized, that a man who lived alone would have *two* chairs. Had he unconsciously longed for company?

Well, there was only *one* bed. He hadn't wanted a woman. But he had one. Or rather, there was one in his cabin. He didn't think he was going to be having her anytime soon.

"What do you think?" Cale could have bitten his tongue as soon as he said the words. What did he care what she thought? She was just a squaw come to spend a little time here. It was irrelevant whether his cabin met her approval. She would be staying here whether it did, or not.

She still hadn't said anything, and he found himself feeling anxious. Hadn't he come up here to live all alone just so he wouldn't have to worry about some woman judging the way he lived his life? So he wouldn't have to bend over backwards to please a woman who would betray him in the end, anyway?

"Well?" he demanded. His voice was harsh with the disgust he felt that her opinion mattered, and he was angry with her for intruding on the privacy he had jealously protected for the past ten years. "What do you think?"

"It's filthy," Raven said. "And it stinks."'

Cale was stung by her condemnation. "You'll just have to get used to it," he snarled.

"No," she said, shaking her head. "I will not live like this. Even a bear does not sleep in a foul den."

"Is this some sort of excuse for you to break our bargain?" he demanded.

She looked right at him, and he was frozen by the scorn in her dark eyes. "I will abide by the bargain my father made. But I will not sleep in a hovel." She headed for the door.

He grabbed her arm as she passed him and pulled her

close so they were nose to nose. "It's going to get mighty cold outside come dark," he said.

"I do not plan to sleep outside," she retorted.

"You just said—"

"I will clean this place and make it fit for human beings."

As he started to release his grip she added in a soft voice, "You have lived alone too long, my beast."

"What did you call me?"

He saw the flush rise under her peach skin to stain her high, wide cheekbones. Her eyes flashed, first with fear, then with defiance.

"Beast. I called you beast."

He dropped her arm as though she had scalded him. He hadn't thought a woman could wound him again. Especially not one he wasn't in love with. One he wouldn't give a pound of coffee for, let alone a pack of furs.

Only he hadn't given a single pound of coffee. Or a single pack of furs, for that matter. He had given an entire season's catch, nearly two thousand dollars worth of skins, for the privilege of being insulted by this woman in his own home.

Cale found himself helpless to strike her. He wasn't in the habit of brutalizing women and children. But he was angry enough to do it. Which was strange in itself. How had she gotten under his skin so quickly? He felt humiliated by her accusation that he lived like an animal. He wasn't an animal. He was a man. Maybe his habits had become a little slovenly, but there had been no one to please but himself. And he hadn't been a harsh taskmaster.

He looked again at his cabin. Instead of feeling pride for the strong, hand-hewn table and huge pine bed he had made with his own hands, instead of remembering the satisfaction he had felt the first time he lit the black, potbellied stove he had taken the trouble to cart all the way up into the mountains, he felt shame.

Dozens of beaver traps lay in piles on the floor. Willow frames for stretching fur hung haphazardly on pegs. The pot on the stove was half-filled with the stew he hadn't finished before he had left the cabin. That must be responsible for at least some of the stench she smelled. The bedcover he had stitched around grass ticking was stained with mud, but he remembered having put his dirty moccasins on it a time or two. Of course, there was a layer of dust over everything. He often worked with the door open, and he considered dust a fact of life.

Even though he was willing to concede the place was a mess, he didn't like feeling guilty for it. For a second he considered forbidding her to touch anything. But that would have been cutting off his nose to spite his face. After all, if she wasn't going to let him take what he wanted from her, he might as well get some good out of her over the next few months. If she wanted to play maid of all work, that was fine with him.

"If you don't like what you see, you can clean it up."

"Will you help me?"

"Hell, no! I won't!" Cale was surprised at the force of his response. He couldn't remember the last time he had shouted. He felt a little ridiculous when he realized who he was shouting at and how she had provoked him into it.

"You want it clean, you clean it," he said emphatically.

"Where is your broom?" she asked.

"I—" He didn't have a broom. Hadn't seen the need for one. Until now. "I'll make one for you," he said between clenched teeth.

She nodded in that smug, superior, self-satisfied way a woman had of looking at a man when she had made her point.

"All right, so I live like a pig. Welcome to the sty!" With those words he marched out the door, unable to face the pitying, sympathetic look she plastered on her face, as though he were some poor, feebleminded simpleton who didn't know any better. Well, he wasn't quite simple yet. He was smart enough to get the hell out of here before she made him feel like an insect, instead of just an animal.

Raven watched Cale's flight from the cabin with ill-concealed triumph. He had abandoned the field of battle and left her the victor. When she looked around at the hovel she had won, she felt more despair than hope. She hadn't exaggerated when she told Cale his cabin was little better than some animal's burrow. She feared she would never get the stink out of it.

Raven had taken only one deep breath, and it had been enough to force her to resort to shallow panting. The cabin reeked. The smell of muskrat caught her in the nose, making her wrinkle it to trap the smell, and then flatten it to force it out. But the stench of beaver was worse. The smell caught in the back of her throat, making it impossible to swallow.

Raven noticed Cale had left the door open when he stomped out. She crossed to the threshold and stood there breathing deep. Here the fresh scent of pine exhilarated her. Perhaps she had been wrong wishing for a permanent home all those years she had been a wanderer. Indians moved their camps away from the offal that collected over time. Orrin had moved because he was always one step ahead of whoever he had most recently flimflammed.

She had come across a cabin one bitterly cold winter as a child and imagined what it would be like, snug and warm inside. It had been a fantasy of hers for years, to live in such a home. Now she was condemned—that was the only word she could think of that fit the awful circumstances—to live here until the first snowfall.

She looked around her. The dirt could be cleaned away, the clutter could be put away, but the smell? She eyed the skin that covered the window. Perhaps if she removed it a breeze would blow through and take the worst of the stench with it. She headed for the window without thinking about what Cale would say when he discovered what she had done.

"What the hell do you think you're doing?"

Raven froze with the parchment skin rolled and tucked under her arm. Cale loomed in the doorway with a make-shift broom in his hands.

"I guess I don't really need to ask what you're doing," he continued when she didn't answer him. "I can see for myself. What I have to ask is, why?"

Cale felt foolish standing there with a broom in his hand, and he felt a rising rage at her violation of his home. "I figured you'd want to sweep the place out, not take it apart," he said with an ironic twist of his lips.

"I only wanted to get some more fresh air inside." She gave a little shrug. "Taking the skin from the window seemed the fastest, easiest way to accomplish that. I promise to put it back again."

She held the skin out to him, as though he would know what to do with it. She gave him a teasing smile and said, "It won't bite."

He felt a shimmer of something dangerously like desire traverse his spine. That smile of hers was lethal. It gave a man ideas that could get him into serious trouble. Cale wasn't someone who took chances. He traded her the broom for the skin and stalked outside, away from the threat she posed. Once he was back in the sunshine he stared at the skin as though it might, indeed, bite him. And wondered what he was supposed to do with it. He set it down near the door.

"Hellfire and damnation," he muttered. He unpacked the mule, then took his horse to the shed to brush it down. When he was done, he stepped out of the lean-to and stared at his cabin. The door hung wide open. She had been here only an hour and already she had taken it over. He was afraid to cross his own threshold because *she* was in there. Well, he'd be damned before he'd let her toss him out like so much garbage.

Cale stomped back inside his cabin, stood there for a moment staring at the bare floors, then headed for the pot-bellied stove to heat himself a cup of coffee. Which was when he saw the coffeepot was missing.

He refused to ask her where it was. It had to be here somewhere. He walked over and stood beside the stove and looked around. He couldn't find it anywhere.

Which was when he noticed the raggedy sleeve of some old long johns protruding from the stove lid. *She was burning his clothes!* He wasn't about to call her on it, knowing she would be bound to point out the obviously worn out condition of the garment.

"Can I get you something?" she asked.

"I want a cup of coffee," he said. "I can make it myself, if you'll tell me what you did with the coffeepot."

"I left it down at the creek, with the other dirty dishes, to soak. I will go get it now. You sit down and be comfortable while I am gone."

She stood the broom up against the wall and started out the door.

That was when the guilt hit him. He couldn't very well sit there doing nothing while she traipsed down to Wolf Creek all by her lonesome. Anything might happen to her. Old Three Toes was out there, not to mention savages, and who knew what-all. "I'll go with you," he said, hurrying for the door.

"There is no need for both of us to go," she said. "I will stay here and keep on working. You will find everything straight down the hill from the front door. The dishes ought to be well soaked enough now to scrub out easily with a little sand."

Cale wasn't sure how he had been bamboozled. He only knew he had. Here he was on his way down to the creek *to wash dishes*. And he didn't even have the woman for company! He couldn't remember the last time he had actually washed his dishes. He sort of wiped them clean with his fingers, or waited for the food to dry and scraped it out. One year? Two? Probably more than that, he realized. Maybe she was right. Maybe he really was an animal.

It was a disturbing thought, and one which Cale chose not to contemplate as he washed the dishes. Considering how long it had been since they had seen sand and water, they came clean surprisingly easily. He wondered when he had stopped observing the rules of a more civilized society.

Cleanliness was an easy one to let go, because it was a sin of omission. One merely had to *not* do something. Like wash dishes. Or bathe. It dawned on him suddenly, that if she had found the house odoriferous, she might have made the same judgment about *him!*

Before he could stop himself, he pulled off his moccasins. Then he yanked off the long john shirt—it was the same bloodstained one she had only rinsed out after stabbing him—then shimmied out of his buckskins and long john drawers. He waded into Wolf Creek, remembering immediately why he had given up bathing.

The water was frigid. It was fed from a mountain spring and stayed cold all year round. He splashed himself a couple of times but realized as he looked down at his skin, that it was as dirty as his dishes had been, caked with grime that had layered over years of neglect.

Cale hissed as he lowered himself until he was sitting in the stream. The water barely came to his waist here, and it rushed by, leaving goose bumps the size of hen's eggs on his arms. The bottom of the stream was more rocks than sand, but by moving a few out of the way he came up with a handful of pebbly sand that he used to scrub briskly at his skin. He was careful to wash around his stitches, but he rinsed them clean with the cold, clear water.

He rubbed until the flesh on his arms was raw, and finally saw, beneath the grit, his own pale skin. He would have been hard pressed to identify his feelings at the moment. Disbelief was foremost. How could he have gone so long without a bath? How had an Indian woman shamed him into taking one? And if, as he had told himself over the years, bathing wasn't important, why did it feel so good to be clean again?

Raven hadn't intended to maneuver Cale into washing dishes, and when she thought about it as she swept the cabin, she began to regret the impish impulse that had provoked her into sending him down to the creek. It was an indisputable fact that washing dishes was woman's work. Maybe that partly explained the filth. She knew a man could lose face with other men if he was caught doing a job that was meant only for women. Cale had been without a woman for years; thus, the woman's work had remained undone.

Raven snorted in disgust. She couldn't imagine a *woman* living in such filth because a *man* wasn't around to help with the work! She had never understood men, and she supposed she never would. It had surprised her when Cale hadn't argued about washing the dishes. But he had been gone a long time and still hadn't returned. Perhaps she should go and find out what was keeping him.

She stopped outside the small, one room cabin and turned to admire the construction. That, at least, had been done with care. The logs were fitted snugly at the corners and were chinked with mud and grass to keep out the cold winter winds. Of course, she mused with a smile, the same windproofing that kept the cabin warm in winter was what had kept in the rancid smells that permeated the place.

She was still smiling when she reached the creek. The smile slowly faded as she realized the odd stone in the creek bed wasn't a stone at all. It was moving. It had arms and legs and a furry beard. Cale Landry was sitting buck naked in the middle of the water. He was taking a bath!

Beside the creek, stacked haphazardly, were the dishes she had sent him to fetch. They were clean, she quickly noted. As he soon would be, as well.

Her smile returned, and with it a bubble of laughter.

Cale was appalled to discover Raven standing on the bank gawking at him. More to the point, he was astonished that anyone had been able to sneak up on him like that. Over the years he had honed his senses to detect even the slightest noise. Staying alive depended on staying alert. So how the hell had he ended up getting caught with his pants down like some Eastern yokel?

"Shall I come in and wash your back?" she teased.

Cale had a vivid image of what it would be like to have her standing behind him, equally naked, scrubbing his back. Despite the cold water, his pulse leaped. "Come on in," he said.

The smile froze on her face. "The water's cold."

"I ought to know," he replied. "I'm sitting in it. Come on in," he urged. "My back could use a scrubbing."

He hadn't expected her to comply. After all, she hadn't done much else he had asked of her. To his amazement, she slipped off her moccasins and waded into the water. The fringe of her dress floated on top, acting like lures for the fish, as she walked toward him.

She traversed a wide berth around him, so she ended up behind him. He tensed, waiting for the first touch of her fingertips against his skin. The water didn't feel cold any more. On the contrary, he had lit his very own bonfire. Cale was chagrined at how swiftly and powerfully his body responded to her presence. He brought his knees up to hide his arousal. He didn't figure it was any of her business.

Raven told herself that the only reason she had succumbed to Cale's taunt to wash his back was because she would be the one to benefit. After all, so long as she was cleaning the house, she might as well go all the way and clean the man who lived in it.

As she stood there, staring at his broad, muscular back, she felt an urge to caress the smooth skin that covered bone and sinew. Instead, she reached down and scooped up a handful of coarse sand, applying it to his back and rubbing energetically.

"Ouch! You're going to take off a layer of skin," Cale protested.

"And four layers of dirt," she retorted. "When was the last time you took a bath?"

He didn't answer. He wouldn't lie, and he wasn't about to tell the truth. Instead, he sat there in mute defiance, daring her to rub him raw.

She damn near did.

Once she was started, Raven took her work to heart. She used all her strength, rubbing until Cale's skin was pink all over, a sign that it was finally clean.

Then she scooped handfuls of the frigid water and rinsed off the sand, painfully aware that the water had to be stinging his raw skin.

He never made a sound.

She suddenly felt remorse for her harsh treatment. Surely Cale didn't deserve her anger. It was her father who had put her in this position. The mountain man had not been given much choice. It was either take her or forfeit any payment at all for his skins. Of course, he could simply have killed her father. All things considered, he had chosen the more humane alternative.

So why had she scrubbed his skin raw? More to the point, why had he allowed it?

Raven was confused by her conflicting feelings about the mountain man. She should have been terrified to be alone with him, naked as he was. Instead, she had been drawn to touch him more. She had been rough because she was daring Cale to respond with roughness. That would have given her the excuse she needed to put him in the same category as Ribbon Jack.

But Cale had endured her ministrations without so much as a grunt of discomfort. In so doing, he had planted a small seed of trust, the suggestion that with this man she did not need to fear his strength. His calm acceptance of her hands on him led her to indulge her curiosity about how it would feel to touch what she found so attractive to the eye.

Raven ran her fingertips soothingly over Cale's pinkened shoulders. Down across the muscular back. Then back up the narrow indentation along his spine. His skin was warm and resilient. The muscles flexed involuntarily beneath her fingertips, and she could feel his massive strength.

Cale tried not to move, because he didn't want her to stop what she was doing. She was caressing him, touching him in ways that made his body sing hosanna. As much as he wanted to return the favor, he felt certain that if she realized what she was doing, she would stop. So he held himself still, as though he had come upon a fawn in the forest, and didn't want to spook it into running.

Her fingertips slid up to his nape, and his neckhairs stood on end. A frisson of desire skittered down his spine. He couldn't stand it. He would surely die if he couldn't touch her soon.

"Dammit to hell!" He rose in a flurry of spraying water and turned to grab her in his arms.

It was then he realized why she had stopped. She was staring with a look of horror at the opposite bank.

It was occupied by Old Three Toes.

6

Raven's glance had snagged on the immense grizzly that stood on its hind legs, sharp-toothed jaws agape, a malevolent presence. They were trapped without weapons, virtually helpless, in the center of Wolf Creek. She would have screamed, except she was too frightened to draw breath.

Cale's leap from the water had startled the beast, which turned and fled.

Unfortunately, it didn't go far.

"We're trapped," Raven cried. "We'll be killed!"

"Shut up," Cale hissed, "and stay behind me."

He didn't have to ask twice. Raven was happy to put anything she could between her and the ferocious jaws and claws of the grizzly.

"Three Toes has a long memory," Cale said. "He won't have forgotten what happened the last time we tangled. Just don't move."

"You *know* this bear?" Raven asked incredulously.

"In a manner of speaking," Cale said. "He gave me this little souvenir last time we met." He reached down to draw his fingers across the claw marks on his chest. "I returned the favor, of course. Let's hope he thinks twice about repeating the experience. Best thing to do is call his bluff."

"You aren't scared of him?" Raven queried.

"Me? Scared?" he scoffed. "Naw."

He was lying. Raven had her arms around his waist from behind, so she could feel the tension in him. He was only saying that so she wouldn't be afraid. There was danger, terrible danger, here.

Raven's first instinct was to run, but she realized Cale had kept her from making that fatal mistake. To run was to invite the bear to chase them. That could end only one way. Instead, Cale was challenging the bear, confronting it beast to beast. To her amazement, the bear backed down.

Three Toes dropped down on all fours and sauntered away into the forest.

Cale exhaled, a long deep breath of relief.

Raven snorted. "You stupid, foolish man. To face a bear unarmed! That was a crazy thing to do!"

"What choice did I have?" he snapped back. "I knew what I was doing, Raven."

"But to be caught without a weapon—"

"I was taking a damned bath!" Because she had said he stunk. Or at least, insinuated it. "I agree, taking a bath was an idiotic thing to do. You won't find me making that mistake again!" And if he stank to high heaven, that was her tough luck!

Cale would have stomped out of the water, except the rocks on the bottom hurt his tender feet. He was forced to mince his way back to his clothes.

"You cannot put those filthy clothes back on!" Raven cried in alarm.

"They're all I've got," he said through gritted teeth. "You just burned the rest!"

Raven watched in dismay as he yanked on the dirty long johns and pulled on the blood-stained shirt. On top of that he added the bearskin coat.

The beast was back.

Cale picked up his Hawken which, she now realized, had never been far from hand, and marched up the hill toward the cabin.

He hadn't gone any great distance before he stopped abruptly. He turned and scowled at her. "Are you coming?

Or are you going to stand there and wait for Three Toes to come visiting again?"

Raven made her way to the edge of the creek and sat down to slip on her moccasins. She felt Cale's angry gaze as she gathered up the dishes he had washed and started up the hill after him.

"The clothes I burned were rat-bitten," she said to his back, in an effort to assuage his fury.

He halted in his tracks and turned to confront her. "If I didn't care, why should you?"

"I plan to make new ones," she retorted, her temper mounting.

"With what?" he demanded. "I haven't got any flannel for long johns."

"I thought you could bring me deerskins—"

"Looks like you've got my whole damned life planned for the next couple of months," Cale said with a snort of disgust.

He started marching toward the cabin again. When he reached the door he stopped to wait for her. "Get on inside."

He could see she was losing her hold on the dishes. Any second they were going to tumble into the dirt. He reached out and grabbed a few of the ones teetering on top of the stack.

"Get on inside," he repeated.

He hadn't planned on coming inside with her. He needed time alone to think. But he couldn't very well toss the dishes in after her, so he followed her into the cabin.

He dropped the dishes on the table and barely caught a tin cup that rolled toward the edge.

"I can make you some coffee now," Raven offered.

It was obviously a peace offering, but he wasn't sure he ought to take it. He looked around the cabin, which had suddenly shrunk in size with the two of them inside it, and decided it was way too small for the both of them. Especially when one person didn't much like the other.

Only, what if she had liked him a little better? Now that he was clean, he thought of putting his skin next to hers. Something of what he was thinking must have shown on his face, because her eyes suddenly grew wary.

He wanted her. He could have her if he took her by force. From her previous attack on him, he knew she would fight him, but she was small, and he could overwhelm her in the end.

Suddenly Cale knew he couldn't stay here another minute, in the cabin she had made too much like a home, with a woman he wanted but wasn't willing to take by force. He needed time to think, time to plan what he was going to do. But there was no earthly reason for him to be leaving his cabin. He had just gotten home!

Only she had given him a reason. And she could hardly complain that he was leaving if he was only doing her bidding.

"Forget the coffee," he said. "I've got to go."

He felt immeasurable satisfaction at the stunned look on her face. "Go? Where?"

His lips curled in a wry smile. "Hunting. You asked for deerskins. I'm going to oblige you."

"How long will you be gone?"

"As long as it takes." Cale didn't know himself how long it was going to take him to figure out what to do about Raven. She had turned his whole life upside down, and he wanted time to sort things out on his own.

"It is not necessary to go far, is it?" she asked. "Or to be gone very long."

He had his mouth open to say he wouldn't go at all if she was afraid to be left alone. But he felt an invisible noose tightening around his neck. Before he could change his mind he said, "How far I go and how long I'm gone is my business. I don't owe you any explanations."

"But—"

He felt a part of himself surrendering to the anxiety in her eyes. He was on the verge of relenting, of staying to keep her company. There was another part of him that still chafed from the knowledge that he was no longer all alone. That after ten years as a solitary man, there was someone for whom he was responsible and to whom he had to answer. The thought both terrified and infuriated him.

"Let's get something straight right now," he said. "I'm the one in charge around here. You do as you're told, and you don't ask questions. I decide where I'll go and when and how long I'll stay gone. Is that clear?"

"Go!" she said. "Go! I do not need you here. I do not care if you ever return! I can take care of myself!"

Cale stared at Raven. Her chin was upthrust, her eyes lit with fire, her whole body poised in a stance of defiance. Her finger pointed him out the door. It was plain she didn't need him around. He must have mistaken the troubled look in her eyes. Well, so be it. If she wanted him gone, he was damned glad to accommodate her.

"I'll just get a few things I need, and I'll be out of here." He wasn't even sure what he was grabbing. He was still too agitated.

A mile away it dawned on him that he had been kicked out of his own house.

Cale wasn't sure where he was when he woke. He smelled coffee, though, so he figured he must've found company. Or company had found him.

" 'Bout time you woke up," a deep voice said.

"Laidlaw." Cale rubbed the sleep from his eyes and yawned.

He had shot three deer the day he left. He could have gone back home that same night. Only his pride wouldn't let him. He figured he would give Raven time alone to stew. Then maybe she would be a little more grateful for his company when he returned.

Every night as he had made himself a pallet on the cold hard ground, he had promised himself he would go home the next morning. And every morning he awoke determined to stay away for at least a month. It was becoming a damned matter of honor.

"Thought you'd be tucked up in bed all right and tight with that Injun squaw," Laidlaw said. "What're you doing down here roaming around the valley?"

Cale stretched out the kinks another night on the ground had put in his muscles. "I left," he said flatly.

Laidlaw laughed. "Threw you out, huh?"

Cale grimaced. "I told you I *left.*"

"Yeah. And I'm Julius Caesar."

"Damned woman was obsessed with cleaning," Cale complained. "Washing dishes. Sweeping. Throwing things out. *Burning* stuff!"

"That's a woman for you," Laidlaw said. "Nest builders, every one."

"I already had my nest feathered the way I wanted it," Cale muttered.

"How long you been gone?"

"A week," Cale admitted. A week of nights spent dreaming about a woman with dark eyes and shiny black hair. A week of days spent feeling the softness of her hands against his flesh. A week of regrets for his foolish pride.

"What have you been doing with yourself?" Laidlaw asked. "Why didn't you come back to the rendezvous? There was enough whiskey around to float a canoe, horse races, arm wrestling. Rip-roaring good fun. Only broke up yesterday. We could have raised the roof together."

"I wanted to be alone."

"Missed her, huh?"

"I didn't say that!" Cale snapped.

"See it on your face," Laidlaw said philosophically. "You're wound up tight as a bowstring. Only one thing does that to a man. You need a woman. Bad."

"I don't need her," Cale retorted. "Damned if I do!"

Laidlaw squinted at the low, dark gray clouds that scudded just across the tips of an ancient forest of fir and lodgepole pine. "Gonna rain, I think." He tightened his horsehair coat—the one he had made from the skin of his favorite gelding when it was killed in a fight with a mountain lion. "Stay here, and you're going to get a real dousing."

"I don't care," Cale said stubbornly.

"You planning to find another place to spend the winter?"

"Her father's coming to get her when the first snow falls," Cale said sullenly.

"Too bad."

"You want to come hole up with me?" Cale asked.

Laidlaw laughed, a deep guffaw that came up from his belly. "Never thought I'd see you scared. And of a woman!"

"I'm not scared! I just thought—"

Laidlaw shook his head to cut off Cale's flimsy excuses. "You're going to have to face her sooner or later."

"Damned woman stiffens like a board when I get near her. Threatened to cut me up if I touched her." Cale was appalled at how much his need for Raven escaped in his voice.

Laidlaw cocked a brow speculatively. "Are you telling me you don't know how to woo a woman into bed?"

Cale felt the telltale heat under his skin. "I know how. Doesn't mean I want to."

"You want to," Laidlaw said with certainty. "Woman's gotta be made to feel like sleeping with a man's her own idea. Then she's happy as a bee in clover."

"I'm not sure I can wait that long," Cale admitted in a

quiet voice. "I'm afraid . . . I might do something I'd be sorry for later."

Laidlaw shook his head. "You aren't the kind of man who hurts something weaker than himself."

Cale's eyes hooded. "Once I would have agreed with you. Where Raven's concerned . . . I'm not sure of anything."

"I've got faith in you."

Cale snickered. "That's a comfort." He reached for the coffeepot and ended up wrenching his barely healed stab wound. He drew back and worked the sore muscle by rolling his shoulder. He had yanked the stitches out himself, wishing the whole time for Raven's gentle touch. *Damn it, I miss her!*

Cale hadn't realized he had spoken aloud until he saw the cheeky grin on Laidlaw's face. He scowled. "I want her," he admitted. "I haven't had a woman in a long time."

As if any woman would do. Cale knew good and well there was only one woman he wanted. She had dark eyes and hair the shiny black of a raven's wing, and she was waiting for him in his very own cabin up the mountain.

"With your luck, she won't even be there when you get back," Laidlaw said.

Cale froze. The thought had never even crossed his mind. Or rather, he hadn't allowed it to cross his mind. Raven had agreed to the bargain. And, after all, she had the whole damned cabin to herself, along with all of his supplies. Why would she want to leave? He felt a cold terror at the very idea.

"Hey," Laidlaw said. "I was kidding."

Cale had already torn his ground cloth off the bed of pine boughs and was shoving it into his saddlebags. He grabbed things from the makeshift camp and packed without regard to neatness.

"Can't you stay for a cup of coffee?" Laidlaw asked.

"I've been gone too long already," Cale said. "I have to get back. Help yourself. I'll leave the pot."

"So long," Laidlaw said, clearly amused at Cale's headlong flight. "I'll see you at the next rendezvous."

Cale didn't even wave goodbye as he headed up the mountain toward his cabin. As he rode, he thought of all the things that could have happened to Raven. If she had stayed, that is. Three Toes might have come hunting berries and caught her unawares. There were Blackfoot and Arikara roaming the hills. She might have hurt herself chopping wood. Or slipped and fallen and broken her leg.

His mind created horrors he wouldn't have believed in a more rational state. But there was nothing logical about his need to return to the cabin. He was a lemming headed over a cliff into the sea. Raven was his. Pride didn't matter any more. Nothing mattered except getting back to her.

Raven hadn't worried at first when Cale didn't return. When her father was sulking, he always wanted to be alone. When a full week passed and Cale still hadn't returned, Raven had cause to wish back the words she had flung at him, to wish that she had left his dirty old cabin the way it was and not gotten him so upset.

She had never been completely alone before.

On the one hand, it was lovely to be able to sleep past dawn if she wanted, to wait well into the morning before breaking her fast. It was wonderful to be able to do exactly what she wanted, when she wanted. She took advantage of the opportunity to explore the open area around Cale's cabin. She found a tiny meadow dotted with an abundance of wildflowers, including lupine and Indian paintbrush and fireweed and late-blooming primrose.

Beyond the meadow, a virgin forest of fir and pine and aspen loomed high above her. The wind in the trees sounded like the exhale of some great beast. It made her shiver when she listened at night. And reminded her of another beast that growled when he was angry.

Raven wasn't afraid to be alone, but she was a little lonely. For the first time in her life there was nothing she needed to do. It gave her a chance to sit and think. She had known for a long time that she would never have a home or a husband or children. She knew her father would never allow it. But that didn't mean she hadn't dreamed of those things.

Since the time she was old enough to bear children, she had imagined herself with a husband whose eyes glowed with love for her, watching as she suckled a babe at her breast. Sometimes—before Ribbon Jack—when she had seen a white man look at her with admiring eyes, she had imagined what it would be like if he courted her, if he married her and took her to live in a wooden cabin like the one she had seen as a child.

But the admiration had always turned to lechery. And after Ribbon Jack, no white man had looked at her with anything except fear and loathing. No man, that is, except Cale Landry.

To her chagrin, Raven had begun to weave dreams around the man, despite his bestial looks, despite his bear-like behavior. She pictured them living in his cabin, with their children playing outside.

But the picture wouldn't stay in focus. Because it *was* a dream. Because being with Cale was only temporary, until she had paid her father's debt. And there was no love in his eyes when he looked at her, only lust.

And loneliness.

She didn't forget the loneliness. It made him vulnerable. It kept him from being, in fact, a beast. It made him human.

Raven pondered why she felt differently toward Cale than she had toward any other man. Even when she had dreamed of a husband, he had been a sort of protective figure who watched over her, nothing more. She had never dreamed of joining with a man, even though that was necessary to create the child in her dreams. It seemed strange to her that she should want to couple with Cale, but she did.

His face was not particularly attractive. Actually, she had never seen the face hidden beneath his thick black beard. She had a fervent desire to see it, though. His nose had a bump at the bridge where it had been broken and healed crookedly, but it was otherwise straight and not too large. His teeth were good and mostly straight. She imagined they would make quite a splash of white if he ever smiled. So far she had only seen him bare them in pain.

His mouth was hidden by his beard, but she had seen his lips flattened in disgust. The lower lip seemed more full than the upper, but that could be an illusion created by his mustache. His eyes were deep black wells where fierce emotion often surfaced. She liked his eyes.

His body was powerful, his hands large and callused, his legs long and muscular. She could not find fault with any of them. In fact, she already knew that touching him was pleasurable. But she had been given too little chance to let her fingers roam. She wondered what would have happened if they hadn't been interrupted by Three Toes.

On the other hand, it was probably a good thing the bear had shown up.

Raven had a dreadful fear that, once in the throes of sexual fever, Cale might turn into the sort of wild-eyed, brutal animal Ribbon Jack had been. She had no other experience with a man. She knew that beasts in rut would fight to the death to secure a mate. She had seen for herself the wild light in Ribbon Jack's eyes as he tore at her clothes and clawed at her flesh. She had writhed with excruciating pain as her body resisted his penetration. If she had not reached her knife in time, Raven knew he would

have torn her in half with the sword he had wielded so un-
mercifully. What if the same thing happened with Cale?

She didn't trust Cale enough ... yet ... to believe he
would not turn into a ravening beast. So her dreams were
going to have to remain dreams, until the man returned to
prove himself one way or the other.

Assuming, of course, that he did return.

Raven had begun to doubt he would. She put her
dreams aside and headed back toward the cabin. It, at
least, was real. She had made it as nearly into the home of
her dreams as she could. It was a pity that when the first
snow fell, she was going to have to leave it.

7

Cale didn't recognize his cabin. It had changed, like a
plain green caterpillar into a spectacular butterfly.
Where before there had been clutter, now neatness reigned.
His traps and stretching hoops hung from pegs on the
wall. The bed was neatly made up with a quilt that had
been laundered so the pattern was visible again, the mat-
tress stuffed plump as a partridge with fresh grass. The
plank floor had been scrubbed clean. The potbellied stove
was burning, and delicious smells emanated from a Dutch
oven on top of it.

Obviously Raven had taken advantage of his absence to
make changes. Not all of them bad, he admitted. The shadows he had taken for granted had been banished. Sunlight
streamed inside, revealing dust motes and, if he was not
mistaken, a fresh hatch of mosquitoes. Raven had never
returned the scraped skin to the window, apparently prefer-

ring the fresh air and light—and bugs—to the odors and gloom that had permeated the closed cabin.

Cale leaned over to sniff the wildflowers Raven had put in a canning jar on the table. The floral scent reminded him of her and made his groin tighten. Where was she? He knew she couldn't be far because there was food on the stove. He was chagrined to find everything so much in order. Apparently his race back to the cabin had been a fool's jaunt. She had managed just fine without him!

Cale dropped the pack he carried, which included three deerskins and about half the venison from the deer, which he had smoked. The rest he had eaten or left for the wolves. He resisted the urge to call out to her. He didn't want her thinking he had missed her. Even if he had.

On his ride back to the cabin, Cale had decided that, assuming he found Raven where he'd left her, he might as well enjoy her company. It beat to heck his other two choices: avoiding her or arguing with her. Remembering the beautifully crafted beadwork on her dress, he thought maybe he was going to fancy having a set of buckskins made for him. If the smells coming from the stove were anything to judge by, she could cook. And he already knew she had a real talent for cleaning.

"Hello."

Cale wheeled, surprised again by how silently Raven could move. He would have admired her for it, if he hadn't found it so disconcerting to be caught unawares.

"Welcome home."

It was amazing how powerful those two words were, what images they conjured in Cale's mind. A rocker by the fire. A hot meal on the table. A warm bed with a woman waiting for him. His throat tightened. Once upon a time he had expected all those things. Over the past ten years he had given up hope of ever having them. Now there was a woman in his cabin, and a bed and hot food on the stove.

All he needed was the rocker, and he could make that himself if he set his mind to it.

Raven leaned down to pick up the three rolled deerskins. "Oh, you brought them after all."

"Did you think I wouldn't?"

She flashed him a quick grin. "I wasn't sure. You were so angry when you left . . ." Her voice faded, as though she were afraid that by mentioning his anger she would bring it back to life.

Over the past week Cale had moved past anger and frustration to acceptance. He was just going to make the best of a bad situation. From the looks of things, it wasn't going to be nearly so difficult as he had feared.

"Is there enough for me?" he asked, gesturing to the pot on the stove.

"You are hungry!" She dropped the deerskins and hurried to get plates to set on the table. "Take off your coat and make yourself comfortable," she urged.

Cale felt a rising irritation. It was his home. He ought to be the one offering her hospitality, instead of the other way around. He bit back the retort that was on his lips. *No arguing,* he told himself. He was determined to keep things on an even keel.

Raven dished up stew and set it on the table in front of him. She scooped up a bowl for herself and joined him, after pouring each of them a cup of coffee.

"The hunting was difficult?" she asked.

"I got all three deer the first day," Cale confessed.

"Then why . . ."

"I spent the rest of the week figuring out what to do about you."

Raven flushed. "I did not think you wanted anything to do with me."

"I made a mistake bringing you here, that's for sure."

The color that had so recently rushed to Raven's face fled, leaving her pale. "My father will not come until the first snowfall," she reminded him. "I have nowhere else to go."

Cale sighed. "I know. That's why I figured the best thing to do is for us to cry peace and be friends."

"You want to be my . . . friend?" Raven had never had many friends, and of the few she had, none of them were male. Her eyes narrowed suspiciously. "What does that mean, friends?"

"You know. Talk together, work together, play together."

"Sleep together?" Raven asked cautiously.

"Under the same roof," Cale said.

"But not in the same bed?"

"No," Cale said evenly. "Not in the same bed."

"But there is only one bed here," Raven pointed out.

Cale glanced over at his bed. She had her things set out all around it. Plainly, while he'd been gone, she had claimed it. His lips curled cynically. "I'll take the floor."

"All right."

She had agreed to that damn quick, Cale thought. But why shouldn't she? He was the one who would end up on the cold, hard floor.

"Shall we shake on it?" Cale extended his hand across the table, wondering if she would dare to touch him. He saw the effort it took for Raven to place her hand in his. Her skin was soft, though the tips of her fingers were callused from hard work. She barely gripped his hand, and he returned the slight pressure before letting her go. She withdrew her hand quickly, and her grin flashed.

"Now we are friends," she said. "I shall make a buckskin shirt for my friend from the skins he has brought me."

"Is there something I could make for you?" Cale didn't know why he had offered, except he didn't want to be in her debt, and if she was going to make him a shirt, then he ought to do something for her in return.

She shook her head. "I need nothing. Only . . . only there is something you could do for me."

"What's that?"

"Would you read to me from your books? I have looked at the pictures in some of them, and I wish to know the story also. But I cannot read."

"Sure." Cale saw himself sitting in a rocker with her in his lap, her head snuggled under his chin and a book in front of them both. He shoved the image away. In the first place he didn't have a rocker. In the second place, she could barely stand to touch his hand, let alone sit in his lap. In the third place, he had no business dreaming about a woman who was only going to be around until the first snowfall.

She spent the afternoon outside working on the deer hide, scraping the skin to make it smooth. There were several more steps, she explained, before the skin would be ready, but she had made a start.

For a while Cale merely sat on the threshold of the cabin and watched her, marveling at the strength in hands that were so slim and feminine. Her hair blew freely in the wind, but she apparently tired of shoving it out of the way. He watched, entranced, as she quickly braided it in a single, silken tail that hung halfway down her back. Soon, beads of sweat appeared above her lip. He had the craziest urge to taste her skin, to lick away the salty drops.

That was when he decided it would be better not to watch her so closely. Not when he had declared they should be friends and had shaken on the deal.

He had wood to chop for the winter, and he figured the hard work would keep his mind off the girl. Cale spent the afternoon splitting pines and cutting them into manageable pieces. As he worked he couldn't let go of the thought that he could use some of the wood to make himself a rocker. Soon he had the rails for the back, then the slats for the seat and the legs. Finally he sat down to work on the curved rockers. By dusk, he had all the pieces cut out. It only remained to shape and smooth them and put them together.

Raven had noticed Cale's eyes on her, and it had made her feel a little frightened at first. What if he decided he wanted to do more than look? But he never made a move toward her. She snuck a peek at him once or twice, and saw that his eyes held only admiration. It was a look that made her feel warm inside. Or perhaps it was only the sunlight that made her wish she could bathe her face in the creek.

Raven noticed immediately when Cale left his seat by the door. He worked steadily with his ax, chopping with sure, steady strokes. Soon he had shed his shirt. The first time she raised her eyes and found herself staring at his bare chest she drew in a sharp breath. Her beast was a truly magnificent animal.

The scar where she had cut him was still pink, but his injury didn't seem to affect the smooth swing of the ax. His muscles flexed and relaxed as he worked. His strength and grace were impressive, and she had to force her eyes away from him and back to her work. She hadn't been looking at him with the eyes of a friend. Friends didn't want to touch the way she wanted to touch.

She consoled herself with the thought that she would have felt the same way if he had been a superb stallion. She would have wanted to confirm the supple beauty with her hands. It was safer, she decided, to keep her eyes and her hands to herself.

Raven hardly noticed the coming of dusk. She was so involved with what she was doing that she jerked unconsciously when she felt a touch on her shoulder.

"Cale!"

"Who did you think it was?" he asked, unable to keep the exasperation from his voice. She had jumped as though he'd scalded her. But he supposed that was to be expected, considering what she had been through with Ribbon Jack.

"I'm sorry," she said. "I forgot where I was. I know you would never—That is—"

"I'm not Ribbon Jack," he said flatly.

"No," she said faintly.

He wished now he had killed the man. He had been a fool to feel the least bit sorry for someone who had left such shadows in an innocent woman's eyes. Cale tried to make himself look less threatening, but he didn't know how. He was big. He was strong. There was no changing that. But he held out a hand to her, palm up, submitting his great size and strength to her will.

"It's time for supper," he said. "Shall we go inside?"

He felt a tightness in his chest when she reached out and took his hand. He could see from the look in her eyes what courage it took for her to reach out to him. He shook inside when he thought of how fragile she was, and how easily he could hurt her. Not that he would. But it was clear now, if it hadn't been before, that she was a person with feelings—and fears—that would have to be dealt with.

She allowed him to help her to her feet, but freed herself to gather her work. He busied himself putting away his ax, then joined her in the house.

Raven had crossed some invisible hurdle when she took Cale's hand. He had offered it in friendship, and she had accepted. She was willing to give him her trust—until he proved himself unworthy of it.

At the supper table, she found herself telling him what she had done to pass the time while he was gone, about the flowers she had found, and the time she had spent doing nothing at all.

He told her about meeting Laidlaw and the rendezvous breaking up and how he always looked forward to it and then after a day or so couldn't stand the crowds and had to leave.

"I like living alone," he confessed.

There was an embarrassed silence, while his words hung in the air. It was plain to Raven that she had intruded on his privacy. Even if it wasn't her fault. "My father will be coming—"

"I don't mind having you here," he cut her off. "I mean, I like living alone, but it's nice having company, too. A man gets tired of the silence." *A man gets lonely,* he thought, only he couldn't tell her that. Besides, he wasn't lonely with Raven around.

She managed a small smile. "Will you read to me tonight?"

He nodded. "Is there any particular book you want me to read from?"

She went to his bookshelf and pulled one out. "This one."

It was an illustrated edition of *Robinson Crusoe*. How apt that she had chosen the story of a man marooned alone on an island. It was a book that celebrated the strength of the human spirit, the ability of man to rise above adversity. It had kept Cale from going mad one winter when he had been snowed in for two months.

Cale pulled the lantern on the table closer, so he could see to read. He expected Raven to sit across from him, as she had at supper. Instead, she pulled her chair around to his side.

"I want to see the words when you say them," she said. "And look at the pictures."

She was closer to him than she had been all day. Close enough that he could see the way her lashes fanned out over her cheeks when she lowered her eyes. Close enough that he could see there were several freckles on her nose. Close enough that he could feel the warmth of her thigh next to his.

He read slowly and tried to make his voice rise and fall with the story. She was quiet in a way that reminded him of the reverence people have in church. She made little noises to punctuate the story, the only evidence he had that she was listening. He had no idea how long he read. He stopped when he felt his throat getting hoarse.

"That's enough for tonight," he said.

"Will you read again tomorrow?"

He took one look at her face, at the childlike expectation, and knew he would read again even if he croaked like a frog. "Of course," he said. "But I'm done in tonight."

It was bedtime. He settled himself on the buffalo hide in front of the fire, and covered himself with his bearskin coat. It wasn't comfortable, but he wasn't about to complain. He had made a deal, and he was sticking to it.

Raven saw Cale on the floor and knew she couldn't make him sleep there. He would be cold. And the floor was hard. If he had wanted to take advantage of her, he could have done it at any time. There was some risk in offering him a place on the bed, but she had decided earlier in the day to trust him. And it was a very big bed.

She took off her moccasins and slipped under the covers and over to the far side of the bed. "Cale," she whispered.

"Yes, Raven."

"There is room here for more than one," she said.

"I know."

"I would be willing to share with you."

Cale came up on one elbow. "Thanks, but no thanks. I can't guarantee that I won't roll into you during the night. I'd just as soon not end up with a knife in my ribs."

She pulled the knife from the sheath that never left her thigh and brought it out from under the covers. "You can take my knife," she said, holding it out to him. "If it will make you more comfortable."

Cale sat up, surprised by her generous offer, but still wary of accepting it. "Are you sure you want to do this?"

Raven nodded. "I am inviting you into this bed only to sleep. I . . . I trust you. We are friends, after all."

Cale took the knife from her and struck it into the wall beside her. "It's there if you feel you need it." He slipped under the covers beside her and blew out the lantern beside the bed.

After awhile he heard the steady breathing that meant she was asleep. It was a long time before he could get his own unruly body to relax.

Friends, he thought as he finally drifted toward sleep. Cale had never had a friend that he wanted to hold in his arms and kiss and touch. It was a unique experience. He thought he could get to like it.

Raven woke in the middle of the night. Her hair was caught beneath Cale's shoulder, and she couldn't move her head. That was when she realized she was snuggled up next to him. Like most large animals, he was warm. She knew she ought to wake him and free herself. But then she would have to give up his warmth. Tomorrow morning would be soon enough for that.

If he tried to touch her . . . but she didn't think he would. After all, he had left her knife within easy reach. He was a strange man, her beast. Imagine wanting to be friends with a woman! She should be afraid of him, but she wasn't. Even this closeness did not raise the terror she had felt with Ribbon Jack. But then, it was not necessary to be afraid of a friend. It was a unique experience to be so comfortable with a man. She thought she might grow to like it.

Raven sighed and burrowed more deeply against Cale's side. He grunted, then shifted and slung an arm around her. She tensed for a moment, until she realized he was still asleep. Then she allowed slumber to claim her once more.

Cale kept his breathing steady, and didn't move a hair until Raven relaxed once more beside him. He had felt her awaken, felt her stiffen as she realized where she was. He had been ready for a knife in the ribs. Instead, her hand had slipped onto his chest, and her nose had burrowed into his shoulder.

He wanted very badly to kiss her, to touch her in all the places he could imagine touching a woman to bring her pleasure. But he wouldn't for the world have violated her trust in him. Maybe, with time, she would be able to accept him as more than a friend. She had to learn that he would never hurt her. He had to bide his time, and hope there was enough of it left before her father came to get her.

Cale shifted restlessly. He wasn't a patient man. However, he had learned over his ten years alone how to wait. The snow melted. Spring always came. But it couldn't be rushed. So it was with Raven. She would be his. Eventually.

He closed his eyes and thought about how Raven had looked sitting beside him at the table after supper. How the story had been so much more exciting with her listening, as though he were hearing it for the first time himself. It was too bad she couldn't read. Too bad he didn't have time to teach her.

Suddenly Cale realized what a bad bargain he had made with her father. It wasn't enough. A few months just wasn't enough. He wondered if the snow would fall early this year, stealing even the little time he had with her.

His arm tightened reflexively around her, and Raven made a grunting sound. He loosened his hold, and she sighed. He would be damned if he let her go. Orrin Schuyler owed him more than a few months of her service. The man had stolen a whole year's catch of furs! Cale had been besotted by a pretty face, and Orrin had taken advantage. He would have a talk with the old man when he showed up and would drive a better bargain.

8

It rained for a whole week, and the weather was colder than usual for summer. Cale put the skin back on the window temporarily to keep out the weather, but he made a point of lighting every lantern in the place. If Raven wanted light, she would have it.

She worked on the buckskin for his shirt, pulling it through rings that were smaller and smaller until it was smooth and supple and the color of butter. "Now I have to measure," she said, as she came toward him with a long string of rawhide. He held his breath, letting her check the length of his arms and the breadth of his chest and the distance from his nape to his buttocks. She looked adorable with her tongue caught between her teeth. It was all he could do to resist kissing her.

"When will it be done?" he asked.

"I can sew the pieces together and cut the fringe in a day or two," she said. "But the beadwork will take longer."

"You're going to decorate my shirt? What design will you use?"

"I have not decided." An impish smile curved her lips and she added, "Even if I had, I would not tell you. I want it to be a surprise."

He raised his brows. "I'm not so sure I like surprises."

"You'll like this one," she assured him.

Raven was amazed at her temerity with the gruff mountain man. Slowly but surely, as the days and nights passed and Cale kept his distance, she was losing her fear of him.

More than that, she was growing to like him. He could be bristly at times, but even when he was angry she never felt herself in danger. She began to let herself dream about what it might be like if they lived here forever, if he took her for his wife and planted his seed inside her.

She was still afraid to lie with him, but she began to believe she might overcome even that fear, if only she had time enough with Cale before her father came to get her. If Cale would only give her some indication that he wanted her to stay, she would defy her father. But he never said a word one way or the other.

For a week Raven had watched Cale making something out of the pieces of wood he had cut the day he returned to the cabin, but she couldn't figure out what it was. She pointed to the curved piece of wood in Cale's hands and asked, "What are you making?"

"It's a rocker." He set down the bottom rail of the rocker and showed her how the chair would move.

She looked at him quizzically. "Why would anyone want to sit in a chair that will not stay still?"

His lip curled in a wry smile. "You'd have to sit in one to understand," he said. "It's soothing. Like being on a limb swaying in the breeze."

"I would be worried about falling off," she said tartly.

"That's why we sit on a rocker, instead," he said with a grin. "It isn't going to dump you on the floor unexpectedly."

"It seems like a stupid thing to me," she said.

"Just wait," he said. "And see."

The day Cale finished his rocker he invited Raven to be the first to sit in it.

She shook her head. "You go first."

He sat down, leaned back and gave the rocker a push with his toe. It creaked against the wooden floor. The rhythmic sound was as soothing to his ears as the rocking was to his body. He closed his eyes and took himself back to a time when he had lived in Virginia and his parents had each sat in a rocker on the front porch of their plantation. He wasn't aware of the smile that formed on his face, but apparently Raven was.

"I'm ready to try now," she said.

Cale got up and held the chair still while she sat down very gingerly.

"You can let go." Raven shoved with her toe and the rocker began to move. She had a deathgrip on the arms of the chair until she realized she wasn't going to tumble out of it.

"I suspect this reminds us of when we were babies being rocked in the cradle," he mused.

"Indian babies aren't rocked in cradles," Raven said. "But sometimes a papoose in a backboard is tied to the limb of a tree, and the breeze will make it sway." She leaned back in the rocker and let it move her gently to-and-fro. "It must feel very much like this," she said in a dreamy voice.

"I can see I should have made two," Cale said ruefully.

Raven's eyes flashed open, and she would have leapt from the chair except Cale put his hands on the arms and kept her captive.

"It's all right," he said. "You keep rocking. I can use it later."

"But—"

He brushed her cheek with the back of his hand. "I'm just glad you like it."

He saw her eyes widen as he caressed her, but she didn't try to escape. Not that he hadn't made it virtually impossible for her to do so. But there was no fear in her eyes, as there would have been if she had felt truly trapped. So maybe he was making progress after all.

"I like this . . . rocker," she said, "but you didn't make it for me."

He stepped back. "Didn't I? Well, we can always share it, you know."

"We can? How?"

"Stand up," he said, backing away to give her room.

She stood obediently, and he sat down in the chair.

Her hands shot to her hips. "You have a strange way of sharing, my beast."

Cale grinned and held out his arms. "You can sit on my lap."

She shook her head. "The rocker will break. I have work to do outside," she said.

She was gone before he could offer the chair back to her.

He read to her every night at the table. She still didn't completely trust the rocker. The way she didn't yet trust him. *Someday,* he thought. *Someday she'll want to sit there with me.*

But the days were passing more quickly than he would have liked. He watched every move Raven made, felt his heart thump wildly when she was near. But he didn't make a move toward her that was the least bit sexually threatening, even though he often lay wide awake for hours after she had fallen asleep in the bed beside him.

Cale was amazed at Raven's patience with the tiny beads she was sewing on his shirt. She wouldn't let him see what she was doing, but it pleased him to sit in his rocker and watch her in front of the fire, her head bowed, intent on her work. He caught her rubbing her neck one night and lowered himself onto the floor behind her. He laid his hands on her shoulders, which tensed at his touch.

"May I?" he said.

She nodded.

He had never been so conscious of his strength or the size of his hands. He moved her hair out of the way, exposing the skin at her nape. He was as gentle as he knew how to be, as he massaged her aching shoulders. She sighed once, and he heard another sound of satisfaction deep in her throat as his fingers pressed against her flesh. He watched her set the shirt aside, and her hands, for once, lay idle in her lap.

He couldn't take his eyes off the skin at her nape. It looked soft and silky and utterly enticing. He lowered his head and pressed his lips lightly against her flesh. He felt the tremor that ran through her, saw her hands slide to her sides.

"Raven?" he whispered.

She turned and looked at him over her shoulder. Her dark eyes were liquid, not frightened, but watchful. Her lips were parted, her breath coming in shallow pants.

He could have kissed her. Could have done that and maybe more. But it wasn't what he wanted most. More than anything, he wanted to hold her in his arms.

He stood and picked her up and walked with her back to the rocker. He sat and settled her in his lap. She hid her face against his chest, and her fingers tightened on handfuls of his shirt. He didn't rock at first, just sat there, marveling at the wonder of having her there in his arms, where he had always imagined her.

Then he began to rock. The floor creaked under the chair. That, and the fire popping, and the rustle of the aspens outside were the only sounds to break the silence.

He held her like that until she fell asleep in his arms. He looked at her with his heart in his eyes. How had she come to mean so much to him? How was he going to let her go?

He managed to put her to bed without waking her and joined her there. He had made his dream come true. But for how long would it last? He had made a bargain with her father. He would have to give her back. Unless she wanted to stay. But why would she? What kind of life could he offer her? Cale held Raven gently in his arms as he fell into a troubled sleep.

Three days later, just before bedtime, Raven presented Cale with his shirt.

"It's a wolf!" he exclaimed, as he examined the intricate beadwork.

"A lone wolf," she agreed.

"He's howling at the moon," Cale observed.

"He's calling to his mate," she said quietly. "Asking her to join him on the hunt."

Raven wondered if Cale could read into her gift the message she was sending to him. *I will be your mate, Cale Landry. I will hunt with you.*

His fingers lovingly traced the beadwork, but he said only, "It's exquisite. Can I put it on?"

She forced a smile. "Of course. I made it for you to wear."

He yanked off his shirt and pulled on the buckskin. It fit him well at the shoulders and across the back, yet gave him room to move. "Thank you," he said. "Words can't express what I'm feeling right now."

For a moment Raven thought he was going to kiss her. She wondered if she would let him, but he drew back. She felt disappointed and realized that, ever since that night before the fire, she had wanted him to kiss her. More than that, she had wanted him to see her as his mate.

How foolish. He only wanted to bed her. She knew that. But it was not enough, and she would not settle for less. She wanted it all, the husband and the home and the children. So perhaps it was better that he had not kissed her. Her father would be coming for her soon, and she would have to leave this cabin and Cale. Better not to leave her heart behind as well.

9

Being friends with a woman, Cale discovered, was damned hard work.

On a sunny, Indian summer day in mid-September, Raven talked him into taking a walk to gather the last of the wildflowers in the wood. He had never heard of doing anything so silly, but she held out her hand to him, and he took it.

"Come with me. We will be carefree for one day."

Before he knew it, he was on his way into the forest with the picnic she had packed for them carried in a burlap sack slung over his shoulder.

Cale was astounded at the number and variety of wildflowers they found. What was even more beautiful was the pleasure shining in Raven's eyes. A lump filled his throat from just looking at her. Another, even more obvious tightness rose somewhere else. He reminded himself they were friends and kept his hands to himself.

Later, after they had eaten, she invited him to lay his head in her lap and relax. When he was settled, Raven placed her cool fingertips on his brow and gently smoothed it as she talked of her life among the Nez Perce.

Cale was appalled at the hardship and deprivation she described.

"How could your father have left you with them so long?" he demanded. "Six years must have seemed forever to a six-year-old child. Did you mind leaving when your father finally came to get you?"

Raven's brow furrowed. "I did not wish to stay longer

with my uncle. He was not kind to me. And I longed for adventure. I wanted to travel and see more of what was beyond the mountains."

"Was your wish fulfilled?"

"I saw more than I wished to see," she said in a bitter voice. "There is much hatred and cruelty in the world."

Her fingertips were laced in Cale's hair, and he reached up to draw her hand down and press her palm with his lips. "I'm sorry you've suffered from that hatred and cruelty," he said.

It was the first reference he had ever made to the incident with Ribbon Jack. Raven stiffened, and if he hadn't been holding her hand, he knew she would have pulled it away. Cale suddenly felt barriers between them that hadn't been there for weeks. He sought a way to bring them back down.

"Was there ever a man you wanted to uh . . . a man you wanted?" he finished hastily.

The sweetest smile curved her lips, and she twirled a lock of his hair on her finger. "Yes. One."

Cale experienced a stab of jealousy that surprised him. Curiosity goaded him to ask, "What was he like?"

She stared off into the distance, as though picturing him in her mind's eye. "He's tall and very strong-willed," she said. "He has eyes that see beyond the surface of things and a powerful spirit that can be gentle when there is need."

"He sounds like a saint."

She laughed, a tinkling, vibrating sound that worked its way down inside him, shattering walls that had stood for long years. "Oh, no. He is a very earthy man. I have often thought him more beastlike than human."

"How can you want a man like that?" Cale demanded.

She smiled enigmatically. "It is easy. When you . . ."

Cale thought she was about to say *love,* and his stomach turned about three flips. He didn't want her to love another man. He wanted her to love him. Well, hell, he could want a woman to love him even if he didn't love her back, couldn't he?

"What about you?" she asked, resuming the caress of his temples that was both soothing and exciting. "Was there ever a woman you thought to have for your own?"

Cale debated the wisdom of answering her question. He had never told anyone—except Laidlaw, when they were both drunk—about Charlotte Anderson. Maybe it was time he did.

"There was a woman back in Virginia," he said. "We were engaged to be married."

"What happened. Did she die?" Raven asked.

Cale snorted. "She chose another man instead."

"Foolish woman."

Raven's statement, scornful as it was of Charlotte's choice in men, did more than anything in ten years to assuage Cale's bruised pride.

"Has there been no other woman?" Raven asked.

"No." It had been a long and empty ten years, Cale realized. He had fled after Charlotte's betrayal and found solace in the mountains. He hadn't once looked back, hadn't once questioned his decision to leave the world with its false women behind him. He had satisfied his sexual urges with the Indian women at the annual rendezvous who were willing to be paid for their favors, but he had not chosen another life mate. Charlotte's perfidy had taken a toll far greater than stolen pride and a broken heart. She had snatched away his chance at happiness with a woman.

Now, by a quirk of circumstance, he found himself with another woman who was slowly but surely stealing her way into his affections. Somehow Raven had become much more than just a friend. Only, this time around he would be more careful. This time he wouldn't give her his heart.

Cale realized he had been staring at Raven's mouth the

whole time he had been thinking, wondering what it would taste like. He had waited long enough. He didn't allow himself time to change his mind, just curled a hand around her nape and drew her down as he lifted his head toward her. If she fought him. . . .

Their lips met somewhere in the middle, just a touch, a fleeting taste of wonder and delight.

Cale felt his pulse pounding as he glided his tongue along the edge of her closed lips. She moaned softly as she opened her mouth, and he slipped his tongue inside. He slowly stroked her mouth, and she made a whimpering sound in her throat. Then her tongue sought his, and he felt his groin tighten with desire.

Cale wasn't sure who broke the kiss first, but he took a shuddering breath as their lips parted.

He had kissed her, and she had been willing.

Cale kissed her again, not as a friend, but as a lover. And yet, the kisses he shared with her were all the more pleasurable because he knew and liked the woman in his arms.

So this was kissing, Raven thought, stunned by the feelings Cale evoked. She had never imagined his mouth could be so soft, yet demanding. Or the surprising warmth and wetness of his tongue. Or the way her belly drew up tight as his tongue stroked in and out.

It wasn't physical fear that made her turn her head away to escape his kisses. It was the knowledge that she was very close to losing her soul to the beast. She wanted husband and hearth and children. Cale offered none of those things. Only this, the brief joining of man and woman, the coming together of friends. It took every resource she had to keep her heart safe from lips that persuaded her to surrender it.

When Cale reached for her mouth again, Raven didn't—couldn't—deny him. She let him kiss her. And she kissed him back. She felt herself yielding. If it hadn't been for his beard, she might have been lost. It was just bristly enough to be uncomfortable. That discomfort brought a measure of reason to what had become a devastating sensual experience. Raven sighed and put both hands to her pinkened face.

"Your beard tickles," she said with a breathy, half-delighted, half-frightened laugh. She wrinkled her nose. "And it scratches."

Cale sat up and rubbed the coarse hair that covered his face. "Do you want me to shave it off?" Where had that offer come from? He hated shaving. Living in the mountains alone gave him the excuse to avoid it.

"Would you?" she asked. "I have wondered how you would look without your beard." Raven rose and put some distance between them. Cale read the signals she was sending and stayed where he was.

Raven took a deep breath and then another, and managed a crooked smile. "I think I will wait for another kiss until I see what you look like beneath that beard," she teased.

She began to gather up the remnants of their picnic. But before they went back she reached out to touch his arm. Her eyes were lowered demurely. Cale held his breath, waiting for her to speak.

"I like your kisses, Cale," she admitted in a soft voice. Then she turned and began walking back to the cabin.

Cale stared after her. He had been a little awed himself by the powerful feelings Raven had roused in him. He began to wonder whether it was fair to take what he wanted from her without giving anything in return.

He didn't shave right away. In fact, it took him a whole week to work up the courage. Even then, he went off alone to do the deed. When he returned, Raven stared at him as though he were a creature from the deep woods.

"Well?" he demanded. "What do you think?" He asked

the question with bravado, unwilling to admit her opinion mattered.

Raven quickly covered the distance between them and put her hands on either side of his clean-shaven cheeks. It was a gesture of reverence, of great gentleness and—the word *love* leapt to mind. Cale stood still beneath her caress, but the earth moved beneath his feet. The world shifted on its axis, and he saw things in a whole new way. An immense realm of possibilities appeared before him, and Raven was a part of it all. What if he kept her with him? What if they spent the rest of their lives together?

"You are beautiful," she said. "Not a beast at all," she added under her breath.

He ignored the second half of her statement and focused on the first. Even that wasn't exactly the sort of compliment he had hoped for. What man wants to be *beautiful?*

"Beautiful?" he complained.

"Yes, beautiful." She nodded for emphasis. Her deep brown eyes glowed with approval that warmed a cold, bottomless place inside him.

This time *she* curved her hand around *his* nape and drew him down for a kiss. He slanted his mouth across hers, which was already open to him. His tongue stroked inside to be greeted by hers. Passion rose swift and strong, and his arms closed around her and pulled her tight against him, so that his hardened shaft was pressed against her belly. He reached for her breast and felt the weight of it soft and heavy in his hand. His thumb skimmed the crest, and her nipple pebbled beneath his touch.

Raven pulled away from him abruptly, and he let her go. She was panting, and her eyes showed white around the edges. He suspected she must be remembering what had happened with Ribbon Jack. It wasn't what he had already done to her that she feared, he deduced, but what was to come.

He reached out a hand to touch her and saw the courage

it took for her to keep from flinching. He cupped her cheek in his callused hand, willing her to trust him. "I would never hurt you, Raven. Is this the first time. . . . Have you ever lain with a man?"

He was asking if Jack had raped her. He was asking if she had given herself to that other man—the one she had described in such glowing terms.

"You would be the first," she admitted in a soft, shy voice.

Cale felt the awesome weight of responsibility for assuaging her virgin fears, along with a heady joy. No other man had touched her. He would be the first to bring her to ecstasy, to put his seed inside her and claim her as his own.

But he would have to move carefully if he didn't want to frighten her. Raven was willing. He had seen the evidence of that. But she was also frightened. His seduction would have to be accomplished with gentleness and consideration. It was a new experience for Cale.

Not that he hadn't taken his time wooing Charlotte, but Charlotte had been years beyond Raven in experience before he even met her. And, he suddenly realized, he had never worried about Charlotte's feelings the way he worried about Raven's.

"Have I told you that I think you're beautiful, too?" he said to Raven.

A faint pink climbed her throat to her cheeks. "Do you think so?"

He bent his knees and tried looking into her eyes. She lowered her lids demurely. "I definitely think so."

Instead of laying her down under him, he made up a chore that took them out of the cabin. At the last moment, he had gotten cold feet. He was afraid that he wouldn't be able to still her fears. That she might turn to stone in his arms, or become hysterical and fight him, thinking he was Ribbon Jack. He didn't think he could endure that.

He backed off. As the days passed, he saw the confusion in her eyes, but he didn't know how to explain his fear to her. Men were the strong ones. They weren't supposed to be afraid. Cale became the most avuncular of friends. That was the solution, he had decided. If she truly trusted him as a friend, she wouldn't be afraid. But, as he held their relationship in abeyance, he was conscious that time was running out.

With his beard and mustache gone, it had quickly become apparent that his hair was too long. Finally, that morning, he chopped it off, too. His efforts were rewarded when he presented himself to Raven. Her wide smile and gurgle of pleased laughter wrenched his insides with a torrent of need. It was hard not to touch her. He searched her eyes, looking for something; he wasn't sure what. And he found it. Willingness. Trust. They were there in full measure. His hands began to tremble, and he turned from her to regain a measure of calm.

She warmed water for him to shave with and sat at his elbow, avidly observing him as he removed the dark beard that had grown overnight.

"Don't you ever get tired of watching me do this?" he asked her.

"No," she said. "It reminds me you are not a beast, that you are a man."

He frowned. "Was there ever any question of that?"

She grinned back at him. "You *were* awfully hairy when I first met you."

Cale punished her by grabbing her up in his arms and nuzzling her with his bristly cheek. She giggled with delight and fought him—not much and not long—until his mouth found hers, and her laughter turned into a moan of pleasure. Their tongues mated as his hands found her breasts. She arched herself into him as he thrust his body against hers, teasing them both, taunting them both, with hints of what their ultimate joining might be like.

She surprised him by pushing his long john shirt up out of the way and sliding her hands up his belly to his ribs. Her fingertips traced the bones that protected his heart, giving pleasure and seeking it in return. He paused to stare at her.

"Does it not please you?" she asked, her eyes wary.

"It pleases me very much," he assured her. "I was only surprised because ... well, because you've never done it before."

"But I have wanted to touch you," she said.

He saw from her lazy-lidded look that she was indeed enjoying herself. There was no fear in her eyes, no caution in what she was doing. So he had not been mistaken. He had earned her trust. The waiting was over at last. He felt such a burst of jubilation that it was all he could do not to shout aloud.

"Help yourself," he said with a lopsided grin. "Touch me all you want."

He hadn't dreamed, when he issued his invitation, that she would take him at his word. Or rather, he'd had no notion of what it was she really wanted to touch. Because before he could say Sam Jackrabbit, her hand slid down the front of him, across the bulge in his buckskins.

It felt so good he bit his lip to keep from groaning. She slid her hand back up and the groan slid out anyway. Was there anything that felt as good as a woman's hand on a man's body?

His fingers clutched her waist, where he forced them to remain as she investigated his body thoroughly. She must be damned curious, he thought, to need so much touching to figure the whole business out. His eyes drifted closed as he focused all his attention on the feel of her hands, measuring the length of him, moving lower, seeking out the sac that drew up tight as her fingers closed around it.

Then her hand was gone, and his eyes opened to find her staring curiously at him.

"Did I hurt you?" she asked.

"No," he managed to grate out. "Why would you think that?"

"The look on your face . . ." She reached up to smooth a brow he hadn't realized was furrowed. "And your mouth," she said, suiting deed to word and tracing his lips with her fingertip. "It looked as though your teeth were clenched."

Cale didn't doubt that. It took every ounce of control he had not to lay her flat and take her right then and there. "What you were doing felt good," he admitted grudgingly. "It's hard for a man if he can't finish what he's started."

"Oh," she said.

But she didn't offer to help him out. She just backed herself right up and said, "I need to go pick some wild onions."

She hurried out the door and didn't come back. He left the house shortly after her and didn't return for lunch.

He wasn't sure why she had fled. Maidenly shyness? Virginal fears? It had to be one or both, he thought. But neither were the reasons he had been keeping his distance. Those were fears he could handle. She had given him all the encouragement any man could need. He knew that when he returned to the cabin, she would be waiting for him.

It was late September. The aspens were turning gold and some had already lost their leaves. Their white trunks stood like beleaguered sentinels waiting for the first snowfall. The bull elk had begun to bugle their challenge, eager to fight for the right to mate with the females in their harem. The haunting, shrieking sound pierced the forest, heralding the onset of winter.

The first snowfall might come as soon as early October. Of course it would melt away; the snow usually didn't stay on the ground until late November. But Orrin had said he would come with the first snowfall. That could be a week from now, maybe two, but surely not longer than that. Cale knew he couldn't wait any longer. Raven might never be totally unafraid. He was willing to take the chance that she was ready to be loved by him.

Tonight he would make Raven his.

10

Raven knew she had been playing with fire this morning. It was the heat that drew her close. In the past she had kept enough distance not to get burned, but now she wanted more. And she was willing to risk the flames for the ecstasy that all her teasing, titillating experiences with Cale had promised her she would find if she leapt into the inferno.

She had marveled anew each day when she saw the striking planes, the bold cheekbones and strong chin that emerged when Cale scraped away the dark growth of beard that had grown overnight. It was a strong, hawklike face, and she had lost her heart for good the moment she first saw it clean shaven.

Once, Raven had named the things about Cale that made him a lovable man. It was a very short, but significant list. Strong and brave, he was a man whom a woman could be proud of. He was a good hunter, and there was always meat for the table. He was not cruel.

On the other hand, he was not always gentle. Before he shaved each morning he looked the beast she had once believed him to be. He was stubborn and impatient. He wanted his own way and argued to get it. He had loved only one woman, and it appeared he would never love another.

Yet, she had fallen in love with him, true and deep and forever. Not only because of who he was, but also because of how he made her feel. Beautiful and desirable and cherished. To Cale she was special, an irreplaceable person, unique and individual. It was something she had never experienced before.

With the Nez Perce, she had merely been a child among many, welcomed when she arrived and dismissed when she was taken away again. To her father, she was a cheap and ready source of labor, an irritant at times and valued only because she could serve him. With Cale, she had the sense that if she were gone, there was no one else who could please him, who could tease him and taunt him and kiss him, in exactly the same way.

Raven never felt so much a person of worth as when she was with Cale. It was a feeling she liked, which she was loath to lose. Above all things, she wanted to mate with him. She knew he wanted her. She also knew that time was short for both of them.

This morning she had known for sure that making love to Cale would be worth the pain that would come when he broached her. She had overcome the terror of lying under a man who had the power to brutalize her. She supposed that meant she had learned to trust Cale. Because, although her fear was real, it was manageable. And Raven wanted a memory to take with her when she returned to her father.

Soon, the day would come when she would not see Cale again unless they happened to cross paths at a rendezvous. The comfortable home she had arranged for them in the cabin would be a memory. The children laughing and playing around them would remain a cherished dream.

Her chest ached when she thought of a lifetime without Cale. But her father would never willingly give her up, and she feared that, while Cale had welcomed her company for this brief time, he would be equally glad to return to the solitude he had treasured for the past ten years.

She glanced out the window and saw the first snow-flakes falling. They were tiny and delicate, and she stuck her hand out through the open window to let them drift onto her skin. It was time to tack up the oiled animal skin that covered the window in bad weather, to shut out the snow, and with it, the light. The house would become dreary once more. When she left, she supposed Cale would revert to his old habits, and the cabin would smell of beaver and muskrat and man.

Raven felt a thickness in her throat that made it difficult to swallow. She forced her thoughts away from the future. There was still today. And tonight.

Raven wasn't sure how she knew that Cale planned to come to her tonight. From the looks that had passed be-tween them before she had fled, by the kisses and touches, she knew the time had come. It would have happened this morning if she had not run away. Wild onions, indeed! She had picked enough to put in *ten* stews.

When she had returned to the house, Cale had been gone. Now it was nearly dusk. If he didn't return soon, he was going to get caught in the season's first snowstorm.

Raven busied herself tacking the oiled skin over the window. When she was done, she lit a lantern, even though it was still daylight, to keep the shadows at bay. She set the leftovers from the midday meal back on the stove. Cale would be hungry when he got back.

And cold.

Raven built up the fire until it was roaring. She stoked the potbellied stove so it radiated heat. With the window covered, it was almost toasty inside. She could no longer see her breath in the air.

He entered the house in a flurry of wind and snow-flakes, slamming the door shut and latching it behind him.

"It's colder than blue blazes out there."

"Give me your coat," Raven said.

Cale slipped the bearskin off his shoulders, and Raven hung it on a peg by the door.

Cale shook his head like a dog, flinging snowflakes off his hair and eyebrows. Some had already melted in the heat, and his face was covered with droplets of water. Raven grabbed a cloth and began dabbing him dry.

He stood silent under her ministrations, and it wasn't until she had no more excuse to touch his face that she realized his eyes, watching her, were avid with desire.

Raven didn't want to wait for supper or nightfall and maybe lose her courage.

"Cale," she said, tracing his eyebrow with her fingers. "Cale," she repeated as her fingertip found the slight bow in the center of his upper lip. His tongue dipped out and caught her unawares. She drew back with a startled laugh.

There was no humor in his eyes. Only a fierce, white-hot need that burned in the darkness.

"Raven," he said in a grating voice. "I . . ."

"Yes," she said. Only that one word.

But it was enough.

He caught her up in a crushing hug and found her mouth with his. His tongue thrust possessively, staking his claim. His hands roamed her back and one slid up to capture her head and keep her still for his kisses.

Raven moaned, a soughing sound deep in her throat as her body drew up tight. She returned Cale's kisses, parrying his thrusting tongue with her own, until she was gasping for breath and her whole body quivered with desire.

"I want you," he rasped. "I want to feel your skin. I want to touch you."

"Yes, Cale. Yes, please."

Then he was stripping her bare, and she was glad of the roaring fire that made it possible to stand before him naked and not be covered with goose flesh.

His eyes were heavy-lidded, his gaze fierce and posses-
sive as he ravished her body without laying a hand on her.

Raven felt her nipples peak, and her heart pounded as
Cale ignited a fire in her blood with his eyes.

"I want to see you, too." She took the two steps that put
her within arm's reach and began to undress him. He
didn't give her a chance to finish, quickly stripping himself until he stood naked before her. He was an intimidating sight, muscle and sinew and bone. And he was
aroused, his shaft standing amid a nest of dark curls. She
reached out to close her hand around him. He was warm
and soft and hard all at the same time.

Cale gave a ragged sigh and slipped his hand between
her legs to cup her dark curls in an equally intimate way.
She gasped when he slid a finger inside her. Raven was
astonished at how easily he had done it and how good it
felt. She looked up and found his features taut with pleasure, his smile a little crooked, his eyes focused on her
face.

"I want to say don't let go," he said as his smile broad-
ened, "but I think if you don't, this is all going to be over
before it's started."

He removed his hand from its intimate resting place and
reached to free himself from her grasp. Raven released
him with reluctance.

Cale lifted her into his arms and headed for the bed. "I
think we'll be more comfortable here." He lay down beside her and stared at her without touching.

She felt shy under his perusal and would have covered
herself except that his hand reached out to stop her.

"You're beautiful," he said. "Your nipples are such a
rosy brown, and your skin is so smooth and pleasing to the
touch." His hand stroked her body, his callused fingers
rough against her silky skin. Her body quivered as he ex-
plored the underside of her breast, the shape of her ribs,

the hollow of her belly, the backs of her knees. He left no spot untouched.

She took advantage of the opportunity he had given her to return the favor, feeling the washboard hardness of his belly and playing with the coarse curls on his chest. She was amazed to discover that his nipples peaked when she accidentally brushed them. She indulged herself by testing the texture of his skin with her lips. She tasted the faint salty sweat and smelled the musky man-scent that was his alone.

"Raven, sweetheart," he murmured. "You're killing me."

She looked up and realized he wasn't anywhere near dead. "I want to touch," she said.

"Turn about's fair play."

She found herself flattened beneath him, with his hips caught in the cradle of her thighs, and then he slid down far enough to cup her breast with his hand and to close his mouth over the nipple.

He sucked.

She groaned and writhed.

Cale made a sound deep in his throat as Raven arched high and hard against his shaft. He shoved her knees apart with his legs and thrust quickly and surely, knowing where he wanted to be. Only he hadn't ever had a virgin before, and when he would have pressed home, he found the way blocked.

Raven cried out. "Cale! You're hurting me!"

Cale withdrew and rolled onto his back beside her. He covered his eyes with his arm and willed his body to stop its throbbing. He was panting, and took several deep breaths to catch up with his need for air.

Raven lay staring at the chinked log ceiling. She should have kept her mouth shut. She should have borne the pain in silence. Now look what had happened.

She glanced over and saw that Cale was no longer

aroused, and when he caught her staring at him, he grunted and turned onto his side away from her.

"I'm sorry," he muttered.

"It is I who am sorry," she said in a quavery voice. "I . . . I did not know it would hurt so much."

"I didn't think it would either," he admitted with a shaky sigh.

"Do you want to try again?" she asked.

He rolled onto his back and then onto his side, facing her. "Do you?"

She nodded.

He sat up and pulled her into his lap. "We'll go slower this time," he promised. "I'll try to be gentle." He swallowed hard. "There will still be some pain. There's a barrier . . . I'll have to break through it."

She swallowed back the acid bile of fear. "It will be all right," she assured him, because she could see he needed the reassurance before he would touch her again.

"I . . ." He had been about to say *love,* Cale realized with astonishment. It wasn't love he was feeling right now; it was gratitude for her sacrifice. He knew it was going to hurt her, yet he wanted pleasure to be part of their joining. So he was going to couple with her as gently as he could. To become a woman, she had to be broached. And better him, who cared for her pain, than some other man.

"All right," he said. "We'll try again."

Only this time Cale could feel there was none of the compliance in her body that had been there earlier. She was stiff and dry, and his task was a hundred times more difficult.

"You have to relax, Raven," he murmured.

"I am trying!"

He was tempted to give up then and there, but he knew it wasn't going to get any easier. So he took his hands off her and put them on the pillow on either side of her head and settled himself in the cradle of her thighs. Then, with his mouth alone, he began to woo her with kisses. Small, sweet kisses on her eyebrows and cheeks. He traced the shell of her ear with his tongue and was satisfied to feel her shiver.

He kissed one side of her mouth and then the other and finally teased her lips open with his tongue. Then he began to mime the sex act with long, slow thrusts. He felt her body melting beneath his as the stiffness left her. Her hands found their way into the hair at his nape, and he felt his own passion rising.

Cale forced himself to tether his need, to hold his desire in abeyance while he concentrated on Raven. His hands formed fists as he forced himself to go slowly. His mouth moved from her throat to her collarbone and inched down to her breast, where he once again suckled a rosy nipple.

Her hands clutched at his shoulders, and her body began to undulate beneath him. He figured it was okay now to touch her with his hands. He started at her waist, with just a little pressure on either side, but one hand found its way up to cup a breast and shape it for his mouth, while the other forayed across her belly and down to tease the nest of curls between her legs.

He felt her tense and moved his hand away again, down to her soft inner thigh where the flesh was silky and warm against his callused fingertips.

He teased his way back up again until he found the tiny nubbin that he knew could bring her ecstasy. He was careful, soft and gentle as he had never been with another woman. Because he knew she was afraid. Because he wanted her to feel pleasure, not pain. Because he wanted her ready so she would never feel the thrust that finally made her his.

His mouth returned to hers and, as his fingers probed her, he could feel that she was slick and wet and ready.

But he wanted her distracted. His hands sought out her breasts, and he caressed them and caught the nipples between his fingers with just enough pressure to cause a ripple of both pleasure and pain.

He took that moment to push himself a little way inside her.

He felt her stiffen and try to break their kiss, but he sucked hard on her lip and then slid his tongue along the underside of her upper lip until she gasped with delight and resumed the kiss.

With her hands clutched at his shoulders, her nails digging painful crescents in his skin, he thrust with all his might.

It was over quickly. He was through the barrier and sated to the hilt. He caught her cry of surprise and pain with his mouth, and held himself still, taut with need, until her body acclimated itself to his. He felt the slow easing of tension in her belly and thighs. He released her mouth to croon soothing words to ease her over the shock of his intrusion.

"Are you all right?" he asked at last.

"I feel . . . strange," she admitted.

"Does it hurt?"

She furrowed her brow as though she were considering the matter. "Not exactly. I feel . . . full."

It also felt right, Raven admitted to herself. It had hurt. She couldn't deny that. But the greatest pain was over now, and she instinctively knew that it was a passing thing, never to be endured again. Which gave her the courage to say, "Are you done now?"

Cale smiled. Then he laughed. "No, sweetheart. I'm not done." He sobered. "But if you want me to stop now, I will."

Raven had some idea of the sacrifice Cale would be making if he quit what he was doing. His body was rock hard, his muscles tense, his body poised for action. She was glad he had asked, but she wasn't about to stop now.

"I want to experience everything," she said.

"Everything?" he asked with a wolfish grin.

She smiled back. "Everything."

He moved slowly inside her. It was as exquisite as it was exciting. Raven sought out Cale's mouth and kissed him with all the feeling she had for him. He returned the pleasure.

As he moved inside her, as his fingertips caressed that special spot between her legs, Raven responded with increasing ardor. It was as though her body knew what it wanted and sought it out. Her breasts arched to his hands and mouth, and her hips drove upward to meet his thrusts.

She could feel the urge to do . . . something . . . to find . . . something, but she wasn't sure what it was.

Cale knew where he was going and wanted Raven there with him. He wanted her to feel everything he felt, the rising excitement, the need for release. So he teased her and taunted her and aroused her for far longer than he had ever done with another woman.

He was rewarded in his moment of extremity by feeling her convulse around him. It was something he had never felt before with a woman, something so powerful, so overwhelming, that he cried out with the tormenting pleasure of it.

Raven was caught in the throes of an ecstasy so profound it sucked the breath from her. She gasped for air as the blood pounded in her temples and her body squeezed and tightened around Cale, capturing him as he planted his seed in her. Then she was floating, her body not quite earthbound, and she realized she did not want to return to firm ground.

Cale rolled over and pulled her into his embrace, keeping her snug against him. Their sweat-slick bodies were chilling quickly, and he pulled the quilt up to cover them both. Before she could find the words to tell him about the powerful feelings she had experienced, he was asleep.

Raven didn't worry. There would be time enough when they woke to talk about what had happened between them. She looked forward to the exhilarating experience of making love to Cale again. She would turn to him and he would kiss her and it would happen. Only next time there would be no pain.

She snuggled under his arm and closed her eyes, confident for the moment of what the future held for them.

Sometime later, a sharp knock on the door woke them both. It was shoved open before they had time to do more than sit up in bed.

"Well, well," Orrin said. "What have we here? Two lovebirds, I see. Time's up, Cale. I want my daughter back."

11

Cale rose from the bed like a menacing beast, heedless of his nakedness. "What the hell are you doing here?"

"First snowfall," Orrin said, whipping his hat against his thigh and brushing flakes from his hair. "I came to get my daughter. Seems like you two got along just fine." Orrin crossed to the stove and took a tin cup from a peg and helped himself to some coffee.

Cale dragged his long johns on over his feet, then added his buckskin trousers. He figured that made him decent enough for company.

The whole time he was thinking *It's too soon. I'm not ready to let her go.* Could he live the rest of his life without her? Could he go back to being alone?

No.

He heard his next words as though they were being spoken by someone else. "I've decided to keep Raven. I'll pay for her. Name your price."

He ignored the gasp from the bed. Raven would be happier with him than with her father, he told himself. He would make sure she was. Only, how could he expect Orrin to set a price on her? There weren't enough furs in the territory to pay what she was worth.

"Whoa, there, son. Hold your horses. Who said I'd be willing to sell her?" Orrin demanded. "She's my flesh and blood. To tell the honest truth, the thought of selling her never crossed my mind."

Cale was stunned when he realized the gist of what Orrin had said, of what he himself had said. *Buying Raven? Selling Raven?* If anyone else had suggested such a thing, he would have flattened them. But it was different for him. He loved her. Furthermore, he was determined to have her, and that meant offering whatever it took to get Orrin to release her.

"I'll give you my catch for the next six months. Hell," he said, shoving a hand through his hair, "that isn't near enough, is it? I know she's worth far more." Cale bit his lip. You didn't tell a man how much you were willing to pay when you were trying to bargain with him. Only it didn't seem right, suddenly, bargaining for Raven. How could he possibly measure her worth in monetary terms? Except, he didn't know how else to free her from her father.

Orrin's eyes narrowed speculatively. He slipped into a chair at the table. "Well now, son, I'll tell you, I didn't realize till Raven was gone just how much I need her to help me out. It was like losing my right arm to be without her."

Cale settled down across the table from Orrin to dicker in earnest. "I know you can't set a value on her in worldly goods. But I'd be willing to give you all of next year's catch to keep her with me."

"Now, son, I'm sorely tempted to take you up on that," Orrin said. "But a year's catch?" He made a *tsk*ing sound. "I'm afraid that wouldn't last me very long."

"I've got gold buried under this floor. Enough for you to hire someone to help you out. It wouldn't be the same as having Raven. Hell, I know that! She's worth more than all the furs and gold I've got or ever hope to have." Cale heard the desperation in his voice. "You have to take the money. You have to set her free."

I need her. I can't live without her.

Orrin shook his head. "I'd only gamble the gold away," he said. "I think I'll keep the girl. Come on, Raven. Get your things together. It's time to go."

Once upon a time Raven would have obeyed her father. She would have gone with him and never thought twice about it. But she had been listening to Cale, and his words were music to her ears.

You can't set a value on her in worldly goods.

She's worth more than all the furs or gold I've got.

Because of Cale she had allowed herself to dream. He had held her and cherished her as someone worthy of his respect and love. She had begun to see herself as a person with needs and desires she was entitled to fulfill.

"I think the choice of whether I go or stay should be up to me," she said.

Orrin gawked at her as though she had grown a second head.

"What did you say?" Cale asked. It had never occurred to him that Raven might want to leave him. Or that she might stay if he simply asked her to.

"It should be up to me what I do," Raven repeated.

Sometime during his conversation with Orrin, Raven had gotten dressed. She had never looked more lovely to Cale. Her cheeks were still flushed from sleep, her hair tousled from lovemaking. She stood with her shoulders back, her chin held high in that regal way that made him think he ought to bow to her. He was willing to do that, just as soon as they were alone, and press his head to her breast and wrap his arms around her waist and love her as she had never been loved before.

That is, if she gave him the chance. That is, if she didn't leave with her father. He understood now that she was entitled to that choice. He could never force her to stay against her will. If she wanted to go, he couldn't—wouldn't—stop her. He had meant what he said to her father. There was no price he would not pay to keep Raven with him. Except, how did you measure the worth of the woman you loved? He would do anything to ensure her happiness. Even if it meant helping her to leave him.

Of course, he wanted her to stay. But he hadn't asked a woman for anything in ten years. And he wasn't sure he could now. Pride was a terrible, awful burden for a man.

"The decision is yours," he said in a voice that sounded like a rusty gate. "I'll support whatever you choose. If you'd rather go back to your people than stay with your father, I'll make sure he lets you go."

"Now look here, son—"

"Shut up, Orrin," Cale said.

Raven felt an awful, sinking feeling of defeat. Cale hadn't bothered asking whether she wanted to stay. He had simply assumed she would want to go. She stared at Cale with her heart in her eyes, willing him to speak, willing him to ask her to stay. She even considered telling him that she loved him. But it would be foolish to admit she loved Cale before he had voiced his love for her. He was never going to love another woman. Perhaps it was better this way.

She turned her back on the two men. "I will go back to the Nez Perce. It is where I belong."

Orrin snorted in disgust.

Cale heaved a long, heavy sigh. Raven had made her decision. He would have to abide by it and make sure that Orrin did, too. He would have to let her go.

The hell he would.

Cale was across the room in two strides. He grabbed Raven by the arm and whirled her around to face him. He caught her shoulders in a deathgrip and fixed her with a fierce look from dark, angry eyes.

The price of having her was higher than he had ever dreamed. But he realized, suddenly, it was one he was happy to pay. There was one thing he hadn't offered her, one last inducement to convince her to stay. He could offer himself. He could offer love.

"Don't go, Raven. I love you. I need you, and I want you to be my wife."

Raven stared at his beloved face, taut with worry. His eyes were anxious as he waited intently for her answer. Her heart was in her throat, making it hard to speak.

"You want to be my husband?" she asked. "To live here in this cabin and have children together?" It was her dream come true, and she held her breath, waiting for his answer.

"Yes. Yes, Raven. You'll sit in the rocker with a child at your breast and I'll make another rocker and sit beside you. We'll rock together until we're old and gray. Will you marry me, Raven?"

"This is very interesting," Orrin said.

"Shut up, Orrin," Cale repeated. His hands were trembling and he balled them into fists. "Well, Raven? The decision is up to you."

She smiled. "Oh, yes, Cale, I will marry you. I lo—"

"Now, hold on a minute," Orrin interrupted.

"Shut up, Orrin." Cale's eyes softened, his hands relaxed and his lips curved into an answering smile. "Now, what were you about to say, Raven?"

"I love you, Cale," she said. "I have for a very long time."

He kissed her, passionately and possessively. She was his woman, a pearl beyond price. Cale intended to make sure she never doubted it in all the years of their lives.

"This might not turn out so bad after all," Orrin finally said, a greedy, speculative gleam in his eyes. He rose and headed for the door. "Two's company, three's a crowd," he added with a wink at Cale. "I'll just be taking myself off."

"You do that." Cale kept Raven tucked beneath his arm, her hip pressed tightly against his.

"See you in the spring," Orrin said as he let himself out into the snow. "I'll be back then to hold my first grandchild."

Cale just growled at the old man.

"You will be welcome, Father," Raven replied.

Cale shoved the door closed and turned to lift Raven into his arms. He stalked toward the bed, a feral animal in possession of its quarry. There was no doubt in Raven's mind that Cale would take what he wanted from her, that he would mate with her and claim her as his own.

She smiled. He was the beast again, wild and dangerous. As he laid her on the bed with gentle care, her heart swelled with love for him. She sought his eyes and found them filled with a savage need that was barely leashed. She slid her hand into the shaggy hair at his nape and pulled his mouth down to meet hers in a kiss that was all the more powerful for its tenderness.

"I love you, Cale," she murmured against his lips.

"I love you, Raven," he snarled in reply.

Raven moaned as his lips found hers and claimed them.

The beast had found his beauty, and all was well.

Joan Johnston

I'm currently indulging a lifelong dream by living high on a mountain near the Grand Tetons in Wyoming in a wood and stone house surrounded by a forest of hundred-year-old Douglas fir, very much like the characters in my story. Several beaver traps actually used by mountain men like Cale are displayed in a museum in Moose, a hop and a skip from me. I live three miles from the base of the Teton Pass, over which Cale and Raven travel after leaving the rendezvous at Pierre's Hole.

My time in the mountains has taught me the wilderness can be as frightening as it is exhilarating. My son was recently prevented from getting to the school bus stop by a moose and her calf blocking the road. The snow gets twelve feet deep here, and we frequently have to dig our way out. Luckily, I can spend my time in front of the fireplace writing, or in my office watching the gentle drift of snow.

I can count the number of weddings I've attended on one hand, my own being one of them, but I would never miss one to which I was invited. There is something special that occurs in the moment when a man and woman pledge their lives to each other. They are each secure in the other's love, and they hold out great hope for a future

filled with happiness. That is a moment we should all celebrate. I hope you enjoyed living that moment with Cale
and Raven.

The Ninth
Miss Noddenly

Kasey Michaels

1

Jonathan Wetherell, the fourteenth earl of Mayfield, was not a happy man.

He was rich, almost sinfully so, and always had been; so that wasn't his problem.

He was handsome, most definitely sinfully so, and although he never gave much thought to his extreme good looks, certainly his physical attractiveness could not be blamed for his unhappiness.

He had scores of friends both male and of the gentler persuasion, enjoyed equally London life and his time spent on his various estates, had set up a stable of admirable quality, was well respected for his ability in whatever sport he graced with his participation, and had delighted in his carefree childhood that had left him with fond memories of his deceased parents.

His mind was sound, as was his body, none of his molars pained him, he could not so much as claim a slight case of the sniffles in a dozen years; and his boots fit admirably well as he strolled down Bond Street on this late May day.

In short, there was no earthly reason why the earl of

Mayfield should feel as if he had acquired his own personal thundercloud, one which hung just over his head night and day, robbing him of his usual good humor and making him wish, generally, that he had stayed in bed rather than take on another day in London society.

No earthly reason indeed, unless one considered the fact that Jonathan Wetherell, fourteenth earl, etc., etc., was for the first time in his three and thirty years, deeply, madly, and—or so it appeared—*hopelessly* in love.

"Jonathan? I say—*Jonathan!*"

Mayfield became aware that someone was calling his name and stopped, frowning, for he did not wish to speak with anyone at the moment, or in any time soon. He was busy, damn it all anyway, busy feeling sorry for himself, and the last thing he needed was for one of his friends to greet him, say something funny, and ruin his self-pity.

"God's teeth, Johnny, I've been calling after you for nearly a block. Out of breath, now, you know, for I detest running. Sets up a cursed burning in m'lungs, which can't be good, can it? What's the matter? Someone dear to you die? You look ready to cry."

Sir Pitney Fox. Mayfield paused before turning around, caught between the knowledge that the last thing Lord Fox could ever be accused of was trying to cheer someone else's spirits and the realization that it was just that same thought that was even now bringing a smile, unbidden, to his lips.

"Pitney, old man," he said as he turned, holding out his hand, half-afraid Lord Fox would otherwise throw himself into his arms, panting for air. "How grand to see you up and about. I could have sworn I'd heard you were at death's door. Or was that last week?"

Lord Fox, a short-ish, thin-ish, blond-ish, bland-ish man—the most thoroughly "ish" person in all of England, in point of fact—had the further distinction of being known far and wide as the sick-*ish* creature in creation.

Always ailing, constantly doctoring, perpetually complaining of his ill health, Fox had the pale color of the invalid, the deep pockets of an only, orphaned son, the personality of a turnip, and the appetite of a full regiment of fighting men.

If Lord Fox did not soon drop dead of one of his many imagined ailments, he would most probably be the cause of several suicides within his beleaguered staff and more than a few deaths by terminal boredom of his unfortunate partners at the dinner table.

Lord Fox waved off what was surely his dear friend's concern for his welfare, innately incapable of recognizing a joke at his own expense. "Never fear for me, Jonathan," he pleaded, releasing Lord Mayfield's hand and quickly wiping his fingers with a clean handkerchief—to ward off contamination, you see. "I am once more stout as a barrel, if it weren't for this small, distressing rash I have discovered on my—"

"Please, Pitney, spare me the details," Mayfield broke in hurriedly, no longer amused by Lord Fox's usually distracting presence. "I am laboring under some small indisposition myself at the moment and would rather, quite frankly, be alone."

Lord Fox prudently backed up a pace and raised the handkerchief to cover his nose and mouth. "Oh, do say you aren't contagious, Johnny," he pleaded earnestly from behind the crisp white linen, once more calling Lord Mayfield by that most loathed pet name from their days at Eton.

"I can't be sure, Pitney," Lord Mayfield replied, one side of his mouth lifting in a self-deprecating smile as Lord Fox only slowly returned his handkerchief to his pocket. "Is love catching?"

The moment he had spoken Lord Mayfield wished the words back. Clearly he was heading for a sad decline, to be so overset that he would stoop to speaking personally with Lord Fox, who was, although an acquaintance of many years, never to be considered one of his lordship's set.

"Love, is it? You, Johnny?" Lord Fox all but chortled. "Oh, don't tease me so, else I'll have palpitations. You'll never fall to Cupid's dart—not you, Johnny. Why, I have it on good authority that our friend Wiley is in the book for a monkey, saying you'll never wed."

The fact that Sir Wiley Hambleton was, first-off, not a bosom chum of either Lord Mayfield or Lord Fox and was, secondly, an unreformed rake well past the age where rakes could be considered either romantic or dangerous, rankled Lord Mayfield more than he would wish Lord Fox to know.

"I hadn't known Wiley to be so absorbed in the happenings of my life," Lord Mayfield said, stepping back, tipping his hat, and bowing politely as Lady Hertford and her maid passed along the flagway.

"Wiley?" Lord Fox inquired, his expression revealing his disbelief that Lord Mayfield could put forth the notion that Sir Wiley Hambleton was not interested in everything to do with such a respected member of the *ton.* Indeed, the man dined out on his vast store of gossip, where his checkered youth and spotted middle age in places otherwise could have caused his name to be dismissed from the invitation list, especially if there was a marriageable daughter in the house. "Oh, on the contrary, Johnny. The subject of marriage is very much on Wiley's mind these days, yours or anyone else's, I suppose. Haven't you heard?"

Lord Mayfield was fast regretting having not lost his hearing due to his exposure to cannon fire on the battlefields with Wellington. Would this fool never shut his mouth and let him be on his way? "No, Pitney," he answered, sighing. "I haven't heard. Or have I? I suppose there is nothing else to do but for you to tell me what *you've* heard, and then I shall know for certain."

Lord Fox was clearly enraptured with the notion that he knew something Lord Mayfield did not. "Wiley has to marry, of course," he whispered confidentially, his watery blue eyes dancing. "His great-aunt, Miss Earlene Hambleton, has decreed it, else she will leave her fortune to some worthy society for rehabilitating whores. Or was that schoolboys?" He gave a dismissing wave of his thin, long-fingered hands. "Either way, Johnny, Wiley will be all rolled up if he doesn't find a young lady of good family to bracket his ramshackle self to within the year."

And that is when the sun came out. Oh, it had risen above the horizon hours earlier, but this was the first Jonathan Wetherell, fourteenth earl of Mayfield, had noticed its golden glory. "Wiley *must* wed?" he asked, his heart pounding so that Pitney, had his own heart beat half so fast, would have sat straight down on the curbing, sure his time on this mortal coil had run out and he was about to be called to his fathers.

"Then you don't know after all," Lord Fox proclaimed, happy to be the bearer of such delicious news. "I would have thought the only person in all of Mayfield still without that knowledge would be Knox—whom everyone knows does not know anything of any importance. Poor Knox. The man has so little conversation, don't you agree, even if he talks *incessantly,* prosing on and on and on about the minutiae of life until, I swear, a man could— Johnny, why are you looking at me so strangely? Oh, dear, that's right. You've told me you're in love. Such a coup. I shall be like Wiley, and dine out on this story for a sennight—if only you will tell me the details, Johnny, the details. But hurry, do, for I have an appointment with a new doctor here in Bond Street at two, and would not like to be above ten minutes late. He's just down from Edinburgh, and said to be ever so clever. I think I will show him my rash. Yes, I do think the rash would be an excellent place to begin."

Lord Mayfield was beginning to feel a crushing head-ache squeezing at his temples. Lord Fox seemed to be in the process of doing a creditably stultifying imitation of Knox Bromley, the man Lord Fox had mentioned in pass-ing, the man who could occupy himself and bore his audi-ence for a quarter hour just in saying hello.

"Would you and Knox and Wiley care to join me in the country next week for a small house party, Pitney?" he asked quickly as Lord Fox stopped to take a breath. "I will tell you then about my descent into love's clutches, and we will have a bruising time, I promise. Damn it all, you may even bring your Edinburgh quack if you so desire. I am feeling particularly congenial, Pitney, but do hurry and an-swer, before my better self reminds me how very little I like any of you."

Lord Fox was momentarily speechless, clutching at his chest in amazement—and to assure himself his heart still beat in its dreadfully calm way, just as if he wasn't daily at death's door. "You—Wiley—*Knox?* Why, Johnny, I never thought . . . I never imagined . . . but of *course,* we shall all be delighted! Next week, you say? At Mayfield? I have never been, you know. You've never invited me. *Must* I bring Knox and Wiley?"

Lord Mayfield smiled blightingly. "They are your ticket of entrance, dear Pitney," he said bracingly. "Can you achieve this small feat, as I don't in the normal course of events see either of them? It might help if you told Wiley that I shall have an array of eligible young misses there for his delectation. As for Knox, just tell him I wish to hear his opinion on Prinny's Pavilion in Bath. That should give him conversation enough to keep his jaw well oiled for the fortnight I plan."

Lord Fox was all a-quiver, his unfortunately long nose twitching as he apparently took up the scent of intrigue. "You've got something a-foot, don't you, Johnny? Some-thing to do with this tumble into love you've taken? Oh, yes. I sense a fine tale here somewhere, some deep machinations. Dare I ask?"

"No," Lord Mayfield said cheerfully. "You may not. Only know that you shall be well entertained. Now, Pitney, if you don't mind, I do believe I must be off." He looked Lord Fox's ill-fitting ensemble up and down, ending, "I suddenly feel like a long visit with my tailor. You don't as a rule deal with Weston, do you?"

"Weston? At his outrageous prices? Indeed, no. I have discovered a tailor just off Piccadilly, who makes up my clothes from designs I draw him myself."

"How you comfort me, Pitney." He gave the man a slight bow. "You will, naturally, seek your own transportation to Mayfield. Arrive on Monday morning, if you please, prepared for a fortnight's stay. Toodle-oo, Pitney, old friend, and thank you. You have truly made my day."

Lord Fox waggled his fingers at Lord Mayfield's departing back, not knowing if he should be delighted at his lordship's invitation or frightened by the intense, assessing look the man had given him before he took off down the flagway, a definite lilt in his step.

But then, as the hour of two was fast approaching, and his rash was now plaguing him in a place where polite gentlemen did not, in public, scratch, he pushed any misgivings from his mind and went off to visit his new doctor, who would most certainly tell him if country air would do his pesky nasal drip any good.

Miss Virginia Noddenly sat on the window seat in her small bedchamber, the one overlooking the mews, and wondered how fate could be so cruel.

Aged eight and ten, with fiery red hair and skin so fair it had been compared to finest marble, Miss Noddenly was still charmingly unaware of her beauty, which also included wide, green eyes as calm and serene as the sea at dawn, a small, pert nose, a delightful heart-shaped face, and a petite, trim figure many debutantes would willingly sacrifice their doting mamas to possess.

For all the good any of this beauty and perfection of form would do her. Poor Miss Virginia Noddenly. Poor, *poor* Miss Noddenly.

Yet, perhaps this maidenly lack of insight into her physical charms was a good thing, for if she were to dwell on the physical, if she were to consider the delights that bodily perfection could gain her, the children she might bear, the life she might have at her loved one's side, she might just break down and weep.

For Miss Virginia Noddenly was destined to be an old maid.

The ninth Miss Noddenly. That's what she had heard herself called by some vicious cats in one of the withdrawing rooms the single night her papa had allowed her to mingle with society.

The ninth, the last, the most unfortunately positioned Miss Noddenly, daughter of Sir Roderick Noddenly, the most stubborn, pigheaded, although adorable man this side of Perdition.

"My girls will marry in the order of their birth," Sir Roderick had decreed many years ago, and almost daily since then.

"First Faith, then Hope, then Charity—good names all, but then I had never bargained on more than three—then Lucille, then Marianne, then Lettice Ann, then Myrtle— named after my sainted grandmother, who always said if I had enough girls I'd finally come through and honor her— then Georgette—after my grandfather, as fair's fair—and, lastly, my sweet Virginia. I've said it, and that is how it shall be. I shall brook no opposition!"

Faith had wed first, as ordered, and now had five little ones, all of them thankfully living in Lancashire, far away from the family home in Sussex.

Hope was wife to the local doctor, Charity had snagged

herself an earl, and Lucille was the proud wife of a dean at Cambridge.

Marianne had wed a sea captain and now lived in far off Boston, rarely writing her dear papa, who had made her wait until Lucille and her "twit of a schoolteacher" had put the cart before the horse and Lucille was at last marched down the aisle, one bun already in the oven.

All these marriages had left Sir Roderick woefully short of funds for Lettice Ann's dowry, so that her entrance into society had been delayed for more than three years, leaving the incongruously named Lettice Ann and her always slight but now rapidly cooling beauty free to pursue the Noddenly gardener, who did not return her affections.

It wasn't as if this delayed entrance to the "marriage mart" had bothered Myrtle, who was in no hurry to be put on the block, having long ago, and as repeatedly as her father, put forth the declaration that she'd much rather remain unfettered, the better to devote her time and affection to her horseflesh (which, sadly, she much resembled).

This left Georgette, a most charming but die-away miss of twenty, a young lady never more content as when she was ailing, having learned in her youth that one sure way of gaining herself attention amidst this gaggle of females was to cough, or sneeze, or groan wearily, or even sigh as if this long, sad breath might be her last.

Georgette would very much like to be married—and secretly envied her sister Hope's success at snagging herself a doctor, although she would, of course, marry a decidedly *superior* physician, one who didn't rudely tell her to get herself up and out in the fresh air and stop behaving like some die-away goose when she was as sound and strong as any of Myrtle's mares.

Three unmarried sisters. Three spinster sisters who must somehow be led or pushed or threatened to the altar before the last sister, Virginia, would be allowed to wed.

Virginia sighed, not as deeply as Georgette, but with

much more credulity, and wondered if the year's worth of pin money she had saved would be enough to bribe the Noddenly gardener into eloping with Lettice Ann.

Not that such a bold action would solve all Virginia's problems, for next to be popped off would then be Myrtle. Marrying off *that* Noddenly sister would be akin to waving her hand and parting the English Channel so that all of England could stroll barefoot to Calais.

Perhaps Virginia should consider introducing her sister to a jockey? Myrtle might tower over the man, but at least they'd have something in common.

Leaving Georgette-Vinaigrette, as Virginia privately called her next oldest sibling, who was often to be seen waving a bottle containing that vile-smelling restorative as a precaution against her frequent fits of lightheadedness.

Who would ever wed that tiresome whiner? Would it pay Virginia to place an advertisement in the London papers requesting an unexceptional gentleman who longed to be a supporting prop to an invalid in exchange for a life of unremitting complaint?

Or would it be easier to apply for such a man at Bethlehem Hospital, for only a certifiable lunatic would ever wish for such a fate.

Fate. Yes, that was what Virginia was thinking about this fine afternoon.

Fate, that had chosen for her to be the ninth, the last, Miss Noddenly.

Fate, that had brought her to London with her older sisters now that her mother was deceased and Sir Roderick could see no reason to leave anyone behind in Sussex when it would be considerably more economically prudent to keep all his servants under one roof.

Fate, that had allowed her that single night in Society when Georgette had complained of an earache and decided to remain home, a roasted onion stuck in the offending ear.

Fate, that had put one marvelously handsome Jonathan

Wetherell, fourteenth Earl of Mayfield in her path, love in her path, only to snatch it away again with the knowledge that their love could never be.

Ah, but how absolutely wonderful those first few weeks had been.

The stolen moments in a quiet corner at Hatchard's Book Depository.

The sweet whispers in the dark when he had come to stand beneath this very window.

The single kiss they had shared in Hyde Park, when Myrtle had been too busy admiring the Prince Regent's carriage horses to notice that her younger sister had sneaked off into the trees.

The vows of undying love told to her by Jonathan Wetherell, the most perfect, most wonderful, most *confused* gentlemen in the history of the world.

Jonathan hadn't wished to fall in love, and most certainly not with a green-as-grass girl from Sussex. Virginia knew this because he had told her, quite honestly, still personally amazed at the depth of his emotions.

He was a man in his early thirties, firmly committed to bachelorhood until it was absolutely necessary to set up his nursery, and a man jaded by Society and a dozen Seasons of insipid debutantes.

Why he had seen Virginia, seen her "glorious hair, her heartbreaking smile" and immediately succumbed to this debilitating emotion he would, he swore, never know.

He only knew that he loved Virginia Noddenly, loved her madly, passionately, and would trod bootless across broken glass in order to gain her hand in marriage.

What he hadn't been prepared to do was to take that trek over the collective bodies of Lettice Ann, Myrtle, and Georgette-Vinaigrette Noddenly.

He hadn't been prepared for that eventuality at all, and so he had stated when he had approached Sir Roderick to petition him for leave to press his suit.

"My girls will marry in the order of their birth," Sir Roderick had told him most firmly. "First Faith, then Hope, then Charity—good names all, but then I had never bargained on more than three—then Lucille, then Marianne, then Lettice Ann, then—"

Virginia had smiled at Jonathan, sadly, knowingly, and told him there was no necessity for him to repeat her father's speech word-for-word.

Jonathan had been nonplused, or so he had told Virginia when next they met—which had been their first truly secret meeting, for Sir Roderick had refused to allow his youngest daughter back into society for fear a lovesick Lord Mayfield might attempt something rash, like a moonlight elopement to Gretna Green.

"You've a look in your eye I find most disconcerting, young man," Sir Roderick had proclaimed. "A fierce determination I cannot like, much as I admire your promise not to ask for a dowry and the offer of an allowance the size of which my Virginia wouldn't have the faintest notion of how to spend, her being a simple lass, and not the sort to squander my blunt on silly fripperies the way her sister Georgette does. Therefore, until my other girls are bracketed, I forbid you to see Virginia. If you still want her once those three are popped off, come see me again. I would very much enjoy you as a son-in-law. Have one earl in the family already, you know, but two wouldn't hurt."

Virginia surreptitiously raised a hand to wipe at a single tear that threatened to reveal to her maid, Clara—a motherly woman shared by all four Noddenly girls—that she was breaking her heart over "his beautiful lordship again, knowin' full well it won't do a lick a' good to weep buckets, for Sir Roddy won't budge."

And, Virginia knew, taking a deep breath and steeling herself for her coming meeting with Jonathan tonight after everyone was in bed, Clara was right. Papa would never allow a breach of his plan to marry off his daughters according to their order of birth.

Why, the man wouldn't even accept change in his personal routine now that they were living in this rented town house on Half Moon Street. He still rose each morning at dawn, just as if he were going to ride out and inspect his fields, and he still retired each night at ten, after evening prayers, in preparation of another early morning.

Which was very convenient, Virginia concluded, smiling, for it did make it so much easier for her to slip down the servants' stairs and out into the mews for those stolen moments with Jonathan.

But even those moments were an anguish to her now. For Jonathan came to her from his nightly rounds of parties and routs and visits to the theater, his fine clothes seeming to mock her as she stood before him in her old dressing gown (just in case Clara or another servant happened to see her and she could plead sleeplessness, saying she was on her way to the kitchens for warmed milk).

He was going on with his life, mixing with the beauties of the *ton* who all gushed over him and pursued him and had a much better chance of marrying him now that the notion of marriage had entered his mind, while she could do nothing but sit back, gnashing her teeth, and wait for her sisters to wed one, by one, by one.

It wasn't fair. That's what it wasn't—it simply was not fair!

And, apparently, Clara didn't think so either.

"Here, Miss Ginny, wipe those eyes," Clara said in her gruff country way, jarring Virginia back to attention by shoving a lace-edged handkerchief in front of her mistress's face.

"And stop lookin' like the end of the world is comin' tomorrow and you have an engagement to go ridin' out with the prince next Friday. Your young lordship is coolin' his heels in cook's sittin' room, and you'd best pin a smile on that pretty face before you set him runnin' for shelter."

"Jonathan? He's here?" Virginia asked, not knowing if she was more surprised by her beloved's appearance in the middle of the day or Clara's seeming compassion for the tribulations of true love.

But as the maid turned away, and Virginia saw the glint from a shiny gold piece Clara slipped into her pocket, the younger woman only smiled, knowing that, once again, her dearest Jonathan had found a way for them to be together.

She ran to the mirror and hastily inspected her simple sprigged muslin gown for wrinkles, then pushed at her curls which were, as she was not dressed for company, held back from her smooth brow only by a satin band and allowed to fall freely past her shoulders.

Did she look too young? Too much the country miss? Jonathan had said he adored her simplicity after being forced to endure the artificially enhanced beauty of the endless crops of debutantes at Almack's. Was he only being kind? No. Jonathan wouldn't lie to her. He would never lie to her. He didn't have a malicious bone in his body!

"Where's Papa?" Virginia asked, her hand on the doorknob, as the firm common sense she had possessed in abundance until meeting Jonathan belatedly prodded at her lovelorn brain. "Is he anywhere about?"

"Sir Roddy's at his club, boring everyone there to flinders with his stories about his girls, I have no doubt," Clara informed her, beating at the cushions on the window seat to plump them. "Miss Lettice Ann is pinin' in her room for her dirt-digger, in case you'll be askin', Miss Myrtle is polishin' tack in the stables half way down the mews—made friends with one of Lord Chesterton's grooms, or so I've heard—and Miss Georgette is in the sittin' room, checkin' her pulse to make certain she ain't dead yet. Go on, Miss Ginny. Shoo! It's not a good thing to keep such a pretty man waitin'!"

Virginia gave a quick bob of her head, grinned at the maid, and ran hotfoot for the servants' stairs that led directly to the kitchens. Once there, she hesitated only a moment as Cook winked and pointed with a wooden ladle toward a narrow corridor, then deliberately slowed her gait to a ladylike stroll as she approached the small private sitting room.

She stepped inside the dim room, for it was on the ground floor and the high walls of the surrounding houses literally blocked the afternoon sun, and nervously looked around for Jonathan.

"Surprise!"

Suddenly a bouquet of yellow rosebuds was in front of her and Jonathan stepped from behind the door, grinning with such unmitigated glee that she instantly knew he had done something wonderful.

"Jonathan!" she cried happily, taking the bouquet from him and burying her face in the fragrant blooms for a moment before smiling up at him, her heart in her eyes. "They're beautiful!"

"No, my sweet love. *You're* beautiful. Why, if you listen closely, you will hear these poor roses weeping in despair, knowing how you outshine them." He took her hand and led her to the shabby couch, pulling her down beside him. "I have news."

She gloried in his closeness, daring to squeeze his hand as she worshiped him with her eyes.

"Tell me, Jonathan," she whispered, wishing he would kiss her again as he had done that special day in the park, even though he had sworn on his honor that he would never betray her trust in him by taking undue advantage of her.

Until they were wed, of course. At that point, he had informed her, grinning boyishly, he would take great delight in introducing her to enchantments the likes of which her maidenly heart could not dream!

"I've just left your father at his club," he told her, his eyes so bright she now knew for certain that he had accomplished a brilliant feat. "I couldn't tease you with my idea without first gaining his seal of approval, for that would be too cruel, for both of us, dear heart. But Sir Roderick has agreed. Darling, sweet Ginny—I am going to marry off your sisters!"

She looked at him, unable to believe what she'd just heard. "How? Who? Georgette-Vinaigrette? My heavens— *Myrtle?*"

"Never fear, I have it all in train. I only wonder why it took me so long to see it. We marry them off, and then we are free to begin our own life together. I'm even giving them each a dowry, an expense that would be cheap at twice the cost. Listen," he said earnestly, leaning closer as he told her his plan.

Virginia listened, slowly beginning to smile. She had been wrong. Her Jonathan did have a few malicious bones in his body after all. And she couldn't be happier for them!

2

"There's a *dreadful* draft in my rooms, of course," Georgette announced fatalistically as she wearily toddled into the drawing room at Mayfield after hounding Clara for a solid hour as to the whereabouts of all her medicines, which had been carefully loaded in a large trunk specially fitted to hold the dozens of vials and papers of powders, then temporarily misplaced. "I shall most probably take a *dreadful* chill."

The young lady dropped tragically into the nearest chair, pressing the back of one hand against her brow. Georgette Noddenly would have made a tolerable actress, for she was a most convincing invalid, with her slight frame, halo of blonde hair, and pale cheeks; although the fact that her abilities were confined to playing die-away consumptives would, of course, have somewhat limited her roles.

"How *dreadful*. Oh, stifle yourself, Georgie," Lettice Ann Noddenly grumbled offhandedly, still perusing the map she had somehow already secured from the Mayfield library. The sunlight pouring through the bank of windows facing west did nothing to enhance her meager beauty, but only highlighted her unfortunate resemblance to her long-nosed sire. "I knew it. I just *knew* it! We are even farther from home now than when we were in London. However will Bertram find me?"

"That's Bert, Lettice Ann," Myrtle Noddenly pronounced flatly as she strode long-leggedly into the drawing room, smelling slightly of horse, as she had been at the stables, personally supervising the placement of her mares in the stalls.

"Or Bad Bertie," she continued, "if you want to call him by the name the chambermaids have given him. He's only a gardener, but he has plowed many a field with our female servants, if you take my meaning," she continued, winking at Georgette, whose immediate high-pitched giggle signaled that she had gotten the joke.

"How dare you, Myrtle?" Lettice Ann protested, her sallow complexion paling rather than flushing prettily at this insult to the love of her life—her unrequited love, but then no one had asked that, had they? "Bertram has always been a perfect gentleman to me."

Myrtle unconcernedly inspected the broken and rather dirty nails of her left hand. She never wore gloves when she rode, liking the feel of horseflesh under her fingers, and rarely wore a hat either, which explained the badly freckled face beneath her mop of shortly cropped, carrot-orange hair. Yet, for all of it, she was a handsome enough female, if sometimes off-puttingly mannish in her manners.

"That's because he don't favor you, you widgeon," Myrtle answered, her penchant for manly, blunt speech now woefully in evidence. "Otherwise he would have tumbled you long since. Give it up, Letty. Papa wouldn't let you have him even if Bad Bertie wanted you, which he don't. Maybe he has half a head on his shoulders after all, and doesn't live entirely between his legs."

"Oh, how I loathe and detest you," Lettice Ann declared from between clenched teeth. "Just because you have no notion of marrying, you feel free to poke fun at my devotion to Bertram. Or do you plan to mate with one of those filthy nags you favor? I can see your child now. He'd be even more horsy-faced than you!"

"Oh, the noise, the noise! I feel the headache coming on!" Georgette-Vinaigrette moaned, her hands cupped over her ears. "How I am made to suffer! What I would not do to be shed of the pair of you."

"You could die of one of your half-dozen ailments, Georgie. That would get you free of us," Myrtle supplied helpfully. "Although the worst of your ills, that of having bats in your belfry, is rarely fatal."

Georgette immediately began searching in her ever present reticule for her vinaigrette, weeping softly, for she was surrounded by heartless, persecuting creatures, no one save her late mother ever having truly appreciated her delicate constitution.

Perhaps if she coughed a time or two, Virginia would notice her distress and say something kind, for Virginia was the best of her sisters. Never Myrtle. Why, Georgette was convinced that if she were to swoon at this moment and topple onto the floor, Myrtle would only step over her on her way to dinner.

Virginia Noddenly, who at the moment was rather wishing Georgette *would* faint, if just to shut her up, and who had been hoping for better from her three older sisters while knowing she had doomed herself to disappointment, sighed and said, "Please, girls. Don't quarrel. His lordship will be joining us at any moment, and I wouldn't wish for him to take a poor opinion of my dearest sisters."

"And that's another thing," Myrtle said accusingly, wiping at a brownish stain on her skirts, which Virginia passionately hoped had been deposited there by some spilled stringy beef and greasy gravy they'd had for luncheon at their hasty stop at an indifferent inn along the roadway, and not garnered from contact with any vile thing her sister had brushed up against while in the stables.

"Another thing?" Virginia asked, avoiding her sister's penetrating stare. Myrtle's eyes were most unfortunately close set on either side of her thin, aquiline nose, and her gaze could be fierce, and unnerving. "I don't know what you mean."

"She doesn't know what I mean," Myrtle responded, singsong. "Oh, the feigned innocence of the young. How thoroughly unconvincing. All right, Ginny, I'll ask again, and this time don't fib or try to fob me off, or your nose will grow as I tweak it."

Virginia bit back an angry retort, knowing it would be senseless to tug caps with Myrtle, who was known to box an ear now and again to prove her point. "Yes, Myrtle. Ask again."

"I will. What does the Earl think he's about, dragging us all down here? If he intends to play matchmaker for the three of us in order to get to you, he's in for a rude shock. Letty here won't marry any save her Bad Bert—which is the same as to say she'll be putting on her caps any day now—I will marry no one at all, and there isn't a man in all England who hates himself enough to take on our wilting Georgie. I wouldn't have tagged along for this farce at all, except I've heard it bruited about that his lordship keeps a bruising stable of hunters."

Myrtle's suppositions (right on the mark) and her conclusions (also frighteningly true) served to rouse Georgette from her self-pitying sniffles. "Is it true, Ginny? Is his lordship going to try to marry us off so that you and he might—that you could possibly—"

"*Marry,* Georgie," Lettice Ann broke in, her voice dripping venom. "Our youngest sister is out to sacrifice all our mortal bodies to be violated for her own ends. As if I would give my precious chastity to anyone but my dearest Bertram."

"Save your precious chastity much longer, Letty," Myrtle sniped, picking through a dish of sugarplums with her dirty fingers, "and only the worms will be crawling in and out of that aging body. Come to think of it, that might appeal to Bad Bertie, seeing as how he's always digging about in the dirt. Ginny," she went on as Lettice Ann glared daggers at her odiously foulmouthed sister, "do you perhaps care to share with us the names of the gentlemen his lordship will be serving up for our inspection?"

Out of the corners of her eyes Virginia spied Georgette leaning forward in her seat, eagerly awaiting her sister's answer. For a moment, just for a moment, Virginia considered fibbing to her sisters yet again, denying any knowledge of this hastily put together gathering at Mayfield to be anything but what it had been purported to be—a small party meant to give some respite from the hectic rounds of a London season.

But then, knowing Myrtle would not swallow such a line, and would make her life a misery if she dared to attempt to hook them with an untruth, Virginia turned to Georgette, the least threatening of the trio, and recited, "Knox Bromley, Sir Wiley Hambleton, and Lord Pitney

Fox. They will be arriving tomorrow morning, or so I believe."

"I'm going home," Lettice Ann announced flatly, rising. "Not back to London, where our scheming papa is probably already celebrating his release from his last four daughters, but home—to Bertram. I refuse to stay here and be paraded about for the salacious inspection of three men I do not know and am certain I will not like."

Myrtle took up the dish of sugarplums and sat herself down on a white-on-white striped couch, immediately putting paid to its pristine beauty. "Oh, sit down, Letty. It's not as if any of them will favor you in any case. So, Ginny, Sir Wiley Hambleton is to be one of our small group. I should have known. I hear he must marry or else be cut off from his eventual inheritance. Georgie—there's a catch for you. Not only is he eager, but he has enough blunt to keep you in burnt feathers and restorative tonics all your days. He'll be sure to take a dead set at you, seeing as how he'll think you'll drop stone cold at his feet within a year. Should I tell him you're stouter than my best mare, and bound to live on, moaning and whimpering, into your eighties. Or wouldn't that be sporting?"

"No one knows! No one cares!" Georgette cried piteously, her handkerchief to her mouth as she fled the room, nearly cannoning into the earl of Mayfield as she headed for her assigned chamber and the solace of Clara's clucking, if grudging, commiseration.

Jonathan stood back, one expressive ebony eyebrow raised as he followed Georgette's departing form with his amused gaze, then entered the drawing room, greeting each of the remaining ladies in turn and apologizing for having left them alone while he discussed the preparation of three more guest chambers (and the strategic placement of gentlemen prospects close by possible prospective brides).

Virginia looked toward her darkly handsome suitor, resplendent in casual hacking jacket and fawn-colored riding breeches, his Hessians polished to perfection, and was instantly soothed by his confident manner.

"Miss Noddenly," he said pleasantly, bowing over Lettice Ann's hand. "Miss Myrtle," he continued, turning toward the grinning woman but not going so far as to grace the back of her dirty paw with his kiss.

"Miss Virginia," he ended with another bow, a graceful move that was accompanied by a wicked grin and a wink he knew would go unobserved by the other two Noddenly women. "Will Miss Georgette be recovered by the dinner hour, do you suspect?"

Miss Noddenly, as Lettice Ann, as the eldest maiden Noddenly was called (a title that had been passed down the line of sisters far too many times for it to retain much in the way of specialty), sniffed and said, "Oh, Georgie's always recovered in time to stuff her face. You wouldn't know it to look at her, but that girl can eat Papa under the table. Isn't that so, Ginny?"

Virginia cringed inwardly at Lettice Ann's frank speech in the company of her hopeful beloved, for they had enough on their plate trying to marry off the three elder Noddenly sisters without each of them taking turns tearing each other down within earshot of their prospective swains. "Georgette possesses a most becomingly healthy appetite," she said politically, smiling at Jonathan.

"Are you importing Bad Bertie?" Myrtle asked preemptively from around a mouthful of sugarplums. "Ginny has told you about him, hasn't she? Not that popping off Letty will do you much good, for I'll be no man's chattel. Better for the pair of you to marry over the anvil and be done with it, that's my advice. Not that I mind being here. You've got yourself a prodigiously fine stable, my lord."

Virginia felt herself melting into the cushions of her chair, so embarrassed was she for her sisters, who had never been known to make sterling first impressions on the opposite sex—or on anyone at all, for that matter.

"I believe, Miss Myrtle," Jonathan began, inwardly wincing at the sound of "Miss Myrtle," for it so easily rhymed with "Miss Turtle," and the young woman did have a certain snappish way about her, "that you are suffering under a misapprehension. As I told your father before we completed our arrangements for this small party, I have no intention of foisting marriageable gentlemen on any of his daughters. Save Virginia," he added, smiling at his beloved.

Myrtle gave a horselike laugh that clearly stated her opinion of this statement.

"I," Jonathan continued doggedly, "only wish for you to be agreeably entertained as I shamelessly use you as chaperons whilst I steal some precious time with Virginia. I live, you see, in constant hope of changing your father's mind on his determination that you lovely ladies marry in order of your birth."

"Oh, Ginny, he's *wonderful!*" Lettice Ann exclaimed, her clasped hands pressed to her woefully undersized breast. "No wonder Clara says you moon and sigh all the day long. And how sad it is you will perish a spinster. My lord," she said, her eyes bright, "if you are serious in your pursuit of my baby sister, might I have a word with you later, in private? I believe I can help speed your plan."

"Don't do it, Mayfield. Allow Letty to convince you to help her to marry Bad Bert and not only won't you gain Ginny's hand, my lord," Myrtle said warningly, yawning widely as she scratched at an itch at her waist, "but your man will be digging bits of Papa's horsewhip from your pretty hide for a fortnight."

Virginia fought the insane urge to pick up two of the lovely lace runners from the mahogany side tables and stuff one in each of her sister's mouths. "Jon———that is, my lord Mayfield, I have been admiring your gardens from the window. Would it be possible for you to give me a short tour of them before the dinner gong rings? Your roses are particularly attractive."

"That's it, Ginny," Myrtle congratulated. "Get him up and out of here before we disgrace you even more. And take a look around for his head gardener while you're about it. You never know, Letty here might be more enamored of the occupation than the man, and be willing to transfer her affections. An earl's gardener might hold more sway in Papa's mind, so that he might allow the match."

"You're rude, crude, and totally despicable, Myrtle Noddenly," Lettice Ann accused as Jonathan took Virginia's hand and led her to the French doors that opened onto the gardens. "Worst of all, you *enjoy* it!"

"Exactly, Letty! What looby was it said you never got the straight of anything in your life?" Myrtle asked as Jonathan gently closed the door on the female bickering, wondering if he should have searched for enemies rather than merely irritating acquaintances to match up with the three Noddenly sisters. After all, were Knox Bromley, Sir Wiley Hambleton, and Lord Pitney Fox really deserving of the fates he was wishing on them?

Jonathan and Virginia walked side by side in silence for some minutes, their fingers brushing together until Jonathan took her hand in his and lifted it, palm upwards, to his lips.

"How lovely you are, my sweet darling," he said, gazing down into her liquid green eyes, still silently wondering how such a confirmed bachelor as he could be reduced to spouting such romantic nonsense, and *meaning* it.

"Will you still say so in twenty years, when my dear papa is gone to his reward and you are at last free to wed your aged beloved?" she asked, her bottom lip quivering under the strength of her emotions.

He cupped her chin in his hand and dropped a light kiss on her cheek. "How little you trust my determination,

Ginny, my love. We'll get your sisters bracketed, if I have to compromise the lot of them."

Virginia's toes curled in her white kid slippers and she laid her head against his broad chest. "I cannot believe you love me so much," she said truthfully.

The rumble of his deep-throated chuckle tickled her ear as it laid against his chest. "Neither can I, my sweet," he admitted, daring to tempt fate by slipping his arms around her back, stroking her comfortingly. "I feel as if someone has lugged me to the top of St. Paul's spire and dropped me down on my head. But I'm not complaining. Besides, according to my friends—not the odd assortment of characters who will be arriving tomorrow, but my true friends—marriage will be the making of me."

"We won't put any such silly strictures on our daughters, will we, Jonathan?" Virginia asked, pulling slightly away from him to admire his handsome face, to drink in the affection that glowed in his dark eyes.

"Our daughters," Jonathan repeated, smiling. "Gad, to think that I should be considering daughters. A single son fathered on a woman I married for convenience was all I had ever aspired to in this life. But daughters? We shall have an even dozen, my sweet, if they all could be as beautiful as you."

This slightly silly, disjointed, and definitely sappy sort of conversation went on for several more minutes, little of it of concern to any save the two involved, until the proximities of their bodies and the dawning knowledge that they were safely ensconced behind a leafy, concealing tree came home to the two parties and the inane, rambling words slowly ceased, to be replaced by a telling, and decidedly more interesting, silence.

Virginia faced the intriguing knowledge that she wished for more from her beloved than sweet words and chaste kisses, while Jonathan, who was already well acquainted with the realm of earthly delights, knew himself to be entering onto a new, higher plane, where passion and love combined, rendering him nearly powerless to deny his desire to crush Virginia to him, and kiss her, and love her, and touch her, and—

"Ginny—" he groaned in real pain, his hands gently cupping her slim shoulders, his thumbs playing against the soft skin just above the modest scoop of her bodice. "Ginny, I know I promised. I swore to you, to myself, that I would wait, that I would be patient, but—"

She pressed her fingertips to his lips, silencing him, suddenly feeling the older, the wiser of the two. "My mother always told me it is not wise to make rash promises, especially when that sort of promise is almost always impossible to keep. I love you, Jonathan. You love me. It is only natural for us to wish to be together."

He took hold of her hand, feverishly kissed her fingertips, then laid their clasped hands against his chest. "Brave words from such a daring innocent," he told her, remembering their first meeting and his immediate attraction to her modesty, her youth, her beauty, and, mostly, her clear-headed intelligence.

But their desire for one another to one side, he knew he had to forget sweet seduction and concentrate on the matter at hand, even if he had to frighten Virginia with his confession of longing. "Dearest child," he warned, turning his mind from the feel of her soft body pressed tightly against his own, "you can have no real idea of what I am so boorish as to want from you at this moment."

Virginia smiled, wondering how such an otherwise brilliant man could be so silly. "I am the youngest of nine girls, Jonathan, and girls do talk. I have known the mechanics for ever so long, but until now I have never understood the desire for such intimacy. Until you, Jonathan. Now I know why my sister Marianne smiled so on her way down the aisle to her sea captain. I love you, Jonathan, and it is my greatest wish to show you just how much I love you. Is that very forward of me?"

"Slightly, my love," Jonathan admitted, watching her full, pink lips, remembering how they had tasted the afternoon he had stolen that first, mind-destroying kiss. He really should step away from her, and he would, only not just yet. Not for another few moments. He was a strong man, but he was not bargaining to make himself into a martyr.

"Your candor is part of your charm, however," he teased. "Do you remember telling me very matter-of-factly, when first we met, that I should seek elsewhere for feminine companionship as you were already destined never to marry? I immediately took your words as a challenge, as if you had dared me not to fall in love with you. I've never so enjoyed losing at anything."

"And now I have presented you with the ultimate challenge, haven't I, Jonathan?" Virginia asked, sighing as she thought of her three incorrigible, uncontrollable, depressingly single sisters. It appeared she was not going to be kissed, so she might as well talk about Lettice Ann, and Myrtle, and Georgette-Vinaigrette. "Do you consider it merely another challenge, trying to marry off three such sad specimens?"

"Ha! If you think they're bad, my love, wait until you see the sad specimens I'm carting down from London to match with them. We may have to yet import Lettice Ann's gardener and risk your papa's wrath."

"Or we could elope, as Myrtle has suggested," Virginia said, her gaze sliding away from his.

"And have you suffer the whispers and snide remarks of society? Never, my sweet. We will go about this as your papa has decreed it, and we shall triumph. If not with the three loobys I've invited here, then with three others. No matter what, I have promised myself that we shall be married before the month of June is out."

Virginia so adored it when Jonathan was masterful. His delightfully kissable square jaw seemed even stronger, his dark eyes shone, and his expression became almost that of Wellington as one portrait depicted him on the eve of Waterloo. Impulsively—or not, as Virginia was not by nature an impulsive miss—she stood up on tiptoe and kissed Jonathan squarely on the mouth.

Once again all conversation, inane or otherwise, ceased, as Jonathan's better self instantly succumbed to his baser, more physical self. He slanted his mouth against hers, gripping her tightly with both arms, crushing her enticing body against his own from chest to hip.

No kiss from any daring debutante or willing courtesan had ever shaken him like this, to the very soles of his Hessians. And when Virginia opened her mouth slightly on a sweet sigh, he readily deepened the kiss, sending new rockets firing deep inside him, lighting fireworks of passion no mere mortal should have to endure, knowing that there could be no explosive climax, but only the damp rain of frustration as a finale.

"I say, Mayfield," came a voice from somewhere behind the Earl, "who are you mauling in that way? Have I come at a bad time? I had thought to travel down with Wiley and Pitney, but as there was nothing on in Mayfair save another crushingly boring night at my club, I rethought the matter and decided to toddle on down today. Lovely trip, too, except for the fact that my leader threw a shoe partway here and I was forced to twiddle my thumbs for two hours while my man went off to secure another horse. Do you know the cost of rented carriage horses these days? Shocking, that's what it is. Absolutely shocking. Not that you won't reimburse me totally, for, after all, it was your idea that I come down here. Not that I'm not delighted— truly ecstatic—to have been asked."

The entire time the man was speaking Jonathan had kept Virginia's face pressed firmly against his chest, feeling her shoulders shake in ever increasing mirth as the man's droning, monotone voice went on, and on, and on. At last, when sweet silence reigned once more, Jonathan turned Virginia about, carefully keeping her features out of sight of his newly arrived guest as he shooed her down the path and back toward the house.

Only after she was gone did he steel his shoulders and turn about, his hand extended. "Knox, my good fellow, how pleased I am you've agreed to grace my humble home with your presence."

"Yes, well," Knox Bromley countered, attempting to peek past the earl's wide shoulders to catch a glimpse of the fleeing Virginia, "you did ask, didn't you? About that money for the horse—"

"You have only to present the bill to my man of business." Jonathan flung an arm around Knox's shoulders, deliberately steering him away from the house. "Shall we walk while we speak?" he asked the man, an unforgettable figure of rather short stature, a premature pot of a belly already in evidence, his gold-rimmed spectacles owlishly enlarging his pale blue eyes.

"You're not going to tell me who that gel was, are you, Johnny?" Knox asked. Then, without waiting for an answer, he pushed on. "Pitney is bruiting it all over London that you've taken a dart straight to the heart. I said it ain't true, that good old Johnny would never marry until he had to, but now that I'm here—"

"You say Pitney and Wiley will arrive in the morning as planned?" Jonathan interrupted, wishing the man would take the hint and allow him to change the subject. "Are they aware that you won't be traveling with them?"

Knox rolled his eyes as if to comment on the absurdity of Jonathan's question. "I sent round a note to Pitney in Berkeley Square early this morning. You know, Johnny," he went on, "I gave this whole matter a great deal of thought on the ride down here—and most especially whilst

I was waiting for the new nag. Did I tell you how much that horse cost me to hire?—and I started thinking, what does Johnny want of me? He doesn't like me, not above half, and never did, even when we were lads at school. It was you what put that dead chicken in my bed, wasn't it? Had my toes on it before I realized there was a lump under my blankets. Had nightmares for weeks, full of feathers and beaks. So, I asked myself, remembering the chicken, and remembering how you barely bow to me in passing on Bond Street, why do you think, Knox, my good man, Johnny has gone out of his way to bring you to Mayfield? And do you know what, Johnny? I think it has something to do with those Noddenly girls. I've heard it rumored you're arsy varsy in love with one of them, but can't marry her until her sisters are wed. Now, I asked myself, I asked, Knox, do you think Johnny wants to matchmake in order to grease his own way to the altar?"

Listening to Knox's monotone whine, and hearing him call him "Johnny" in that hateful way, Jonathan found it easy to smile convincingly and say, "Knox, old man, you constantly amaze me. In a fit of nostalgia for my salad days I ask three of my schoolboy friends to a small party and I am immediately become the subject of question as one of those three men—the *best* of those three men— accuses me of ulterior motives. I'm aghast, Knox, aghast and, well, to be truthful about the thing—hurt."

Knox Bromley flushed a deep, unflattering red to the top of his rapidly balding head. "Johnny, good friend, please accept my most profound apologies. But the Noddenly females are here, ain't they? That was one of them I saw you kissing just a few minutes ago, wasn't it? I don't care, truly I don't, for I've heard you keep a tolerable cellar, and I could use a few days away from the crush of London, and the importunings of my creditors. Just tell me which of the ladies I'm to court—for a fee, naturally. Five hundred pounds, perhaps? Make it an even thousand, and I'll go so far as to marry the chit, for it's time I settled down and your thousand and a dowry from Sir Roderick would do my pockets a world of good. Just so long as she don't talk too much. I never could abide a female what talks too much . . ."

3

Sir Wiley Hambleton had never been so thrilled to arrive at the end of a journey as he was this sunny May afternoon, hopeful as he was to be shed of Lord Pitney Fox before he was constrained to shoot the man and put them both out of their misery.

"This coach is too stuffy by half, Wiley. Pray put down the window before I aggravate my rash," Pitney had complained upon entering the vehicle in London.

"I detest being a bother, Wiley, but could you raise the window? The country air stuffs up my head most abominably this early in the morning," he had said not five miles out of the city.

"Do you think me overly cautious in bringing Doctor Fitzhugh with me, Wiley? Johnny said I was free to do so, and the man is a jewel, a positive jewel! But I wouldn't wish to appear to be hanging from the last swinging hinge of death's door, now would I?"

"No one could possibly think such a thing, Pitney," Sir Wiley had assured the man through clenched teeth. "I imagine most gentlemen of three and thirty tote their own quack with them wherever they wander. I must be the exception. I only ask that you forgive me my health."

Sir Wiley had held his famous temper firmly in check

for the first leg of the journey, only wishing to strangle Pitney twice: when that man had complained that the bouncing of the coach was making him nauseous and, a scant fifteen minutes later, when the man had proved himself to be truthful—all over the shiny black paint on the outside of Sir Wiley's treasured traveling coach.

But when his lordship had insisted upon sending his meal of roast pigeon back to the traveling inn's kitchens because "pink meat serves as a purgative for the bowels, you know, Wiley, and as I have been most regular in my habits this past week or more I should not like to risk an upset," Hambleton had lost his temper, threatening to dunk the man head and ears in the horse trough in the stable yard.

And so it was that, although he had begun his journey with misgivings (still confused as to why Lord Mayfield should wish to assist him in his search for a bride), Sir Wiley was hard put not to drop to his knees once the coach had reached Mayfield and kiss the crushed-stone drive.

Instead, he comforted himself with curtly informing Lord Fox that he would be detained at the stables for a few minutes, settling the bay gelding he had only recently purchased at Tattersall's and brought with him from London in hopes of a few good workouts across open fields, and would join his host later.

"Once I can unclench my teeth long enough to say hello to Johnny, that is," Sir Wiley muttered to himself as he lightly hopped back into the coach, the bay gelding still tied up behind it, most happily leaving Lord Fox, Doctor Fitzhugh, and his lordship's mountain of baggage behind at the front door to Mayfield.

Sir Wiley still could not believe the cruel twist Dame Fate had served up to him in Aunt Earlene's ultimatum that he either marry or lose her fortune. The fact that his embarrassment had become common knowledge within the *ton* seemingly within moments of his aunt's declaration had only served to depress him sufficiently so that he had leapt at Lord Mayfield's backhanded invitation.

A wife? What on earth could he possibly do with a wife? One woman, a single woman in his bed night, after night, after night. The same face. The same voice. The same body. He'd perish of boredom within a month—a week!

For Sir Wiley Hambleton was a rake, and delighted in his reputation as a "bad, dangerous man."

Watching society's clucking hens hastily tucking their innocent chicks beneath their wings at his approach was a balm to his soul.

He gambled deep, played high, rode hard, fought bravely, and bedded whom he chose—although tumbling the wife of any of the stodgier peers was a particular pleasure.

Green as grass lads from the country idolized him, his tailor discounted his purchases because his lordship's broad shoulders and straight legs showed his creations to such advantage, and if he was sometimes shunned by the "nicer" people in society, he could never say he didn't enjoy himself at his many outlandish pursuits.

After all, if a straight-speaking man who openly gloried in life's pleasures was to be condemned by such morally upright, boring high sticklers, he must be doing something right!

But marry he must, and marry he would. He didn't particularly care who was to become Mrs. Wiley Hambleton. He just needed a warm female body on his arm when next he visited Aunt Earlene in Wimbledon, may the old dear suffer a hard, lingering death.

Sir Wiley popped open the door to the traveling coach and hopped down before the vehicle had come to a full halt in front of the enormous, whitewashed stable.

"You, there—boy!" he called out imperiously as he

made for the open door, to pick out a fitting stall for his prize gelding. "See to untying my mount. There's a copper in it for you."

"Stuff your copper straight up your nose, why don't you," the tall, carrot-haired groom, who was in reality Miss Myrtle Noddenly dressed in her favorite old shirt and breeches, called out, turning away from him.

She knew Sir Wiley, of course, having seen him riding that same bay gelding in the park just the other day—not remembering the man, precisely, but never forgetting a fine bit of horseflesh. And she wasn't insulted that he had mistaken her for one of the Mayfield grooms. Myrtle simply didn't care for men. Not at all. Not a jot.

She was supposed to be in the drawing room at the moment, sitting side by side with her two thimble-brained sisters, all decked out in ruffles and lace, awaiting the gentlemen who were on their way down from London.

She was supposed to be smiling politely while Mister Knox Bromley sat across from her and droned on and on about every boring subject under the sun, the man seeming to have an unnatural interest in the cost of everything from tallow candles to chamber pots.

She was supposed to be being, as she and her sisters had agreed late last night, "cooperative, if just for poor Ginny's sake."

Yes, well. The world was also "supposed" to be a place where a reasonably intelligent person should not have to willingly sit in the company of idiots!

And so she had deserted her sisters within an hour, discarded her hated gown on the floor of her bed chamber, and come out to the stables, where she could be assured of some peace and quiet.

Until Sir Wiley Hambleton had shown up to clog the scenery with his presence, of course.

Intent on retrieving a currycomb she had been using on one of her mares, Myrtle had uttered her irreverent remark and then continued purposefully walking toward the stable, only to be brought to an ignominious halt by a hand coming down heavily on her left shoulder, yanking her up short, then turning her around.

"I've a better idea, you overgrown guttersnipe. Why don't I shove this copper straight up your—God's teeth! You're a female! I don't believe it!"

Myrtle looked nearly straight into Sir Wiley's black as pitch eyes—for she was a tall woman, and the top of her short-cropped head came nearly to the bottommost tip of his aristocratic nose—and said, laughing in real amusement, "Oh, close your mouth, Wiley Hambleton. You're going to catch flies on your tonsils."

Virginia sat on a stone bench in a corner of the gardens, safely away from the Mayfield music room where her sisters and the three London gentlemen—plus Doctor Angus Fitzhugh—were discussing plans for a small entertainment the following night, a Christmas in May celebration including a masquerade and pantomime of sorts.

The idea of only four women and five men dressing up in costume and not being able to identify each other as they recited conundrums from behind masks seemed silly in the extreme to Virginia, but when Myrtle had agreed to the scheme—and Myrtle agreed to precious little that was anyone else's idea—she had decided to stroll out into the gardens and let them all have a go at it.

Besides, she was confident that Jonathan would join her as soon as he could be shed of Lord Fox, who had requested his removal to another guest chamber because his present one was decorated all in green, an unfortunate color which invariably made him bilious.

Virginia smiled as she looked about the vast gardens, envisioning a day when she would be mistress at Mayfield, her children at her feet as she brought her embroidery with her to this bench and waited for her beloved husband to return from riding the fields with his estate manager.

They would sit here together, talking over the day's events, and then the children's nurse would sweep them away to their evening tea and she and Jonathan would be alone. Blessedly alone. The way they never had been these past four days, since the gentlemen had arrived and they had been busy from morn till night mentally attempting to match miss with mister.

If only she had not promised her dear mother on that gentle woman's death bed that she would obey her father's strictures about marrying in order of birth.

If only Jonathan weren't such a gentleman, refusing to open her up to censure by marrying her over the anvil.

If only her dratted older sisters would be more cooperative!

Lettice Ann had been barely civil to any of the gentlemen, sitting in corners like a little mouse, pining for Bad Bert—as if she could ever have him.

Georgette had been somewhat better, seeming to have taken Lord Pitney Fox and his traveling chest of medicines in slight affection, the two of them comparing illnesses over the dinner table until Myrtle had begun to beat at Georgette-Vinaigrette with her soup spoon.

Myrtle. Now *that* was the sister who confused her. She had been walking about all day with a wide smile on her face and a kind word for almost anyone—which was not to say that she was being all that polite, only that she was not so cutting and direct in her comments. Why, she had not even balked at Clara's suggestion that she allow the maid to try to "do somethin' with that mop you call your hair."

Yes, Myrtle was being strange. Very strange. Perhaps, Virginia thought, she might ask Doctor Fitzhugh to have a look at her sister tomorrow, just to be sure she wasn't suffering some sort of fever.

Banishing thoughts of her sisters, Virginia concentrated on a more pleasant thought, thinking back to the first night she had met Jonathan, marveling yet again at the kindness of the gods that had made her single journey into society so magical.

She had been sitting on the very edge of the dance floor, for her father had told her she was not allowed to dance or in any way draw attention to herself when settling Lettice Ann was the order of the evening.

Virginia hadn't been bored, for watching the dancers gracefully swirling and dipping as they whirled around the room was most entertaining, even if her toes had been tapping in time with the music as she wished someone would come along and sweep her into the waltz.

"What a lovely, winsome smile," a male voice had commented as she stiffened, for the owner of that low, melodious voice was already in the process of sitting down on the chair directly beside hers. "You will forgive me if I flaunt convention and join you, I hope. I'm avoiding a most determined young female and I am assured that when she sees me in the company of the most beautiful creature in the room she will be discouraged and return to her mama. By the bye, my name is Jonathan. And yours—"

Virginia smiled now as she had then, remembering how she had turned to look at Jonathan and drawn in her breath in shock, for he was quite the most handsome man she had ever seen. The man of her maidenly dreams, to be blunt about the thing.

Devastated by both his proximity and her instant attraction to him, she had blurted out the first thing that came into her mind.

"Do you remember telling me very matter-of-factly, when first we met, that I should seek elsewhere for feminine companionship as you were already destined never to marry? I immediately took your words as a challenge, as

*if you had dared me not to fall in love with you. I've never
so enjoyed losing at anything.*"

Yes, that was what Jonathan had said to her the other
day. She had issued him a "challenge" that first night. Innocently. Not meaning to be cute, or coy, or even mysterious. And, with that first exchange of names, of looks, of
information, they had started down the road that had led
them here, to Mayfield, doing their best to fob off three
Noddenly sisters to any man who might be so generous as
to take them off their hands.

Was it terrible of them? Or was it a necessary means to
a mutually pleasurable end? At the moment, Virginia decided, it didn't very much matter what it was. As long as
it worked!

Virginia was drawn from her reverie as she felt a gentle
pressure along her leg and looked down to see a fuzzy
gray and white kitten rubbing itself against her. "Oh, you
little darling!" she exclaimed, picking up the kitten and
burying her face in its soft fur.

The kitten took exception to being squeezed and gave a
sharp cry, turning its head to bite Virginia's thumb. "Forgive me!" she told it, cradling the animal more gently
against her breasts, so that it began to purr. "I know how
prodigiously oppressing it is to be held too tightly, as I am
to the bosom of my family," she said, smiling. "Is that
why you're out here alone? Have you run away from all
your sisters, daring anything for a life of your own?"

"Is that who I am, my sweet? *Anything?*" Jonathan
questioned her quietly, coming up behind her and dropping
a kiss on her nape. "Are you running to me only to escape
your sisters, and your papa's confounded rules? Why, I do
believe I am crushed. Totally destroyed."

Virginia smiled up at him as he came around the bench,
to sit down beside her. "No, you're not," she told him.
"You're sweet, and wonderful, and kind, and generous—
and probably twice as disgusted with what we are at-

tempting to do as I am. Or have you discovered that you really do like my sisters and their prospective husbands?"

Jonathan reached down to stroke the kitten's head. "I'd like to tie them all up together in a very large sack and dump them in the lake," he offered with a grin. "All of them save Georgette and Pitney, that is. They probably wouldn't drown, but only catch a chill, and spend the remainder of our lifetimes sneezing in our faces."

"Unless they broke out in spots from the rough material of the sack," Virginia teased. "Then they would drive the pair of us to despair by sitting around all the day, scratching." And then she sobered, asking, "Do you still think this will work, Jonathan?"

He shrugged. "As a child, I believed in miracles. Once I had reached my majority, I gave up that belief—until I met this remarkably beautiful red-haired, green-eyed creature one fine night and lost my heart to her. Now, my pet, I believe anything can happen."

Virginia allowed her head to rest against Jonathan's shoulder, sighing as she watched the sun slowly dropping behind the trees, the coming of dusk lending them a heightened feeling of privacy in the gardens. "Oh, Jonathan, how I love you!" she told him, sighing contentedly.

"That's fortunate," he told her, slipping an arm around her waist, "for I must inform you that, once they are all safely married, I doubt if I will allow any of your sisters or their husbands across my threshold."

"Amen," Virginia answered, sighing once more.

"Here's the script," Georgette said, waving a sheaf of papers for all to see. "Oh, listen to the names of these characters! I had forgotten how amusing Park's Twelfth-Night Performers can be. "Mrs. Strut, Lord Lollypop— Countess Fly Away! We shall have such *fun!*"

"And I say if it's not *truly* Twelfth Night, we can't *truly* perform in these costumes," Lettice Ann declared as the small party sat around the half-dozen open trunks the servants had grudgingly lugged down from the attics just five months after they had lugged them up there following the Christmas holidays.

"We don't necessarily have to perform, Miss Noddenly," Lord Fox assured her, a handkerchief to his nose lest the dust from the trunks set him off into a fit of sneezing. "We'll just each take a costume and use it for the masquerade. Surely there are masks somewhere."

"In the smallest trunk," Jonathan supplied helpfully, sitting on one of the couches beside his beloved, busying himself by playing with an enticing tendril of hair that had escaped her coiffure to tease him as it curled against her long white throat. "They are only simple eye masks, but they could easily be decorated by clever hands."

"Oh, what fun!" Georgette cried, clapping her hands. "We could use bits and pieces of lace and material and even feathers! Except for Myrtle, of course, who is simply *dreadful* with a needle. Shall I fashion yours for you, Myrtle?" she asked her sister, who was holding up a pair of black satin breeches and eyeing them with interest.

"But then you'd know me, you widgeon," Myrtle pointed out reasonably, dropping the breeches. "Wiley, do you see anything here you like, or are you thinking, as I am, that this is very nearly the most asinine exercise you have ever contemplated, sober?"

Sir Wiley smiled over the rim of his wineglass. "Now, Myrt, don't ask me for the truth. I wouldn't want to send the ladies screaming from the room."

"Why not? It seems a fair idea to me," Myrtle said, smiling at him while, Virginia noticed in shock, actually *batting* her short, nearly colorless eyelashes at the man. "Mr. Bromley, what do you think?" she inquired, turning to Knox, who had slapped a cardboard crown covered in gilt paint on his head. "Is this not the most ridiculous notion—dressing up and pretending not to know each other when anyone with half a candle lit in his noodle would know I'm the tallest female in this company, and you are the shortest man?"

"And the fattest, Myrt," Sir Wiley inserted quietly, but not so quietly that Virginia and Jonathan, who were seated closest to him, didn't overhear. Turning to each other, they smiled, believing that they scented a most unusual romance in the air.

"You do have a point, I suppose, Miss Myrtle," Knox Bromley said, taking a deep breath which, to his companions, was the only warning they would receive that he was about to launch on another of his marathon ramblings. "I am the shortest male. However, I am also the only male who requires spectacles to see the tip of my nose. This, naturally, rules out any notion of my wearing an eye mask. Coupling this with the fact that you, Miss Myrtle, are indeed the tallest female, we two are already effectively unmasked. However, as neither you nor I wish to destroy the fun for the rest of this lovely party, I suggest you do your best to stoop, whilst we men all endeavor to locate masks that will not disclose which one of us is wearing glasses. As for the rest of it—I also now suggest we all, save one of us, leave the room while the remaining person selects his or her costume. Then, one by one, each will enter the room and select his or her costume, until we are all satisfied with our choices. Isn't that simple?" he ended, beaming at each of them in turn.

"Lord, if my mares were as long-winded I should enter both of them in the Derby," Myrtle said, rolling her eyes in disgust.

"You did bring up the subject, you know," Sir Wiley told her, handing her a glass of sherry, which the irrepressible young woman threw back in one swallow.

"Well, I think Mister Bromley has had a wonderful idea," Lettice Ann said firmly, so that Virginia quickly glanced in Miss Noddenly's direction, amazed to see a hint of color in her sister's cheeks.

"Thank you, Miss Noddenly," Knox said, bowing over her hand so that his crown slipped from his balding head and landed in her lap. "Whoops! Sorry about that. Perhaps we should leave the others to choose first, as I know I shall have no trouble taking whatever is left. Would you care to stroll in the gardens?"

"I should like that above all things—Knox," Lettice Ann answered, blistering Myrtle with a withering stare that dared her not to say a thing, not a single *thing*, before taking Mister Bromley's hand and walking with him out the already open French doors.

"Did you see that, Ginny?" Georgette exclaimed, shifting about on her chair to watch as Lettice Ann and Knox disappeared down the flagstone steps and into the garden. "I vow to you, I'd rather she eloped with Bad Bert than to marry that odious man." She then sat back in her chair, fanning her cheeks in the afternoon heat. "Ah, well, perhaps they'll *bore* each other to death, and take our perennial spinster, Myrtle, with them. Then, perhaps, *I* shall be allowed to think of marriage."

"What? And give up your invalid status?" Myrtle scoffed, walking past Georgette and giving her a light tap on the top of her head. "Wives must be prepared to sacrifice, Georgie. Give her husband children. Drag herself away from her vials and potions long enough to attend the odd dinner party now and then. Recover from her third fatal illness of the week to hostess a ball every second season. You don't have it in you."

Lord Fox, who, still with his handkerchief to his nostrils, had been rummaging about in one of the trunks, using a poker from the fireplace so as not to contaminate himself, dropped his hand and came to Georgette's rescue. "I know, I know," he said, shaking his head. "Life puts such unbearable strains on the frail constitution. But a loving, caring, understanding husband could be a supporting prop to a delicate female, delighting in her mere presence, reclined on her own drawing room couch, and not wishing for more. Especially when he knows that she will likewise be solicitous of *his* uncertain constitution."

"I think I might be ill," Jonathan whispered in Virginia's ear.

"Don't tell me," she whispered back to him. "Just go describe your symptoms to Georgette or Pitney. I'll wager both of them have suffered the same sort of upset—only twice as often and three times as badly."

"Well, I've had about as much of this as I can take," Myrtle announced suddenly if not unexpectedly, slapping down her empty glass and rising. "Wiley? You up for a gallop before dinner?"

"Naturally. Shall we outrun the groom again, Myrt?" Sir Wiley asked, taking her arm. "Then we can stop at that inn we saw, and have a meal in the common room. Perhaps even fleece a farmer or two at cards?"

Virginia hit Jonathan on the forearm, wordlessly telling him that he must put a halt to such wanton behavior, but she might just as well not have bothered, for Jonathan merely covered her hand with his own and wished Sir Wiley and Myrtle a pleasant evening.

"Why didn't you stop them?" she asked as Georgette and Lord Fox began an earnest discussion of the merits of a few drops of laudanum mixed up in a tooth glass with a measure of water over that of a dish of warmed milk when trying to ward off insomnia.

"Why?" Jonathan responded, lifting her hand to his lips. "I don't know if Lettice Ann has been smitten by Knox or is merely doing us all a favor by taking him into the gardens, intending to conk him over the head with a shovel to shut him up, but I do know blossoming love when I see it. Dear heart, Wiley and Myrtle will be posting banns within the week!"

Virginia sat back against the cushions, considering Jonathan's declaration. It did seem possible. She couldn't ever remember Myrtle being so happy unless she was in the process of teasing Georgette to death, and Sir Wiley did seem to enjoy her company, even calling her "Myrt" in a most affectionate manner. "But if Lettice Ann doesn't marry first—"

"Then I'll import Bad Bert, bribe him with the offer of his own set of green houses in New South Wales or some such distant place if he marries Lettice Ann—and hang the consequences," he answered, feeling more lighthearted than he had in several days as he observed that someone besides Lord Fox (who was busy at the moment in pressing a hand against his forehead and testing himself for a fever), someone who had barely spoken these past five days, was sitting unnoticed in a corner and looking at Georgette Noddenly with something more than polite interest in his eyes.

4

In the end, the idea of a Christmas in May masquerade was discarded and the Mayfield servants found themselves grumbling as they carried the boxes and trunks up to the attics once more.

But there was nothing else for it, because almost overnight Mayfield had become the uncomfortable setting of a "delicate situation," and there could be no time for mindless frivolity when Miss Lettice Ann Noddenly and Mister Knox Bromley had disappeared.

Not that they hadn't left a note. A rather long, prodigiously boring note, obviously penned by Knox, who had not stinted in his use of the earl's best stationery in his efforts to explain the reasons behind his departure just before dawn, Lettice Ann at his side.

Jonathan, upon waking early that morning, had discovered the informative missive that had been slipped under his door sometime during the night.

Knox, or so he had written, had been surveying the Noddenly females these past days and had come to the conclusion that Georgette's vaporish disposition would drive him to distraction within a fortnight, Myrtle was so outré in her manner that he was left speechless as to describe her shortcomings (and with the man's overusage of words, that was saying something!), and Lettice Ann was too old, too plain, and too much in love with a quite unexceptional young country gentleman named Bertram to be considered as reasonable wife material.

"You couldn't have known that, Johnny," Knox had written, "or else you would have had this Bertram fellow as one of your party."

However, Bromley's letter continued, considering the fact that Miss Noddenly was the eldest of the three (Miss Virginia being already taken by dear Johnny), it had become "clear as crystal" to him that she must be married off at once. And that, Knox related, his crabbed handwriting now suffering badly in his agitation, was when he had been "struck by a mutually beneficial inspiration!"

Dear Johnny did remember that thousand pounds he, Knox, would receive if he took one of the Noddenlys off his hands, didn't he? And shouldn't that sum be doubled, seeing as how Miss Noddenly didn't want to marry anyone other than this Bertram gentleman, and considering that it had been he, Knox Bromley, who had ferreted out this important information and taken it into his mind to help the lady on her way?

What Knox meant by all this, "in short" (Lord, how

Jonathan, now reading the fifth page of Knox's letter, had wished the man could mean it), was that Knox and Lettice Ann were even now on their way across country to the Noddenly estate in "the pursuit of true love. After all, Johnny, you didn't say I had to *marry* one of 'em. You didn't say anything at all on the subject, come to think of it—not outright. But we all three of us, Wiley, Pitney, and myself, know what you want. I'm just helping you to get it. You can forward the two thousand to my solicitor by way of thanks."

"He's not eloping with Lettice Ann," a horrified Virginia exclaimed as Jonathan finished reading the letter aloud to the assembled company prematurely roused from their beds and now gathered in the breakfast room. "He's only helping her to elope with Bad Bert—who doesn't want her in the first place. And they'll have to spend a night on the road before they reach our estate! Oh, poor Lettice Ann. She'll be crushed when she realizes she has gone and ruined herself with Knox Bromley—and all for nothing!"

"Never mind that. What's this about two thousand pounds?" Lord Fox asked, meticulously picking at his heaping bowlful of coddled eggs with his fork, in search of any vagrant sliver of shell that might impale his tongue. "You made no such promise to me—or to Wiley here, for that matter, not that either Wiley or I needs the blunt. Wiley just needs a wife to parade past his Aunt Earlene. Ain't that the right of it, Wiley?"

"You know, I never did like you, Pitney," Sir Wiley stated, his tone soft as velvet, so that Virginia felt a frisson of fear skip down her spine. Hadn't she heard somewhere that Sir Wiley had once fought a duel? But who would have thought that he'd take umbrage at something that was common knowledge? Unless, of course, he was afraid her sister Myrtle might take offense at being seen as a bride of convenience? That was a comforting thought.

"He—Lord Mayfield—offered Knox Bromley *money* to court us?" Georgette asked, two spots of highly unhealthy looking color rising in her cheeks, as Lord Fox mumbled a quick apology and dropped his gaze to his bowl. She clasped her hands to her breasts, reeling in her chair. "Oh, why did I come here? Why did I allow this to happen? I shall die of this embarrassment. I shall most assuredly *die!*"

"There, there, Miss Georgette," Lord Fox commiserated, abstractedly patting her hand, although he still didn't look up, perhaps in fear Sir Wiley might still take it into his head to throttle him. "No one has ever perished of embarrassment. I have it on good authority. Now, eating bad shellfish is a different matter. Why, I remember the time— remember it as if it was yesterday—that I took a bite of some bad lobster. Well! You want to speak of *dying?* I was wishing for the sweet release of death, I tell you, lying upon my rack of pain, retching until I thought my—"

"Oh, shut up, Pitney, you ridiculous baboon! I don't care a fig about your stupid shellfish!" Georgette fairly screeched as she pulled her hand free—any thought of her delicate lungs blown to the four winds by her sudden explosion of temper.

And she had thought Lord Fox to be a kindred spirit? Nonsense! He was nothing but a selfish old woman, intent upon his imagined ills—boring, and stupid into the bargain! "That's all you do," she told him hotly. "Prose on and *on* about your delicate constitution, your restorative tonics, your mustard plasters, until everyone is totally *sick* of listening to you. You're the most depressing man I've ever met. Well, I'll tell you this, Lord Pitney Fox. I only wish there were a whacking great bone in those eggs you're pushing all around your bowl—and you *choked* on it!"

"God's teeth, Wiley, do you hear this?" Myrtle asked, grinning from ear to ear. "I never would have believed it.

The little twit has a spleen after all. Do you think she already realized she sounds just like him, or are we witness to some major breakthrough this morning?"

"Me? God's waistcoat, Myrt, who cares? But I'll tell you what I do think. I think I'm ready for a morning gallop," Sir Wiley responded, rising and throwing down his serviette in the general direction of his now clean plate for, although no one else seemed disposed to eat after hearing about Knox and Lettice Ann's flit, he hadn't seen anything so terrible in the news that it should put a person off his feed. "You coming, or do you want to sit here and watch the second act of this ridiculous farce?"

While Lord Fox frowned—for he had thought his courtship of Miss Georgette to be going along famously, seeing as how they had so much in common, and Miss Georgette belatedly set to, tackling her own breakfast of fried eggs and country ham with a will, Virginia and Jonathan looked to each other, sighed, and reluctantly got on with "the second act of this ridiculous farce."

"It has already gone nine, you know, and one of the grooms has told me Knox and Miss Noddenly left at a quarter to six—Lettice Ann being slightly tardy because she refused to leave without all of her luggage being securely tied down on the wagon for the trip to the nearest posting inn. It is more than time we go after them," Jonathan announced fatalistically as a worried Virginia nodded in agreement.

"Oh, must we, Johnny?" Sir Wiley asked, looking pained. "I'd be the first to suggest it, if there were more sport in the thing. As it is, we'll find them in less than an hour, if I know Knox—who has probably hired a ramshackle carriage and two broken in the wind nags for his flit, so that they are no more than five miles from here, being passed on the road by farm wagons and adventurous tortoises. Never saw a man with so tight a purse. Surely you can effect the rescue without me and Myrt here having to ruin a fine morning on such a sad chase."

"Papa's going to be prodigiously angry," Georgette pointed out around a mouthful of ham (a sentiment Jonathan shared, but rather wished had remained unspoken), then added thoughtfully, "Why, when all is said and done, he might just make Lettice Ann marry Mister Bromley."

Once more Virginia and Jonathan exchanged looks, but this time they smiled. If Lettice Ann were to be compromised into marriage, and if Myrtle and Sir Wiley (still thought of by Virginia and Jonathan as a pair matched by the stars) were to be considered all but engaged, why, that would leave only Georgette-Vinaigrette still to be settled!

It would appear Jonathan would have to import another possible suitor for the girl, however, as Lord Fox was most definitely out of the running. Ah, well. That was a simple matter. London was clotted with men who could be depended upon to look hopefully upon marriage to a pretty, if pale, blonde lass of reasonable dowry.

But then Virginia and Jonathan both frowned, for they were basically good-hearted people, and knew that they could not in good conscience sacrifice Lettice Ann's happiness for the sake of their own.

"We must go after them at once," Virginia and Jonathan said as one, rising to quit the dining room.

"Well, Lord Fox?" Georgette asked, her tone stinging. "Are you going to be a gentleman and accompany them, or have you just remembered that you are highly allergic to good deeds?"

"Good girl!" Myrtle chortled, giving her sister an affectionate clap on the back that nearly sent Miss Georgette reeling head first across the width of the table. "It *is* a miracle! Georgette is turning human. I'm impressed, I tell you. Who'd ever have believed it? Come on, Georgie— ride with us. It will be a grand lark."

"I—I," Georgette began, suddenly looking faint, as if all

her exertions of the morning were beginning to take their toll on what she still believed might be her faint constitution, even if exposure to Lord Fox's constant complaints had served to make her realize that she was not garnering attention with her avowals of fragility, but most probably only making everyone around her nauseous with listening to her.

"I shall be happy to bear Miss Georgette company while everyone rides to the rescue."

Six heads turned as one at this short speech, for everyone had forgotten that Angus Fitzhugh, physician, was in the room, and had been for some time.

Virginia tilted her head to one side, her green eyes narrowed as she looked to the doctor assessingly. Really, all things considered, she was beginning to feel distressingly close to a race track tout, and wondered if she should ask the good doctor to open his mouth so that she could inspect his teeth.

But the doctor did seem to be a good enough sort, quiet, almost taciturn, yet rather handsome behind his unusually full mustache; his eyes a lively blue, his thick sandy hair falling forward over a smooth brow. Papa would approve of a doctor. They already had one in the family—Hope's husband, Joseph—but, as Papa was wont to say, another "couldn't hurt."

"Why, thank you, Doctor Fitzhugh," Virginia said quickly, as Lord Fox had already opened his mouth to protest—for although he had already decided to quit Mayfield this very morning and return to London, where his nerves would not be so put upon by screeching ladies of indifferent looks, only mild fortune, and unexpectedly volatile temperament—he hadn't counted upon making such an exhausting journey without his personal physician.

"That settles it then," Myrtle stated, slapping her thighs as she rose without Sir Wiley's assistance even though he was standing directly beside her chair. Sir Wiley was like that, never going out of his way to treat her like some helpless infant just because she'd been born a female. She liked that. By and large, Sir Wiley's lack of consideration for her was one of his most shining attributes. "Yoiks, tally-ho and away, and all that bilge! We're off for the hunt. Wiley, would you like to share a quick stirrup cup before we ride out?"

Jonathan, not believing being female equated with being helpless, but a firm devotee of the good manners his late mother had drummed into his head during the course of his formative years, hesitated in order to offer his beloved his arm, then passed by Lord Fox to whisper, "Have a good journey back to London, Pitney, old man. Oh, and by the way—good riddance to you."

"Well!" Lord Fox exclaimed as he watched his host leave the room, Miss Virginia hanging on his arm, her face turned into his sleeve as she gave way to a fit of giggles. "I have never been so insulted in my life."

"Oh, no? Then this is a day of revelations, for you'll be even more insulted in just a moment!" Miss Georgette pointed out, lifting his lordship's bowl of eggs ("they must be runny, no lumps") and dumping it over his head, bowl and all.

"My goodness gracious sakes," she then commented, smiling broadly as rivulets of unlumpy eggs ran down Lord Fox's thin cheeks and long nose, "I do believe I have not felt so robust in ages. Doctor Fitzhugh—Angus— might I avail myself of your arm as we remove to the morning room for a second cup of tea?"

"It would be my very great pleasure, Miss Georgie," Angus Fitzhugh said, and they, too, departed the breakfast room, leaving Lord Pitney Fox behind to contemplate the dilemma of either allowing the remaining coddled eggs to ooze out slowly from beneath the upturned bowl now snugly seated on his head or to lift that bowl and have his unpleasant bath over with all at once.

* * *

Virginia had always enjoyed riding, even if her mare, Plum Pudding, was a three-time, hand-me-down sixteen-year-old from her sisters and well past anything save a wheezing trot, so that sitting sidesaddle aboard one of Jonathan's prime mares was a real treat. Almost as much of a treat as riding alongside her beloved, who cut a most dashing figure up on his huge red stallion.

They were clipping along the main turnpike leading away from Mayfield at a brisk but safe pace, Sir Wiley and Myrtle having long ago outstripped them on their own mounts, Myrtle not being one to hide her light beneath a bushel in her blatant attempt to outride Sir Wiley.

"Are you sure we will be able to catch up with Lettice Ann, Jonathan?" Virginia asked nervously as they rounded a turn in the road only to see it empty in front of them. "I believe I'd like less to see her wed to Knox Bromley than I would if she were to marry Bad Bert. But she is compromised, isn't she?"

"Not if we can reach them soon," Jonathan told her. "After all, none of us is going to bruit it about London that Lettice Ann has gone off alone with Knox. Unless Lord Fox takes it into his head to run his mouth off once he's back in London."

Virginia drew in a quick breath. "Would he do that? Would any gentleman be so cruel?"

"First, dear heart, we have to consider whether or not we wish to consider Pitney a gentleman. No," he added, shaking his head, "now that I've considered it—he's *not* a gentleman. But he isn't entirely blockheaded either. In the normal course of events modesty would make me refrain from saying this, pet, but it is worth more than Pitney Fox can spare to have him cross me."

"You're so socially powerful," Virginia said, ashamed to find herself feeling slightly smug—for her beloved *was* the earl of Mayfield, and he wished to make her his countess.

How lovely. How very, very lovely. Not that she was a mean sort, to wish ill upon Lord Fox, but if the man dared to lay his tongue on any of her sisters she could stand back, applauding, as he was run out of London on a donkey's back. "Could you ruin him, Jonathan? Could you break him?"

Jonathan smiled at her, sending shivers of delight from her head to her toes. "I could *bend* him, dear heart," he told her reassuringly. "So we won't worry about Pitney. Instead, I think we should spend a moment thanking our lucky stars. Look, Ginny. Isn't that your sister Myrtle coming toward us? Up there—peek between the branches of that small stand of trees just before the next bend."

"Where? Oh, yes, *yes,* it is Myrtle! And look—there's Sir Wiley." She leaned forward over the mare's neck, trying to peek around the bend in the road now that the two horses had hit the straightaway once more and were heading directly for them. "But where is Lettice Ann? I don't see a carriage following after them."

No sooner had she uttered the words than Myrtle spied them out, shouting, "Yoo-hoo, fellow rescuers. No need to call out the hounds. All's well."

"Told you it wouldn't take us long to ferret them out," Sir Wiley called, reining in his mouth ten feet ahead of Jonathan and Virginia. "They're just a small stretch back the way we've come, stuck tight in a ditch. Always said Knox was a cowhanded driver."

"Is Lettice Ann all right? She isn't injured in any way, is she?" Virginia asked, all concern, for her sister would not have been put in such desperate straits if she, Virginia, hadn't been so selfish as to wish all her sisters married.

"She's fine as ninepence, Ginny," Myrtle assured her, "although I can't say the same for that gudgeon Knox Bromley. We'll be heading to Mayfield for a wagon in order to fetch him back."

"Broke his leg falling from the curricle," Sir Wiley said, looking to Jonathan. "A curricle, Johnny! Did you ever hear such nonsense? The man can barely handle one in the park, yet alone on the highway. But a coach and driver would have cost him, cut into the two thousand he planned to cut out of you, so he decided to drive himself. That mountain of luggage didn't do him a heap of good, setting off the balance, but he was bound to come to grief sooner or later. Well—Myrt and I will be off now that you've come to bear them company. You know, it's too bad old Knox didn't break his jaw. He's moaning nineteen to the dozen about how he sees the whole debacle as your fault, Johnny, and how he intends that you should pay. And you will, I suppose, if only in being forced to have Knox kicking back his heels at Mayfield until he's mended. We'll send a wagon—in about an hour, I suppose. See you later, Johnny."

And then Sir Wiley and Myrtle were off, spurring their horses into a gallop, leaving both Jonathan and Virginia behind in a shower of road dust as they breezed by.

"Tell me again how terrible it would be to take you to Gretna Green and have done with it, pet," Jonathan pleaded from between clenched teeth. "I believe I need to be reminded that we have chosen the *easy, sensible* approach to our problem."

"Oh, poor *Johnny,*" Virginia teased as their mounts rounded the bend, at last allowing them sight of the tilted curricle, Knox Bromley lying on a grassy bank, moaning, and Lettice Ann ministering to him. "Poor, *poor* Johnny!"

"I'm leaving."

Virginia's head jerked up in shock at this tersely uttered announcement. "Leaving, Myrtle? To go where? And why? I don't understand. I thought you and Sir Wiley were getting on so famously?"

"Famously? That just goes to show what you know,

Ginny." Myrtle threw herself into a chair, her long legs, thankfully covered by her split riding skirt, flung out in front of her, her chin jammed down hard against her chest. At times like this, with Myrtle flinging herself about, Sir Roderick had been heard to say that Myrtle was the son he'd always wanted.

"Oh, yes, Ginny," she went on, glaring at Virginia. "Let's hear it again, shall we? *Famously.* We laugh, we joke, we ride, we even drink together. We're the best of friends. I call him Wiley and he calls me Myrt. We're bosom chums, actually—kindred spirits. So why is he going to return to London and propose to some little bit of frippery named Araminta Sedgewick? Answer me *that*, Ginny!"

Virginia bit her bottom lip as she saw tears standing bright in Myrtle's pretty but close-set eyes. "He is?" she asked, her heart breaking for her sister. "And you love him, don't you, Myrtle?"

Myrtle fairly leapt out of the chair and began furiously pacing the drawing room. "Love him? Are you daft, Ginny? I don't love *anybody.* I don't want to marry anybody—not now, and not *ever.* Haven't I told you that often enough?"

"Yes," Virginia answered consideringly. "You have told me that. You've told everybody. Have you said as much to Sir Wiley?"

Myrtle stopped her pacing and sliced her sister a curious look. "Yes, as a matter of fact, I have. We've had several discussions about marriage. He wants it as little as do I, and wouldn't even be thinking about it if it weren't for his Aunt Earlene. But you know all that. That's why Jonathan invited him here in the first place. What of it? Oh," she exploded, "why am I standing here talking? I should be upstairs right now, packing up my whips."

Virginia held out her hands as if to detain her sister, saying, "Don't go yet, Myrtle. Just sit down a moment, and bear with me while I think aloud, all right? Please? I think I might be able to help."

Myrtle set her chin at a belligerent angle and glared at her baby sister. "Why? I don't love him, you know. Why should I need any help?"

"Then why are you running away?" Virginia countered, and knew she had won when Myrtle's gaze slid away from hers and the woman sat herself down once more.

"All right, all right. Damn the man for a tinker—I love him. And he sees me as his friend, and no more." She glared at Virginia. "Now what?"

Virginia was silent for some moments, wondering if it were more than her physical safety was worth to say what was on her mind. "I think," she said slowly at last, "I think we should go see Letty, and Georgie—and Clara. It is time, Myrtle, that you were turned into a *woman*."

Myrtle's eyes grew wide with fear as her mouth dropped open and she began slowly shaking her head. "Oh, no," she declared, burrowing back into the cushions of the chair. "Not that, Ginny. I know what you mean. You mean scented baths, and lace, and hair ribbons, and silly white gloves. Oh, no. Not me. Not Myrtle Noddenly."

Virginia tipped her head to one side appealingly. "Even if it meant that Sir Wiley realized that his good friend Myrt was not only a great companion but also a lovely woman—a woman he could be proud to introduce to his Aunt Earlene as his wife?"

Myrtle began worrying the side of her rather dirty thumb. "Do you really think Wiley doesn't know I'm a female?"

"I think he knows you're great fun—the sort of friend a man such as he would never tire of," Virginia said, sensing a victory. "Now it is up to you to show him that you are an attractive, desirable, *eligible* young lady. Men can be obtuse, Myrtle. It is up to us to show them the road best taken. You remember Mama telling us that, don't you?"

Myrtle nodded, looking down at her roughened hands and threadbare riding skirt, then ran her fingers through her shortly cropped hair. "To be fair to Wiley, I've never gone out of my way to remind him I'm a female," she said consideringly.

Then she slapped her hands down hard on the arms of the chair and stood. "All right. Let's do it. Only no hair bows. I draw the line at hair bows, I swear it, even for Wiley!"

5

It would be difficult for the casual observer to see that the lovely estate of Mayfield was in reality a hotbed of intrigue, the very air almost pulsating with plans and schemes and not a little unfulfilled love.

Lord Pitney Fox, his tail neatly between his legs (and bits of egg-white congealing behind his left ear) had departed within an hour of his unfortunate experience in the Mayfield breakfast room, leaving behind his "personal" physician and a terse note stating that "I shall be rusticating at my estate in Surrey until the fall, regaining control of my shattered nerves. It would be best, I believe, for all parties concerned if no mention of the goings-on of this past week were to be made public, if you take my meaning."

Knox Bromley, fortunately, also was no longer a part of the scene. In a burst of inspiration, Jonathan had shunted the injured man straight from the turnpike to a local hostelry, happily paying down the blunt that would keep Mister Bromley, his broken leg, and his tiresome tongue in reasonable comfort until the bone knitted or the innkeeper decided no amount of Lord Mayfield's money was worth the aggravation of having to deal with the plaguey man and sent Bromley off to London in a hired coach.

Either way, Jonathan believed he would be getting off cheaply.

That left Doctor Angus Fitzhugh still in residence, and still most solicitously attentive to Miss Georgette Noddenly, who had taken to the notion that good health just might be good sense—especially when one was being courted by such a handsome man as the doctor. And did anyone know that Doctor Fitzhugh's great uncle in Edinburgh was something called a "laird," and the dear doctor was his only heir?

Yes, there would be time and enough for Georgette to catalog her list of ailments *after* the wedding ceremony—if those ailments were to make a comeback. As it was, Miss Georgette Noddenly had been surprised to find herself feeling as fit as a fiddle these past three days, capable of long walks in the gardens, late evenings in the music room, and even a visit to the local village to purchase a few badly needed female fripperies for Myrtle—all these exertions taking place with the good doctor at her side.

Jonathan, at the behest of his beloved, had convinced Sir Wiley Hambleton to stay on in the country for another week, pointing out that marriage proposals were nothing to rush into, even with a pot of gold (Aunt Earlene's fortune) awaiting him at the end of the aisle of Saint George's.

Sir Wiley had agreed, but only reluctantly, for Myrtle Noddenly had been curiously unavailable to him these past three days, "indisposed," or so he had been told, although she was sure to be up and about in time for dinner this evening.

And it was about time, too, Sir Wiley had told anyone

who would listen, for he was bored to flinders without his boon companion "Myrt" about; to go riding with across country, to regale with his jokes, to slip away with in the evenings for a visit to the village taproom—Myrtle laughingly done up in her old breeches and acting so rough as to fool any but the most trained eye as to her sex.

Little did Sir Wiley know that tonight, after three long days spent in seclusion—her face and hands being treated with freckle creams made of sweet cream and crushed strawberries, her body repeatedly dunked in rose water, her hair snipped and curled into something vaguely resembling the popular *Titus,* her mind assaulted with the do's and don'ts of polite manners, her body subjected to pinches and pulls as she learned how to sit, stand, and eat correctly—Miss Myrtle Noddenly, *female,* was about to make her debut.

"This will never work," Myrtle said as Georgette tucked a vial of vinaigrette into her sister's reticule and placed the slim gold chain over her sister's arm. "Look at me, will you! I look ridiculous!"

They were all gathered together in Virginia's bedchamber, where they had remained almost exclusively for the past three afternoons, working more in tandem than any of Wellington's crack artillery units in planning their strategy to bring down Sir Wiley Hambleton—known in the bedchamber only as "our target."

"No more than usual, Myrtle," Lettice Ann said in answer to her sister's wailing lament. As Miss Noddenly was still smarting from the regular ear-banging lecture delivered by a terse Lord Mayfield upon being ignominiously returned to the estate, a virtual verbal tour de force on the folly of trying to fool a fool (meaning her sad tale of her love of the "country gentleman, Bertram," related to Knox Bromley in order to gain his sympathy), her pettiness might be excused.

"Letty, don't be cutting," Virginia said around a mouth full of pins for, even if it was almost dinner time, she and Clara were still making last minute adjustments to the hem of the simple gray and blue batiste gown.

It had been nearly impossible to coax Myrtle to remain still for fittings on the new gown, with the young woman alternating between rebellious threats of bolting from the estate and entirely female histrionics concerning her unrequited love for Sir Wiley, both of which invariably ended in tears and stomping exits from the bedchamber.

"I'm prodigiously sorry, Myrtle," Lettice Ann said now, sighing. "It's just that although Georgie and her doctor seem so happy, and you and Sir Wiley will be settled before the week is out—for I have no doubt this plan will work—in Papa's mind I will still be left firmly on the shelf. You do all realize that none of you may marry until I am settled, don't you?"

Lettice Ann immediately became the center of attention as three sets of female eyes turned on her as if measuring her up for possible suitors.

"Knox Bromley is still in the neighborhood," Virginia told her, not with any great hopes that this already known information would thrill her sister, who had called the man "an impossibly obtuse, verbose, stultifyingly *boring* ignoramus" before leaving him lying at the side of the ditch and threatening to walk back to Mayfield if she would otherwise have to ride in the same vehicle with Bromley.

"Oh, *please,* Ginny," Lettice Ann groaned, rolling her eyes. "I'd rather take myself off to a nunnery." She frowned. "Do they take non-Catholics, do you suppose, not that it matters? You see—"

"How about Lord Fox?" Georgette questioned her sister, giggling. "I think he could be made to forget what I did to him if you were to ask about his rash and cluck your tongue a time or two as he told you it was much better, but now his liver might be spotty due to eating five slices of rum cake the other night at dinner."

"Don't be wasting our time with such nonsense, Georgie," Myrtle admonished, stepping off the low stool, nearly dragging Clara across the room along with her as the maid attempted to put another stitch in the hem of the blue and gray gown. "Come on, Letty. Speak up. If Georgie gets her sawbones, and if Wiley comes up to snuff over this ruse we're pulling, trying to make a silk purse from this sow's ear, and with Ginny's earl already so arsy varsy over her that he's willing to put up with settling us—it only seems fair that you give it a try. We all know you want to get spliced to someone before you're too old for anyone to care. Counting out Bad Bert—which you must do—who else have you seen in London who interests you?"

Lettice Ann lowered her eyes and concentrated on pleating the fabric of her skirt. "I thought the Earl of Royston to be rather pleasing when I saw him dancing at Almack's," she said quietly, wishing she could snap her fingers and have all her nosy sisters disappear—or *listen* to her. Didn't they realize she was laboring under a great strain, trying to tell them something?

"Royston, huh?" Myrtle considered, knowing herself to be desperate, but not *that* desperate. "I suppose we could kill off his wife for you, Letty," she teased. "Samantha— ain't that her name?" She looked to her sisters as if for assistance. "Anyone here know of any good, quick-acting poisons?"

"This is no time to be joking," Georgette said, dabbing at her eyes, for she had been walking with Angus again this afternoon and he had hinted, only slightly, of course, for he was a gentleman, that her cherry lips rivaled the famous Mayfield roses for purity of color. "Letty—isn't there somebody else? There *must* be somebody else. You've been going out in society since April."

Lettice Ann said something, but spoke so quietly no one could understand her.

"What?" Myrtle fairly exploded, taking hold of her sister's shoulders and giving them a mighty shake. "A name, Letty! Give us a name!"

As Lettice Ann broke into loud sobs, Georgette so forget herself as to scrabble in Myrtle's reticule for the vinaigrette; Clara, still on her knees, took several quick stitches before biting off the thread and quitting the room (still on her knees); and Myrtle glared with those intimidating too close-set eyes. Virginia saw herself as the sole repository of sanity.

"That will be enough, Myrtle," she said decisively, pulling Myrtle back and kneeling in front of Lettice Ann. "Forgive us, Letty. We've become no better than a gaggle of quarrelsome cats. You do not have to marry just so that the way may be cleared for the rest of us to approach the altar. We'll go to Papa—all of us, together—and explain how unfair his rule is. He'll see the sense of suspending the rule if it will allow him to marry off three daughters within a single season."

" 'My girls will marry in the order of their birth. First Faith, then Hope, then Charity—good names all, but then—' "

"Oh, stifle yourself, Georgie," Myrtle ordered as Georgette began reciting the well-known rule. "We all remember how it goes. Besides, Ginny might have a point. Getting himself shed of three out of four in a single season might just strike Papa as a good trade. And he'd be getting another earl, another doctor, and even a sir—a *rich* sir, and a Noddenly first, as we have none to date."

"I'm already married," Lettice Ann mumbled so quietly that none save Virginia, who was still kneeling in front of her, heard.

Virginia wet suddenly dry lips and looked up at her

older sister. "What—what did you say, Letty?" she questioned her carefully.

"I'm already married," Lettice Ann repeated, more firmly this time. "There!" she said, sitting up straight and smiling, as if someone had just removed a particularly weighty rock from between her shoulder blades. "I'm already married. I didn't elope, if that's what you're thinking. I'm past twenty-one, so I could marry whenever and wherever I so wished, without Papa's permission. And I so wished—I mean, I did. Six months ago tomorrow. So there!"

Virginia batted her eyelids, desperately trying to comprehend the enormity of what Lettice Ann had said while doing her best to banish the sudden image of her father— his face an angry red as he placed them all in their rooms, on bread and water for a month.

Georgette swooned, her suddenly numb fingers unable to uncork the vinaigrette. *For once in my life I truly need the dratted stuff,* she thought randomly as darkness closed in all around her, *and I can't use it. What a pity.*

Myrtle, struck speechless for the first time in her life, plunked herself down on the floor directly where she stood, only to rise just as quickly, for she had sat herself down on a pin. *"Married!"* she yelped, rubbing at her sore posterior. "Who the devil *to?* God's hatstand—not Bad Bert?"

Lettice shook her head. "Not Bad Bert," she told them, smiling at Georgette, who had roused from her swoon and was now sitting very still, taking her pulse (from habit only, for she knew she was fine as ninepence, really). "I only told all of you it was Bert, to put you off the scent. As if I'd have the man. He's even worse than you say— although he did so pay me attention. He pays everything in skirts attention."

"Then who?" Virginia asked, cudgeling her brain for

some memory of seeing Lettice Ann with anyone other than Bert. Lettice Ann had said she'd married six months ago, which would have placed her at home, before the start of the season. "And why have you kept it such a secret?"

"Papa hates him," Lettice Ann told them, her smile beginning to waver.

The three unmarried sisters looked to each other in shock, their eyes wide and incredulous, and cried as one, *"Sean Conway!"*

Lettice Ann stood, her hands drawn up into tight fists, her chin at a determined angle. "Yes. Sean Conway. Do any of you have any objections?"

Sean Conway, an Irish widower of at least forty who had settled near the Noddenly estate and was rapidly in the process of building a fortune breeding horses, had gained Sir Roderick's dislike with his outspoken disdain (rightly so) for the Noddenly horseflesh (save Myrtle's mares, which he deemed "passable").

But Mister Conway had not stopped there. He had imported all Irish workers from his birthplace in County Clare rather than hiring from the locals, and had thrown a large party last Christmas *without* inviting the man who had publicly stated that the Irishman was "a paddy-whacking clodpole who's no better than he should be."

But, at the moment, none of this seemed particularly germane to the question. Did the three remaining Noddenly spinsters, who knew they had to wait until Lettice Ann was popped off in order to marry the loves of their own lives, have any objections to the match? They again looked to each other, consideringly.

"I think it's wonderful," Virginia said, not sure if she liked Sean Conway, but knowing she much preferred him to Bad Bert. "Myrtle? Do you object?"

"Nope," Myrtle said, shrugging. "Not me. Maybe Mister Conway will allow his prize stallion to service my mares, now that we're related."

"Oh, leave it to you to see some advantage for yourself," Georgette complained, then smiled. "But I don't object, not that it would mean anything if I did. It won't mean anything if Papa objects either. Myrtle—it looks as if you're clear to wed Sir Wiley. Straighten your bodice, for goodness sakes. How do you propose to entice a man with your gown falling half off your shoulders?"

"I'd say it's precisely the way to entice a sad rotter like Wiley," Myrtle said reasonably, remembering the man's reputation as a rake—a reputation that was sadly lost on her, whom he persisted in treating as if she was his flat mate from Cambridge.

Virginia, caught between wanting to rush off to find Jonathan and tell him her good news and the sneaking suspicion that, now that she had begun her confession, Lettice Ann was not quite finished with her revelations, said, "When are you and Mister Conway going to tell Papa the truth, Letty?"

"Soon, I suppose," she said, sighing. "That's why I was trying so hard to get back home. I wanted Sean to know before I told anyone else. I couldn't be sure last month— not positively sure—but now that it has been two months, ever since we came to London, as a matter of fact, I am quite convinced."

"So am I," Myrtle said, bending to pull the last remaining pins from her hem. "I'm convinced you're to let in your attic. For goodness sakes, Letty, try to say something that makes sense."

"I'm increasing!" Lettice Ann exclaimed, pressing her hands against her still flat stomach. "Clara knows, of course, but now you three do, too. Isn't it marvelous?"

"Marvelous?" Myrtle cried over Virginia's objections. "You're *pregnant*, and you haven't even told Papa that you're *married*—to a man he detests? Oh, yes. Yes, indeed, Letty, that's marvelous. Bloody marvelous. Papa will be in alt, won't he, girls? Georgie—lend me that vinaigrette, will you? I never had 'em before, but I think I feel a fit of the vapors coming on."

Virginia quietly slipped from her bedchamber as Myrtle, Lettice Ann, and Georgette applied the finishing touches to their toilettes, intent on seeking out Jonathan to tell him that they'd already had one matrimonial success—without even knowing it.

She sought him out in the usual spot—the Conservatory behind the music room, a glassed-in area devoted to greenery and the odd orange tree—and was delighted to see that he had arrived before her and was waiting, a small bouquet in hand, to meet with her.

"I have news," she told him, standing on tiptoe to kiss his cheek. Virginia was beginning to consider herself one half of an old married couple, riding herd on the younger generation and doing her best to find time alone with her similarly beleaguered spouse.

There was barely time for passion anymore, especially since the defection of Knox Bromley and the ouster of Lord Pitney Fox. Every moment had been dedicated to the marrying-off of her three sisters, to the detriment of her relationship with Jonathan, the love of her life.

But that did not, it appeared, mean that Jonathan had resigned himself to prudish pecks on the cheek—not when he and the beautiful Virginia were alone in the Conservatory. "Your news can wait, my love," he told her, gathering her close. "I, on the other hand, have waited all day to see you and refuse to be fobbed off with that one miserly kiss."

"Mm," Virginia sighed once he had released her from a most satisfying embrace, "I do so adore it when you're masterful. Thank goodness my sisters are such lackadaisical chaperons. But I must tell you what I've learned. Brace yourself, Jonathan—Lettice Ann is already married. And soon to make me an aunt for the twelfth—or is it the thirteenth time?"

"Already married?" Jonathan shook his head, unable to believe what he'd just heard. "And you're to be an aunt?" He closed his eyes a moment and did some mental arithmetic. "That leaves out Knox, thank the good Lord. Or is it worse? Has she eloped with Bad Bert?"

"Neither," Virginia told him, taking his hand and leading him to a nearby bench, the scene of several mutually pleasurable exchanges these past days. And then, in between kisses, she told him the tale of Sean Conway, Irish horse breeder.

"Well, that's two down," Jonathan said when she had finished, nuzzling her neck above the soft silk collar of her gown. He sat back and told her, "You see, I have some good news for you too."

"About Doctor Fitzhugh and Georgette?" Virginia asked hopefully.

"Yes, puss, although I would appreciate it if you were to allow me to pretend you hadn't noticed, and then praise me as if I'd had some scant something to do with our second success."

"Sorry, darling," Virginia said, not the least repentant.

"Apology accepted, puss. Angus came to see me this afternoon, seeking my opinion on his chances of gaining your father's approval for a marriage to Georgette. It seems he's only in London for a year, learning some of our medical techniques. Then it's back to Edinburgh for him. Back to his *castle,* as it turns out. He took one look at Georgette and tumbled top over tail in love. I told him I believed your father might just fall on his neck with happiness at the match. The thought seemed to cheer him mightily, although it's difficult to tell with Angus. But I did catch a fleeting glimpse of very white teeth beneath that bushy mustache, so I assumed he was smiling."

Virginia was so pleased she kissed Jonathan again, this time squarely on his lips, which effectively put a halt to any further discussion for some minutes, until the gong had rung the first time, calling them in to the drawing room in preparation for being summoned to their dinner.

"Oh dear," Virginia cried, adjusting the bodice of her gown, just lately the scene of an expeditionary foray by her beloved. "We must go. I promised Myrtle I'd lend her emotional support as she makes her entrance."

"Your attempts to soften her hard edges have met with so little success?" Jonathan asked, doing his best to undo the havoc Virginia's roving fingers had done his neck cloth.

Virginia took hold of Jonathan's hand and unceremoniously pulled him to his feet. "Don't be so quick to fear the worst, darling," she admonished him as they made their way back through the music room and along the corridor leading to the drawing room. "I believe Myrtle looks"— she cudgeled her brain for the correct words—"quite uniquely attractive."

"Uh-huh," Jonathan said, wondering if falling in love had turned him against his own sex. Otherwise, without his own marital future hanging in the balance, he most surely would have warned Sir Wiley of what was about to transpire in the drawing room. Warned him, and given him the option of high-tailing it back to London before the sight of Myrtle Noddenly rigged out in lace and bows drove him straight to the drinks table.

"I mean it, Jonathan," Virginia protested, knowing that even three solid days of trying had only marginally succeeded in turning Myrtle into an unexceptional young lady of fashion. That sort of success would have taken a year of dawn to dusk labor, at the least. "And you promised to be supportive."

"And I will be supportive," he said with a straight face, entering the drawing room. "I will be supportive of poor Wiley as he tumbles into a dead faint at the sight of his good chum Myrt in hair bows."

"Wretch," Virginia whispered. "As if Myrtle would allow hair bows."

They greeted the good doctor, who had arrived in the drawing room in advance of them, Virginia going up to the nervous looking young man at once to tell him how very well pleased she was to be the first Noddenly to welcome him to the family.

"Thank you, Miss Ginny," Angus Fitzhugh said, bowing over her hand. "I love the woman dearly, you know. And she's got wide hips. She'll bear me many strong sons."

Virginia considered this for a moment, then gave a slight nod of her head. "If that makes the two of you happy, Doctor—*Angus.*"

Sir Wiley Hambleton was next to enter the room, a glass in his hand and a certain glow to his cheeks that stated to even the uncurious that he had been imbibing steadily for most of the afternoon.

He was a sad sight, this normally active man made to cool his heels while his "Myrt" was hiding out above stairs, doing Heaven only knew what instead of bearing him company as he tore about the countryside, looking for mischief in the manner of a youth half his age. In point of fact, he might as well have been visiting with his Aunt Earlene, for all the sport he'd had.

"Evening all," he said, heading straight for the drinks table. "Depressing evening, isn't it? Sun still above the horizon, the air cool and crisp, and the lot of us stuck looking at each other yet again. I've a mind to bolt, Johnny, no matter what I promised you, and if Myrt ain't going to show up tonight, I'll do just that."

Jonathan took Sir Wiley's glass and replaced it with a smaller one he'd filled only partway with wine. "She'll be down directly, Wiley," he promised, looking hopefully toward the foyer, already rethinking what he'd done and wondering if it wouldn't be best if Wiley were half-blind with drink when Myrtle showed up. "You know, for a man who has stated his intention to propose marriage to one woman, you're acting deucedly like a fellow in love with another woman who is much closer to his heart."

Sir Wiley screwed up his face in puzzlement. "You mean Myrt?" he asked, incredulous at the suggestion. "She ain't the marrying sort. No more than me. Only I have to, and she don't."

"True enough, Sir Wiley," Virginia agreed, approaching the two men with every hope of helping her beloved bring home his point. "But, much as Myrtle protests, she is a woman, and all women desire to someday fall in love. Once that joyful moment occurs, there is no end to the compromises she will make in her convictions in order to be with that one special man who has captured her heart."

Sir Wiley peered owlishly at Virginia, then looked to Jonathan. "What'd she say, Johnny? Is she saying that Myrtle might want to marry me?"

Jonathan glanced quickly to his beloved, who nodded her head a single time, giving him permission to speak what was, after all, the truth. "You're a hellion, Wiley, and have justly gained the reputation of a ne'er do well, but you do, I suppose, have a certain appeal to a woman of Myrtle's singular tastes," he said, not wishing to jump straight into the water when it might be more prudent to test its temperature first with a single toe.

"Young girls have always liked me," Sir Wiley said in

all modesty, for truth was truth, no matter how thick you sliced it. "It's the danger they see in me, I suppose, the silly creatures. But not all of them. Araminta Sedgewick is scared spitless of me, but her father likes my aunt's fortune well enough to turn a blind eye to my past. I've stuck mostly to matrons, those ladies who know what they're doing. But now I have to marry—and you're telling me I might be able to marry Myrt? I could be that lucky? I thought a rake had to pay for his sins."

"Then you do love her?" Virginia asked, all but bursting from her skin in her excitement. They were within Ames Ace of doing it—of marrying off all three remaining Noddenly sisters. Who would have believed it?

Then she frowned, remembering the past three days, and all the sisters had gone through trying to make Myrtle presentable. "For goodness sakes, Sir Wiley, *why* didn't you say so?"

Sir Wiley looked suddenly sheepish, avoiding everyone's eyes as he said quietly, "I'm a rakehell, a ramshackle bounder, a man with more past than he knows how to hide and barely a regret save that I didn't start my rambling about at an earlier age and do it twice as much. I'm an unrepentant reprobate who'll probably be switching signposts for sport when I'm in my dotage. Myrt's too good for me, and that's a fact. Too good, too beautiful. And much too honest."

"Good grief, Ginny," Jonathan said, laughing. "The man's in love for certain! There is nothing so moral as a reformed rake—or so self-serving as a rake who wishes to continue raising a ruckus."

Virginia didn't quite understand all of what she was hearing (as no woman could), but she had assimilated the two most important points. Sir Wiley loved her sister. And Sir Wiley already believed Myrtle to be "honest," and "beautiful."

"Oh, my stars!" she blurted out, turning for the door, hoping to warn Myrtle off before she appeared in the room, resplendent in her new gown and new hair and soft white hands and at least partially smooth, freckle-free skin. Myrtle, Sir Wiley's "beautiful, honest" Myrtle, had been the recipient of every beautifying artifice known to her sisters, and she had to be stopped before she presented him with her altered appearance—and most probably frightened him off once and for all!

But it was too late, for Lettice Ann and Georgette were already entering the drawing room, smiling broadly as they shielded all but the top of Myrtle's carroty head from view.

"Sir Wiley," Georgette trilled merrily, "we have a marvelous surprise for you. A *visitor*—someone you will swear never to have seen before this moment. Isn't that right, Letty?"

"Oh, yes. Yes, indeed," Lettice Ann seconded. "Why, if our host, the earl, weren't already spoken for, I would shudder with fear that he would defect to our newcomer, breaking dear Virginia's heart."

"Letty—Georgie," Virginia fairly hissed beneath her breath, "leave off. Sir Wiley already loves her—*the way she was!*"

"*What?*" Lettice Ann and Georgette were parted like the Red Sea as a transformed Myrtle unceremoniously pushed them to either side and stepped up to Virginia, glaring at her as if she wished her stuck in her own tub of rose water for three days, her hands and feet and knees scrubbed until they nearly bled in order to rid them of callouses. "I've gone through the tortures of Hades for *nothing?* And this was all your idea, wasn't it, my dear, sweet, *meddlesome* Ginny?"

Jonathan, still standing at the drinks table, stared disbelievingly across the room, impressed with the sight of the horsey-faced Myrtle of the too-close eyes and un-gainly manners. Not that a miracle had been wrought, but there was a noticeable improvement in the woman's appearance. Of course, if she could have been made a mute for the evening it might have been considered more of a success.

He looked to Sir Wiley, who was standing as if made into a statue, staring bug-eyed at his rough and tumble be-loved, who now looked ready for nothing more strenuous than some fast-paced tapestry embroidering. "God's teeth, Myrt," he said, his voice rather strained, "what in blazes have you done to yourself? You look just like everybody else!"

Myrtle tore herself away from her sisters (who were mightily glad to see her go, for they were worried she might box their collective ears at any moment), and ap-proached Sir Wiley at a near gallop, her forefinger point-ing straight at his nose. "This is all your fault, Wiley Hambleton. I thought you wanted a lady."

"A lady?" Sir Wiley responded, confused. "What rot! What would I do with a lady? I want you, Myrt. But you said you'd never marry, and I believed you. You have to take a man at his word, you know."

"I'm *not* a man, you idiot!" Myrtle shot back, wiping the back of her hand across her mouth, smudging the care-fully applied lip rouge Georgette had sworn would appear so natural that no one would ever believe the color to be anything but nature's own. "I'm a *woman!*"

"Well, you don't act like one!" Sir Wiley countered, shouting even louder than Myrtle, who now stood chin to chin with him as the rest of the party looked on. "Why else do you think I love you?"

Myrtle stood back, momentarily speechless. "You love me? You *really* love me, Wiley?"

"Yes, I do. But I'd love you better if you'd nip off upstairs and climb into your breeches. If we ride hard, we can make Gretna in less than a week. I've a mind to marry over the anvil, just to shock Aunt Earlene. Can't let her have it all her way, now can we?"

"That's a deal," Myrtle said, holding out her hand to Sir Wiley, who looked at it for a moment before taking hold of it and pulling her tight up against his chest— whereupon, with everyone watching, he kissed Miss Myrtle Noddenly until her newly soft, white toes curled inside her wretchedly bothersome silk stockings.

Virginia wiped at her moist eyes with the corner of the handkerchief her beloved had wordlessly slipped into her hands, then asked, "We aren't going to let them run off to Gretna, are we, Jonathan?"

"Yes, my love. We are," he answered, pulling her close against his side. "I think we owe it to them. It may not be what we want, but I believe we have gotten more than any two people could hope for. Lettice Ann already married, Myrtle to be wed within the week, and Georgette soon to follow the two of them to the altar. You'll be a June bride, my dear, as promised. And if your Papa doesn't like it, then he'll just have to take it up with Myrtle. Lord knows he'd be a stronger man than I if he tried it."

"You have a point, darling," Virginia said, sighing romantically as Sir Wiley and a clinging Myrtle exited the room without a word of farewell, and Georgette and her doctor wandered off into the garden, undoubtedly inspired by the kiss that had passed between the eloping pair. "Do you suppose we could return to the Conservatory for a while before we're called in to dinner?"

Jonathan looked down at her, winking. "Do you have a hankering to inspect the oranges, my sweet?"

"Not really. But I do have a *hankering* to have you continue with what we were doing when the dinner gong first rang," Virginia told him, refusing to be embarrassed by her own forwardness. "It was, as always, a most inspiring interlude."

Jonathan Wetherell, fourteenth earl of etc., etc.—a most happy and soon to be fulfilled man—was pleased to comply with his affianced wife's suggestion.

Kasey Michaels

Thirty-one long or short years ago this June (long, if I'm thinking about the trials and tribulations; woefully short when I look at Mike and still feel that indefinable "tingle"), I married, as the saying goes, "my best friend."

At the time, I wasn't looking for friendship.

At nineteen, I was more than happy to settle for the "tingle."

But life has a funny way of taking care of fools who rush in, somehow gifting them with mates who believe love will conquer all—the midnight races to the hospital with a desperately ill child, the overdue bills, the fifteen-year-old "baby fat" from that last pregnancy still clinging to his once svelte bride, a man's love for golf that could lead lesser women to drink, the unexpected metamorphosis of a once full time, if indifferent, housekeeper (who now barely "house-keeps" at all) because she discovered, years too late to be a child prodigy, a burning need to write.

At nineteen, I married for love, for passion—maybe even for a little bit of good, clean lust. Thirty-one years later, I know I married my best friend, a man who cheers for me, turns a blind eye to my faults, holds my hand, talks to me and, best of all, *listens*. I wish all my readers, and all my heroines, this same dumb luck—which is another way of saying that following your heart, heeding that "tingle," maybe ain't such a bad idea after all!

Happy anniversary, darling.

Avon Romances—
the best in exceptional authors and unforgettable novels!

FOREVER HIS   Shelly Thacker
                          77035-0/$4.50 US/$5.50 Can

TOUCH ME WITH FIRE   Nicole Jordan
                          77279-5/$4.50 US/$5.50 Can

OUTLAW HEART   Samantha James
                          76936-0/$4.50 US/$5.50 Can

FLAME OF FURY   Sharon Green
                          76827-5/$4.50 US/$5.50 Can

DARK CHAMPION   Jo Beverley
                          76786-4/$4.50 US/$5.50 Can

BELOVED PRETENDER   Joan Van Nuys
                          77207-8/$4.50 US/$5.50 Can

PASSIONATE SURRENDER   Sheryl Sage
                          76684-1/$4.50 US/$5.50 Can

MASTER OF MY DREAMS   Danelle Harmon
                          77227-2/$4.50 US/$5.50 Can

LORD OF THE NIGHT   Cara Miles
                          76453-9/$4.50 US/$5.50 Can

WIND ACROSS TEXAS   Donna Stephens
                          77273-6/$4.50 US/$5.50 Can

Avon Romantic Treasures

Unforgettable, enthralling love stories,
sparkling with passion and adventure
from Romance's bestselling authors

COMANCHE WIND *by Genell Dellin*

76717-1/$4.50 US/$5.50 Can

THEN CAME YOU *by Lisa Kleypas*

77013-X/$4.50 US/$5.50 Can

VIRGIN STAR *by Jennifer Horsman*

76702-3/$4.50 US/$5.50 Can

MASTER OF MOONSPELL *by Deborah Camp*

76736-8/$4.50 US/$5.50 Can

SHADOW DANCE *by Anne Stuart*

76741-4/$4.50 US/$5.50 Can

FORTUNE'S FLAME *by Judith E. French*

76865-8/$4.50 US/$5.50 Can

FASCINATION *by Stella Cameron*

77074-1/$4.50 US/$5.50 Can

ANGEL EYES *by Suzannah Davis*

76822-4/$4.50 US/$5.50 Can